Elite

The Satellite Trilogy   Part II

L e e
D a v i d s o n

For Nana.

Your love for books, stories, and writing in general

has been an inspiration like no other.

I miss you.

Contents

Did you never know, long ago, how much you loved me—

That your love would never lessen and never go?

You were young then, proud and fresh-hearted,

You were too young to know.

—Sara Teasdale, Did You Never Know?

Prologue

Jonathan Clement sits in his ceilingless, octagonal office, re-inking his pen and scribbling notes in a book. When the door opens, his dancing feather halts on the page and Jonathan looks up from his desk.

"Great to see you, Beaman. Any news today?" Jonathan asks.

"None sir. He seems to have forgotten everything."

Jonathan is pleased by Beaman's response. He rolls his chair back a few feet, removes an iron rod from the fireplace behind him, and stamps the cover of a book before responding. "I foresee some obstacles in his future. Would you mind continuing to monitor him?"

"Not at all. Should I still report daily?" Beaman asks.

Jonathan dips his pen into the ink well. "Yes, thank you."

Beaman narrows his eyes on the feather. "You do know we're in a digital age now, right?"

Jonathan laughs. "Ah, yes. Old habits die hard, it seems."

1. It's the name of the game

Willow

"You wanted to see me?" I wish my candlelit dinner with Troy wasn't being interrupted.

"Yes, thank you for arriving so promptly, Willow." Jonathan stops a few feet from the K hall in the grand marble lobby. "I am in need of your assistance with an assignment."

Anxiety hits quick, making my heart rate spike when my mind ticks through all of my Tragedies. "For who?"

"I am saddened to say, Tatum Jacoby. She is careening off course once again."

Tate. I'd bet the farm she is off course. Things like this tend to happen when the natural order gets altered. "But you said…never mind. What's going on with her?" *Aside from the fact that she erased all of Grant's memories* is what I want to say, but don't.

"Grant's inherent memory loss is a natural part of the process," Jonathan says, using his unnerving mind reading ability—he can deny having this gift all day long, but I'll never believe him.

"We both know the way his memories were erased was not natural," I taunt.

"Despite how his memories were taken, losing them

1

was essential, especially now that—"

"Now that he's an Elite," I mumble, knowing Jonathan is right. Probably, anyway.

"As a member of the Elite team, distractions in our work can be treacherous. Wouldn't you agree?"

I hesitate before nodding. Regular Satellite assignments are strenuous enough. The kid has no idea how agonizing the road ahead is going to be. "Working towards the greater good," I say with phony enthusiasm.

Jonathan smiles. "That's the spirit. I would like you to accompany Liam on Tate's assignment until we can get her advancing forward again."

"I'm guessing you need me to go now?"

Jonathan nods and squeezes my shoulder.

So much for my chicken marsala, and more importantly, my husband-time.

"Thank you. You are one of our most exceptional, though you mustn't need me to tell you that."

How is it that this guy knows flattery always brings him forgiveness? "Oh, come on Johnny, you say that to all the Satellites," I tease. "Am I expected in training?"

"Unless you feel the need, I think you can manage without. I'm here if you need anything. Good luck."

"Will you get a message to Troy that I'll see him at break?"

When Jonathan nods, I thank him and dig in my bag. When my fingers find Tate's gold necklace, I whisper, "Displace," and fall through the dark marble floor of the lobby. On my way down to Earth to save another Tragedy, I think of

Troy. At least he will understand. God love my husband. He's more than a girl could ever hope for and I'm somehow lucky enough to get eternity with him. Not a bad trade for missing out on a few years of my mortal life.

I breathe deeply to pull the zooming wind into my lungs and then I grin. Being a Satellite will always be a close second to being with my husband. As the houses below quickly approach, I still find it difficult to believe there really is something better than this. Six months ago, before I was reunited with Troy, I didn't believe it myself.

When Liam almost jumps out of his Sketchers from the shock of my landing, I can't help but snicker.

"Bloody hell, woman!"

"What's up?" I ask beautiful, British Liam. Shocked expressions always look silly on him. He should really lose the hat; his wavy, sand-colored hair is too perfect to be covered. I shift my eyes toward Tate. "I hear our girl is still going all mental-ward on us."

Tate appears normal enough, minus the black jeans, black tee, and black make-up. The protruding ribs aren't overly flattering either. Not that I can blame the poor thing, having lost first her fiancée and then her brother within a few short months. If she knew Grant and Elliott were both Satellites and that she would see them again, it would make my job a lot easier. Until then, Liam and I will have to keep her slogging on through life. "She's still on the black kick, huh? Pity. She wears color so much better."

"Her attitude is as dark as her clothing. I can't believe I'm saying this, but I'm glad you're here. I could certainly use the help."

"I can see that. Have you been coding during breaks?"

"Yeah, but my relaxed state is usually diminished within the first ten minutes of being with her." At the same time Liam says this, Tate cranks her radio up to ear-piercing volume. "Here she goes again," Liam shouts over the noise.

"I got this one," I yell back and focus on pulling in my filter. When my energy is formed into a pretty, purple ball floating in front of me, I say, "Haze," and then send my thoughts to Tate through the film than has enclosed the two of us.

Turn it down.

Oh, it hurts! My body clenches in pain. *Labor, Willow, labor!* Remembering childbirth always snaps my mind back into the game.

"Block." The connection between Tate and me is severed, making the vapory filter fall to the carpet in droplets before vanishing.

In my head, my arms raise in victory when Tate spins the volume dial down.

When she switches her attention to the family photograph on her nightstand, I ask Liam, "Has Elliott forgiven Grant yet?"

Liam shakes his head. "I can't blame Elliott. The bloke put down his sister."

"He didn't really put her down. According to Clara, Grant just said something along the lines of 'so what if Tate was a Rebellion.'"

As usual, Liam isn't buying my downplaying attempt.

"All right, his tone probably wasn't super-sweet."

"A *Rebellion,* Willow. The worst-case-scenario for a Tragedy, and Grant pretty much told the girl's brother he didn't care. Don't forget, he and Grant were almost brothers themselves. It was cold."

"I understand Elliott's point, but in the kid's defense, his memories of her are gone, so he really didn't know what he was saying."

Liam lets out a loud breath.

"I guess this means you're still mad at Grant, too?"

"I had to endure watching Grant here, remember?" He points his eyes at Tate. "He broke every rule we have to be with her, even leaving his own Tragedy—whom he should have been watching—unattended."

I wince, knowing my own son was left unprotected while Grant was making illegal visits to Tate. Liam continues and paces around the room. "She erased his memories one by one. She destroyed all the reminders of him from her life: photographs, music, even her clothes."

"I know!" I immediately regret my sharp tone that was merely a result of wishing he'd stop with the rehash. "I'm not cool with how his memories were wiped from his mind either; it's not the way they were supposed to disappear, but there's nothing we can do about that now. The fact is they're gone like they should be, like how it is—or was—for all of us. It's not his fault and it's not fair of you and Elliott to blame him."

"He's changed," Liam says in a quieter voice.

"We all changed when we became Satellites, Liam. It's

the name of the game. You forgot your life, I forgot mine. That's what Programming is for: to return our memories when our loved ones join us. You weren't so quick to lose your memories either, and as I recall, you were able to keep more of them than a lot of people around here." Oh Lord have mercy; I wish I could take the words back as soon as they are out.

Liam squints his eyes and his hand freezes on his ball cap. "Do you think I want to remember my death?"

"No, I'm—"

"Do you think I want to remember the look on my son's face when he pulled my body from the water?" Liam shouts.

"No! I'm sorry. But how about the alternative, Liam?" I yell back before I'm able to calm myself. "How about not remembering you had a son at all? How about not remembering you died while giving birth to him?"

We both retreat to our respective corners, speechless.

"Just try to cut the kid a break, Liam," I finally say. "Being a Satellite isn't always an easy road. If it were, there'd probably be a lot more of us."

I take the next block, which is better than any apology I could give him. His grateful expression says so.

2. Now that we all know each other, let's get down to it

Grant

A single knock at the door jerks me from my coma-like state and forces me up from the puke-green sofa. I swore I'd destroy the atrocious couch my mentor left me, but the truth is, the thing's too comfortable to part with. I'd never admit that to Willow, though, because if her head got any bigger, it'd explode like a firecracker.

When I check the door, the hallway is empty except for an abandoned roll of parchment at my feet, delivered, no doubt, by the magic of Progression. On my way to the kitchen, I untie and drop the leather cord on the hardwood floor, knowing it will disappear, compliments of, yes, the magic of Progression. The musty odor of the curled letter is quickly covered by the scent of coffee.

Dear Grant,

We are honored to welcome you to the Satellite team of Elites. Please go to the courtyard at break to begin your training. Also, please commence reading *your assignment. You know we only ask because it is important.*

—S

I laugh out loud, recalling a similar note from S, when I missed a block on my first—and, so far only—assignment. Apparently, the life-planning Schedulers are fully aware that I haven't started my reading yet. Imagine that.

In truth, I have been putting off getting acquainted with my next Tragedy because I'm nervous about what lies ahead. My time protecting Ryder wasn't what I'd call easy, and that was a normal case. I can only imagine what an Elite assignment will entail.

I gulp down the extra strong coffee on my way back to the sofa, then trade the mug for my assignment on the dilapidated trunk used as a coffee table (another of Willow's eclectic touches). The book is too heavy for its size, much heavier than Ryder's book was. I try not to think too much about what this could mean.

My eyes move past my name and label *Assignment Two* on the dark purple cover, getting stuck on the third line: *Elite*. I reluctantly open the book and the binding creaks as if in defiance. I skim past the first page and am greeted with the familiar, neat handwriting.

Dear Grant,

It is with great appreciation that I welcome you to the Elite team of Satellites. You have proven to be a remarkable

Satellite. Your qualities of integrity, empathy, and kindness will be pivotal in your upcoming assignments.

Being chosen as an Elite is the highest honor in this program. I have great hope that you will gain a respect and appreciation for your fellow Elites.

If you should need assistance at any time, please do not hesitate to contact me.

All My Best,
Jonathan Clement

The Beginning graces the next page in bold text above the instructions for dummies. I flatten the spine and do as I'm directed, placing my hand, fingers splayed, on the page. The drawn outline of the hand suits mine precisely.

The tugging starts lightly, but it doesn't take long before my arm feels almost dismembered. When I'm yanked into the book, my eyes clamp shut as I move through the constricting, black space. I know better than to try and breathe. Instead, I make an effort to focus on anything other than the invisible needles scouring my body.

When my feet finally hit the dirt in the circular room that resembles the inside of a well, the dank smell is calming. The blackness overhead, however, makes me uneasy. "Well, let's go," I say out loud, anxious to get out of this stone, claustrophobic prison of rusty doors.

GPS Jeanette, the automated voice of choice in Progression, chimes through the space, "Welcome, Grant Bradley. Please hold while I configure your assignment."

A rumble prompts the circular wall to spin into a gray blur. I focus on my boots and the dirt ground, thankful that both remain stationary.

With a ding, the wall stops and leaves just one door. "Your assignment begins in the year 1976, with the introduction to your Tragedy, Meggie Ann Lotashey. Please proceed through the door ahead," GPS Jeanette instructs.

I suck in the smell of earth. The door that remains includes *1976* in iron numbers. When I turn the handle, an electric current vibrates through my veins. The room on the other side welcomes me with nose-burning antiseptic and bright lights. My breath swims like smoke each time I exhale, even though the temperature is as comfortable as Progression.

Six gender-neutral doctors in blue scrubs and matching masks crowd around a small table. Taller than all of them, I lean between two shoulders to see what has their attention, but cringe away in shock.

"More suction," a male voice says, followed by a dry sucking sound that turns to a gurgle.

Probably because I'm a guy and, therefore, fascinated by gore, I go back for another look. A heart the size of a walnut frantically pulses inside a tiny, open chest.

"Clamp," the doctor says and somehow finagles a silver instrument into the area.

Putting space between myself and the group, I grip the stainless steel table and swallow. The gore is one thing; twisting implements into the infant's body is entirely different. I could never be a doctor.

After barking more orders, a male voice finally says, "Happy Birthday, Meggie. I think you're going to be quite a fighter." He takes a step back and pulls his mask down. "Close her up. Good work."

My feet come out from under me and I grab at the air as I'm yanked out of the room. My boots hit the hard earth and the metal door closes with an echo.

The stone wall cyclones around me again. When the familiar ding halts the movement, instead of saying, *it's now safe to move about the cabin,* GPS Jeanette says, "Please proceed to 1980," in her creepy-calm voice.

I push through the door, past the shock of the handle, and step into a yellow kitchen. Balloons and bodies fill the tiny area.

I push myself against the wall and exhale vapor, glancing through the doorway into an even smaller room that's been taken over by a sea of pink bows, decorations, and wrapped boxes.

The crowd in the kitchen finishes belting out "Happy birthday, dear Meggie, happy birthday to you," and the girl at the table shows her approval by baring all of her white Tic-Tac teeth.

"You belong in the zoo," a boy beside her sings after Meggie half blows, half spits out the four candles. He's double her size in both height and width, but has the same white-blond hair. If the boy on Meggie's other side wasn't wearing a red shirt instead of blue, I'd swear I was seeing double.

"Max and Ryan!" Twenty bucks says the woman is momma bear, as no one else in the room has hair as blond as the three kids.

Meggie sticks her tongue out at the twins.

I'm sucked away and the thunder of metal follows. When the cyclonic walls halt, GPS Jeanette tells me to move on to 1984. I step into the living room that had moments ago been filled with birthday gifts. A rancid odor hangs in the air. A piercing shriek makes me stumble and my back hits the drywall beside the couch.

"You're a worthless excuse of a woman!" The voice belongs to a charmer who's wearing the source of the smell on his shirt. The ugly stains match his weathered face. He rocks over momma bear while she hunches over little Meggie like a shield.

My instinct is to block him until I remember this is the past; blocking this scene would work about as well as trying to block the events of a movie.

Blood is matted in momma bear's hair and her shoulders jerk in silent sobs. Little Meggie, however, wastes no energy trying to keep her shrieking quiet. My fingernails sting my palms when Mr. Drunk spits on the wall. He exits the room like a slow and swaying elephant.

Momma bear jumps when the door slams and rattles the walls. The pictures above the sofa go crooked. With her back to me, the blond woman unfolds her wary body. She motions silently for Meggie to stay and then tip-toes across the tiny room, holding her lower back with her left hand. She peers around the doorway before disappearing into the kitchen.

My stomach twists into a knot and I keep my eyes on

little Meggie for almost a minute. I turn toward the doorway to see what has made her eyes so big.

My hand clamps over my mouth, but even muffled, my groan is loud. Every part of me wants to chase after the monster, to make him regret what he did to this woman.

"Momma?" little Meggie's voice squeaks.

My feet are kicked out from under me and I hit the hard earth, doubled over. As I hurl onto the dirt, a cloud of dust lifts into the air and the remains of my meal disappear. The image of momma bear's face, battered like she'd been bludgeoned with a meat tenderizer, is seared into my brain.

The room must have already completed its spin-cycle, because GPS Jeanette says, "Please proceed to 1989." I wipe my mouth with the back of my hand, not wanting to face another door. Taking a deep breath, I reluctantly turn the handle.

The sound of a beeping monitor raises goose bumps on my arms and knits my insides together. I so hate hospitals. Meggie's asleep in the bed. Her mom, whose face features a sagging left eyelid and a deep scar along her cheekbone, is sitting on one side of Meggie's bed. The twin boys are sprawled in chairs on the other side.

Meggie's mom stands when a middle aged man, wearing a tie that is spotted in a Dalmatian pattern, comes into the room. He opens a folder and skims across a page inside. Thirty seconds later, he puts the folder under his arm and says, "I am very pleased with the results we've gotten back on Meggie's heart. I know these outbursts are scary, especially with Meggie's past heart surgery, but her heart is as healthy and strong as a normal thirteen-year-old girl. This is good news." The doctor pulls a pen and small pad of paper from his pocket and scribbles something while he talks. "I'm prescribing a sleeping pill that should help."

Meggie's mom turns toward Meggie and barely nods. In a soft voice, she says, "It doesn't matter how many times I tell her he's not coming back, her nightmares won't stop."

My feet are clotheslined out from under me and I'm jerked back into the stone room. After the usual cycle, I reluctantly push myself into 1992, which is not a room at all.

My foggy breath fills the backseat of what would better be described as a go-kart than a car. My knees shove into my chest like a closed folding chair.

The guy in the passenger seat beside Meggie has a protruding Adam's apple and a deeper than expected voice. "Now release the clutch and push the gas. Ea-si-ly."

The car jumps and we jerk forward so hard my chin hits my knees.

Meggie's thin, white eyebrows crease apologetically. "Better?"

He laughs. "Not yet, but you'll get it…or my clutch will burn up. Either way, you owe me dinner."

After the car jerks forward three times and then dies, the guy smiles. "How about you pretend *not* to be a rabbit."

I'd laugh if there were actually room.

Meggie smacks the guy on the arm. "Brody, you're not helping!"

I'm sucked out of the car and back into the musty room, relieved to stretch my legs. The drill is repeated and the door to *1994* appears.

A hoarder would look like minimalist in this room. Posters and photographs cover every inch of wall space. The stereo, playing at a low volume, is almost as big as the bedroom.

Brody, whose body has grown into his Adam's apple, managed to find a piece of carpet amid the strewn clothing. Meggie sits on the bed behind him and rubs his shoulders. She's taller and thinner, but not at all lanky. Her light hair is longer and sports a side ponytail.

"What's the big deal? Just take the test again," Meggie says.

"My score isn't going to get any better," Brody replies, seemingly to the carpet.

"Sure it will."

"It won't. I'm not like you!"

Meggie leaps back on her bed and shrinks into the corner. A second later, Brody's up and towering over her, causing her to mimic my position in the backseat of the car a few minutes ago.

"Whoa." Brody holds his palms out like he's trying to calm a wild horse. "I'm sorry."

There's fear in her blue eyes when he inches closer. "I'm sorry," he repeats and then lunges. She disappears under his embracing arms while he talks into her hair. "I'm not him. It's OK, I'm not him. I would never hurt you."

My heart sinks as my body is pulled back into the stone room. The door slams and the thunderous sound echoes off the curved walls.

"Thank you, Grant. This will end your first session. Please return after break," GPS Jeanette's voice says. I'm yanked up into the blackness before I can prepare myself. My lungs constrict under the pressure and I fight to catch my breath.

I land hard, but at least I'm on my feet when the book spits me out. The binding thuds to the hardwood floor and the cover flops closed. At the same time, my calimeter buzzes to signal break.

I scratch through my hair and wonder if that will ever become bearable, not sure if I'm referring to the traveling or to glimpsing into a Tragedy's past like Meggie's.

———～～———

With coffee in tow, I take the elevator down to the sprawling marble lobby. GPS Jeanette, whom I've had enough of for one day, wishes me well when I step out of the golden box.

I glance at Benson on my way to the courtyard, wishing I could pop in and see the crew. I almost talk myself into it, but figure Jonathan won't be happy if I'm tardy to my first day of training.

My heart rate quickens—from nerves, I guess—when I'm in the courtyard hall off the lobby. The giant doors welcome me to a tree-huggers' paradise. The air smells like dandelions, even though there's not a single weed along the manicured lawn.

Down the stone path and across the vast training field,

a small group is hanging out. My nerves ramp up my heart rate even more when I realize I haven't given much—OK, any —thought to training. Willow's image flickers in my head, her lunatic voice demanding, *Again,* over and over when she trained me to block. I shudder on my way to the field, forcing my shoulders and back straight.

Jonathan is one of the five on the grass, dressed casually like always. I guess a group this size is too small for a formal bleacher meeting. He smiles and the severity of his jaw line lessens. "Welcome, Grant."

I recognize the other four from *Elite Force Seven*, the video game of choice around here. I wonder if I'll make an appearance in the game now. The thought is horrifying.

Jonathan points to a plain, but very pretty girl. Her thick, reddish-brown hair is haphazardly tied into a bun that's the size of Texas. "I'd like you to meet Trina. She's been with our team sixteen years."

"As a Satellite or an Elite?" I ask to no one in particular while her hand, as delicate as her frame, gets lost in mine.

"As an Elite," Jonathan answers. "And Reed. Thirty-three years."

I overlook his sharp, spiky hair and multiple piercings to shake his hand, recalling our meeting a couple months ago and the helpful advice he offered Willow for my coding problem. Now that coding comes so easily, it's somewhat embarrassing to think of the trouble it once gave me.

"Thanks for helping me out with that problem," I say to make conversation.

Reed's eyes dart briefly to Jonathan and when they are

back on me his expression changes; he may as well be calling me the village idiot. Normally this might bother me, but coming from a guy who shares Willow's fashion sense—God love her—I don't put much stock into it.

Jonathan steps between us and pulls my attention to the other girl on the field. "And this is Evelynn. She'll have been with us an impressive forty-two years next month."

This girl isn't dressed casually like the others; there's not a shred of cotton on her body. Instead, she's clad in some sort of painted-on, shiny material. Maybe training won't be too strenuous after all. One can hope.

Evelynn's tongue slides over her bleached teeth. Her eyes move up and down my body like she wants me for dessert. Her seven-inch heels make her exactly my height, so we are eye to eye when we shake. Our hands don't break apart until Trina overdramatizes a sigh.

"And not to forget Jackson, who has proven himself exceptional over the past twenty-one years," Jonathan continues.

Feeling embarrassed and unsure why, I turn back to Jackson. To say this guy has any sort of build would be a lie. He's not only small, he's awkward. Not in a subtle way, either. Like trouble-tying-his-own-shoes awkward.

Jackson looks from Evelynn to me and grins, nodding like a bobble-head. I consider digging a hole right here in the field and hiding inside it as two other guys approach, looking more like the type I'd expect to see here. If it weren't for the stark contrast in their skin color, they could be twins, by size anyway.

"Last, but certainly not least, meet Lawson, thirty-nine years, and Billy, nine years," Jonathan says when they reach us.

Everything but Lawson's extended arm, heavily muscled and black as his T-shirt, remains frozen. His grip tightens and he nods once. When he releases my hand, I turn to the other guy.

With his bumpy nose in the air, Billy squints at me like I smell bad. He ignores my hand at first, then clutches it as I'm pulling away. I grit my teeth while the veins in his tree-trunk neck pop out. Billy finally releases his grip. Instead of splaying my fingers, I turn to Jonathan and bite the inside of my cheek until my hand stops tingling. Note to self: stay away from that guy.

Jonathan seems oblivious to the transaction between Billy and me. "Now that we all know each other, let's get down to it. First, let's get Grant acquainted with how things work."

Evelynn has materialized beside me, so close her warm, bare arm brushes against mine. I'm surprised a star-bright *glint* doesn't bounce off her teeth when she smiles.

"Grant, Elites convene for training every other day. This practice is instrumental in building your blocking tolerance and keeping that tolerance elevated." Jonathan scans the others. "As you may have heard, Grant is, historically, our most inexperienced Elite."

Billy muffles a laugh and his partner in crime, Lawson, fails at concealing a grin.

"It would be wise not to discount this," Jonathan says in the direction of the Hulks. "Grant has proven himself quite impressive in his previous training. His mentor was not easy on him."

Ha! Try unrelenting. Or insane…unstable…mental…

Jonathan reacts to Billy's arrogant smirk with a warning look.

Billy's laughing now. "Sorry, was that eye roll out loud?"

"Grow up," Trina says to him.

Billy winks at her.

"Did I mention that Grant established a new record for the number of blocks on a first attempt?"

I didn't know this—nor do I care much—and wish Jonathan would stop already. His cheerleading isn't helping my fan base.

Billy is now chili pepper red, and it's clearly not a result of embarrassment. His crimson cheeks are taut. "Yeah, we've all heard it. So he's Boy Wonder. Big deal." There's not a trace of nice in Billy's grin.

"Let's be mindful that we are a team." Jonathan pauses and then uses a stern tone. "Billy."

Billy's grin finally dissolves.

Jonathan turns back to me. "Building a tolerance is important. Training with Willow was just a glimpse into what an average day will consist of with your Tragedy."

An average day? What the heck happens during a *bad* day?

Unaware of my worries, Jonathan continues. "Let us pair off for blocking drills."

"I'll partner with him." Evelynn breathes the last word

in my ear, sending chills down my arms.

"Actually, I would prefer that you partner with Lawson today."

Whew. Thank you, Jonathan.

Evelynn isn't pleased.

"Jackson, would you be so kind as to instruct Grant? Billy, Trina, why don't you two pair off and work out some of that aggression," he suggests happily, despite Billy's and Trina's blatant disapproval. "Reed, please be our Watcher today."

When everyone breaks off into pairs, Jackson and I head to the far right side of the lawn. He skips along to match my pace and beams up at me. He's so small I could step on him.

"Were you super-stoked when you found out?"

I refrain from laughing at his high voice and shrug my answer. After learning what an average day will be like, I'm even less keen on this whole Elite thing.

"Man, it was over twenty years ago that I was chosen, but it feels like yesterday. No one ever thought a guy like me would be an Elite. Not even me, if I'm being honest. Which I am, by the way. Being honest, that is."

I raise my eyebrow.

"Sorry, am I rambling? I am. I ramble when I get nervous. At least that's what people tell me. Not that I always believe what people say. You shouldn't, you know? It doesn't matter what people say. You should never—"

"Jackson," I interrupt.

"Yeah?" he asks.

"You're rambling."

"Oh. Sorry."

He takes two silent strides to my one until we reach the other side of the field, far from the other two groups.

Billy and Trina have already started working in the distance. When Billy charges towards her, the image of Meggie's dad pops into my head. Billy isn't sloppy, though, which worries me.

Trina looks bored, twirling a long curl that has escaped from her bun. A waterfall-like haze extends out from her and encloses them both. When the filter dissipates, Billy falls on all fours and shakes his head like a dog.

My laughter halts as soon as he stands. Even from here, the darkness in his eyes is dangerous. Trina's stance, no bigger than a kid compared to his monstrous size, doesn't help matters and my stomach does a nervous flip.

When Trina's next concocted filter evaporates into bouncing water droplets around them, Billy falls on his butt. As Trina mockingly bows at the giant, it's apparent he'd like to maul her.

"Um, you ready?" Jackson says.

"Huh? Oh. Yeah."

"We'll just be doing standard blocking drills. Should be pretty easy, right? You want to go first or should I? Because it doesn't matter to me either way. Whichever you choose is fine. Personally, I—"

"I'll block first," I interrupt, remembering how unnerving it was when Willow got into my head.

"Cool," is all he says and positions himself fifteen feet away. I hope that from this point on, Jackson will keep all his answers to one word.

His boyish face is all business. "We'll keep it simple, I mean, if that's all right with you? I'm going to come at you, so try to stop me, OK?"

If I could get past his height—or lack thereof—he'd be easy to take seriously, but I'm looking down at him wondering how someone so small could do any damage as I take my stance, certain that this is going to be easy.

Jackson's short legs carry him faster than I expect. I collect my energy as I've done so many times now and tighten my visualized blue filter into a perfect ball. "Haze," I say and a rippling waterfall rushes from my body, enclosing us and muffling all distant sounds.

Sit, sit, sit, sit, SIT, SIT…

While Jackson comes at me, the paralyzing electric jolt hits, sharp and strong. I try to think, to remember the word that will make the pain halt, but the current holds my brain hostage.

"Block!" I finally shout when Jackson's shoulders are three inches from my chest.

He sits on the ground, stunned for about thirty seconds. "Not bad. Let's test your stamina, if you're cool with that. Or, we can take a few minutes to rest if you…"

"I'm good."

He pushes himself up from the grass and returns to his previous position fifteen feet away. "Ready?"

After I nod, he begins his approach.

When the translucent, blue ball obstructs my vision, I shout, "Haze," and the undulating barrier separates us from the rest of the world.

Turn back, turn back, TURN BACK…

A hot knife cuts through my muscles and my scream can't break free from the electrifying pain. *Think, Grant, THINK!*

"Block," I finally manage, breaking the connection and causing Jackson to turn.

I hunch over to relieve my rubbery muscles. I look up from my boots, panting, as Jackson stops and turns. He smiles, as if the fact that I got into his head doesn't bother him.

"Can you go again? I understand if you can't, two in a row can be tough…" he's saying as I stretch my shaky arms.

"Just give me a minute, OK?"

Jackson stops talking and I welcome the silence. While my muscles recover, he jogs in place and watches the others work in the distance. This guy is a ball of energy. I have to wonder if it's possible for him to sit still. After about five minutes of watching the others work, I feel rested enough to go again. "Let's do it."

We go three more rounds and my muscles scream in agony.

"Man, you're really good. Really. That's a lot of blocking for someone so new. Seriously, wow, I can't believe—"

"I'll try again," I say, exhausted but curious to see how long I can last.

"Really?"

That's it? One word? I nod. I'm already dead, what's the worst that can happen, aside from losing all muscle control?

Jackson's short legs pivot back into position. He doesn't give me a heads up this time, just advances.

"Haze!" I shout when the blue filter comes, lighter than before.

The bubble forms around us and I watch Billy and Trina through the waterfall, distorted and now just a few yards away. Whatever Billy is saying is too muffled to comprehend.

You, idiot, you're too late! I scold myself and react the only way I can, by digging my left foot behind me to brace for the impact.

Jackson groans when he hits me, but despite my flaming muscles I barely budge. When the haze that never carried a thought evaporates, the roaring sound of someone's laughter increases.

I ignore the others approaching us. "Sorry, man." I pull Jackson up and mentally ream myself for missing the block.

Jackson brushes himself off. "Totally cool, no sweat. You all right? I didn't mean to hit you so hard. I totally thought you had it. If I had known, I would have gone easier on you. I mean—"

"I'm OK," I interrupt, but because Billy won't stop laughing at him, I mock a pain in my stomach. "That was a heck of a hit."

"I'm sorry I hurt you. That was a head-on blow and—"

"I think I'll be all right," I say in my nicest voice.

"You've got some mad skills," Trina says.

"Seriously, that was really something. *You're* really something." Evelynn adds.

I shift awkwardly while everyone gazes with approval; everyone but one, anyway. Billy, who has stopped laughing, is glaring like he wants to rip me in two. Or ten. When he retracts his venomous stare, he turns to Lawson. "You may as well ask him out, you pansy."

"Watch it, Billy," Lawson warns in a deep voice.

Jonathan clears his throat and steps between them. "We have many years ahead. I would advise that we all try to get along." His smile doesn't do much to lighten the mood. "That will wrap up our session today. Grant, the others will be returning to their assignments shortly. I suspect you have some work to complete in getting acquainted with your Tragedy."

In response, I lock eyes with Billy.

"See you all in two days. Safe journeys everyone," Jonathan says as his dismissal.

Billy breaks the staring contest first, but snickers before whispering something to Lawson.

On the way back inside, Evelynn glues herself to me. Her smooth arm keeps meeting mine no matter how much I veer away. "You really were something out there. That's some great stamina, especially as a newbie." Evelynn squeezes her hand around my biceps muscle. "I'm interested to see what other tricks you have up your sleeve."

I pull my arm away and step to the left, giving Trina what I hope is a 'help me' look.

Trina smiles like she gets it and moves to put herself between Evelynn and me. Evelynn is reluctant to take the hint, but eventually falls back, becoming the receiver of

Jackson's rambling.

"She's a persistent thing. She'll be all over you until she's absolutely sure you're not interested," Trina says.

I scowl. "I guess I'd better let her know sooner than later."

Trina undoes her hair and wild curls sprout in every direction. Something tugs inside me. Why is she so familiar? Maybe I've seen her around Benson and just don't remember. That doesn't feel right, though. Hair like that would be difficult to forget.

When we get through the doors, Billy's shoulder rams into mine.

"Watch yourself," he hisses in my ear when I straighten. "Don't count on doing so well in training next time." His lips pull over his pointy teeth like a wolf before he turns and stalks away.

3. Whatever it was, it must have been really bad

Keeping my distance from Billy—because he could probably take me and he obviously hates me—I cross Benson when I spot my crew. Before I get to the table, Clara, Liam, and Rigby puff into nothingness while Owen and Anna say goodbye to one another with their tongues. After allowing them sufficient slurping time, I glance down from Benson's floating lanterns to see the now-abandoned table. Sigh.

My backpack feels heavier on my way out of the dining hall. It seems like ages since I've talked to everyone and now I'm stuck waiting another day.

A strange, almost anxious pull in my gut manifests as I find myself walking through the middle doorway of Alogan. My footsteps are the only sound in the church-like room and I sit in one of the back pews. The marble altar where Jonathan gave his orientation speech seems bigger now that the place is empty. Scarlet tanagers, the State Birds of Progression, fly like flames across the sky that, by all accounts, should be a ceiling.

Being in this room and recalling Jonathan's welcome speech, my thoughts turn to Willow. I twist in the pew, expecting to see her brown dreadlocked hair that's almost as big as her personality, her tattoos nearly as colorful. But the doorways are as silent as the heavily-columned room. Odd, since the birds are usually trilling unless Jonathan has something to say.

An orange, black-winged bird lands on the pew just a foot from my shoulder. I keep still, amazed that it would land so close to me. Its glass eyes shine, reflecting my own image. The bird chirps once and then flies into the sky. My scars prickle and a cold tingle percolates through my T-shirt and jeans, accentuating the anxious feeling in my stomach.

Exasperated, I stand and shrug on my backpack, wishing I knew where the twin, tear-shaped marks on my chest and knee came from.

I stalk down the B hallway and ride the elevator up to my room. After two minutes of banging around in the kitchen for coffee, I'm on my favorite green sofa staring at the dark purple book on the trunk.

The addition of the *Elite* label unbalances the way that my name appears, embossed on the cover. I feel unbalanced myself, remnants of the strange feeling I had while sitting in Alogan.

"May as well get on with it," I say to the empty room.

I grab the heavy book and open to the hand-shaped vacuum portal. Funny how non-threatening the page looks. I turn my head like I'm about to get a vaccination injection and reluctantly press my palm into the hand outline. Instead of searching for light that doesn't exist, I focus on the insides of my eyelids and remind myself that my lungs won't actually implode.

When I open my eyes, dirt is swirling around my legs from my landing, making the musty smell of the circular room even stronger.

"Welcome back, Grant," GPS Jeanette says before the wall of doors spins into a blur. The sparse blades of grass around the stone edges dance from the tornado.

Ding.

"Please proceed to 1999," GPS Jeanette chimes.

The handle shocks me with an electric spark when I enter through the only door the cyclone left behind. The temperature doesn't change, but the air feels thick in my lungs when I step through.

On the blacktop driveway, Meggie has her hand fisted tightly around a large envelope. "You read it," she orders to Brody.

"Come on Meg, you were top of your class at Maryland." He pries Meggie's fingers free and rips the envelope open, scanning over the letter.

Meggie's face is colorless. "Well?"

Brody's smile prompts Meggie to shriek in such a high pitch I doubt I'll ever hear again. "Hopkins!" she yells and then squeals again. "I. Got. Into. Hopkins!"

Brody hugs her and then spins her around until she finally stops squealing. "Congratulations, baby. I'm so proud of you."

I'm sucked away and the metal door slams. The spin-cycle completes and GPS Jeanette orders me into 2000.

Blood is pooling at the foot of a hospital bed and I cringe away from the metallic smell. Meggie, donning pink scrubs, pushes sweat-matted hair from a woman's forehead. The woman in the bed alternates between holding her breath and screaming. The doctor and the two other nurses are as despondent as Meggie.

"Give me a big push as soon as you can," the doctor instructs.

The woman's knuckles turn white as she crushes Meggie's hand. Something covered in slime and blood sloshes into the doctor's hands. It can't be, it's too small to be...

I focus on the dated linoleum while the new mother's cries pierce the room. When a man—out of place in his suit and tie amidst the massacre—rushes in and joins the nightmare, the room is soon flooded with hysterics from the would-be parents.

I follow after Meggie when she hurries out of the room. Her back slaps against the cinder block wall before she hunches over and sucks in air. Someone closes the door to block out the unthinkable devastation, but the barrier is not enough to muffle the couple's wailing entirely.

I'm too numb to notice the pull that sucks me out of the hospital or the spinning room that follows, but the current of the next door pulls me from my stupor. I walk into 2001, into a world of white.

I've got to hand it to Brody; Meggie in that lace wedding dress really is something. Meggie's brothers, all grown up now, along with three other groomsmen, face me as they watch Meggie walk down the aisle. One twin has blond hair that hangs below his shoulders; the other has hair so closely cropped that it makes Rigby's look long. Their faces, though, are as identical as their white suits.

The bastard who used Meggie's mother to catch his swinging fists is in the back corner of the ivory church where no one is likely to notice him but me. He's no raging bull now. Heck, he'd probably have trouble beating an egg for an omelet. Still, my muscles tighten and I have to remind myself this is the past, not the present. He's gone through the trouble of tucking in his shirt and his oily hair shows predominant comb lines. I'd bet money no one knows he's here. I'd also bet his invitation didn't get lost in the mail.

I watch the ceremony and can't help but smile along with Meggie and Brody. I laugh with them when Meggie trips on her dress on the way back from lighting the candle on the altar. Meggie is the definition of a glowing bride. Just as the priest announces the newly married couple, I'm sucked out of the church.

The roulette wheel lands on 2004 and places me in another hospital room. I swallow, not wanting to witness another death. It might not make sense for a dead person to have trouble witnessing death, but my reaction is far from apathetic.

I'm not sure whether to be happy or scared to see Meggie in the spotlight this time. While she's screaming obscenities, I gauge the overall atmosphere to be upbeat and I relax a little. A nurse ignores Meggie's foul mouth, and studies the paper graph spitting from the machine next to the bed.

Meggie pulls her legs to her chest. "Janine! I want more drugs! Now!"

The nurse laughs and I don't even want to know what

she finds under Meggie's hospital gown.

"He's almost here. I'll go grab Doc Walt. Take a look Brody, it's really something. The glory of a new life and all that..." she trails off on her way out the door.

Brody extends his arm so Meggie can maintain her death-grip on his hand while he leans toward the end of the bed.

Meggie groans her disapproval just as an eighty-something year old doctor shuffles calmly into the room, followed by a slew of chatty nurses.

"This is it, Meggie..."

"I can't believe..."

"...so glad I was on shift today."

"Brody, are you all right?"

Meggie disappears amid a sea of pastel-colored scrubs, but her volume remains at maximum, screaming obscenity after obscenity. After a few grunts, a baby cries, causing an eruption of *oohs* and *ahhs*.

"I love you guys," Meggie says in her sweetest voice after a few minutes. Apparently babies have a magic ability to restore sanity.

I'm pulled back into the stone well and directed into 2007.

I huff a visible sigh into a room that may as well be the same as the last. The good news is that Meggie appears to be playing it cooler this time and Brody actually has some color in his face.

"My mom is bringing Josh in later," Meggie tells the nurse who's typing on the computer beside the bed. "He's so big you'll hardly recognize him and he's so excited about meeting—"

Meggie breaks off and—*Holy Mother!*—the obscenities that follow from Meggie's mouth are impressive, albeit unflattering.

The doctor shuffles into the room, even older and slower than last time. He asks if everyone is having a lovely day.

Meggie answers with a slew of curses.

"Are you ready?" Grandpa Doc asks, sitting at the foot of the bed that's been transformed into some torturous, stirrup contraption.

With fewer spectators than before, I have more of a view than I ever wanted. Brody and two nurses encourage Meggie while her face changes from red to purple and then back to red.

Meggie relaxes, sucks in a breath like she's about to go under water, and then her face contorts again. A nurse counts down from ten and at number four the baby slips out, covered in red slime. Sweet Meggie returns for about thirty seconds, then reverts back to sailor mode. Someone needs to give this girl a bar of soap.

"Almost finished. Give me another one," Doc says.

Another what? She's already—

Oh Lord, twins run in the family!

I'm waiting to be sucked out of the room while the babies are taken care of and Meggie is put back together, but nothing happens. Meggie's mom comes in with big brother, Josh, and they are introduced to Sophie and Harper. Josh is as white headed as Meggie with the same close-set eyes, but his face is square like Brody's. Little Josh's mood sours when the attention shifts off of him and onto his new sisters. While I'm chuckling at his impressive temper tantrum, the powers that be call for a switch-up by sucking me away.

GPS Jeanette's chiming voice directs me into 2009, which is finally somewhere other than a hospital room.

This may be worse.

After letting one vaporous breath out, my lungs freeze, unwilling to let the assaulting stench of sweat, feet, and urine enter my air passage.

Josh, a toddler-sized, blond-haired girl, a freckled boy, and I are squeezed into a human-sized hamster cage. I crawl backwards into the blue tube, hitting the smudged, convex window and wishing I was anywhere else.

"What did you call her?" Josh's threatening tone is humorous because he's no thicker than a straw.

The freckled kid is confused. "What?"

"You called my sister an idiot," Josh says.

"So?"

Josh socks him in the arm. "Don't call her that!"

"But…you call her that all the time," the freckled kid whines.

"I'm her brother!"

Baffled, the freckled boy turns to maze through another stinky tunnel, mumbling, "Whatever."

Meggie's head appears from the green tube. She's up here by choice? She crawls to Josh and pulls him into a hug. "I'm proud of you, baby."

"I found a penny up here!" Josh says like he didn't hear Meggie. "Heads up, too!"

"You find those everywhere. My little penny boy."

When I'm pulled back into the stone well, I take advantage of the fact that I can breathe again and revel in the earthy air. I've been on farms that have smelled better than that place.

The stone spins in a blur around me. When the circuit is complete, GPS Jeanette says, "Please proceed to 2012. This will be your final door."

Yes!

I step from the circular room onto a brick patio. My breath hangs as heavy in the air as the smoke from the grill. The screen door bounces closed behind Meggie and she sets a tray of raw meat on the table beside the grill. Brody wraps an arm around her and takes a swig from his beer bottle.

With her head resting on his chest, Meggie watches their three kids in the backyard. Josh is making a dump truck fly, barely missing the girl who is having a full-blown conversation with her Barbie dolls. Their other daughter is digging through the rocks, concentrating like she's in search of something.

Meggie steals Brody's bottle and takes a drink. "What did we do to deserve them?"

Brody takes the bottle back. "Whatever it was, it must have been really bad."

Meggie jabs her elbow into his ribs and he hunches in fake pain.

"We're so lucky," Meggie whispers a minute later.

Brody kisses the top of her head. "I think that every day of my life, baby."

My feet kick out from under me and I'm more than thrilled about it being my last ride for a while.

"Thank you for your time and best of luck in your assignment," GPS Jeanette says.

Strike that, there's one ride left: a black, constricting one. My muscles tighten and I squeeze my eyes closed, silently saying *adios* to the stone dungeon.

Flying upwards through the nothingness, I keep my eyes locked shut. The suffocating ride ends with the book hawking me out like a loogie and flopping closed.

I stuff the book into my bag before sinking into the sofa. After a few minutes, it's obvious that my attempt to relax is failing, so I decide to head down the hall to the coding room instead.

Sitting on the black mat that contrasts against the light hardwood floor, I study my reflection in the mirrored wall and try to tame my messy hair. Giving up, I cross my legs, rest my hands on my knees, and close my eyes.

The faint hint of lemon in the air relaxes me. After a few breaths, my shoulders and back loosen and I'm surrounded by a forest. From my tree stand, I have a full view of the clearing below. To my right, the antlers come into view before the giant buck himself does. There's no possible way I could be any more relaxed than I am while I watch this animal.

The surrounding trees strangely fade away, leaving me standing in a bedroom. I blink my eyes, sure that my vision is tricking me. Is this my old bedroom? Feeling like I should recognize it more, the unsettling déjà vu sensation makes my muscles tense. Crossing to the open closet, I inventory the clothes. The jeans and shabby cotton shirts are similar to items I would wear. On the carpet below them are a pair of worn boots identical to my own; same brand, same worn leather, same laces. Confused, I go to the dresser to scan the picture frames. I suck in a sharp breath when I see a photograph of myself. Ice-cold air assaults my lungs and goose bumps rise on my arms.

"Grant," a raspy voice whispers.

I groan from a freezing, muscle-gripping pain like I've never felt before. When my eyes pop open, I'm back in the coding room. My teeth won't stop chattering, yet sweat is running down my face and dripping from my hair, leaving dark spots on the mat. My mystery scars feel frozen, so I rub my chest and knee hard to warm them. When my head lifts, I stop moving altogether.

Was the guy in the photograph really the same person as this panting, crazed stranger in the mirror? And who was the girl beside him?

4. As luck would have it, here you are

I peel off my wet shirt and methodically hit the shut-up button on my calimeter, shocked—but very glad—that break is here. The scar on my chest, now more white than pink, is still cold. The one on my knee is probably the same, but I'm not checking. No need to confirm the sick feeling that something is seriously wrong here.

On my elevator ride down to the lobby, the haunting, unfamiliar voice that spoke my name replays in my head. When my heartbeat reaches an uncomfortable pace, I focus on breathing and push the unsettling event out of mind. Instead, I think of telling my friends about my new role as an Elite. I hope that any hard feelings about my lack of experience won't generate bad vibes among us.

"Dude, you look like trash," Rigby says when I join the table, and then resumes gnawing on his toothpick. Thankfully, no one else comments on his observation since looking like garbage is common around here if someone has a particularly difficult day with a Tragedy.

Owen, the black-haired bulldog, leans over the table and shakes my hand. "Congrats on making the team, man."

Looks like I don't need to share the news. "Thanks," I mumble and try to gauge the others' reactions.

Clara beams at me in her usual overly-admiring way that makes me uncomfortable. Rigby, seemingly put off by Clara's reaction, clamps down on his toothpick so his jaw flexes into a sharper angle. So far so good on the normalcy around here. I relax and settle into my chair.

Liam must have just eaten something rancid. "How's Tate?"

Never mind about normal.

Before I can reply, Clara says, "Cut it out."

Liam's problem—whatever it is—is his deal, not mine, so I turn away. "How's it going with you, man?" I ask Rigby.

He flips his toothpick between his teeth. "Could be worse. How's training?"

"Relentless. It's like training with Willow." I shake my head. "Nah, it's not that bad."

Recalling our first training session when Willow publicly humiliated me, Rigby laughs.

"I'm so proud of you!" Against her olive skin, Anna's smile is as white as Evelynn's, but the quality of it is completely different. Probably because Evelynn's carries zero sincerity. I don't recall having any siblings while I was alive, but if I had I would have wished for a sister like Anna. I'll never get what she sees in Owen—I've seen monkeys with better manners than that guy—but he makes her happy, and that makes me happy.

Liam's chair scrapes across the gray, wood plank floor and Anna and I watch him stomp out of Benson.

"What's with him?" I ask when he disappears through the middle archway.

Owen shrugs, but the silent exchange he and Anna share makes me uneasy. "You know Liam. His assignment's probably getting hairy. What'd you think of that little guy, Jackson?"

Height-wise, Owen and Jackson could almost be brothers. In width, though, Owen looks more like he ate Jackson for breakfast and transformed him to arm muscles.

"He talks a lot," I say.

Owen bounces up and down like he's about to pee his pants. "Man, I still can't believe you're an Elite. You realize how great this is, right?"

Relief washes over me, and my guilt about being chosen over my friends, who are much more deserving of the position, dissipates.

"It's amazing," Clara adds before I say anything, her clear blue eyes seeming to sparkle against her silver eyeshadow. "And to step into Willow's shoes—I mean, replacing your own Legacy—I don't think that's ever happened before."

"Not in my lifetime. Dude, I can't believe they picked *you!*" Owen barks this loud enough that the neighboring table stops their card game for a second.

I press my hand on my heart in mock pain, but drop it quickly when I feel the cool scar through my shirt. "I was surprised, too." Uneasiness about my scar shifts to my upcoming assignment. "I don't have the experience like you guys, and now things are weird with Liam. I hope he's not jealous. If I had the choice, I would have given him the position. Lord knows he's a better Satellite than me."

"Oh, I don't think he's jealous," Clara says under her breath.

"Why else would he be so pissy?"

Clara shifts in her seat. "Liam's just being…Liam." She sits up straighter and the bright pink tank top elongates her super-model body. "He'll get over it."

Unsure, I shake my head. "I just want things to be normal."

"Not gonna happen, man. You're an Elite now," Owen says.

Clara and Owen make their usual exchange, which is a Clara look-of-disgust met with an Owen smirk.

"That's not true." Clara goes on like she needs to console me. "You didn't even know Willow was an Elite until I told you."

Owen spits a mouthful of milk across the table, barely missing Rigby. "Are you kidding? How could you not know?" he questions like I'm the dumbest person in existence. He may be right.

My expression cracks and I'm laughing before I can stop myself. "I had no idea," I confess.

The others succumb to full hysterics, too.

We finally calm down and I wipe my eyes. "I'm going to get a steak. Anyone hungry?"

Rigby, the only taker, mazes around the crowded tables with me to the best room ever. Every food imaginable, plus a million others I've never heard of, are displayed upon long buffet tables. Sharp mountains beyond the glass wall serve as the perfect backdrop. Rigby follows me past four tables and plops a thick slab of meat on his plate. Man, I love this place.

"Hey Rig, what's really going on with Liam?" I ask when we move to another table.

After the mashed potatoes slide from the serving spoon and splat onto his plate, he stalls by pretending to be preoccupied stirring the gravy. Finally, when the gravy has turned to a watery consistency and the toothpick between his teeth is mangled, he talks. "Here's the thing, man. He's not jealous that you're an Elite. He doesn't like that you've changed."

He thinks I've changed? I'm about to deny this, but Rigby goes on before I can open my mouth. "Your memories didn't disappear like the rest of ours, and you were wrapped up in this chick from your past named Tate. You don't remember any of this," he explains to my blank expression. "You even went to see her a few times."

"Oh, come on, not you, too? Liam's told me this whole fairytale, and frankly, I can't believe you'd buy into it. How would I even go see someone from my past?"

"You displaced to her using your picture frame. I gotta admit, that was an ingenious idea."

All this time, I thought Rigby was a sensible guy.

"Personally, I don't get what Liam's deal is. I mean, you're following the natural order." Rigby shrugs and rearranges his tray to make room for a plate of fries. "So what if it's a little later than everyone else?"

Whitfield, a redhead from our orientation group, pushes herself against Rigby and reaches around him for a roll.

"Rigby," she says in his ear.

"Whitfield."

She chews on her lower red lip and walks away.

I decide against spending any more energy entertaining the made-up story, and ask instead, "Does this mean you're over Clara?"

"Huh?" Rigby dumbly watches Whitfield ladle soup into a bowl two tables over.

I laugh and punch his arm. "Come on, man."

Back at the table, Owen's already dealt Rigby and I into a hand of Sats.

"You guys know Rig is into redheads?" I joke.

Owen twists around in his chair and watches Whitfield talking with some girls a few tables over. "I knew it, man!"

"Whatever," Rigby sneers and scoops up his cards. "Let's play."

"She's really pretty. You two would be great together." Clara slides a card into the fanned set in her hand and winks at me.

As usual, break ends too soon. When the thousands of Satellites have vaporized to save the world, I head out of the empty hall figuring I might as well take Owen up on his offer to use his gaming system. There's nothing else to do now that my introduction to Meggie is complete. If Jonathan doesn't release me soon, I very well may lose my mind.

Owen's décor made me laugh the last time I was here,

and my reaction hasn't changed. The floral sofa and chair, outdated enough to make my green sofa modern, just don't match his personality.

I grab the binocular-mask contraption, hop up onto his black counter, and strap the atrocity around my head. The device powers on with a series of chimes, and the icon for *Elite Force Seven* appears. Apparently no one plays any other games around here. The characters begin scrolling past and—

Oh. My. God.

You've got to be kidding me! Not only am I included in the game, but someone has pulled a really bad joke designing my character, which is anime at its worst. The scar through my left eyebrow is the only thing that is actually dead on. My arms and chest are so big they're bursting through my shirt and the lines of my jaw are also exaggerated. A lot. And my brown hair…it's never been so…metrosexual. Ugh.

I try to forget that other people are actually playing this game and slide my finger through the air to shoo my image from the screen. I cycle through the other characters and scowl because their images are more accurate.

Sour about the embarrassing way the game depicts me, I chose to play as Billy. Then I intentionally lose three games in a row.

Deciding to play for real, I choose Trina's character. She's compact but defined, and her out of control curls couldn't be any sexier.

Did I honestly just think a cartoon character was *sexy?* Someone commit me. I shake my head and start the game, punching through the air in the correct sequences to make the blocks. The longer I play, the better I get.

I'm on level nine, after spending at least an hour stuck on eight, when there's a knock on Owen's door.

"Owen's not here!" I yell mid-block, and my concentration cracks. Forgetting the rest of the sequence, I yank the goggles off to find Jonathan standing in the kitchen.

"Oh, hey. Owen's not here," I say, a little out of breath from so much air punching.

"Actually, I am here to see you," Jonathan says.

His uncanny ability to find someone whenever he wants is enough to raise my eyebrow.

"As luck would have it, here you are," he says.

Yeah, luck. "What's up?" I ask and hop off the counter.

"I received word that you've completed your reading."

My introduction to Meggie was nothing like reading. "Is that what we're calling it?"

He laughs and holds out his hand. "I'm here to bring you this." He passes me a heart-shaped locket that's so tarnished the gold has turned to a dull green.

"My tocket, I'm guessing?"

Jonathan nods.

I turn the heart over in my palm, noting it's even smaller and more convenient than Ryder's granite rock. Chain free, too, which makes it easy to slip into my pocket.

"So I'm released?" I ask eagerly. I probably shouldn't be excited, but anything is better than hanging around here all day, no matter how fun *Elite Force Seven* is.

"Yes. Can you go now?"

Is he kidding? "Of course."

"Excellent. Meggie's life is going to be permanently altered within the hour. Do you have your book?"

I fish the assignment book out of my bag and eye it suspiciously because my biceps muscle now strains under the weight. The appearance of the book, however, has not changed at all.

"Please complete your reading upon your arrival. Good luck."

The urgency in Jonathan's voice makes me edgy, which quickly eclipses my previous excitement. My imagination plays through scenarios of what Meggie's going to endure. When I get to a few that are too awful to think about, my mind shuts down completely.

"Staying here will alter nothing," Jonathan says. "I will see you on the field at break."

I swallow and nod while the edges of the locket dig into my palm. "Displace," I whisper and the floor drops out.

I plummet to Earth in a blur, hardly noticing that my stomach has leapt into my throat. Meggie's life is about to take an unimaginable detour. I scowl with regret for being excited about—

Bam!

My feet land in Meggie's world, not like in Flashbacks-o-Meggie, but for real. The red numbers on the clock float in the blackness as my eyes adjust: *4:49.* I'm surprised that the floor didn't break under my boots or that the shallowly breathing bodies in the bed haven't startled from the jolt.

I reposition my bag on my shoulders and flip through

the weighty book. The pages may as well be illuminated now that my Satellite night-vision has kicked on. I read through *The Present* in less than a minute and the heavy book falls from my hands, landing soundlessly. I pick it up, open to the page I just read, blink a few times, and read again. The text refuses to bend to my will.

I close my eyes and keep them that way for a full two minutes until the roaring starts. The rumbling overwhelms my brain, but my body never feels the heat, even when the flames have climbed up the stairs.

Fury kicks in and I shove the book into my bag. "Wake up! Come on, wake up!" I scream, pacing at the foot of the bed to fill the void a smoke detector should occupy.

When the coughing starts down the hall, I lean over and cover my ears, but the scratchy barks still get through.

"Wake up!" I yell into my knees.

Finally, Brody and Meggie start coughing, too.

"What's happening?" Meggie croaks.

I see Brody's figure out of the corner of my eye when he heads to the door.

"Don't touch the knob," I say under my breath.

He does, of course. The cursing that follows proves it. I assume he finds something to use as an oven mitt because the roaring becomes overwhelming for two seconds, followed by a slamming door.

"WE HAVE TO GET THE KIDS!" Meggie shrieks.

"Jump!" Brody's voice yells over the roaring fire.

I lift my head to watch their exchange by the now opened window.

"The kids!" she pleads.

"It's the only way to get to them! Jump!" He all but pushes her out the window, hanging onto her forearms to lower her as much as possible before releasing his grip.

I take a few steps and ghost my head through the drywall and insulation in time to see Meggie two stories below limping around the side of the house. I step through the wall and float to the grass, staying close to Meggie as Brody sprints past us.

When we reach the front yard Meggie eyes up the only tree, surely wishing the sturdy limbs were closer to the second story windows, while Brody disappears around the other side of the house.

I keep my eyes on Meggie when Brody returns, looking away only to watch Brody prop a ladder over the bushes, climb up, and break through the window with his elbow.

Meggie's face is painted with so much worry it ages her pale skin. I ball my fists in anger, all too aware of what's coming next.

Brody does his best to carry Josh down the ladder. Limping across the yard, he lays Josh at Meggie's feet like a dog dropping his game. I concentrate until the blue filter clouds my vision. "Haze!" I yell and order the only thing I can.

Calm, calm, calm, calm, calm…

After I'm zapped with a voltage that would kill me if I weren't already dead, my heartbeat echoes in my ears, carrying the searing current throughout my body. I find the smallest fracture in the wall of pain and spew my next order. "Block!"

Meggie's coughs and cries lessen and the wailing sirens grow louder. Like she's just been jerked awake, Meggie switches from mom to nurse. If she could actually hear my voice, she'd know pumping on Josh's chest will do nothing.

I turn away again when Brody returns with one of the girls because the ruffled pajamas and ash-colored curls are too much to stomach. Meggie's screams overwhelm the approaching sirens and Brody disappears again. A few of the neighbors have joined the nightmare, crowded around two small bodies in effort to help Meggie.

I center my filter to summon the waterfall effect. "Haze," I yell angrily.

Calm down, calm down, calm down...

Pain ignites my already boiling blood. My muscles fight, but the strength seeps out of them anyway.

"Block," I somehow manage and the rippled water surrounding us falls, the droplets bouncing on the grass before vanishing.

Meggie's volume dials down a notch, but she's still frantic, shaking Josh's limp body. The horror on her face is like nothing I have ever seen. She resumes feverishly pumping Josh's tiny chest.

After thirty seconds, I realize the scream pounding though my head is my own.

Meggie growls at the medic as he tries to wrestle her off of Josh, so I block her again and ready myself for more torture. I'd take a lifetime of the electrocuting shock if it would bring even a thimble of comfort to Meggie.

Step back, step back, step back, step…

Zing!

"Block," I groan.

Meggie's arms fall to her side and her face contorts in even more horror when a firefighter returns from the house carrying Brody. Behind them, another yellow-suited man is carrying her third child.

The fifth body removed from the second story window confirms that there will be no break for my trembling muscles.

While I'm performing another block, one of the seven medics who have joined us jogs halfway through me. They attend to the lifeless bodies on the lawn while the Mount Airy firefighters direct water into the house. Meanwhile, Meggie's shedding enough tears to extinguish the murderous flames herself.

The sun is up. Meggie and I are bumping along in the back of the first ambulance. Josh lies on the gurney. Flashing lights from the truck carrying Sophie and Harper spiral through the back-door windows and the mix of sirens is deafening.

After the medics call time of death, I perform seven more blocks. The drive takes only twenty minutes, but when the doors of the steel dungeon open, I'm shrunk between the gurney and oxygen tank, convulsing.

Two nurses, one of whom I recognize from the twins' delivery, collect Meggie when she falls out of the ambulance under the St. Mary's Hospital Emergency sign. When Josh's body, a mere lump under under a sky-blue sheet, is rolled by, both nurses fall to their knees on the sidewalk with Meggie in effort to comfort her, or at the very least, shield her from the nightmare. Four more stretchers follow and I force myself from the truck, cursing my lack of strength. The blue filter is barely visible when I center the translucent ball.

"Haze," I choke.

Pull it together, pull it together, pull it together...

I'm not sure if I'm sending my thoughts to Meggie or myself when I break the connection and my useless body collapses. Somehow willing my crippled muscles to work, I pull myself up and trudge behind the nurses assisting Meggie through the sliding doors.

Before anyone is even aware of what's happening, Meggie has an energy surge that pushes her around the medics and into the room where her three lifeless children lay together. When I reach her, she's staring at the lumpy, ash-smudged sheets. Unimaginable hysterics follow and, running on pure adrenaline, I break what has to be Progression's blocking record.

5. I've got something really special planned for you this time, Princess

The massive, twisted-limb doors bang behind me as I cut across the field like a chisel plow on steroids. Just past the bleachers, seven pairs of eyes follow me like I'm a lunatic. Their allegation couldn't be more accurate.

"What the hell?" I roar on my way to them.

"Grant," Jonathan says calmly when I reach him.

"They were just kids!"

"Awe, that's sweet. This isn't proving to be too much for Princess Grant, is it?" Billy sings in a just-got-kicked-in-the-nads, high-pitched voice.

I lunge to take care of his smile, but someone catches my arm just before it springs forward to kill Billy's ugly face.

"Let me go!" I yell, having no luck squirming out of Lawson's brown, stone arms.

"Grant, please calm down," Jonathan says in an easy tone that burns through me like acid.

Billy steps back when I struggle harder against Lawson, but still smiles. "Kids your weak link, then?"

"She lost all of them," I snarl. I'll kill him when I get free, or whatever the equivalent of death is in this place.

Lawson will have to let me go eventually.

"Show some sensitivity," Trina says narrowly to Billy.

Billy's grin begins to fade and I relax under Lawson's iron grip. Lawson releases me and I lunge, but am caught within seconds.

"He'll continue to restrain you until you've gained control," Jonathan states matter-of-factly. "I would advise that you save your strength for training."

I give up after a few minutes of struggling and Lawson hesitantly releases me. Everyone stands stiffly, presumably in preparation to break up a fight. Everyone except Jackson, that is; he's collecting his eyeballs from the ground.

"Let us take a walk," Jonathan says to me, and then to the others, "Hang loose for a few moments."

I refuse to match his easy-going stride when we cut across the lawn. The tips of gray mountains just beyond the forest pierce the fog and the air seems thicker than usual.

"Facing death is never without challenges," Jonathan finally says after we've stopped.

I'm only able to keep my voice level because I understand what's done is done. "They were too young. It's not fair."

"When you think in Earth terms, yes."

I shake my head and scowl at the manicured grass.

"I agree, the story is one-sided from down there," Jonathan says and nods at the ground.

"And down there the other side is never revealed. It's cruel."

"It can certainly seem that way."

"It *is* that way!"

"There is a grand purpose for every person who passes, as well as for every person who remains living."

I'm seriously getting hit with this again? "Yeah, I get it. The whole 'everything-happens-for-a-reason' thing," I say mockingly. "Meggie's a train wreck. She'll never understand."

"Yes, I was there with her," Jonathan says in a solemn tone.

Is he playing me for an idiot? Being at Meggie's side the entire time, I would have seen him.

"She will," he says a few seconds later.

"She will, what?"

"One day, these events will be vindicated."

"Right." My voice is fully-loaded with a mix of sarcasm and poison.

"Please realize, after a few hundred years together, their time on Earth will be nothing more than a blink."

He doesn't see me roll my eyes because he's focused on the mountains again.

"In the meantime, let's be sure Meggie continues on course." He squeezes my shoulder before directing me back to the others. I'm too frustrated to argue.

When we reach the gawking Elites, everyone but Billy jumps into dramatic, overly enthusiastic conversations to pretend they weren't trying to eavesdrop on Jonathan and me. The image of Meggie's tiny, blond haired kids pops into my head. Kids. They were just kids! Whatever purpose they have could have waited another ten—or sixty—years.

Jonathan's voice halts the Elites fake dialog. "Let's pair

off for blocking drills. Jackson, would you be our Watcher today?"

"Totally. Thanks Jonathan. That's really great. I won't let you down…"

Jonathan breaks Jackson's babbling with a simple, "Thank you."

"I'll take Billy," I say dryly. My line of sight is stuck on Jonathan, but I know Billy's smiling. His expression is so loud, I can feel it vibrating through the air.

Jonathan considers, probably calculating the risks. "Billy, is that acceptable to you?"

"Absolutely," Billy answers with too much enthusiasm.

My tongue slides over my teeth to keep my anger under control.

"May as well get it over with," Jonathan finally says with a tired sigh. "Jackson, please see that they mind the rules."

Jackson follows up the instructions with a slough of jabber, thanking Jonathan again. His voice mutes as Billy and I walk toward the heart of the sprawling field.

Billy doesn't pounce when we cross the field, even though I wish he would. "How you wanna play this, Pretty-boy?" he asks when we stop.

"I'm coming at you. Block me if you want," I say when we've taken our positions like Old West gunslingers.

"Works for me," he says through his pointy teeth.

Fury rolls through me, and my limbs twitch. I charge, making his great-wall-of-chest grow bigger and bigger…

"Haze," Billy hisses when there's just three feet keeping me from annihilating him. Then he grins like he knows something I don't.

The world goes black and goose bumps rise on my skin. My head fills with foreign thoughts; thoughts I would never think, yet it's my voice, no doubt.

I stop in mid-lunge and twirl before sitting on the grass.

Yes, I *twirl*. A graceful, three hundred and sixty degree circle with my arms over my head—like a ballerina!

When Billy explodes into hysterics, Jackson, now just a few feet away, smacks his hand over his mouth to cover his laughter. "Sorry," Jackson muffles to me, gaining control over his reaction.

In the distance, others are also finding humor in my display. Lawson and Evelynn are folded over at the waist, not even trying to hide it like Reed is. Only Jonathan and Trina are straight-faced.

I ignore all of them and narrow my eyes at Billy. "Again!" I demand, internally shuddering by how much I must sound like Willow when she lost her marbles in training so many months ago.

"Sweet! I've got something really special planned for you this time, Princess."

Acid rushes through my veins when Billy winks.

"Haze," he says as I charge him.

A black wall of ice engulfs me. The darkness clears a millisecond later and I'm overcome with thoughts of dancing. I've never been a dancer. Why, I wonder? It would be so fun. I have to try it. Right this instant.

No! My voice screams to itself.

Dance! My alter ego yells back.

No!

Dance!

A deep growl escapes while my mind is stuck on *No!* and the blue filter I see when I'm blocking clouds my vision. I lunge at Billy.

We both groan when I crash into him and my sight snaps back to normal. Surprisingly, the giant falls over. So surprisingly, in fact, that I freeze above him. His face is worth a thousand, priceless words.

"You dance," I snap.

His expression morphs from shocked to enraged and he pushes off the ground. "Beginner's luck," he says.

"I'm not a beginner," I reply, feeling much better because (a) I've kept him out of my head, and (b) I've gotten to maul him. A win on all accounts.

We repeat the cycle and I run at him again, preparing my mind to fight off thoughts he sends to impersonate my own. The temperature drop, mixed with being blinded for a couple seconds, warn me he's about to get in, but my legs are weighted and tired. I need to sit right now. If not, I'm going to fall over. My muscles have never needed a break so badly.

No! Lunge, you fool!

Sit!

Lunge!

Sit!

Lunge!

I follow the tennis match fought in my own voice. Billy and the landscape behind him turn blue, and I force myself ahead against my fraudulent will. My shoulder slams into Billy's chest. When he doesn't fall, I take a swing and catch him in the mouth. He returns the blow.

"Guys, guys! Come on! Stop! Hey…" Jackson rambles in the background.

"Enough!"

Billy and I drop our arms at Jonathan's discordant voice. Then Billy takes a cheap shot at my face while I'm wondering how long the others have been circled around us.

Jonathan's vexation keeps me from mauling Billy. Trina appears to share Jonathan's viewpoint, whereas Evelynn and Lawson seem impressed. Jackson is clearly terrified, and Reed picks at his thumbnail like he couldn't care any less about what has transpired.

"We're a team," Jonathan says, keeping his voice level while Billy and I focus on the grass and pant. "I'm disappointed that we are not behaving as such. Training is concluded."

"But what about—" Jackson starts.

"We're done for today," Jonathan says firmly and turns away.

None of us move until Jonathan has gone up the curving sidewalk and through the massive doors. I push on the tender, swollen skin surrounding my left eye and wonder if it looks as purple and mutilated as Billy's. At least Billy keeps his distance when we cut across the lawn. I wish I could say the same for Evelynn.

"Great show out there, Charmer," she says and bumps her hip against mine. Apparently, she decided that a slippery, gold piece of material and eight-inch heels would be suitable for training. Her matching earrings have more surface area than her dress and she carries a shiny bag large enough to hold her tockets and assignment book, along with the whole get-up she's wearing.

I stomp harder on the stone path. "It wasn't meant to be a show."

"That's what was so great about it." Her seductive wink only annoys me more.

I stop before we reach the door and turn to her. "How do you do it?"

She mocks innocence. "What?"

"Act like this. You're an Elite, so you're obviously good," I say, knowing that after today's assignment there is only one person who has mistakenly been put on this team. "How can you be so numb to everything?"

When she shrugs, the sun, which has burned off the distant fog, hits her metallic earrings and blinds me like her smile. *Glint*. "It's easy after awhile. You'll become desensitized soon."

I shake my head, trying to imagine becoming as crass as her. "I don't want that."

"Of course you do. Look at you; you're a mess. You know what you need?"

Evelynn has no idea what I need. I half expect her to say a make-over.

"A distraction," she says instead, an inch from my ear, and blows her cinnamon-spicy breath in my face.

Full-blown angry now, I push past her like a kid in

mid-tantrum. "Excuse me. I have to go deal with a broken mother who just lost all of her children."

"Which is why you need a distraction," she calls after me.

I stomp through the lobby and into Benson, thrusting a chair out from the table where my friends are sitting.

"Dude! What happened to your eye?" Owen sounds both disgusted and impressed.

I don't answer. Clara, Liam, Anna, and Rigby gauge my bad attitude and leave me alone for the remainder of break. When my calimeter beeps, I dig the tarnished heart out of my pocket and say the magic word to make the gray, weathered wood floor disappear. Blurs of other Satellites surround me, plummeting to Earth like shooting stars. A gold streak bumps against me and the trilling laughter is clear even as it pushes further away. Evelynn is as blinding in motion as she is standing still.

I take a second to gain my balance after the impact of my landing. Back in the death room, Meggie is still frozen over the tiny, ash-covered bodies. When the electricity pops on, everything but her babies are kick-started back to life with a buzz. Two nurses linger in the doorway keeping watch on Meggie, but also sobbing themselves. While Meggie sits between the beds, bent over and wailing into the knees of her dirty sweat pants, I catch up on my reading.

Deflated, I drop the concrete book into my bag, massage the bridge of my nose (which isn't tender anymore), and prepare for the nightmare ahead.

The delivery nurse I recognize from Flashbacks-o-

Meggie approaches my Tragedy. She probably wants to be here about as much as I do, knowing nothing she could say or do will fix Meggie's broken heart. "Take this," are the only words she has to offer.

Without argument, Meggie takes the water and swallows the pill. A hysterical fit follows and the haze command is out of my mouth three seconds later. My thoughts transfer with a jolt and I sever the connection as quickly as possible.

The next hour is a blur of blocking. A priest arrives and reads a passage from the Bible. He offers a few words that I suppose are meant to comfort Meggie, but turn out to have the opposite effect. When the priest is gone, one of the nurses helps Meggie lift and hold one of her daughters. Meggie sits on the bedside and rocks the tiny body for over thirty minutes. Her cries are the loudest yet, but I don't block Meggie. The rest of St. Mary Hospital should know what kind of hell she's been sentenced to.

When Meggie finally lets her first daughter go, she moves on to the second, spending the same amount of time rocking and hugging that tiny, lifeless body. When she gets to Josh, she cries louder and holds him awkwardly because he's so much bigger than his sisters. Her cries lessen and eventually turn to humming. Meggie then begins half whispering, half singing a lullaby that repeats the words "sleep, baby, sleep." My eyes squeeze closed to prevent stinging tears from trickling down my cheeks.

Meggie calms a little after releasing Josh, either from being able to embrace her children or from the nurse's consolation; maybe both. I turn away long enough for the nurse to help Meggie out of her dirty T-shirt and sweat pants and into a clean pair of scrubs. Facing the door, my ears stay sharp for any indication of another outburst.

"You need to say goodbye to your mom, too," the nurse whispers while she ties Meggie's hair into a ponytail. "I'll take you to her."

"What are we going to do, Janine?" Meggie says in a dead voice.

"I don't know." The nurse, Janine, shakes her head and wipes her own tears. "I don't know." What else can she say?

Three blocks later, Meggie leaves her children behind and Janine helps her into the second death room of the day. After six more blocks, my muscles are screaming and Meggie has said goodbye to her mother's lifeless body.

Meggie will probably blame herself for her mom's death. As her assignment book told it, Meggie asked her mom to stay overnight to babysit the kids in the morning. If the cause of the fire is ever disclosed, Meggie will, no doubt, also blame herself for leaving a candle burning in the kitchen the night before. Too bad she'll never learn the truth about fate's hand in this mess, at least while she's alive. Destiny can be a real bitch.

Another nurse stops Meggie and Janine in the hall and leads them to a room a few hallways over. Meggie pauses before her hand touches the steel door.

"Want me to go in with you?" Janine asks, squeezing Meggie's arm.

Meggie takes a deep breath and shakes her head.

"I'll be right here if you need me." Janine plants her back to the wall and wipes her eyes again.

Meggie leaves the door open behind her. I stand beside Janine for a second to prepare for the upcoming torment.

Janine covers her face and her shoulders bounce up and down when Brody's voice carries into the hall. "The kids?" he asks, dry and hopeless.

"Haze," someone says from within the room.

6. I heard our kid here is quite the scrapper

"What are you doing here?" I'm so caught off guard I've almost forgotten about Meggie and Brody. Almost. Completely forgetting would be impossible because they're both in a full-blown frenzy in a room that's not much bigger than Evelynn's dress.

"Despite what Billy says, I assumed you had half a brain. Guess I was wrong."

"Who are you here for?" I ask Lawson, too shocked to care about his slam on me.

"Here's a clue: it's not Meggie," he mocks in a slow voice. "I bet if you try real hard, by process of elimination, you'll figure it out."

"Brody," I say to myself.

"See. That wasn't so hard," Lawson says.

"Oh good, the chocolate hulk is funny, too," I say dryly when the shock has lifted. "This should be a blast."

His teeth, nearly glowing against his dark skin, make an appearance before Meggie's and Brody's volumes rise to a level beyond disruptive. We block our Tragedies at the same time. Clearly, I'm unconditioned compared to Lawson. Not because he's twice my size, but because his body shows no signs of weary twitching, whereas mine appears to be hooked up to a shock machine.

"How do you control your muscles?" I ask, wondering if he notices the jerking spasms of my forearm.

"You'll build a tolerance. That's why we train."

I nod, glad to know I may not always battle this annoying side effect. "Do you build an emotional tolerance as well?"

His broad shoulders under his green military-style jacket lift and fall. "Depends."

"On?" I ask when he doesn't offer any more.

"On you," he states.

Good God, getting him to talk may be more of a challenge than extracting information from Willow. "You wanna elaborate?"

"Do you want to be emotionally numb?" he asks.

I pause for a long time. "I'm not sure."

"Well, you'll be affected until you figure that out."

"Does it still get to you?"

He barely nods at the speckled linoleum.

"It doesn't seem to bother Evelynn," I sneer.

"She's hardened to this life. Billy, too." Lawson shakes his head. "They're built with this—I don't know—shell or something."

"That just seems…" I dig for the right word. Insensitive is too weak.

"It makes them the best we've got," he says before I come up with anything. "Evelynn has taken an interest in you." He puts his bright-white smile on display again.

"Evelynn seems like the kind of girl who takes an interest in everyone."

His laugh is so deep it's more of a rumble. "No, not everyone. Although she does have a knack for being… affectionate, doesn't she?"

"Affectionate?" I say under my breath. "Try presumptuous."

He grins wider. "Your feigning disinterest is only making it worse."

"I'm not feigning, trust me. She's not my type."

"Not your type? Brother, you must be blind."

I force myself to keep a straight face.

"Oh!" His face lights up like he's just solved a puzzle. "You're gay."

Now I do laugh because his shocked eyes are like twin full moons. "No, man, straight as an arrow. Hence the bad clothes. She's just…too much." I try to picture us as a couple: me in my worn out jeans towing around a six-foot disco ball. The vision is absurd.

A loud noise propels me back to reality. Lawson completes a block before I even process the IV tree crashing against the wall, compliments of Brody. He holds his bandaged hand, probably wishing he would have used the other for his outburst. Meggie rushes to fix the stand and checks Brody's tubes while Janine and another nurse enter the tiny room to help.

"Nice," I say to Lawson's quick block.

"You'll get faster. Trust me, we get plenty of practice."

I sigh at his best-news-ever.

"Did you want to be an Elite?" I ask a few minutes later to tune out Meggie's quiet sobs.

Lawson answers by shrugging. "You?"

"I didn't know it was an option for someone as new as me." I pause, remembering when I found out Willow was an Elite, and then recalling the first time we met. I grin at the memory. "I wasn't so thrilled about being a Satellite, I know that."

"Yeah? Why not?"

I think of my reasoning. Every molecule within me knows I didn't want to die, let alone be here. I was pulled away from something, but what? "Don't know." I hate this answer.

"Well, brother, you're the exception around here. I mean, we may not all aspire to be Elites, but most of us think being a Satellite is pretty great."

"It's not that I don't respect what we do, and sometimes I don't even mind the physical strain, but it feels like there's something from my life I'm missing and I just can't grasp what. It's unnerving."

"It's called your memories, bro. You haven't even been here a full year. That's no more than a heartbeat in Progression. I'm shocked that you were chosen to be an Elite. No offense," he adds as an afterthought.

I focus on the gray speckles in the floor and chew on my lip to keep quiet. Anything I say will probably make me sound ungrateful, which is not exactly what I'm going for.

"Jackson, Billy, and Evelynn are the only ones who really wanted to be Elites. For the rest of us, it's a job hazard that was beyond our control." He pauses and cracks his knuckles. "Jonathan told me once that as Elites, we're genetically built to withstand physical and mental bashing more than others, but that doesn't mean we withstand it easily. Even your girl, Evelynn; she's hardened, but I still have doubts that nothing gets to her. I know there are things that get to Billy. I've seen him crack a time or two."

I huff and ignore the part about Evelynn being "my girl." "I have a hard time believing anything affects Billy."

"He's arrogant, but he's not immune," Lawson says. "Better block your chick."

My eyes shift to Meggie. Her face is scrunched into a wrinkled, pained expression and her fingernails are indenting the vinyl chair.

My blue filter comes fast. "Haze."

Calm down, calm down, calm…

The electric shock paralyzes me. When I finally give the order that breaks the connection, Meggie hugs her arms around herself and relaxes as much as the stiff chair will allow.

"She's had a really bad life. It's not fair." The last three words seem to be my mantra lately.

"The walk of life doesn't matter. Being in a situation like this is never fair."

Brody's coughs advance to uncontrollable, though you'd never know it by Meggie's reaction. She's like a drug addict, zoned in on the thin sheet dangling off the hospital bed as precariously as the way Meggie is hanging on to her sanity. My block must have worked better than expected.

Meggie doesn't even raise her head when a nurse hurries in and feeds something into Brody's tube that sends him to Slumberland.

When the room gets quiet again, I look at Lawson. "You're agreeing with me about this being unfair?"

"You sound surprised."

"Willow never agrees with me, especially on the unfairness stuff. She thinks this is all necessary, part of the greater purpose," I mock.

Lawson's face brightens. "Ah, Willow. I miss that girl."

Another Willow fan. Go figure.

"She's right," Lawson says when I stay quiet. "Fair and necessary are very different animals."

"So I'm learning." I watch my thumbs race around each other and then ask, "Where were you during the fire?"

He nods to the unhappy couple. "In their bedroom."

No way. I would have seen him. "You couldn't have been."

"Not bad on your blocks. For your first Elite assignment, you did well."

"Why didn't I see you?" I mumble, more to myself.

"There was a lot going on. I was crouched in the corner by the bathroom. Typically, I keep my face buried when an initial tragedy occurs, but I couldn't help watching you try to warn them. You'll learn soon enough there's nothing we can do in the first few minutes of these disasters. My advice is to save your energy, lay low, and try to keep what's happening out of your head." He turns toward the window, even though the blinds are drawn. "Easier said than done, I know."

I remain quiet, still unsure if I believe him about being there.

"I stayed inside while Brody made his rounds to all the bedrooms. You and I split up in the ambulances."

Meggie sits impressively still when a middle-aged man dressed in jeans and a polo shirt enters. Introductions tell us he is Dr. Brown, the hospital shrink, though he doesn't use those words exactly. An I.D. tag clipped to an Atlanta Falcons lanyard is the only sign that he is part of the staff here. His printed name is followed by a slew of abbreviations that show his importance.

While Brody sleeps, Dr. Brown chooses my chair to pull over to Meggie. After a swift ride across the small space, I jump up before he sits on me. I walk around the bed and rest my back and head against the wall by the window.

"It wasn't that funny," I say dryly to Lawson, who has gotten a kick out my slow reflexes, or more likely, the shock on my face when the doc caught me off guard.

Dr. Brown talks to Meggie about her enormous loss, but Meggie is too raw to answer the few questions he asks. She stays silent while he discusses the different ways people grieve during these types of tragedies. I spend this time replaying the events of the fire, but remain unable to find any trace of Lawson.

After Dr. Brown wraps up his session and excuses himself, Janine takes his place. Meggie is not zombie-like when she argues with Janine about leaving the hospital for a shower and some clean clothes. Janine finally wins, which is a good thing because Meggie's hair and skin are still tinted gray with soot. A break from this building couldn't hurt either. I say goodbye to Lawson and ride along in Janine's minivan.

Back at Janine's house—because Meggie no longer has a home of her own—I remain a gentleman by staying in the hallway while Meggie showers. Though the total trip takes just a little over an hour, by the time we return to the hospital my tired muscles feel a decade older.

Lawson and I exchange a few words and judging by his relaxed posture, his hour with Brody was easier than mine.

After an excruciating afternoon of blocking, my calimeter finally sets me free. I welcome the buzzing grace, wondering how I ever considered the noise annoying. I push on the top of the watch at the same time Lawson pushes his. The hospital powers down with a fading hum and everything in the room goes dead except Lawson and me because we already are. The tears on Meggie's blotchy cheeks are now frozen beads of glass.

Lawson says, "Displace," a second before I do and we're yanked through the ceiling. The screaming wind fills my ears and my hair flattens to my head.

Along with Lawson, who's morphed into a glowing, bright red blur, distant Satellites burn through the atmosphere in a rainbow of colors. A bright purple line far away makes me think of Willow, though surely she's too busy driving Troy crazy to be checking on one of her Tragedies. My heart feels a little bigger when I think of Willow, but more empty when I realize I miss her.

Lighted streamers converge closely enough to make me uncomfortable before we're all flung into our respective living quarters. My muscles continue their spasms when I land. A quick coding session before heading down to Benson is a must.

In the small room at the end of the hallway, I sit on the black mat and face the mirrored wall. My sight moves from my messy brown hair across the small scar on my eyebrow, compliments of a victorious football season. It figures I can remember where that scar came from, but not the two that are making me crazy. When my gaze stops on the drawstrings of my hoodie, an unsettled feeling slides through me. I should recognize this sweatshirt—I know I should—but why? Could it have something to do with my twin scars?

I blink hard and shake my head, looking away from the mirror. The verdict is in, ladies and gentlemen: I have lost my mind.

Irritated with myself, I force my brain to empty (oh the fun Willow would have with that) and close my eyes. My knotted muscles loosen slowly, then faster, until I'm in my happy place: above the ground in a tree stand surrounded by the wildlife-filled forest. The ropes tying my muscles together pull away as noisy birds sing around me. By the time the monster buck strolls into the clearing, crackling leaves under his weight, my entire body feels like a marshmallow. No more convulsing for me, at least through break.

When I blink, the buck disappears and a dust-covered ceiling fan fills my vision. A lead weight crushes against my body and my fingers claw into the mattress beneath me. Panicked and paralyzed, I jerk my head to the left, catching glimpses of an entertainment center in the bedroom of my past. I blink hard three times, hoping to get back to the coding room and away from the sensation of stinging ice sliding over my abs like a knife. My scream bounces through my head while the prickling cold circles its way up my chest, to my neck, and then my ear.

"Come back to me," a voice whispers in a cloud of freezing vapor, delivering the greatest torment yet.

My yell is so loud it seems to vibrate the bedroom walls before my eyes burst open to see the mirror in the coding room. I claw at my frozen chest and escape the blue hoodie while trying to control my chattering teeth. My skin warms until the ice localizes on my mysterious scars. The raised, tear-shaped welt on my chest is now white instead of pink but is somehow, unbelievably, not split open. I manage to stand and unbuckle my belt, letting my jeans fall around my ankles. The scar on my knee is a twin in every way, including pain.

I avoid the mirror in fear of seeing the expression on my face reflected back.

———

After my scars finally cut me some slack, I pit-stop at my closet to trade clothes because mine are soaked, making the term *cold sweat* actually mean something. My stomach is knotted and uneasy. So much for finding relief by coding.

In the kitchen, I splash fresh water on my face and will my jitters to swirl down the drain, too. They don't so I opt for caffeine, not even bothering to doctor the black coffee. Although the bitter and strong brew would put Willow's battery acid coffee to shame, the edge isn't enough to take mine away, even after an extra tall cup. I'd consider coding again if I weren't so terrified of getting the same, inexplicable results.

I'm pouring my second cup when—speak of the devil—the queen of sarcasm barrels through the door. Of course Willow doesn't knock. This shouldn't surprise me, but I jump anyway and steaming coffee dumps down the front of my fresh shirt.

Years worth of tockets jingle when she dumps her corduroy bag on the floor. Willow skips right over the *hello, how are you* bit and leaps head first into, "Heard about that eye, kid."

I unthinkingly reach for my temple. "What are you doing here?"

She pulls off her sweatshirt to reveal a pink, screen-printed tank that in no way matches her camo pants. "Just popping in to say hi. Hi! I think the beating helped your face. Your nose looks straighter."

"Shut up." I try to say it with a little venom but end up smiling instead. I playfully smack her arm when I pass by her before pulling my coffee-soaked shirt over my head to trade clothes for the second time. "No one even touched my nose," I yell from the closet.

"Who was lucky enough to hit you?" Willow says from the kitchen.

"Billy," I answer.

"Ah. He's quite a charmer."

I really did miss this freak.

Back in the kitchen, said freak is helping herself to coffee. She eyes the puke-green sofa while taking a sip. Like me, she opts for black, straight up and doesn't even flinch from the strength.

"I knew you'd keep it," she says over her cup in her usual I-told-you-so tone.

"I'm not keeping it," I lie. "I just haven't had a chance to get rid of the thing yet. It's been a little busy around here."

"Yeah, I bet." Willow nods, not buying my excuse. "How's your new assignment?"

I push my maroon shirt sleeves up. "Difficult."

"Welcome to being an Elite. Gooooo Team!" she sings and throws her fist in the air. "You eating?" she asks after another sip of coffee.

"Always."

She walks around the counter to me and stands on her toes to mess up my hair. "You're so predictable. Come on, I'll join you. We'd better hurry, though. Only about a half hour before duty calls."

"'Til break? You're kidding?"

"Uh…no. What have you been doing?"

"Coding," I say.

"For an hour and a half?"

"Apparently," I mumble to myself.

"You all right, kid?"

I hate when she acts like a mother. "I'm fine." I collect my bag without looking at her. "Come on."

On our way to Benson, Willow fills me in on her and Troy's garden projects. She lights up when she adds that Troy has been sharing lots of details about what life was like with Mya and Ryder.

"Hey, speaking of, when do I do Maintenance?" I ask.

Willow's expression turns to horror and she stops in the middle of the lobby. "You haven't checked on him?"

My heartbeat bursts into a double-time rhythm while my mind races to the biggest mistake of my short career, the one that almost cost Ryder his life. I ignore the stares of our fellow Satellites—compliments of Willow's volume—while I try to remember how and why I let Ryder stray so off course that his beautiful Shelby ended up wrapped around a tree. How could I have almost failed both Ryder and Willow so terribly?

Willow's voice cuts through my thoughts. "You told me you'd take care of him!"

"But…I didn't know…I mean, Jonathan never said…" I ramble in panic. "I'm sorry. I didn't know!" What if I've failed Ryder again? What if—

Willow's stone face buckles and she convulses with laughter. Then she walks away, still laughing.

"Willow!" The heat from my anger rises to my cheeks.

"I totally had you! You should have seen your face," she yells through her chortling, keeping the interest of the scattered Satellites throughout the lobby on us.

To think I'd actually missed her. "That was cruel!"

"No, that was classic!" she barks over her shoulder.

"You're a nut!"

"You're too easy," she says.

Figures she'd find a way to make it my fault.

79

"Seriously, though, when am I supposed to check in on Ryder?" I ask when we're in the mosaic hallway that connects the lobby to Benson.

"Whenever you have some free time. Your assignment is still new, so probably not for a while. Things will settle eventually and you'll find a window." Then, barely audible, she whispers, "You did before."

"What?"

"Nothing. Jonathan says Ryder's doing great, by the way. Mya, too. One of the perks to getting my memories back is that I get status updates on the kids. Pretty excellent, huh?"

I nod. "That's good news. So, what exactly do I do for Maintenance? I mean, I don't have Ryder's assignment book anymore."

"Just make sure your Tragedy is happy. That's really all Maintenance is about," Willow says.

"And how do I do that?"

"Observe. Determining if someone's happy isn't rocket science, kid."

"And if someone's not happy?" I ask.

"Let Jonathan know and he'll check it out."

We reach the table and Willow's attention shifts to the others.

"What's up stranger?" Owen asks, sharing her always-happy attitude.

"What's up yourself? You guys totally missed me, right?" Willow says.

"Not as much as you missed us," Owen retorts.

"I actually did miss you guys. It's been awhile." Willow

turns a chair backwards before sitting.

"What brings you back?" Clara asks.

"Just checking up on one of my assignments. No biggie."

Liam decides to pay attention now and I swear Willow shoots him a worried look before turning back to Clara. But then Willow's beaming her electric smile again and I question whether I imagined the exchange.

"I heard our kid here is quite the scrapper," Willow says.

"Dude, his eye was raunch city! Billy didn't look so hot either," Owen says.

I can't help but let my exuberance leak out a little at that.

"How long you gonna be around?" Rigby asks Willow before flipping his toothpick over with his tongue.

"Not sure. How you been, Rig?"

"Decent," he says, gnawing on the mangled wooden stick.

"You still scopin' Scarlet over there?"

Rigby glances sideways at Clara and shrugs.

"I'm telling you, man, show Whitfield some of that charisma of yours. She'll be all over you, I swear it," Willow says.

When did these two become BFFs?

Owen jumps in. "Charisma and Rigby? You're kidding, right?"

Rigby gives a pained expression. "Dude, that hurts."

"I think you should go for it, Rigby," Anna says and

loops her arm through Owen's.

Clara pushes a few strands of hair behind her ear. "Seriously, you really should."

I turn away, wondering if Rigby is hurt by Clara's support of a love connection that doesn't include her, when I catch Liam glaring at me. As if one antagonist isn't enough, here comes another one of my fans. At least Liam can share a table. Elliott, on the other hand, switches directions when he sees me. I wish I could take back what I said about his sister being a Rebellion.

"Elliott!" Willow calls, not letting him get away.

He turns reluctantly and makes a point to look at everyone but me when he crosses to Willow. "Hey Willow, long time, no see."

"Hey yourself! How you doin'?"

"Not bad. Where you been?"

"Oh, you know, hanging with the hubs and enjoying the time off."

"Yeah? What brings you back to this group of losers?" Elliott asks, lightening up a bit.

This time I know I'm not mistaking the worried expression on Willow's face before she recovers. "Is a girl not allowed to stop by every once in awhile? Join us, I've missed you." Willow motions to the empty chair between her and me.

Now Elliott looks my way and points the hate in his voice directly at me. "No thanks."

Owen resumes chewing his burger while the others shift in their seats. Liam, who was busy mutilating his tray of food, is motionless.

"Hey, man. I'm sorry about what I said the other day."

Elliott ignores me, leaving our table for another closer to the fireplace.

"That went well." Willow's mumble is followed by a very silent table.

"Anybody in for Sats?" Owen asks couple of minutes later through mouthful of fries.

Clara acts like she just got a whiff of sewage. "Swine."

Rigby, ignoring them both, shuffles and deals the cards. With break close to ending, and the fact that my stomach is still uneasy because of my strange coding session, I opt to pass on food and play Sats instead. While we play, I notice the other Elites for the first time in the expansive hall. They appear as ordinary as every other Satellite, blending into their respective groups. Well, aside from Lawson and Billy, sitting together six tables away. They'd have trouble blending anywhere other than a steroid convention.

Then there's Jackson, on the opposite end of the size spectrum. His volume overcompensates for his small stature. I hear him before I spot him, fully concealed behind a girl who's no bigger than a pixie. His flannel-clad arms, moving as fast as he talks, are all I can see while the six others at his table are engrossed by his rambling. Whatever story he's weaving is as animated as it is loud and he almost knocks over his Mountain Dew can at one point.

Reed is by the fireplace, chatting with others who wouldn't stand a chance of passing airport security with the amount of metal in their faces. Willow would meld nicely into that group, but—though I'd never admit it to her—I'm glad she's with us.

After laying an eight onto the discard pile on the table, I scan the right side of the room for Trina, but find Evelynn instead. She's sprawled on one of the sofas against the back wall, surrounded by a dozen drooling Satellites. While her all-male fan club focuses on her bare thighs, she laughs at something one of them says. The guy who delivered the amusing bit beams, likely thrilled that she's noticed him. She catches me staring and her smile widens. It's a dangerous smile, the kind that says she's going to share a secret that will bring me down with her.

"Yo kid, you're up."

My head snaps back to our table at the sound of Willow's voice and my cheeks get hot. "Huh?"

"Dude, it's your turn," Owen says, too wrapped up in his fan of cards to notice where my wandering eyes had been.

Nothing gets by Willow, though. "You see something you like?" she asks, looking over her shoulder in Evelynn's direction.

"What?" I say, hoping my tone comes off like she's being absurd. "No."

Clara, paying close attention as well, is equally unhappy when she zeroes in on Evelynn.

"You don't need any distractions," Willow states matter-of-factly and returns her focus to her cards.

After laying down my next card, my eyes—as if I'm powerless to stop them—sneak back to Evelynn. She's still watching me and I quickly turn back to the table, hoping

Willow and Clara haven't noticed. Not that their approval matters, but Willow's right; a distraction is the last thing I need right now. My eyes stay on my cards for the short remainder of break.

7. He gives new meaning to the word "bombed"

"Ready for another day?" Lawson asks in his baritone voice.

I answer him by slumping my shoulders until my backpack slides off. Is anybody ever ready for this?

St. Mary's Hospital powers back to life with a flicker of lights and the air conditioner kicks on. I follow Lawson's lead and pull my book out, reading through the future events as quickly as I can. Lawson wins and has his book shoved into his canvas bag before mine is even closed.

"Looks like it's going to be another long one," I say as I'm zipping my backpack closed.

He doesn't answer.

A few minutes later, I perform my first block of the day, which is actually late afternoon here on Earth, though the drawn shades hide the sunlight.

The hours that follow are as I anticipate: no better, no worse. I learn to read Meggie's eye twitch, which conveniently happens before her emotional outbursts. Lawson isn't so lucky and when he's caught off guard on two occasions, he curses Brody. Despite my faster reflexes, Lawson still has me, hands-down, in physical strength. Twice now, he's pulled me up from the floor without a word. No way would Billy be so generous. And Evelynn…heck, she'd probably use the opportunity to jump me.

Lawson and I work silently through the night and into the next day while Brody and Meggie drift in and out of restless sleep. Janine stops by a few times to check on the couple. On her last visit, she tells the broken pair that she's made an appointment for them with Dr. Arnoldson, calling him the best therapist in town. When Brody vetoes the idea, Janine fires back and has the two convinced to go to therapy by the time our calimeters drone. I can't get away fast enough. Even though memories of my cancer-ridden days are vague, I never thought I could hate a hospital more. I was wrong.

"See you on the field," Lawson says before being yanked through the ceiling.

Training day. My muscles tense, wishing for coffee and coding instead. Though, with my recent record of coding, maybe training is the better option.

A couple of minutes after landing, I'm on my way down to the courtyard. Jonathan is already waiting when Jackson and I, the last two of the Elite group, join the others. Billy laughs at me when I mirror his nasty expression. Jonathan breaks us into pairs and refuses Billy's request to partner with me again, teaming me with Reed instead.

While Reed and I are silently crossing the field to a vacant training spot, it feels like a boulder slams into my back. I'm within kissing distance of Billy when I spin around. More than happy for another chance at him, I wrap my arms around his torso and take him to the ground.

"That is enough!"

Rolling on the grass, we pause our swinging arms long enough to observe Jonathan standing over us. His disapproval prompts Billy and me to push off each other with more force than necessary.

"Reed, pair with Evelynn please." Jonathan turns to face us again. "You two must learn that we are a team."

There's no learning curve wide enough.

As if hearing my thought, Jonathan says, "The other option is you become too fatigued to engage in this behavior."

"Whatever," Billy snarls.

"Line up for sprinting drills," Jonathan says evenly, unaffected by Billy's attitude.

Billy's arrogant expression disappears and he groans.

Lawson's deep voice carries to us from a distance. "Oh man. That sucks."

I look around for an explanation, but nobody bites. By the expressions of my peers, Billy has gotten us into something really fun.

"Billy, would you please explain to Grant how these drills work?"

Billy looks like he wants to kill me, so I return the sentiment.

"We run," he growls.

OK. I can run.

"Across the field and back. There are five rounds. After each round, the loser does three hundred sit-ups." He looks me up and down and says, "I hope you like sit ups, Princess."

I take in Billy's massive, angry form and hope that his size makes him slow.

"Please proceed with your training," Jonathan says to the others, all still gawking, before wordlessly leading us to the far edge of the field. The walk is a long one and with every stride, I want to maul Billy more.

Once we're in position, Jonathan points out a tree as our mid-point destination, a speck at the end of the field at least a mile away. The whistle blows and Billy's off before I realize we've begun. I chase after him, pushing myself harder than I ever have. If I was racing anyone other than Billy, I probably wouldn't care so much.

Billy beats me to the tree—which up close is more than seven feet wide—and flashes his most ugly face when he passes me on his sprint back. I push my legs harder and catch him twenty yards from Jonathan, but he kicks into turbo while my lungs threaten to burst.

He gasps for air and then makes a foolish gesture by throwing out his arms and cocking his head to the side. "What's up?" he says arrogantly through his panting.

I hit the ground and try to get my labored breathing in check to downplay how tired I am.

Stay focused. The two words repeat in time with the excruciating sit-ups. I push through the last hundred in fast-forward, not wanting Billy to have more time to rest, but his breathing is already even, giving him the advantage.

I have to beat him.

Back in position, Jonathan's whistle blows and I'm ready this time. We reach the mammoth tree at the same time.

Something inside me unravels and my pent up hate for Billy explodes. I stay focused on beating him instead of what I really want, which is to beat *on* him.

When my victory is announced, I keep my mouth shut. Hunched over and gasping, I watch Billy pumping through his sit-ups. There's something satisfying about seeing him wearing down.

His glower is toxic when he stands beside me. Jonathan's whistle blows and we take off. Billy's concrete arm plows into me and throws my balance. Losing just one stride is enough to yield him the lead. He crosses past Jonathan first and I'm doing sit-ups this time.

He won't win again.

I'm fully prepared to play dirty this time, but Billy chooses to follow the rules. The break did him good and he's sprinting at his fastest speed yet. Unless I'm getting slower, which is a good possibility because it feels like razor blades are murdering my sides.

He cannot win, he cannot win, he cannot win, I think with each labored breath.

And he doesn't. I beat him by a blade of grass, so close Jonathan has to call it for me to know for sure. Billy isn't convinced that I won. He falls to the ground for sit-ups anyway and I narrowly watch him while my body tries to reenergize.

Our last lap couldn't come soon enough. Billy looks terrible and if I look as bad as I feel, my appearance can't be much better. When the whistle blows, I collect all of my strength and take off. Even though Billy's right at my side, I ignore him and focus on the tree ahead. My mind goes blank until nothing but my loud breathing swirls through my brain. My legs keep stride with each breath: *in, out, in, out, in, out…*

I pivot at the tree just half a second before Billy, knowing one misstep is all he'll need to take me. I focus on Jonathan, his shirt just a red dot in the distance, and ignore the fact that my legs are like dry-rotted rubber bands about to snap.

When we reach the finish line, Billy has nothing to say and plunges to the ground to begin the torturous sit-ups.

Even though I swear my calf muscles have detached from the bone, I won't let myself collapse to the ground. Billy will not have the satisfaction of seeing me weak.

"Grant, I expect you will want to code. This would be a good opportunity," Jonathan says sternly. "I hope the two of you will now set your differences aside." Adding nothing more, he walks across the field in the direction of Trina and Jackson.

Billy keeps his eyes toward the bluish-gray mountains, huffing loudly each time he hits the sitting position. As much as I want to, I decide not to stick around to watch Billy finish his reps, mostly because I'm afraid I'll collapse if I don't move soon.

Back in my room, I'm certain that my lungs have ruptured. I guess it's no big deal, seeing as I'm dead and all. I dump my backpack at the door and take my time getting to the coding room.

When I'm sitting on the mat, there's no longer any sign that razors were cutting into my sides just minutes ago. My lungs are already feeling decent, too. Hurray for fast healing. My muscles are still tight, though, so I close my eyes and welcome the unwinding release.

Then it happens again: the hunting field disappears. In its place is my old bedroom, the lead weight on my chest, and the freezing blade circling my abs like spreading frost. Before the cold vapor reaches my ear, my calimeter buzzes and my eyes spring open.

"Dude, about time," Lawson says when I land in the hospital room. The building has already powered on, probably around the time I was trading my sweat-soaked clothes for dry ones. I shouldn't have taken so long to study my scars, which are now translucent-white and still freezing.

Lawson's white teeth contrast with his skin when he smirks. "Sprinting drills. Suck-city, bro."

"Tell me about it." I rub my chest to try and warm the scar.

"Leave it to Billy to get you into that mess. I had to go up against him once myself not long after he become an Elite."

"I thought you two were buddies," I mock.

"I didn't care for the chip on his shoulder when he joined the team. You'll learn to deal with him like the rest of us have."

"Doubtful," I mumble.

"At least you got him out of the way. He's the fastest

we've got. Well, was. He's going to be royally pissed now."

"Great," I say dryly. "What's his beef with me all about?"

"It probably has something to do with you holding the record for being chosen for an Elite in the shortest amount of time. Billy holds a record of his own: the Satellite who waited the longest to join the team, a whopping sixty-eight years. I think the guy wanted it more than anyone in history. His excitement was snuffed out when he realized how insensitive we Elites can be. Let's just say he took a lifetime of jabs in about a week's time. Don't sweat it; he's just jealous. He'll get over it. Although, after the sprinting drill—" Lawson looks at my chest. "You all right?"

I pull my hand away and tug Meggie's book out of my bag for a diversion. "Speaking of sprinting drills," I say to change the subject and nod towards the ceiling, "why are things so painful up there? I can run, heck even fly around on my assignments all day and feel nothing close to that kind of torture."

He shifts positions on the hospital floor, crossing his legs, and I keep my thoughts about contamination to myself. A floor littered with remnants of bodily fluids would obviously never affect either of us. Still, out of habit I opt for the chair in the corner while Lawson talks.

"In Progression our bodies are physically the same as when we were alive. That's why sprinting drills are so effective."

Effective is one word for it, although that wouldn't be my first choice.

"Here on Earth the normal rules don't apply. Our bodies transform as we displace, allowing us to walk through walls and all that."

"Then why is blocking equally torturous in both places?"

Lawson thinks this is humorous even though nothing I've said is funny. "Blocking is a mental pain."

"So mental pain works the same on Earth and in Progression?"

He nods.

"Does it ever dull?"

I take his laugh as a no.

I ramble a question of much less importance. "If our bodies are the same as when we were alive, why aren't we ever hungry?"

"Because we're dead. Food is a survival necessity for the physical body to thrive and grow. Yes, our bodies are the same as when we were alive, but now we're in a frozen state. The same goes for sleep; there's no need to recharge our physical body." He taps his head. "All we have to recharge are our minds, which is why we code. Really, though, I wonder if our muscle pain is a trick our minds play on us. Either way, coding certainly makes us more comfortable."

It did, I think, but keep this to myself. Recalling how sweaty coding has made me lately, I smell my armpits out of habit, knowing I should smell terrible, but don't. "And as for showering and using the bathroom?"

He smirks at this. "I guess someone figured Satellites wouldn't have time to be bothered with such things in

Progression."

By opening his assignment book, Lawson cues to me that he's done talking. I mimic him and read through Meggie's day. Dr. Brown enters and settles in for another therapy session, this time with Brody in attendance because he's awakened from his drugged state.

Lawson and I are silent through the late afternoon and evening, only speaking to block. Brody and Meggie are quiet as well, except for their occasional sobbing outbursts, which are to be expected when they are forced to trudge through this kind of hell.

Max comes by around noon the next day carrying a pizza box, but I'm sure no one will be eating. He's taller than even Lawson, but lankier—of course, anyone would appear lanky next to the giant. Max is a male version of his sister, but he seems younger than Meggie now because Meggie has aged in the past forty-eight hours.

I keep my head down and wring my hands together when Meggie disappears under Max's arms for a crying fit. Brody joins the tear-fest and the threesome's hysterics bring pain to my stomach. I wish I could take all this away.

A third voice joins in when Lawson and I are blocking.

Fire-red Whitfield, standing in the door frame, smiles and nods when the block is complete. "Hey y'all," she says and drops her bag by my chair.

"How you doing, girl?" Lawson says.

"Swell, honey. You?"

"Really? You're going to go there?"

She grins like she gets whatever the heck that means

and says in her deep-south accent, "Hey Grant, didn't expect to see you here. Your first Elite assignment?"

I nod.

"Well, by the looks of it, it's going to be a doozy." She hops herself up on the narrow counter by the miniature sink and studies her fingernails.

"Tell me about it," I say under my breath before I give up my chair to Max and squeeze myself into the corner between Lawson and Whitfield.

A couple of hours and a few blocks later, a doctor joins the already crowded but very quiet room. He places a metal chart under his arm and says Brody's lungs are clear. After explaining that a nurse will need to change the bandages on Brody's hand one more time, he shares the news I've been waiting for: no more hospital!

"Where will we go?" Meggie says to no one in particular when the doctor is gone.

"To Mom's, of course," Max whispers.

Meggie rubs the bridge of her nose before nodding. My energy comes as soon as her eye twitches. I finish the block, the rippling wall of water evaporates, and Meggie's sobs have been soothed. For now.

"Not bad on the fly," Whitfield says, obviously not seeing my muscles spasm.

"Thanks," I manage, and put my bag on my shoulder.

I follow Meggie to the nurses' station down the hall and my calimeter buzzes when she's asking questions about Brody's at-home care. Lawson and Whitfield are at my side when we're launched through the roof of the hospital.

Together, Whitfield, who has blurred into a bright orange streak, combined with Lawson's red trail are like rocketing embers.

Wanting to code after another exhausting jaunt, I eye the hallway suspiciously and weigh the odds of having a normal session. Unsure, I twist my back until my spine pops. Better, but not good enough.

On my way down the hall, I stop at the closet for a quick wardrobe change. This happens to be long enough to reconsider my decision about coding. I collect my bag and am out the door before I can change my mind again.

Benson's still only about half full when I walk in, but the noise level coming from the lobby behind me rumbles as the body count grows.

"You're back," I say to Willow when I reach the table.

She looks terrible, even aside from her dreads and tattoos, which are sufficiently terrible on their own. She and Liam cut off their whispered, top-secret conversation and her expression transforms to so-beyond-enthusiastic it's unnatural, even for her.

I slide into the chair beside hers. "You all right?"

She drops her zeal down a notch. "Fine," she says through a plastic smile and squeezes my arm. "How you doin'?"

Suspicious because she's holding her breath, I answer slowly. "OK."

"Cool. Wanna eat?"

"You're being weirder than usual."

"I'm fine! Come on." Willow pushes up from the table

and strides away in fast-forward.

"You sure you're OK?" I ask when I catch up to her.

"Totally good. Just famished."

We enter the menagerie of delectables and she backs her claim by filling her entire tray with food, consisting mostly of chocolate.

"I'm surprised to see you again," I tell her on the way back to the table.

"Just working on those loose ends," she says, putting her plastic smile back on.

"A previous assignment?"

"Mmm. No biggie. A couple more days should straighten it out. Haven't I ever told you that when you're a Satellite, it's forever?"

"Yeah, I'm sure you've mentioned that. So, what's Troy doing in the meantime?"

"He's staying busy fixing up a Chevelle. It's a total piece. You should see it."

"Lucky guy to have such a supportive wife."

She laughs, appearing normal for the first time today. Back at the table, though, she doesn't touch her food even though she claimed she was "famished." Her conversations with everyone (minus Liam, who has reverted to his no-talk policy) seem forced. Something's up.

Giving in to the idea that maybe I'm just being paranoid, I turn to the only person, aside from Liam, who's not participating in the conversation. "Have you talked to her?" I ask.

Rigby brings his attention back to our table and pulls

the toothpick out of his mouth. "Huh?" He straightens. "Sorry, I was zoning. Tough day. What's new with you?"

"Come on, man, you're not fooling anyone. She's cute. Go talk to her."

"Nah." His jaw tightens around the toothpick.

"Why not?"

His eyes move back to Whitfield a few tables over. "We couldn't possibly have anything in common."

"Are you kidding? Go talk to her!" I push him hard enough that he falls off the side of his chair. Since Clara's not here to hold his attention, now is as good of a time as any. Instead of decking me, he accepts the persuasion, though he shoots a malevolent look back at me on his way to her table. She'd better be nice or I'll never hear the end of it. I don't relax until Whitfield motions for him to sit next to her.

My attention moves to the Ford versus Chevy debate happening between Willow and Owen. Despite having my own stance on the issue, I keep my mouth shut, refusing to agree openly with the nut. This is difficult because defending Chevrolet has always been one of my favorite things to do, especially with my old man.

My thoughts turn to my parents, hoping they are all right, and a prickle of loneliness settles in my stomach. I force myself to eat and try not to think about them, but I don't have much success. My mind wanders to my carpenter days and working with my dad. He was tough, no doubt about it. I'm amazed it was cancer that killed me because back in the day I was certain it was going to be the old man, possibly from working me to death or launching a tool at me when I screwed something up.

I shift to happier thoughts by putting my mom in the spotlight, but this turns out to make me feel even worse. I would give anything to hug her or to have a conversation across the kitchen counter like the millions we had over the years while she cooked for Dad and me.

Break ends too soon, severing my homesick thoughts, and the room clears as everyone heads back to their nightmares. No paranoia about it, Willow is definitely avoiding eye contact when I tell her goodbye. She disappears before I've even retrieved Meggie's locket.

Even though Liam would probably rather see a proctologist than talk to me, I ask anyway. "Liam, you got a minute?"

He gives me his attention like he's actually willing to listen.

"I'm sorry if I did something to offend you."

The room of Satellites quickly empties.

"You still don't believe me about Tate, do you?"

I really don't want this make-believe girl to be the subject of a conversation that will surely go nowhere. "I'm sorry," is the only nice thing I can think of to say.

"Tate's not doing well. She misses you and Elliott. That's why Willow's back, you know?" Liam scans the room. Only a handful of Satellites remain, congregated closer to the entryway.

My irritation no longer stays hidden. "I respect the protection that you want to give your Tragedy, but there's no way I was engaged."

Liam's voice raises a notch. "What would I gain by making this up?"

I open my mouth, but then close it because I have no response.

Liam's face fills with pity, bringing back memories of my human life that I'd rather not have. This angers me. I'm not the guy with cancer that everyone felt sorry for anymore. I never want to be that guy again. "Even if I believed you, what good would it do?" I bark. "It's not like I'll ever be able to go back to that life." I force myself to calm the erupting emotions building inside me. Could this be why I didn't want to die?

NO!

No. I've never been in love, and if I had, it's an event that I certainly would have remembered.

"I know I'm treating you unfairly," Liam says. "It's just that I liked the person you were. Not at first, I'll admit, but those feelings you had for Tate, the feelings she had for you, they were all so real."

I stay quiet when he pauses.

"What bothers me most is that I had those same feelings for my wife. I wish my memories were stronger, but at least a few are still there. You don't remember Tate at all. Maybe if I had never seen you with her, this wouldn't bother me so much, but I did. The way you were with her…she was everything to you. You've become this insensitive prick who thinks he's better than everyone."

"Hey!" I argue. "I don't think I'm better than anyone! You should have been chosen to be an Elite before me. I don't deserve it. I don't even want it!" I force my volume down. "Liam, half the time I don't even know what I'm doing here, let alone as an Elite. You should see me down there, I'm a mess compared to the others. I'm not good at this and I'm so afraid I'm going to fail my Tragedy." A churning inside me settles as I admit my fear not only to Liam, but to myself as well.

I suck in a few long breaths.

"I just wish you remembered her," Liam says slowly.

I say the only thing that seems honest. "If what you say about me and her is true, I agree."

Liam nods like he understands, or at the very least, no longer appears to hate me. "Don't tell Willow I told you any of this, OK?"

After agreeing, I remember Meggie. "I have to go. Are we cool?"

After considering, Liam says, "Yeah, we're cool." He digs his hand in his pocket, retrieving a silver ring that only fits the first knuckle of his index finger.

"Liam?"

"Yeah?"

"Is Tate going to be all right?"

My question catches him off guard. "I hope so," he answers and then whispers the word that drops him through the hardwood floor.

"Displace," I say when he's gone.

I land at the nurses' station and the scrub-clad mannequins have already come back to life, looking busy while Meggie fills out paperwork. When she and I are back in

Brody's crowded room, Dr. Brown comes in to say his goodbyes, leaving his business card with instructions to call if there is anything he can do to help them. Bringing back Meggie's family would be a start, but the ever-empathetic Schedulers have ensured that will never happen.

When the doc leaves, Meggie opens a pill bottle, shakes two out, and gives one to Brody. He tips back the paper cup of water like a shot glass. Bottoms up. Anger sparks inside me because there's no pill in the world that could ease their pain.

Brody's new threads must be compliments of Max because the green T-shirt falls almost to his knees and his pants are cuffed at the bottom.

Lawson's sitting in the corner consumed in his book. Whitfield pulls out hers and her freckles are almost glowing. A possible love connection between her and Rigby, maybe? For Rigby's sake, I hope so. Someone around here should be happy.

I dig out my own book and read until the pages go blank. Lawson and Whitfield appear to share my lack of enthusiasm about the upcoming funeral planning.

Twenty minutes later, we're trudging through the sterile-smelling hallways behind our Tragedies.

"You coming?" Whitfield says.

After realizing I've stopped and am staring at a bald-headed boy as he passes us, I turn away and jog to catch up to the group. The sun is setting when we exit the building and my eyes narrow at the sight of Max's car. Been there, done that, and no way am I doing it again.

"You couldn't bring your SUV?" Meggie whines.

"Ryan's got it. He took Nancy and Janine shopping. You and Brody need new clothes." He neglects to mention that nothing survived the torching, though Meggie and Brody have probably already figured this out.

The door creaks when Max wrenches it open. The only thing spacious about the primer-black car is the amount of room it leaves between the cars parked on either side. Max negotiates himself into the driver's seat like a magician, reaches over and unlocks the passenger door, and slouches until he can fully straighten his head behind the steering wheel.

Meggie sighs and, even less gracefully, climbs into the backseat.

"Just like old times." Brody's joke doesn't lighten the mood like I wish it would.

Whitfield nods toward the car as it backs out.

"No way," I say dully.

Whitfield shrugs indifferently and disappears through the hatchback. Her red ponytail shows up a second later next to Meggie in the backseat. Lawson and I fly behind the toy car into the setting sun, stopping for half a dozen red lights.

Fifteen minutes later, Max turns into a neighborhood of homes so near one another they almost touch. Very few of them have been updated. Of the handful of houses that actually have landscaping, most would be better off without. Ryan pulls up the cracked driveway behind an equally small, silver car under the carport. The sun is hidden by the house, but there's enough light to see that the home is, hands down, the nicest on the street. Only a few patches of grass are brown, unlike the surrounding yards, which are mostly dirt.

We file through the front door and even with the Extreme Home Makeover that's happened, I recognize the inside. No way can this place hold good memories for Meggie. I seriously doubt she would have chosen this as her home, had her own not been roasted.

My eyes lock on the corner of the living room; the image of a young Meggie taking cover under her mom is rooted in my brain like an old tree. The walls have been covered over with celery-green paint. I force my eyes back on Meggie and repress the bloody image of her mom's battered face.

Within two minutes, Lawson and I are blocking. Meggie gains control after four blocks and falls onto the faded, pink and yellow plaid sofa. Lawson is still blocking Brody. What I wouldn't give to yank the emotional triggers off the walls. The photographs, mostly of their kids, just mock what's been stolen from this family.

Whitfield fidgets and picks at her nails while Max hovers around the door. "Megs, I'm gonna get out of here, OK?" he says in a desperate tone.

In a daze, Meggie turns to her brother. "Huh?" She pauses. "Oh. Yeah, sure."

Brody, much to Lawson's relief, falls beside Meggie on the sofa.

Max's hand is already strangling the doorknob. "Ryan will be by later, hopefully with some new clothes. I'll come over tomorrow morning so we can get to the…for the… um…arrangements." He doesn't want to say the bad word: funeral. I don't blame him.

"Take it easy, boys," Whitfield says to Lawson and me as she follows Max out.

Not five minutes later, Max comes back through the front door with a handful of bags, but it's not Whitfield who accompanies him this time. Ugh. This day just keeps getting better and better.

"What are you doing here? Where's Whitfield?" I demand.

"That's Ryan, not Max," Lawson mumbles from the other side of the living room.

Before Janine and a thinner woman I assume to be Nancy come through the door, the light bulb blinks on in my dumb head. Sure, now the twin brothers decide to have the same haircut. Whatever I did to piss off the powers that be must have been bad because here stands Elliott, seemingly employed as Ryan's Satellite.

After glaring at me in disbelief for ten full seconds, Elliot crosses the room and slouches in the corner on the far wall by the window.

I plunk down in the hallway where I can see Meggie, but be out of Elliott's sight, though probably not off his mind. I decide against laughing at Lawson, crammed into the dainty, pink chair, since the current mood is even darker than his ebony skin.

Ryan gives up on small talk and sits on the floor at Meggie's feet while Janine and Nancy busy themselves with de-tagging new clothes for Meggie and Brody. When the women are finished, Janine sits on the other side of Meggie and Nancy settles on the floor beside Ryan. For the next hour, the unhappy group gives Lawson, Elliott and I more job security than we could ever want.

When Ryan finally leaves, Elliott says goodbye to Lawson and walks past me like I don't exist.

I mull over a way to make amends with him until Meggie begins questioning Brody about how the fire could have started. The conversation quickly morphs into in a full-blown cage match between the two, which ends when Brody storms out of the house. Lawson sighs and follows without a word.

Just when I was certain my muscles couldn't ache anymore, a half-dozen more blocks are needed to calm Meggie down.

A little after two a.m., the sound of sloppy singing comes from outside.

Crap.

Unmoving from her position on the pink chair, a china doll compared to when burly Lawson sat in the same place, Meggie opens her eyes three seconds before Brody enters the house. Lawson looks almost as bad as Brody when he stumbles in, but Lawson is still mostly coherent...and standing. Brody, on the other hand—

"He's been at the bar," Lawson says like I really needed the explanation. The fumes radiating from Brody's pores would be enough to intoxicate even the most professional of alcoholics.

"Obviously," I say under my breath while I stand, and grit my teeth in preparation for what is to come.

"You've got to be kidding me," Meggie's tired voice says.

"Hey baaaaby!" Brody trips and smashes into the wall, taking one of the pictures down with him. I wish he would knock them all off; at least then something good would come out of his drunken stupor.

Meggie gets up from the chair and catches Brody before he crashes into the end table, then helps maneuver his leaden body to the pink chair.

He pulls her down on his lap.

"Did you hear about my boy?" he slurs. "He buuurrrrnnn-da."

"Oh, come on!" I yell while, behind me, Lawson gives the order that better shut the drunk up.

Meggie yanks free from Brody's grasp. "Damn you! Getting wasted isn't going to help!"

He points a limp finger at her and spits through his words. "You know what you need? You need a drink, baby. Takes the edge off." His eyes roll behind his lids. When his enlarged pupils reappear he says, "Did you hear about my boy?"

"Make him shut up," I growl to Lawson.

"I'm trying!" Lawson says and gives the order again.

"Just pass out already," Meggie hisses and disappears down the hall.

A minute later, Lawson and I are still both at a loss for words when Brody somehow plucks himself from the chair.

He takes one step and collapses onto the floor. Lawson and I stay frozen for a few seconds before our tense shoulders fall into a more relaxed state.

Lawson is disgusted. "He gives new meaning to the word 'bombed'."

"Should we do something?"

"Are you kidding? He shut up, didn't he?"

Brody lets out a snore that is loud enough to give Ryder a run for his money and then a series of chainsaw grumbles fall into a pattern as he drifts into drunken Neverland.

Lawson sits on the sofa, so small under him it could be a chair. "Probably want to check on your girl," he suggests.

Jealous because his work is done and mine is very well just beginning again, I follow the sobs down the short hall, through the bedroom, and into the microscopic bathroom that was forgotten in the home makeover. I hadn't seen an avocado colored toilet or sink since my great grandma died, and it's plain to see why they stopped making them.

Fully clothed, Meggie sits in the dry, clawfoot tub and hugs her legs, occasionally breaking her sobs with gargled sniffs. She's even paler with the peach wall as her backdrop. I park myself on the black and white checkerboard tile and mirror her position, ready to jump into action when her sobs become too much for my heart to handle.

The rust stains on the outside of the tub hold my attention while anger boils inside me. Meggie cries herself into exhaustion, eventually drifting away in sleep. I remind myself that this is necessary, though I can't find a single reason convincing enough to believe it.

8. *I'm going to kiss you*

The next day is even worse than I feared. Already, the funeral arrangements are catastrophic. Even Max, who's been as emotional as an ice cube, is now a wreck. Whitfield performs almost as many blocks as Lawson and I do. Her freckles are no longer glowing.

Between blocking and refusing to acknowledge me, Elliot isn't fairing so well either. I hate to say it, but I'm glad he is exhausted. When he had the energy to talk to Whitfield and Lawson in the parking lot, the atmosphere was more than a little awkward for me.

Brody, doubly hit by the after-effects of his binge, doctors his hangover by popping a pill every time Lawson blocks him. For all I know, that may actually be the order Lawson is giving.

Needless to say, I'm thrilled to be wrapping up in Death City, a.k.a. the funeral home. I dread coming back here tomorrow and the next day for the big event. I try not to think about why the caskets will be closed.

Back at the house after Max, Ryan, and Nancy leave, Brody apologizes to Meggie for the tenth time about his behavior the night before. He could have stopped after the first time because it was obvious Meggie had already forgiven him. I'm glad about that. The two need each other now more than ever.

With help from Janine, they trudge through the painful task of sorting through shoeboxes of Meggie's mom's photographs for the funeral visitation. Seeing photos of a family so happy and alive is difficult for me and they're not even my kids. I turn my head away more than once to conceal my silent tears from Lawson.

My buzzing calimeter makes me jump in the mostly quiet room. I relax when Meggie, Brody, and Janine freeze, because even though Meggie won't notice the lapse, she gets to be frozen in time just like her children and her mother for a short while.

On the training field, Billy isn't so cocky, keeping his gaze straight ahead when I approach the group. In contrast, Evelynn's attitude hasn't changed. She's already brushing against my side and trying to catch my attention with her dark eyes; a gesture she probably uses often to keep all eyes above her neck. A proper shirt would have the same effect.

I step close to Trina, who saves me by positioning herself between Evelynn and me. Trina smiles up at me when I mouth the words, "Thank you."

"I'll work with Grant today," Evelynn says before Jonathan even tells us what we're doing.

This is the closest Jonathan's probably ever come to rolling his eyes. "Fine." He waves his hand in the air as if to move us along.

Trina appears apologetic and shrugs before I walk, very slowly, across the field.

Evelynn's smile beams like a laser—*glint*—while we cross to an empty place on the lawn. The sparkles on her pink, painted-on dress are blinding when she moves and she somehow manages to keep her five-inch heels from staking into the ground. She must be feeling conservative, leaving the seven-inchers at home.

"Ready?" she asks, still grinning ridiculously huge.

I internally cringe.

"I'll block you, all right?" she continues when I don't answer.

The last thing I want is to have her inside my head, but I'm too exhausted to argue. Regret for not coding weighs on me until I think about my scars.

"Come after me." Oh jeez, her expression is a wicked one.

I shake my head. "I can't do that."

"Oh come on, I can take it."

I continue shaking my head.

"Fine. How about a hug?"

My brow raises. "How about I go to the left," I state, not as a question.

Evelynn considers, sounding a little defeated. "Fine."

I start to walk to the left when her voice chimes the order, "Haze."

A curtain of ice-cold blackness engulfs me, but it dissipates as fast as it came. In its wake is an urge so great I pull in a sharp breath.

A spotlight is on Evelynn and I've never wanted anything more than to kiss her. How had I managed to be this close to her without doing it sooner? Her full-lipped smile is impossible to deny: she wants me, too. *Do it! Kiss her now before you lose your chance, you fool!*

No! My voice screams its rebuff against itself and the battle in my head ensues.

Kiss Her!

No!

Kiss her!

No!

Kiss her!

"*No!*" This time my voice yells out, severing the internal argument. My sight is veiled in the same blue as my blocking filter. "You're not playing fair," I say angrily.

"A girl's gotta try." She's all innocence now as the blue filter fades from my vision. "How strange," she half-whispers to herself. "Let me try again."

I worry about what else the diva has up her sleeve, but doubt I can persuade her otherwise, so I reluctantly agree.

She raises her eyebrow. "You want to attack me now?"

I can't help but laugh. "No. Not even now."

"Fine. May as well go left again."

I begin my walk to the left and when she says the order, I smack into a frigid, black wall. Chills run across my skin, but retreat as fast as the wall itself, as if neither ever happened.

Evelynn is nearly glowing, as everything surrounding her has darkened. She's always been hot, but dang! It should be illegal to look so good. I bite my lip thinking about all the ways I'm going to ravage her. I'll start at her lips, but there's no telling where I'll go from—

No! These are not my thoughts! In fact, these couldn't be further from them.

Kiss her! my voice insists, smaller than before but no less unsettling.

I snap out of the stupor. *No!*

When my translucent blue clears from my sight, I regain my composure. "It's not going to happen, Evelynn."

She's obviously hurt, but before I can feel badly, her expression morphs into anger. "Go left!"

I match her tone. "No! No more. You can't force me to kiss you."

Her eyes grow even darker. "Billy forced you to twirl like a ballerina."

"It's my turn."

Her cold expression turns to a toddler-like pout. "Fine. I'm going to kiss you."

Is this girl for real?

She's sliding her tongue across her teeth when my order comes out. "Haze."

Don't kiss me, don't kiss me, don't...

The pain of the electric current holds me hostage. I force my paralyzed brain to think. If I don't hurry, the pink disco ball is going to be planting one on me and, by her expression, it's going to be an X-rated version.

The magic word completes the cycle. The waterfall that connects us evaporates to droplets that bounce on the grass before disappearing. I have to turn my face to keep her nose from touching mine.

When she takes a step back, her heel actually does stake into the ground. She smiles, but not warmly, and shakes her long, pink fingernail at me. "You're good." She pauses, but keeps her eyes on me. "Try me again."

"I assume your going for the same approach?"

"Mmm. I'm that predictable, huh?"

Sigh.

I give the order and in half a second my mind is made up. She and Billy refuse to play nice. Why should I?

Her mouth is close to mine after I complete the circuit. I fight the instinct to step back when she exhales her minty breath in my face. Her dark eyes, surrounded in pink glitter, move away from mine and she maneuvers herself around me. I turn and watch while her dress works with the sun like a pink reflector as she strides sullenly across the field.

I assume Billy has just blocked Reed, unless Reed is accustomed to performing cartwheels on the lawn for no good reason.

Evelynn jumps out of Reed's way and reaches Billy, grabbing his shoulders and spinning the giant around. She smacks her lips against his almost loud enough for me to hear. When she goes even further by adding tongue, I have about as much luck stifling my laughter as Billy has keeping his wide eyes closed.

When Evelynn finally releases Billy, she wipes her mouth with the back of hand and looks…satisfied. Billy's eyes are impossibly larger.

Catcalls and whistles erupt and Evelynn's glassed-over expression melts away, leaving her alert. And angry.

"You!" This is obviously directed at me.

"Whoa!" My hands shoot up in surrender as she marches her five-inch heels in my direction. "Oh no! Uh uh. You're the one who didn't want to play fair."

"How could you!"

"Don't play with fire, Evelynn. And for the record, I'm not interested in anything more than being your friend," I say firmly, hoping she'll keep her tongue to herself in the future.

Her mouth opens like she wants to say more, but then hinges closed before she takes off across the lawn.

Jonathan is so smug he may as well be nodding in approval. He claps his hands together once. "Well, team, why don't we call it a day?"

Billy, still frozen, is staring at the courtyard door as Evelynn goes through.

On my way across the lawn, I do everything I can to keep my smirk hidden. Trina brushes by me on the curved pathway and winks. "Not bad."

"Dude, I owe you one!" Reed, coming up behind us, puts himself between Trina and me before smacking my back. "Did you see what that buffoon had me doing? I swear Billy is the worst."

I nod in agreement. "He's definitely that."

"Cartwheels," Reed mumbles. "How did you keep them out?"

"What do you mean?"

"How'd you keep them out of your head?"

"Oh. I'm not sure."

"Well, it's impressive. If you ever figure it out, let me

know." He holds the door for me and I step through, wondering the same thing: how did I keep them out?

—— ~~~ ——

Against my better judgment, I walk past Benson. I dump my bag in my room and try to stomp out my stress on the way down the hall. I have to do this, I remind myself, or my coiled muscles will snap.

Parked on the mat, I close my eyes. Please, please, please let this be a normal session.

The chains begin to release my tendons as I sit in my tree stand—my solace—and the feeling of relief justifies the risk. Falling deeper, my muscles may as well be cheering in victory by the time the monster buck enters the clearing. I haven't felt this good since…ever. I needed this more than I realized. When my body feels like Jello, I open my eyes.

Uh oh!

A sharp inhale is replaced with a deep yell that roars through my old bedroom. It takes a minute for me to realize I'm the one howling in agony.

The sensation of a freezing knife cuts through my torso. Around and around it goes, so cold it burns through my flesh. I'd thrash out against whatever was pinning me to my mattress if I wasn't paralyzed. The cold dances up my neck until it consumes me. My brain is so strangled by the ice, I can't even tell if I'm shivering.

"I love you," the freezing vapor says.

My eyes pop open—for real this time—and I all but rip

my skin off trying to remove my shirt. My breath gasps in and out of my lungs as I attempt to rub the stinging cold out of my scars.

When my calimeter interrupts, I do scream. Well, half scream and half groan as I force myself up from the floor.

I try to calm down, snatching the thickest sweatshirt I can find in the closet, and grabbing my bag. With tocket in hand, I mumble the word that will return me to Meggie, hardly noticing the fall because the chill is still swallowing me.

I'm rubbing my chest and knee when I land. Meggie is right where I left her, on the floor with Brody and Janine, holding a photo of her kids; her happy, full-of-life kids.

Why won't my scars warm up?

Meggie's trying to persuade Janine to go home to her family, but Janine doesn't do so until all of the photographs have been selected. When she leaves and my scars have finally gotten closer to room temperature, I pull the book out for my daily reading. Only a few blocks are required by Lawson and me through the night, and those are only for sobbing outbursts. It's the next day that makes Lawson and I pay dearly for our break.

At last count, I am up to fourteen blocks in the suffocating funeral room. No matter how I position myself, I can't keep people from ghosting through me. The emotions running through the room are also weighing on me. The tears of the never ending line of spectators are enough to prompt the Great Flood and I'm shedding more than a few of my own. The only good thing about this day is that Meggie doesn't know that her dad showed up. Brody gained my respect by excusing himself from the receiving line and quietly asking the man to leave, which her father surprisingly did without a fight.

My fracturing heart needs a break as bad as Willow needs a hairbrush, so I couldn't be happier to hear the buzzing of my calimeter. The packed house freezes to match the bodies inside the four boxes placed front-and-center in the fancy, burgundy and gold room.

"Displace," I say weakly.

Between the numbness of my brain and the screaming pain of my muscles, I don't notice the three glowing blurs who fly into the sky beside me, nor do I notice my landing or how long I've been parked on my horrendous sofa. I want to code more than anything, but can't. I am too terrified of the freezing demon that keeps interrupting. More pain is not what I need right now.

I grab my bag and head out the door once I finally stop trembling, but a dull ache still accompanies even the smallest movement. I'm going to have to code again, and sooner rather than later.

Today is definitely one of those days I wish GPS Jeanette wasn't so chipper in the elevator.

I walk as fast as my legs will let me, which turns out to be extremely slow, and cut a path straight to Willow. "Hey, can I talk to you?" I whisper after nodding hello to the others at the table.

"Sure. What's up, kid?" she replies at full volume.

I bend closer to her ear. "Alone?"

Willow sighs before shrugging "whatever" and follows me. We sit in the far corner of Benson and I have to lean both arms on the table to keep my aching back upright.

"You look like rubbish." If there's one thing about Willow, she is eternally honest.

I keep my voice down. "I need your help with something."

"Kid, you need my help with a lot of somethings."

"I'm serious."

"So am I." She doesn't even crack a smile. Lord help me.

"I can't code right," spews from my mouth.

Oh sure, now she gets it. Her shock erases as fast as it came, though, and she twirls one of her braids like she's bored.

"What do you know?" I accuse.

"Why would I know anything?"

"You look guilty." She doesn't, but it's worth a shot. "Do you know something?"

"I know a lot of things. Like, for example, you're wigging out right now." Her stone expression doesn't crack. "You're assignment's got your head screwed up, kid. It's cool, happens all the time."

Either she'll get an Emmy for her acting or she's right.

I relax and sink back into my chair. "I really need to code." I shake my head. "Bad."

"So what's the problem?"

I explain to Willow what's been happening: the freezing ice, the voice. She follows along without interruption—totally out of character—even when I go into detail about my white scars.

When I'm finally done, she says, "Where'd the scars come from?"

My hand instinctively reaches to my chest. "I don't know."

She clasps her hands together. "Well, keep trying. I'm sure it will get better." She's halfway across the room before I can even open my mouth.

"Willow!"

Just when I think she can't get any less helpful, she hollers over her shoulder, "Good luck, kid."

A few people gawk when I belt out a frustrated groan, but their attention turns to their calimeters just as mine beckons me back to purgatory. If there were a way to ditch, today would be the day.

Knowing Meggie needs me more now than ever, I displace and drop to Earth, landing smack inside one of the funeral spectators. I jump to the left to get out of the man's body.

I unzip my bag and dig for Meggie's book while the room powers back to life. Whitfield, Lawson, and Elliott, standing behind their Tragedies in the receiving line, are doing the same.

With an internal shudder, I deposit the heavy book into my bag and perform my first block of the day. Well, my day, anyway.

———

How Meggie and Brody are still standing is beyond me. How *I'm* still standing is beyond me. The unhappy couple moves through the living room like zombies, obediently swallowing the pills from Nancy, their sister-in-law, before settling on the sofa. They try talking, but have nothing to say and both succumb to sleep thirty minutes later. Their bodies are spooned together on the small sofa and Nancy covers them with a blanket before she and Ryan quietly pick up around the house and then tiptoe out.

"Have a great day, Elliott!" OK, I didn't really say it, but I should have.

After about an hour of silence, Lawson and I have a Q and A session, which is really me asking him a lot of Q's. Lawson confirms that this is one of his more difficult assignments. No surprise there; I can't imagine anything much worse than this.

Lawson warns—after admitting he enjoyed Evelynn and Billy's show in training—that neither of them are quick to forget. His advice: whatever I'm doing to keep them out of my head, I'd better keep at it. He gives me the 'Lawson Guarantee' that their retaliation won't be pretty. I had already guessed as much.

The remainder of the night is quiet and my muscles welcome the break. I don't move from my spot in the corner of the tiny living room until morning.

The steady patter of rain is relaxing until a crash of thunder makes me jump and wakes both Meggie and Brody. Lawson and I are up and blocking two minutes later, when reality roots itself into the childless couple like a weed. *Nope, that wasn't a dream you had, Miss Meggie. Good morning and welcome to your nightmare.*

I follow Meggie while she wanders through the house trying to figure out what to do with herself.

When Ryan and Nancy come in an hour later, Elliott makes the tension between us more than a little uncomfortable, but it's worth it to have Nancy here. Nancy helps Meggie with the little things, like brushing her teeth and getting dressed. Otherwise, Meggie would be climbing into her SUV for the burial in yesterday's clothes.

Max and Whitfield, in the black primer Matchbox car, are ready to go when Janine and her husband and teenage daughters show up in their minivan. I jump through the side of the SUV, get comfortable in the backseat, and off goes the world's unhappiest caravan to the only funeral home in town.

Meggie holds up better than I expect through the day. The only explanation is that she's numb. I block her just three times: once when hers eyes freeze on the four rectangular holes cut into the red Earth (a sight so shocking even my own breath is stolen), once when she lays a penny on Josh's casket, and once when it's time to leave. She won't pull away from the shiny pink and blue boxes that hold her babies. As much as I hate to, I have to interfere so she'll accept Max's coaxing to get her out of here. Poor Lawson, Brody's not faring much better.

Back at the house, the luncheon provides enough food

to feed a third-world country, but no one is eating. In fact, I can't recall Meggie eating anything the past three days.

Note to self: make sure Meggie eats soon.

Elliott continues excelling at ignoring me. After three stalker-like attempts, I leave him alone.

The crowded room stills after I silence my calimeter. I and the three other Satellites burn through the atmosphere like an impossibly bright rainbow.

The hardwood creaks under my feet when I hit the floor of my room. Wary, I decide to try coding again, partly because of Willow's advice, but mostly because my muscles need some relief. Just a quick session before training and I'll be on my way. I will not think about the thing I refuse to think about. I will not think about the freezing—

Stop it!

My eyes are closed before I'm even sitting on the mat. One by one, the puppet-string restraints release me. Yes, I really needed this. Before the buck makes his way into the clearing, I blink hard to snap myself out of coding in an attempt to avoid any unwanted diversions and then…

Oh, come on!

I gasp for air but a lead weight is too heavy on my chest. My eyes are the only part of me able to move and they dart madly around my old bedroom, unable to see what's restraining me.

Darkness forms at the outer edge of my vision and closes in until there's nothing but black. Panicked, my wide eyes search for light, but find none. The swirling ice that cuts into my flesh doesn't die with my vision. Instead, it begins to warm. I'll take the warmth over the cold any day of the week.

The temperature increases and increases and increases. Hot, hotter, yikes!

I take it back, I take it back! Give me the cold!

"Stop!" I roar, but my voice is only in my head. My mouth is melting like my skin and the concrete weight pressing me into my mattress is unrelenting. The flames lick up my neck and the imprisoning darkness intensifies the burn.

It's almost over, it's almost over, it's almost over, I repeat, pushing away the image of my skin dripping from my bones like hot wax. The flames move slower, lingering on every inch of my charred neck until they finally reach my ear.

"Grant, please come back to me," the flame whispers.

Liquid ice floods through my heated veins before I convulse with chills so severe I'm sure I'm going to crack in half.

9. What in God's name are you doing

My teeth are chattering when I strip off my shirt. The lunatic in the mirror puffs out a visible breath, but as instant as the coffee around here, my next breath is invisible.

My finger recoils from the freezing, purple blister on my chest. When I touch my knee, goose bumps run down my legs and across my bare chest. Still shivering, I drop my jeans to see a similarly gruesome blister.

I kick out of my boots and walk to the closet in my boxers, pulling on the heaviest sweatshirt I can find and leaving the hood up. I jump into a new pair of jeans and rub my hands along my upper arms for more warmth. I expect to see my breath every time I exhale.

I shiver and put on one of the seven pairs of work boots along the back wall. How convenient that the leather on each shoe is broken in just how I like them. Once dressed, the only thought floating through my head, aside from concern for my blistered chest and knee, is this: must have coffee.

When I inhale the first cup, the heat that swims down my throat is nothing compared to the burn from coding. I drink the second cup a little more slowly. By the third, I'm collecting my bag and am on my way to the courtyard for training.

The field is empty when I push through the doors. Apparently I wasn't the only one who needed to code. I jog the distance to Jonathan, hoping the movement will warm me up to at least a comfortable thaw.

"Grant, how are you? I was wondering if you were going to join us today."

I try to swallow my sarcasm. "Here I am." Insert big, fake smile.

"I can see that." He mirrors my expression. "The others have already been dismissed."

Goodbye smile. "Huh?"

"We had a great session. I suspect you were coding?"

Not for two hours.

"Are you all right? You're looking pale."

My head bobs up and down. "Mmm Hmm." *Feel free to stop nodding anytime, you idiot.*

"How is your assignment? No problems, I hope."

"No, no problems. Well, except that Meggie's children and mother are dead. Aside from that, no." Maybe I should have stopped after the first no, but whatever.

"They're not dead, as you know. I'm glad things are going well," Jonathan says lightly.

I don't recall ever using the term "well." Refraining from an eye roll may be the most difficult thing I'll do all day.

My timepiece hums like fingernails on a chalkboard and Jonathan glances down at my wrist. Certainly he can't hear it. Being subjected to one is torturous enough; hearing all of them would turn a sane person into a window licker. Before I can ask, he's telling me to have a great day and walking toward the doors.

Right. "You too," I murmur.

I throw my coffee mug across the lawn, jealous because wherever it disappears to will surely be better than the nightmare that awaits me. With a deep breath, I close my fist around Meggie's locket, say the magic word, and the neon-green lawn disappears from under me.

As soon as my feet hit the crowded living room hosting death's after-party, Lawson assaults me with questions. "What's up? Where were you today? You didn't puss out because of Billy, did you?"

"Billy? Why would my absence have anything to do with Billy?"

"He's convinced you bailed because you were scared."

I freeze with my hand in my backpack clutching my book. "You're kidding, right?"

Lawson cocks his head. "Why else wouldn't you show?"

"I was coding."

"For two hours?"

Meggie's crying interrupts my thought. Brody is chasing after her and Lawson and I follow them into the bedroom. Brody tells Ryan to give them a minute and closes the door.

"It's not fair!" Meggie yells through her sobs.

Brody reaches for her. "I know, baby. I know." When he gets his arms around Meggie, she jerks away, knocking the bedside lamp over in the process.

She falls backward, landing on the lamp and cutting

her hand on the broken bulb in the process.

Brody locks his arms around her, but she punches against his chest. "Let me go! Let me go!"

"Block!" I yell.

Calm down, calm down, calm...

I think through the pain and manage to sever the command.

Meggie goes limp in Brody's arms, sobbing uncontrollably when Max and Janine come in. I don't bother hiding my tears from Lawson this time. If he's not shedding any, he's the only one in the bedroom who isn't.

Meggie finally calms down and lets Janine clean the deep cut in her hand at the bathroom sink. The gash could probably use a few stitches, but I figure if the nurse isn't going to press the issue, who am I to argue? I slide down the wall and onto the dingy checkerboard tile, wishing there was something more I could do to help her.

Meggie refuses to leave the bathroom so Janine stays with her while Brody rejoins the crowded house in effort of getting everyone to leave. He recruits Ryan's help in the bedroom.

Lawson's cargo pants and boots come into my downcast view thirty minutes later.

"Most of the guests are gone."

I loosen my entwined fingers. "Do you think this will be the worst of it for them?"

Lawson takes up the entire doorway and his deflated expression is enough of an answer. He turns and disappears into the bedroom.

"Good talk," I mumble to my fidgeting thumbs.

Whitfield comes in five minutes later because, apparently, this is the place to be. "Hey, hon. How's it going?"

"Excellent. You?"

She shrugs, not catching my jeer. "All right, I guess. The party's over. I'm heading out with Max. Just wanted to let you know."

"OK." Long pause. "Bye," I finally add when she keeps lingering.

"Umm, you and Rigby are friends, right?"

Ah, her motive has emerged. I nod, knowing I could make this conversation easier for her, but my patience just isn't where it should be today.

"Has he…mentioned me?"

I give her my best don't know/don't care shoulder shrug. "Why?" I am such a jerk.

"Oh, um, no reason." Her face turns as red as her hair and she disappears through the wall.

"Whitfield?" I yell, feeling bad about inflicting my sour mood on her.

She's back in half a second. "Yeah?"

"He's totally into you."

Her freckles light up, making me glad I called her back.

"Thanks! See ya around." She brushes past Janine on her way out.

Fifty bucks says I'll get no goodbye from Elliott.

———

Somehow, Meggie and Janine have fallen asleep in the shoebox-size bathroom, stealing my position on the floor, which leaves just one place for me.

Perched on the toilet, I almost laugh. This so fittingly sums up my day.

Both girls drift in and out of sleep through the quiet night while Brody's snores carry into the room. Meggie moves slow when she pulls herself up from the floor in the early morning. She twists and her backbones crack.

Meggie steps over a sleeping Janine and stops by the mirror to examine her puffy, red eyes. She then unwraps the bandage and opens her hand, making a pained face when she does.

I'm grateful that the rest of the day proceeds uneventfully. Janine helps Brody and Meggie clean up from the after-funeral-party. Later, she delivers the comatose-like couple to the therapy appointment she's scheduled. I get a reprieve from blocking during the hour-long session, figuring that's what Doc Arnoldson is here for.

Lawson and I follow behind the minivan when Janine delivers the couple back home. She leaves an hour later when Meggie and Brody fall asleep together on the sofa. With Lawson and I having nothing to say to each other, I welcome the momentary peace, knowing it surely won't last.

I bypass coding and head straight to Benson when I get back. Liam and Willow are in spy mode, but this time

I have the upper hand because they don't see me coming.

"…it still doesn't make sense," Willow is saying, not noticing me standing behind her.

"You heard her, she asked him to come back. I'm telling you, she could sense him when he was there and now she can sense he's not. It's the only explanation," Liam whispers.

"That's your imagination, not an explanation. How could she possibly know what happened?"

"I don't know." Liam pauses. "But you saw her piecing the torn photograph together and begging him to come back."

"That doesn't mean anything."

"What else could it be? Enough time has passed. She should be showing more improvement than this."

"She did talk to Fish today," Willow says.

"She said, 'Excuse me.' I don't count that. She's hurting, Willow."

"I know. I hate to see her hurting, too. Especially when she treats Fish badly."

"I still think his scars prove that whatever she's doing is working."

"Whose scars?" I blurt out before I can stop myself.

They both jump and spin their heads around.

"Whose scars?" I repeat.

"It's rude to eavesdrop," Willow says.

"You lied! You know something about what's happening to me."

"I didn't lie," Willow fires back. "I really don't know

what's happening."

"So this *is* about my scars?"

"I'm sorry, kid, but I don't have any answers for you." Willow squeezes my arm and stands. "I promised Troy that I'd spend some time with him. I'll see you guys later. Grant, try to stay out of trouble."

"What's that suppose to mean?" I mumble and then yell, "Willow!" but she ignores me.

Liam looks apologetic and says, "I'd better go code."

I want to ask him to stay in hopes that he could offer more information than Willow about my scars, but he's so beaten down, I let him go.

"You guys eating?" I ask Clara and Rigby.

"I am." Owen's voice comes from behind me and he slaps my back.

Clara nods and Rigby says, "Me too."

The four of us head to the back corner of Benson for food.

"Have you noticed how bizarrely Willow's been acting?" I ask Owen after I squeeze a hot dog on my crowded tray.

Owen grabs a dog, too. "As a matter of fact, I did—"

"I haven't noticed," Clara's voice says from behind me, cutting off Owen. She reaches through the space between Owen and me, grabs the ketchup bottle, and gives Owen a look that says he should shut up.

"What's going on?" I try to keep my tone light.

Owen shrugs. "Nothing, man."

Rigby rushes past us with his tray. "I'm gonna sit with

Whitfield today. Catch you guys later."

Before I can question Owen and Clara more, they've skated through the door as well.

Ugh.

Back at the table, I can't help but think that the upbeat chatter during a game of Sats is forced. Frustrated when my calimeter beeps, I grab Clara's elbow before she displaces.

"Can I talk to you for a sec?"

"Sure." Her face brightens. "I actually wanted to talk to you about something, too."

"Ladies first," I say to be nice. My patience about Willow's strange behavior is wearing thin and it's difficult to force a smile.

"Well, I wanted…I mean, I've been wanting…"

"Clara, why the stammering? What's up?"

"It's just, I, um, wanted to ask you about our kiss."

Oh hell.

My body language must reflect my internal feelings because Clara drops her head to shield her disappointment.

Oh no. Please don't cry. Please, please, please. "I'm really sorry, Clara." I instinctively pull her into an embrace, but her arms stay crossed tightly over her chest, rejecting comfort.

"Listen, please believe me when I say you're really great. Your friendship means the world to me, but to be in a relationship—I can't risk having that kind of distraction. My assignment is grueling; it's seriously tearing me apart and I can't let down my Tragedy. Please understand." I suddenly feel like Jackson as I ramble on. Maybe I should go easier on the guy.

Her body remains tense. I pull back enough to lift her chin from my chest, urging her face upward. Her eyes skim mine and then shoot down, freezing on my T-shirt collar.

"So it's nothing against me personally?" To see her sad makes my chest tighten.

"Clara, you're beautiful. I'm not kidding, you're super hot. Trust me, if I were looking for a relationship, you'd be at the top of my list."

"Really?"

"Swear."

Catching myself fixating on her lips when she lifts her head, I internally curse. "So, uh, we should probably get to our assignments."

As if she knew I was thinking about the possibility of tasting her lips again, her cheeks turn pink. When I put more space between us, her hand disappears into her shimmery-silver purse.

I dig into my jeans pocket and make a fist around the metal heart. "I'll see you later?"

"Yeah." Clara's hand reappears from her bag with its prize, but her tight grip conceals the item. "Displace," she whispers and falls through the hardwood floor.

Only when I'm falling through the clouds does it occur to me that I never asked her about Willow's peculiar behavior. Sigh.

Back at Meggie's, the electricity has already popped back to life, but Meggie's mom's living room is darkened by the curtains and quiet aside from the air conditioner unit humming outside. I retrieve the book from my bag and do my reading, grateful to learn Lawson and I will get a breather this evening. Meggie and Brody drift in and out of sleep and eventually they move to the bedroom together.

I'm thankful to be sharing an assignment with Lawson, a man of few words. If I had to be here with Billy, he and I would surely spend our time on Earth trying to kill each other. And Jackson…sheesh, just the thought of his non-stop jabbering is tiresome.

I close my eyes and my mind drifts to my scars, trying to remember where they came from. When that fails, I think about Clara. Then, for the sake of my sanity because I'm spending way too much time imagining her lips, I shift my thoughts to training.

Could Billy have really thought I was scared of him? True, the guy could probably flatten me, but I would never allow myself to back down from such a jerk.

Then there's Evelynn, who's even more dangerous than Billy. I wonder how long it takes her to get over things. If I'm lucky, maybe now she'll leave me alone. Or maybe she's not as bad as I think and I should lighten up. Who am I kidding? She's worse. Much, much worse.

I stop thinking about Evelynn, about everything, and let my mind go blank. There hasn't been much quiet time lately and I plan to take full advantage of it.

When Brody and Meggie wake the next morning, the day starts rough. Brody is the first one to cry. Meggie holds him while he repeats, "Why did it happen? Why are they gone?" into her messy blond hair.

She cries with him for about an hour with Lawson and I occasionally throwing in a block or two to calm them down. When they are both too worn down and dehydrated to carry on any longer, the four of us go into the kitchen.

Brody opens a cabinet and reaches for a cup. Lawson, Meggie, and I jump in unison when the trill of breaking glass fills the small kitchen.

"It's not fair!" Brody grabs another glass from the cabinet, then sends it to the floor with its twin, causing glass fragments to explode across the tile.

"Block him!" I shout at Lawson.

As if he was in a trance, Lawson pops alert and gives the order.

I'm certain that Lawson has calmed Brody down until his hand shoots back up to the cabinet. Meggie is by the oven, covering her face and balling.

"Lawson!" I bark in frustration as another glass meets the floor. This time, the shards come much to close to Meggie's bare legs.

My filter comes fast and Brody is engulfed in translucent blue. Without thinking, I grab for him and push him away from the cabinet. He slams into the island and Lawson has me pinned on the floor a second later. *Me!* Like

I'm the bad guy.

"What in God's name are you doing?" he growls, one inch from my nose.

I push against him. What the heck is this guy built from?

"If you can't control him, I will!" I groan back, trying to wiggle free.

In the silent five seconds that follow, I consider Lawson's next move. He could crush me if he wanted, but I'm hoping he'll come up with something else—something a little less painful.

He lets me go and turns to Brody, who's on the floor at the base of the cabinet. Brody's expression mirrors Meggie's because neither of them have a clue what just happened. Not knowing what I was capable of, I can't deny that I'm a little surprised myself.

Heat is radiating from both palms where they touched Brody, hot enough that my calloused skin should be blistered, but isn't.

On the training field after a much-needed uneventful afternoon with Brody and Meggie, I'm grateful Lawson decided to drop the incident in the kitchen. Even better is that he's being civil to me out here. Trying to imagine a role reversal, I'm not sure if I would be so kind if he touched Meggie.

Evelynn isn't her usual, free-spirited self. If looks could

kill—well, she'd still be too seductive for her own good, even through her seething. She doesn't say a word to me. Thank goodness for small favors.

Billy, however, is vocal, not that I expected anything less. He actually thinks his pretty-boy and princess comments bother me, but he's easy enough to ignore, especially after Jonathon pairs us off for workouts.

Crossing the field with Trina, I notice she's not pierced, arrogant, impossibly huge, impossibly small, or half-naked. I like her. She makes small talk about how I'm doing with my assignment, but doesn't press for details. I ask her the same sort of questions, and I don't press either.

When we're positioned away from the others, she asks if I want to block or be blocked. The real question is whether I want to be tormented by the pain of sending my thoughts or would I prefer to have someone else inside my head? Neither is a great option. Because sending my thoughts hasn't made me any friends, I opt for letting her block me.

She promises to play nice even though she's already a saint compared to Evelynn. This is because of her kindness, and because Trina's T-shirt is made from cotton and covers more than just four inches of skin.

"All right," Trina says. "Come at me."

I force myself not to groan. "Why is this always the direction?"

"What do you mean?"

"I won't come after you. You're a girl."

She puts a hand on her hip. "Think I can't handle it?"

After gauging her expression, I try to disguise my smile.

"No offense, but there's no way you could handle it."

"Really?"

"Come on Trina, you're five foot nothing. That alone should be reason enough."

She charges me. What the—

Somewhere between my laughter and shock, I end up on my back with her standing over me.

"You were saying?" Shadowed from the bright sun overhead, her expression is unreadable.

I take her extended hand for help up and brush off my backside. "I stand corrected."

She smiles. "Good. Now come at me."

I shake my head. "Sorry, I can't."

After her mouth opens soundlessly, she snaps her jaw back into place with a click. "Fine. Sit then. Will that work for you?"

"Perfect."

After she says the order, cold darkness wraps around me, but vaporizes as fast as it came.

Stay standing! my own voice screams in my head. That's what my feet were made for, after all: to stand. Stand, stand, stand, all day long...

Sit, you idiot!

Stand!

Sit!

Stand!

Sit!

The translucent blue filter clouds my sight and I snatch my opportunity, bending my knees before another thought can process.

From the ground, I look at Trina victoriously.

"Not bad." She rubs her chin. "Do it again."

I start to get up and she stops me.

"Stay there for a second."

I obey and she stands up straighter.

"Now get up," she says, followed by, "Haze."

The lights go out and ice floods me for an instant. My butt stays planted on the ground because I don't feel like moving an inch. Why would I? I couldn't be more comfortable. I could stay on the ground forever. I could live here.

Get up, you pansy!

No!

GET UP!

When everything in my vision turns blue, I push off the ground and stand. The cycle is getting easier to distinguish, which makes it easier to resist the foreign thoughts. Even if they are in my own voice, which is extremely weird and creepy, the thought phrases are delivered in a way that I would not think; that seems to be the common tie. Somehow my energy is connected to fighting off the thoughts as well.

Instead of being impressed, Trina is fuming. At her request, we play the game six more times. Each time, I get faster, recognizing the tone changes of my thoughts.

"How about I try blocking you?" I suggest, despite the fact that she's pretty cute when she's frustrated.

Before she answers, Jonathan blows a whistle and motions for everyone to join him.

I bend down to Trina as we're crossing the field. "If it's any consolation, Evelynn and Billy couldn't get through either."

Disgusted, she storms ahead of me.

"What?" I shout after her.

Hoping she'll soften, I stand next to her when we gather around Jonathan. Billy punctuates his approach by slamming his shoulder into my back. With some effort, I only stumble forward a little.

"You should be thanking me," I'm saying to Billy before I can stop myself. "Evelynn would never kiss a troll like you if she wasn't under my influence." My grin widens when Lawson laughs.

"*Really?*" Trina puts three steps between us, not even glancing over to see the unspoken apology on my face.

Jonathan wraps up with a "Go Team" speech and dismisses us. Trina bolts before I can stop her, leaving an opening for Evelynn to slide in beside me. This time, Evelynn manages to brush more than just her arm against me.

"Is this your way of saying you're not ignoring me anymore?" I sneer.

"I saw you with Trina today. Impressive. How do you do it?"

No way I'd share any secret with her, especially this one. "I don't know," I lie. Well, mostly lie, since I can't be sure exactly how or why I seem to be the only one able to fight against blocks.

"You're different than everyone else."

"Why? Because I don't want you?" That's what I want

to say, but I stay quiet.

She pushes her invasion of my personal space to the next level as we cross the lobby. In the mosaic-tiled corridor of Benson, she grabs my arm before I step through the far right archway. Moving fast, she has me pinned between her almost-naked body and the wall.

Her hot breath is in my ear and there's a wicked smile in her whisper. "Relax."

My muscles tighten and I try to push lightly against her, not wanting to injure her, but wanting her off me. She fights me, though, and the physical force necessary to peel her off would hurt her for sure.

"I said, relax." There's no smile left in her breathy voice.

Her lips touch mine. They're smooth, and soft, and *wrong*. All wrong.

Her tongue slips into my mouth and dances around mine while I stand like a paralyzed idiot. I'd shout "rape" if my lips weren't occupied, not even caring that I'd lose my man card.

When my stupid head finally works, I do the only thing I can to get her tongue out of my mouth without hurting her. Her lips smear against my cheek and I don't turn my head straight until I know she's gotten the message.

Evelynn's smile is bigger than ever. *Glint.*

"Nice, kid," an acidic voice says.

When I find the very-unhappy Willow in the gawking crowd, she stomps away like everyone else seems to be doing lately, or at least those I actually want to hang out with.

"What the heck was that?" I yell at Evelynn.

"Oh, that's just Willow—"

"Not Willow! You!"

She transforms into the poster girl of innocence. "What?"

"Stay away from me. I'm not interested. I like Trina." The realization hits me at the exact time the words fly from my mouth.

Evelynn steps back. "Trina?"

I swallow and nod.

"Trina?" she repeats. "Really?"

My temper builds. "Yes, really!"

Evelynn thinks for a second, while the passing Satellites move to go around her. "Pity."

My calimeter buzzes and I push the mute button. "Yeah. Pity."

As I'm falling to Earth, only one thought bounces through my head: Trina?

10. No offense, man, but you're no Casanova

By the kitchen table, I open Meggie's book while she roots through the refrigerator for leftovers she can heat up for Brody. To my surprise, a handwritten note follows my usual reading.

Certainly you can understand the importance of keeping your hands to yourself.

—S

Nowhere does it say I *must* keep my hands to myself, just that I "can understand the importance" of doing so. I'm cool with that.

I flip the page.

You must keep your hands to yourself.

—S

I'd laugh if I wasn't so creeped out.

———

An hour later, I'm blocking Meggie so she'll eat something with Brody. She takes two bites of lasagna and runs to the sink to vomit. My next block coerces her into the shower. I sit outside the hall bathroom and listen for any signs that she's about to derail.

Janine arrives and lets herself in while Meggie's dressing and Brody's cleaning the dishes. When the women appear through the doorway, my shoulders slump lower. Even in clean clothes, Meggie is so emotionless, so dead looking. She'd cry if she could, but her sunken eyes and cracked lips are proof that she's too dehydrated.

I ride in the backseat of the minivan with Janine, Meggie, and Brody on the way to the seven o'clock therapy session while Lawson flies behind us. Meggie and Brody get through the hour of counseling like champs, dutifully talking about their kids and how much they love them. Meggie almost smiles once at a memory, but then dry sobbing erupts when she realizes her memories are all she has now.

Back at the house, Janine wants to stay, but Meggie kicks her out.

A little after midnight, Meggie wakes and pulls herself and Brody from the sofa and into the bedroom. It takes her an hour to fall back asleep. I block her two times when she wakes up screaming.

Ryan comes over in the afternoon with a bag of lunch for Meggie and Brody. When Ryan goes into the kitchen,

Elliott leans against the front door, avoiding me as best he can.

"Look man, will you at least talk to me?"

"You're an ass," is Elliot's reply.

I think about this. "OK, you've probably got me there."

"Seriously, man. I don't even know you anymore."

Anymore? "What's that suppose to mean?"

His eyes narrow. "I don't get it. How could you not remember?"

I'm not sure what to say.

"It's Tate! My sister! Your fiancée! The love of your life!"

Whoa, down boy.

We've got Lawson's full attention now as he leans over the back of the sofa to watch the show.

"Come on, Grant! Who are you?"

"Wait a minute, how do you remember all that about your sister?" Lawson asks Elliott from the sofa.

Elliott's face is animated no more as he slides down the wall. "I remember everything about her." His eyes lift to me for a second. "And Grant. My memories of Tate started to slip, but they came back and now they're crystal clear. I don't remember anything else from my life but the two of them." Now Elliott's glaring at me.

"Is that," I pause to find the best word, "normal?"

Elliott and I both turn to Lawson for an answer.

"Sure," he says in a no-big-deal way and then appears to be waiting for us to continue with the performance.

A conversation pops into my head from what seems like years ago. "Anna said everyone's memory loss is different," I mumble to myself.

"That's true," Lawson replies.

Elliott and I wait for more, but get nothing.

"And?" I ask. "Any insight you can add that might be helpful?"

He shrugs. "Not really. Just that Elliott should consider himself lucky. Most of us don't get to keep so many memories."

And here's the look where Lawson waits for more drama from Elliot and me. *I'm Grant and I'll be your entertainment for the day.*

"Lucky, huh?" Elliott says. "I don't get how you could forget her. She was everything to you."

Overjoyed that Elliott's at least talking to me, I decide to play along and try hard to sound sincere. "I'm sorry, man."

Elliott mulls something over, but adds nothing so my focus turns to Meggie. Ryan has gotten her to drink a cup of coffee and keep it down, which is more than I've done.

In just over two hours, Ryan actually has Meggie eating. Eating! This guy is good. She has half of a sandwich consumed without making a single trip to the sink when Elliott jumps up.

"I've got it!"

Sitting in the doorway separating the kitchen and living room, I'm much less enthused. "Got what?"

"I'm going to make you remember her."

Yay! That's what he's expecting, I'm sure, but I refuse to humor him. "Oh," is all I say before I'm saved by the bell. I push on the face of my calimeter. "Maybe later."

I blurt the word that sends me sailing into the atmosphere. After arriving in my room, I head down the hall with a new approach, which is refusing to let a little ice—or fire—scare me away. I need the release. Badly.

I take my position and close my eyes. The strain from my muscles is cut away like puppet strings and I sink into my tree stand, into the relaxed state my body has been craving.

Until it changes.

I'm not sure what's more paralyzing: the cold or the blackness. I hate both, but neither compares to the icicle blade carving into my abs. The stinging knife cuts up my chest, lingering on my neck. When it slices my lips, my scream is buried until the piercing cold moves to my ear.

"Grant, where are you?" the frozen torture whispers.

I expect my eyeballs to crack when my eyelids open. In the coding room, I claw at the freezing sting of my scars. Someone may as well have poured liquid nitrogen on them. When I escape my shirt, the deep purple blister on my chest is nastier than ever. The one on my knee is the same. Even a grazing touch has me cringing in pain. I pull my jeans up, careful not to let the denim scrape over the wound, and stalk out of the room.

Frustrated, I roar and punch the wall on my way to the closet. The hole will be repaired in my absence, no doubt, which makes me angrier.

I head to Benson with my own cup of coffee because the crap there is never strong enough.

Willow starts in before I've even reached the table. "Really, Grant? Evelynn?"

This is so not what I need right now. "Drop it."

"No," she replies just as coldly.

"What about Evelynn?" Owen asks.

"They kissed." Willow sings like a toddler.

"Nice!" Rigby cheers in approval.

Owen is in agreement, Liam ignores me, and Clara looks like she's been punched in the gut.

I could strangle Willow. "We didn't kiss!"

"Fine, they were tongue wrestling." She narrows on me. "Better?"

"*We* didn't kiss. She kissed me! Against my will!" I throw in for good measure. There goes my man card.

"What? You didn't kiss her back? This is Evelynn, as in *Elite* Evelynn, right?" Owen says. Yep the man card is G-O-N-E, gone.

Anna smacks Owen hard and he apologizes

I squeeze my eyes closed. "Just drop it."

"She's trouble. Stay away from her," Willow warns.

More than anything, I want to argue with Willow for the sake of arguing, but she's right. "Change the subject, Willow."

"I'm serious."

"Change the subject," I repeat.

"Fine. Did you guys see what Evelynn was wearing today?" Between Willow and I trying to get the last word in, it's a wonder we get anywhere.

I grit my teeth. "Willow."

She pushes up from the table. "I'm getting something to eat. Anyone care to join me?"

"I would love to," I say in a mock-sweet voice.

Clara, the only one who has the jewels to join us, stands. By the time I notice her eyes are watery, she turns and runs away. Never mind about the jewels.

"Clara!" I yell after her, but she's already disappeared into a crowd of Satellites.

"Way to go," I say to Willow while we snake around the tables.

"Don't spin this on me. You're the one who kissed Evelynn."

"I didn't kiss her!" An entire table of Satellites stops eating to watch us pass by. "Honestly, I want nothing to do with that girl," I say in a lower voice.

"Good. Evelynn couldn't be worse for you."

"Since when are you so interested in my love life? You didn't act like this when I had dinner with Clara," I remind Willow.

"That was different. You weren't into Clara."

"And I'm not into Evelynn! And so what? What if I had been into Clara?"

Willow stops in the buffet room and turns to face me. "Things were," she swallows hard enough that her throat moves, "different then. I didn't know everything I know now."

"Which is what, exactly?"

"Look, I just don't want you doing something you'll regret, that's all."

"Why would I regret kissing someone?" I ask, suddenly thinking of Trina.

Willow hands me a tray. "Just drop it, please."

"Oh, now you want to drop it?"

Since she's not enthused, I decide to let it go. May as well try to enjoy the rest of break. We fill our trays in silence before heading back to the table.

I work on my steak and am relieved the topic has taken a new direction, putting the emphasis on Rigby. He's going on and on about Whitfield and doesn't let up until she enters the room. Then he excuses himself and joins her.

"Talk about dropping us like a bad habit," Owen says.

"Lighten up, he's in love," Anna replies. "You know what it's like."

Owen gets all googly-eyed and kisses Anna.

Liam, who has looked better even on some of his worst days, stays quiet and keeps his head down through the small talk that follows. Everyone presses their calimeters just after mine buzzes, signaling the end of break and the beginning of more torture. The agonizing thought makes me brush against the scar on my chest, which I instantly regret. As if my touch was a trigger, ice shoots out in all directions and my face cringes in pain.

"You all right?" Willow asks with her eyes glued on my chest.

I mange to nod.

Sure, now Liam's interested.

———

Elliott must have used his break to work out his plan of attack because he's on me before I even get my balance from landing.

"Let me at least get my reading done," I say.

Lawson, who's stuck in his own book, laughs.

I open to the documented place and scan the page as slowly as possible. There's only one paragraph today, so dragging out my reading is not easy. I welcome the light load, or rather, my muscles will welcome the reprieve.

Elliott finally becomes suspicious of my stalling. "You can be stupid sometimes, but I know you don't read that slowly."

Without the energy to return his blow, I close the book and shove it into my bag, making sure to check on Meggie before he can start. Still at the kitchen table working on her sandwich, Meggie has the closest expression to a smile I've seen since the fire. Thank God for Ryan. I wish he'd move in. Brody spaces out on his Coke can and I wonder if Lawson's day will be as easy as mine.

"So, about Tate," Elliott says.

Strike that thought about Ryan moving in. The new house guest would come with too much baggage.

"I was thinking I'd start off easy. Do you remember what you did in life? You know, for a job."

"I was a carpenter." I get the feeling I'm going to loathe this game.

"Who'd you work for?"

"My dad."

"Did you guys get along?"

I shrug. "Can anyone really get along with my father?" Yes, I loathe this game.

"And your mom?"

My arm muscles bulge, stretching the cotton of my short sleeves. "What about her?"

"Bro, you never talk about someone's mom." Oh joy. Lawson's joining in the fun, too.

Elliott moves on. "You remember anything about high school?"

I open my mouth and run head first into the brick wall guarding my memories. I dig through my head for something, anything. "No," I concede.

"That's where you met Tate. You had an art class together, but you didn't really hook up until after she bashed into your truck."

He may as well be telling this as Lawson's fairy tale because I feel no connection whatsoever to his story. As far as I'm concerned, that's all it is: a story.

"You remember your truck, right?" Elliott continues.

Working construction, the fact that I had a truck makes sense, but I don't remember the vehicle in the slightest. I hesitate before shaking my head.

"You had two trucks, actually: a company truck and a piece-of-crap truck. I was partial to the company truck. So were you."

My face must certainly be blank, because that's how my head feels. Lawson appears to be enjoying story-time.

Elliott's interrogation continues. "Do you remember Fischer?"

"It's cool," he says like he's trying to make me feel better when I don't answer. "I don't remember much of him either, just the parts that had to do with you and Tate. He's my little brother and he was your pawn when you popped the question."

"What question?"

"The *Will You Marry Me* question."

"I can only imagine how that went," Lawson says with a big, fat grin.

"What's that suppose to mean?" I accuse.

"No offense, man, but you're no Casanova."

"Whatever. I bet I'd put a guy like you to shame." My jab fails to affect Lawson's smile.

"Believe it or not, he actually did pretty well." Elliott turns to me. "You asked her during a game of trivia. She had no idea. I can't believe you don't remember her expression. She actually cried! My sister! The only other times I saw her cry were…" Elliott trails off like he's sad. "She just didn't do that kind of thing."

"Oh, she's one of those girls." I visualize Ms. Make Believe in my head as one of those tough-girl feminists.

This angers him. I almost feel bad, but reconsider. He's trying to make me believe in something that never happened. I'm not going to jump on the emotional crazy-train just because he is there.

I'm saved when Ryan, Meggie, and Brody head for the door. Tonight Ryan is the couple's chauffeur to Doc Arnoldson.

To my dismay, Elliott joins us in the Doc's office and parks himself beside Meggie on the arm of the sofa.

"Shouldn't you be keeping an eye on Ryan?" I ask,

hoping Elliott will join his Tragedy in the waiting room.

"Nah, he's always easy when he's close to Meg. Do you remembering anything about the music you liked?" Jeez, he's wasting no time.

I focus on the ceiling as an answer and ignore Lawson's laughter.

"Tate loved music. All kinds. You always bought CDs for her. Remember?"

"Elliott! No, I don't remember! I'll play your story-time game, but stop asking me if I remember. I don't." Period. The end.

"She loved music," he whispers and then keeps his mouth shut for the rest of the session.

Watching Meggie's eye for any indication of a twitch, I don't have the patience in me right now to feel bad for Elliott even though I probably should.

After the appointment, the group of us ride in the SUV silently back to the house, minus Lawson, who has chosen to fly again.

Brody looks about as good as Liam did at break. He moves into the bedroom and Lawson follows.

"I can stay if you want," Ryan says from the kitchen.

"I'm fine. You should go," Meggie urges.

"You're not fine."

"I know, but you should still go. I'm sure Nancy would appreciate the help with the…" Her sobbing resumes before she can get out the painful word: kids. "Oh God, what am I going to do?"

Ryan wraps his arms around her. His presence seems

to relax her, which gives me a break as well. "I wish I had an answer, Meg. I really wish I had an answer."

That makes two of us.

I block Meggie five minutes later because her sobs don't lessen. With so little physical strength left, she would be on the floor if Ryan wasn't holding her up. When she calms down from my aid, Ryan talks her into going to bed.

Ten minutes later, Meggie climbs between the covers beside Brody. Since his face is covered, I can't tell if he's sleeping. Lawson has made himself comfortable in the corner beside the nightstand.

Ryan tucks Meggie in like she's a child and kisses her forehead. "Try to sleep."

She sniffs and nods.

"Max will be by tomorrow. I love you, Meg." He smoothes her hair and gives her another kiss on the head before making his exit.

"See you guys later," Elliott says. "I'm not giving up on your memories, man."

Great.

—⁓—

An hour later, Meggie and Brody have both escaped to Slumberland with Lawson and I on watch from opposing corners of the room.

"Think Elliott will be able to jog your memories?" Lawson asks.

"Doubt it."

"Me too. Trying seems to be helping him, though. It's big of you to play along."

I nod, inclined to think that I owe Elliott something, but can't, for the life of me, figure out why.

———

The next morning, Meggie wakes up in Brody's arms. When she nuzzles into his neck, he tightens his grip around her in such a way that no one would know the nightmare they were facing.

After a long time in this position, Brody pinches the bridge of his nose. "I don't know how to function without the kids."

Meggie swallows and starts to cry. "I need you more than ever. We need each other."

When they work themselves up to getting out of bed an hour later, they both manage to shower, brush their teeth, and take their pills. In someone else's life, this would be no big deal. In theirs, this is huge.

Janine stops by, making four trips to the car to bring in more than a dozen clear baking dishes. She stocks every shelf in the fridge and freezer. With Meggie barely eating these days, it's a shame all that food will be wasted.

Brody snatches one of the oval dishes before Janine loads it into the fridge, grabs a fork, and shovels the pasta into his mouth. Never mind about the wasted food.

Janine stays late into the afternoon, cleaning the house, doing laundry, and paying bills. A very unhelpful Meggie follows behind her like a puppy.

Max shows up with Whitfield and joins Brody, who's on the sofa zoning in front of the T.V. Whitfield, apparently feeling extra chatty, goes on and on about Rigby. I nod like I'm paying attention until my calimeter drones.

"See you in training," Lawson says before the three of us displace like glowing missiles into the sky.

11. I'm trying to jump-start Grant's memories

Training goes as well as training can, meaning I am able to keep everyone out of my head. Jonathan has taken notice and watches Lawson and I the most. Lawson's nice enough at least. His thoughts are nowhere near as evil as Billy's.

Trina catches me on the way off the field and my heart rate picks up.

"Sorry about being so cold the other day," she says. "I was frustrated when I couldn't get in your head. That's never happened to me before."

"It's a known fact that I'm a freak."

Trina thinks this funny. "Aren't we all?"

My coding problem surfaces front and center in my thoughts. She has no idea. When my calimeter goes off, I shift my weight in discomfort. I suck with women.

"You all right?" she asks.

My eyes widen and I nod too many times in order to skirt the issue of liking her. "Yeah, fine. See you around," I blurt out, displacing as soon as my hand is in my pocket.

She's really pretty, I think when I'm falling to Earth, followed by, *You blew it, you idiot.*

"You schooled me out there," Lawson says after he lands.

"Sorry."

"Don't apologize. It was sick!"

"Thanks." I guess.

"How'd you do it?"

I measure him and decide to spill, mostly because of the entire team of Elites he's the closest I have to a friend. Jeez, that's sad. "Something in my head can distinguish the foreign thoughts. Once I make the connection, I fight against them and my energy seems to take over. There's a warning that comes before the thought, when everything turns black and cold for a second." I shudder, thinking about how coding has this same effect.

"Sweet. I'm going to try it."

I grin and we read through the upcoming day's events. Ryan will be back later, which means Elliott will be back later. Sigh.

"Thanks," Lawson says when he closes his book.

"For what?"

"For sharing the goods. You didn't have to."

"It's cool." Yes, I consider him a friend.

An hour later, as documented, Ryan comes in with his wife, Nancy, followed by Elliott walking leisurely behind them. With Janine, Max, and Whitfield still here as well, the seams of the small house are threatening to burst. I'd step outside if I wasn't worried about Meggie.

I was right to stay because Janine's goodbye hug sets Meggie off. The pain of blocking is getting—not tolerable, but expected. My pain is an easy trade for Meggie's comfort, or the closest thing to it that I can give her.

Elliott is back at it thirty seconds after I sever the command. "So we talked about how Tate loved music. She had a million CDs. She never left the house without her iPod, she hated T.V., she loved to read—"

"What are you doing?" Whitfield interrupts.

Elliott loses his train of thought. "Huh?"

"What are you talking about?"

"My sister, Tate, who also happened to be Grant's fiancée. I'm trying to jump-start Grant's memories."

Whitfield bites back her smile. "Oh hon, tell me you're kidding."

I wish.

"Uh-uh," Elliott says.

Whitfield studies him, certainly realizing the guy is delusional. "It'll never work."

Thank you.

Elliott shrugs. "Worth a shot."

Mental sigh. I remind myself that I upset him big time when I took the jab about his sister being a Rebellion and owe him this much. When he continues, I have to remind myself again.

"Anyway…music, she's loves it. Moody, poetic chick singers are her favorite, but don't knock her for that; she'll listen to anything. She plays the violin. She rocks at it, actually.

You never missed a college recital. Ever. You had a lot of fights with your dad about this actually, because you skipped a few days of work for them. Tate always came first. You were seriously addicted to her."

My fingers automatically rub my prickling chest. There's a new warmth to my scar.

Meggie falls into another crying jog and I block her again. In the background, Lawson is blocking Brody. Like watching someone vomit, it causes a chain reaction and in seconds the four of us are barking out commands in one, giant blocking fest. At least Elliott has shut up about his sister.

I lean against the wall in the living room and try to relax my muscles while Lawson and Whitfield do the same. Elliott is also exhausted, but clearly still has the gears spinning in his mind.

"I'll be right back," I say, needing to get away before he starts in again. "Holler if she needs me."

Understanding, Lawson nods.

I walk through the back wall to the dilapidated patio, wishing I could feel the summer heat. The sun is just starting to fall, making the pollution in sky glow bright orange. In contrast to the front yard, most of the ground back here is just dirt and the few spots of grass are crispy and brown.

For no clear reason, I think of my dad. I can picture his weathered face. My mom's, too. Oddly, their images are never side-by-side in my half-memories.

"You all right?"

I suck in a deep breath. "Just getting some air."

"It's crowded in there," Whitfield states like she gets it.

I nod.

Like me, she's focused on the orange sky. "Elliott's bothering you."

"Not really. Story-time's just getting in the way of watching out for Meggie."

"Do you believe him?"

Ah, the million dollar question. "No."

"Why?"

I shrug. "I don't feel anything. How could I have had this deep relationship and not remember it all?"

"Memories can be funny." With that, Whitfield goes back inside.

I stay outside for a long time, not eager to go back through the wall into the mental ward.

———

When everyone finally leaves, well past midnight, the remainder of the night and the next day move quickly, probably because Elliott isn't here rambling nonsense. My calimeter buzzes its reprieve faster than I expect, with zero complaints from me.

In my room, I do a quick clothing change and inventory my scars. The blisters are even more disgusting, scabbed and so purple they're almost black. No way am I going to try coding today.

When I get to Benson, the crowd at our table has grown. I try my best to be positive, but doubt I pull it off.

"Hey," Elliott says.

I don't answer and slump into the furthest chair from him, next to Willow.

"You remember Whitfield?" Rigby says from my other side.

I barely move. "Yeah."

Whitfield, sitting close enough to him that she's almost in his lap, leans over and shakes my hand, followed by a wink.

I ignore Rigby's scowl and turn to Clara. "How's it going?"

"I'm good," Clara answers, way more chipper than the other day.

"Great," I smile for good measure. "Anyone eating?"

"Always," Owen says.

He, Anna, Rigby and I cross the room, walk through the buffet, and emerge with overflowing trays of food. Well, all of us except Anna. Her tray consists of more greens and a lot less meat.

"Hey man, hold up a 'sec."

I stop beside a crowded table to wait for Rigby.

"What's up with you and Whitfield?"

"Excuse me?"

"Why'd she wink at you?"

I lift my shoulders, dumbfounded. I'd hold out my hands in a I-have-no-idea-what-you're-talking-about gesture if I wasn't holding my tray. His intense look gets under my skin. "Why don't you ask her?"

My tray is no longer an issue as Rigby dumps his own and then takes care of mine. How we get on the floor escapes me. All I have time to think about is dodging his hammering fists as they try to make contact with my face.

"Dude!" I manage. "What the—"

Our brawl ends as suddenly as it began because some huge guy straight-jackets Rigby.

"You're a dirtbag! First Clara, now Whitfield? What's your problem? Why can't you pick someone I'm *not* interested in?"

I stand and pull my shirt down. "It's not like that! I'm not interested in either of them! Honestly. There's someone else—"

Crap!

"Clara, wait! I'm sorry. That's not—" Damn. I should have coded. A few more blisters would have been worth avoiding this mess.

Rigby storms away with Whitfield following and yelling her disapproval at him in her thick southern accent. I ignore the dozens of wide eyes fixed on me and force an exit route through the gathered crowd. Looking towards the lobby, I decide that's not my best getaway since Rigby is probably still out there. Instead, I retreat to the buffet room. I get a new tray and choose much less food than before. Nothing is quite as appetizing now.

When I leave the buffet, I plan on heading back to my own room. Only when I notice that the spectators have moved on to other topics of conversation do I reconsider.

"I think it's a great idea," Anna is saying when I grab a seat.

"What's a great idea?" Liam asks as he sits down in

Rigby's place.

"I'm trying to bring back Grant's memories," Elliott tells him.

I stare at Elliott. No, I try to burn holes into him with my eyes. It doesn't work and his reaction is the complete opposite of what I intended to provoke.

"How?" Owen's interested tone sucks, like he wants in.

Elliot sounds like a motivational speaker. "I've been telling him all the things I remember about Tate. Which is a lot, actually."

Owen swallows a mouthful of food. "Cool."

No! Not cool! The furthest thing from cool.

"When have you been telling him?" Anna asks.

"Oh, uh, just here and there." Elliott is clearly worried about breaking rule number three.

Everyone nods, understanding the obvious, except Anna. God love her innocence.

"Our assignments have crossed," I explain to Anna because I feel bad that she's out of the loop. Rules schmules.

When she gets it, her face brightens. "Oh."

Liam ignores us and appears much too enthusiastic about Elliot's zany notions. "I think it's a great idea. I have things I can add, too. Maybe it'll help."

Even Anna has jumped on board the crazy-train.

"It won't work," Willow murmurs.

"Thank you!" At least one sane person still exists. Who knew it would be Willow?

"It might work," Elliott says.

Willow bites into a snap pea. "You're wasting your

time."

Liam is so hopeful he could spontaneous combust. "It's worth a shot!"

"You've got nothing to lose," Anna agrees.

"Except time," I mumble, thinking about playing Sats. Since coding exacerbates the blistered holes eating through my chest and knee, this is all I have to wind down. I don't need Elliott trying to fill my head with trivia during break, too.

"Don't you even want to remember her?"

I keep quiet. Surely, no one wants my real answer.

"What have you told him so far?" Liam asks Elliot and it's game on.

"Just some basics about what she likes, that kind of stuff," he says.

"Did you feel anything?" Liam asks me.

I look up at the lanterns overhead. I hate this game.

When my eyes lower, Liam is giving me the dying-of-cancer pity expression. Then, displaying extra-odd behavior, he uses a friendly voice. "You found a way back to her after you died."

Willow's head jerks up as the others lean in closer. "Liam," she hisses.

I move on to chewing my burger like Liam's said nothing. To further my point that I couldn't care less, I lick a glob of ketchup off my thumb.

"You blocked her when she got upset. You hung out there all the time." Liam points his thumb at his chest. "I had to put up with you."

I almost laugh when Anna sucks in a breath like Liam's just shoplifted a bible.

Willow clears her throat.

Liam lowers his voice and leans further into the table. "Oops. Forget I said that."

"You're her Satellite?" Elliott says to Liam.

"Willow's been there, too." Liam ignores Willow's angry disapproval and keeps talking. "Tate erased your memories by destroying all of the objects that tied the two of you together. She burned her clothes and all the notes you wrote her. Photos, ticket stubs, all kinds of things."

"Liam, this is a bad idea," Willow says and leaves the table.

I watch her walk away as Liam whispers, "Tate hammered her engagement ring to a pulp before chucking it into the river. Willow said Tate almost threw herself in after it."

Elliott flinches. Good. Maybe he'll put an end to this madness.

"She slit her wrist."

When the words are out of Liam's mouth, my scars ignite with heat. Instead of gauging Elliott's reaction, I have to blink away a murky image. I bite the inside of my lip until it bleeds to keep my face from revealing any emotion. The iron taste makes the image clearer, which only intensifies the burning.

I can't breathe.

My chair screeches across the floor and I'm standing and slinging my bag over my shoulder. "It's not going to work." I think I do a decent job of making my voice sound irritated instead of panicked.

It takes all my strength to walk out of the room instead of running. My teeth grit together to fight against the pain. The scars feel like they're melting off my body. When I get into the lobby, out of sight, I bolt. I don't even know where. It doesn't matter.

The hallways get narrower until they may as well be pushing against me, but I don't stop sprinting until I'm sure no one will find me. I slam my back against a wall and try to even my breathing. Whatever the nightmarish image of the murky water was, I hate it. Not only are my scars rebelling, my heart is as well. Thank God I'm already dead; otherwise, I'd surely be having a heart attack right now.

When the flames subdue to a bearable temperature, the tightening in my chest lessens and I stop gasping. I drop my bag and yank my shirt up. The blister that was almost black just an hour ago is now blood-red and hot.

I sink down the wall for the remainder of break and try not to think about anything but breathing.

———

I do my best to act normal back at Meggie's and am able to brush Lawson off when he asks about my brawl with Rigby. Thankfully, the atmosphere stays placid into the evening, with only the sound of the television breaking up the time. I'm not sure how well I would be able to pay attention to anything aside from what happened to me and my scars during break.

Around eight o'clock, Lawson and I move from the living room to the kitchen while Brody heats up two plates of chicken from the fridge. He devours his while Meggie makes some kind of shredded sculpture with hers. When Brody is finished, Meggie dumps the ceramic plates, silverware and all, into the trash.

"Guess that's one way to do dishes," Lawson says, almost humored.

Meggie acts like she needs something to do. If she had salvaged the dishes, at least she could burn some time by washing them.

Brody and she have a minimally worded conversation about Brody's plans to go back to work. Meggie lets him know, in a few more words, her feelings on the issue, despite Brody's plea that he's afraid to lose his contract on a resurfacing project with the highway department. He argues that "the company needs him." Meggie's argument is the same, and she feels that her need for him should win, hands down. Their conversation ends with Meggie accusing Brody of not caring about their dead kids, which puts her and me in a certain tiny, avocado prison for the night. At least Elliott isn't here.

Cramped on the checkerboard floor, I think about this girl, Tate, and reach to my chest. Heat still radiates around the lesion. I close my eyes to put my scars, her, and everything else out of my head.

———

My calimeter finally buzzes after a day so bad I would have preferred listening to Elliott. I'd gladly take his stories over watching Meggie and Brody fight. The couple has been through enough already. The last thing they should be doing is turning on each other.

Back in my room, I decide to code—no, I *need* to code—so it's wearily down the hall I go.

The bindings start to release my muscles as soon as I close my eyes. After just enough comfort, unwilling to go deeper, though my body could certainly benefit, I try to pull myself back from the forest before something bad can happen.

Instead, a strong force yanks me from my tree stand into my old bedroom. Every cell in me fights in rejection, but the effort is wasted because I'm paralyzed under the lead weight. This time the cold doesn't even bother to make an appearance. Heat overwhelms me and I wail from the sensation of a branding iron scorching my chest in a circular motion.

The fire claims victory over my skin, climbing higher and higher, up my neck, to my ear.

"Please remember," the flame whispers and delivers the greatest torment yet.

"Grant, I wasn't sure if we'd be seeing you today." Jonathan says when I'm on the field. When his eyes drop to my chest, I assure myself that he couldn't possibly know about my scar.

Looking past Jonathan, the others are already paired off and working. "How long have they been here?"

"Just over an hour."

Over an hour?

Play it cool, man, play it cool…

I'm grateful when Jonathan turns away from me to watch Trina and Reed. "I've been hoping to talk with you. I hope you don't mind that I seize the moment while everyone is immersed in training."

"Sure." Crap.

"You have quite a skill with blocking. In my many years, I've never seen anyone able to close his mind the way you do. It is a talent, indeed. I have a question to ask and if you have any reservations, please say so." He makes eye contact, waiting for an answer.

"OK," I say, not knowing what he's expecting.

"Would you be inclined to allow each of the Elites to block you today?"

I consider it. The bright side is not having to strain myself with the pain of blocking; the dark side is that Billy gets another shot. And Evelynn, too. I have my doubts that either will play nice.

After a few seconds of weighing the options, I agree.

He claps his hands. "Excellent." He blows the whistle and everyone gathers around him.

"Grant has graciously agreed to let each of you block him today. For some of you, this will be the second time. The purpose of this exercise is to test Grant's stamina…"

Whoa, what? That's not why I signed up.

"...and also to possibly give each of you a healthy does of failure. After many years of success, I think this will prove to be a humbling opportunity on all accounts."

And *I* think Jonathan has lost his mind. My stamina? Meaning, like, we'll go until I fail? Or until my mind cracks in half by way of multiple personality disorder?

Everyone is lining up before I can argue. Billy wears a smile so big he could compete with Willow. He would have been first in line if Evelynn hadn't used her barely-clad hip to knock him out of the way. God, help me.

Jonathan is way too eager about this. "Whenever you are ready."

"Maybe tomorrow," is what I want to say, but before I can, Evelynn has already said, "Do whatever you want."

What the heck does she mean?

"Haze," she says. The black, iced wall is gone as quickly as it came.

Holy—

She's beautiful. And those lips, those full, wet lips. I have to taste them. Now! I can't get to her fast...

No, you moron!

Kiss her!

No!

"No!" I yell, three inches from her face when I gain my bearings and my blue sight. "I thought we had moved past this."

"Doesn't mean I can't still have a little fun with you," she says and smiles. I smile back because of her changed demeanor, which is now more playful than wicked. She huffs her peppermint breath in my face and does a runway walk to the back of the line.

Billy steps up like he's just won the lottery. "Do whatever." He shows his pointy teeth. "Haze."

I hardly notice the darkness or the temperature drop because all I notice is Jackson. He's short, yes, but he's…hot! Who knew someone like him would be my type? Me, that's who! He's gorgeous! There's no other word to describe…

What the heck is wrong with you?

Go get him, Tiger.

Huh?

No! No! No! "No!"

Billy laughs while heated anger crawls up my face. Thankfully, no one else knows what he was trying to plant in my head.

I try to telepathically deliver my thoughts to Jonathan so he'll stop this nonsense, but he's choosing not to read my mind right now. Figures.

I'm unable to make eye contact with Jackson when he steps up.

"Come after me," Jackson says.

Oh, dear God.

"You all right, man?"

"Oh. You mean like attack?" I ask.

Billy's laughter belts out loud enough that the others turn toward the back of the line.

"Yeah, of course. What else—"

"Go!" I yell.

The confusion leaves his face, he gives the order, and the cold, black wall comes for an instant.

I want to back up. Badly. My feet should not be forced to carry me forward anymore.

Back away, man, back away…

No, stupid!

Back away!

Two inches from driving my shoulder into Jackson's head, I manage to stop myself. My breath comes a little faster. "I can't attack you, but I can't back away either. Sorry."

Before Reed gets his chance, Jonathan announces the end of training, but relief doesn't have a chance to set in before he adds that we'll be picking up with the same torturous drill next time. Billy may as well be giving Evelynn a fist bump.

I walk slowly towards the doors, hoping my plan to wait for Trina is not too obvious.

Trina ends her conversation with Jonathan and skips up the hill. When she gets close to me, I say, "Can I talk to you for a sec?"

"Sure," she answers.

I steer her into one of the empty hallways off the lobby, internally freaking out because I have no idea what I'm going to say to her.

She lifts my wrist and opens my hand, revealing the tarnished gold locket I have dug out of my jeans. "It's beautiful." Her green eyes are larger and brighter than usual. A curl has escaped from her ponytail and follows the soft line of her cheek. "Good job out there." She keeps my hand in hers and my heartbeat picks up.

"Thanks."

"You're different."

Yeah, haven't I already told her this? I'm a freak—and not in the tatted-up-and-pierced way, but the screwed-up-in-the-head way, which is far worse. Before I can say anything, she continues.

"You're humble. So many Satellites have this air about them like they're extraordinary."

Looking into her eyes, I forget to talk until my subconscious kicks me in the butt. "Aren't they?"

"Only because of how they're built. What they do comes naturally because of their genetics."

"It's not without effort, though." I'm not really sure why I'm arguing the fact when I couldn't agree more.

"I know. I just feel like what we do doesn't make us more special than anyone else, living or dead."

"I agree."

"You do?"

I nod. "You sound surprised."

"Most people around here don't, that's all." Trina releases my hand, leaving me disappointed.

Maybe it's the red sweater that clings to her in all the right places, or because I can't stop watching her lips. Whatever the reason, before I can think about what I'm doing, I grab both of her hands and lean into her.

Her green eyes widen as she leans forward and, a second later, her lips are moving with mine. I release her hand, push my calimeter to silence it, and wrap my arm around her waist. She pulls her other hand free to grab my neck. Her body pushes harder against me. She feels so good, so right. My fingers work themselves into her ponytail, making tight fists around her curls.

And then—

Ahhhhh!

It takes everything I have not to bite through her tongue from the fire in my scars. I push her back as lightly as I can manage and hunch over in pain.

"Grant?"

I can only imagine the look on my face. If my expression mirrors my insides, deranged would be an understatement.

"I'm so sorry," I croak, fighting to keep from screaming in pain.

I give the order to displace and pray that I'm still holding Meggie's locket. Thankfully, the floor falls out and the whooshing air camouflages my tortured wailing.

12. If Upper Management found out, they'd send you off to the Probing Department

I'm glad Lawson landed in the living room so I don't have to face him. One look at my neurotic state would prompt an interrogation and there's no way I could sanely answer a line of questioning right now. I'm not even sure what happened when I kissed Trina, but the lingering heat in my scars won't go away.

After doing my daily reading, I spend the rest of the afternoon and entire night in the bathroom, wondering what is wrong with me. Three hours after the sun breaks through the peach curtains, I get my first reprieve from my crazy thoughts by blocking Meggie before she makes it to the vanity.

"You look terrible," Lawson says to me when I follow Meggie into the living room.

Meggie speaks before I have to offer an explanation. "I'm sorry."

"Me too, baby. Come here," Brody says from the chair.

Meggie falls into Brody's lap and the two of them silently cry together for awhile.

"I guess it's better than fighting," Lawson says.

I agree and we let the couple share their sorrow until Ryan shows up.

Elliott starts in immediately. "Tate's favorite food is pancakes. Green is her favorite color. She loves fall more than the other seasons. Her favorite…"

Someone help me; he won't let up. I manage to tune him out and focus on Meggie, Ryan, and Brody's conversation in the kitchen. Ryan agrees that Brody should try to get back to work, at least part-time, for some normalcy. Meggie chooses not to argue this time, but ignores Ryan when he mentions that maybe she should do the same.

"…favorite sport is baseball. She loves dogs, all kinds, mostly the big ones. Her favorite subject has always been art. She drives too fast. You hated that. She—"

"*Elliott!*" My tone shocks him into silence.

"Yeah?"

"Stop!"

"I can't. I have to try. It's my purpose now."

"Get a new purpose," I pause, "like watching Ryan."

"Ryan's fine," Elliott answers, but retreats to the far side of the kitchen and decides to leave me alone.

In the silence, my mind goes blank and it's smooth sailing until my calimeter beeps.

"See you at break?" Elliott asks.

"Doubt it." I displace before having to hear another word from him.

When I land in my room, I have two choices; coding or Benson. Coding could possibly kill me—again. On the other hand, Trina is sure to be in Benson. Facing her after the embarrassing kissing disaster may kill me, too. And Elliott will be there. Ugh.

I glance down the hallway and weigh my options while I change clothes, eventually choosing the least of the three evils.

"You got a minute?" I don't let Trina answer and park myself in the neighboring leather chair in a corner of Benson. "I'm really sorry. I don't know what happened."

When she says nothing, I go on. "I liked it. Kissing you, I mean. But something happened. I can't explain it. It was…I don't know…weird."

She marks her page in a book that features an intimidatingly buff guy on the front cover and lays it on the coffee table. "Kissing me was weird?" She winces on the last word.

Do I tell her or not?

She continues to wait silently while I argue back and forth with myself. I lower my voice. "I'm having some issues."

Finally, her expression lightens. "Oh!" After ten more seconds, she adds, "I've heard that kind of, um…problem, I mean issue, happens to a lot of people." Her face blushes darker and darker until her skin almost matches her red-tinted hair.

"Huh?" Oh, dear God, she thinks—"No!" My voice lowers to almost a whisper and I make sure no one is eavesdropping. "Not that kind of issue."

Her expression makes me feel like I have a third eye.

"When we kissed, my skin felt like it was on fire," I

explain, hoping to regain my manhood.

She pauses and then nods. "I thought it was pretty hot, too."

Sheesh.

"No, I mean, it hurt. Physically."

"My kiss *hurt* you?"

I take a deep breath. "Can I start over?"

She waves her hand through in the air and sits back. "Be my guest."

"This goes back to coding, really. I'm having problems in that area." Great. Now she surely thinks I'm an idiot. "I'm getting…interrupted when I code."

She opens her mouth, then pops it closed when my hand signals for silence.

"It starts off fine, but then the scene changes to my old bedroom, the one from my previous life, and I'm paralyzed. A freezing pain, like ice, crawls from my stomach to my ear every time. But lately, the ice has been turning to a scorching heat. Then something whispers to me."

She raises an eyebrow. "Say what?"

"I know how bizarre this sounds."

"Do you?" She's skeptical when she pauses. "What does the voice say?"

"My name, *come back to me, I love you,* things like that. Just recently it said, *remember me.*"

"Is it a guy's or a girl's voice?"

"What kind of question is that?" I accuse. Billy must have spilled the goods about his block in training and… Jackson.

"Chill. It's a legit question."

So I overreacted. A lot. "A girl's voice," I say, nicer than before.

"What does this have to do with our kiss?"

Here it goes. "I felt the same pain when I kissed you."

"Did you hear voices, too?"

When she puts it that way, I sound like I really have lost my mind. "No."

"The pain, did it crawl up your stomach like before?"

"No, it was centralized on my scars."

"Your what?"

Oh, right, my scars. I haven't mentioned those yet. "I have two scars. The pain lingers in them after these episodes. Pretty ferociously, actually. When you and I kissed, my scars burned hotter than ever." There's no way to redeem my sanity at this point, so I add, "They changed color, too."

Yep, I'm insane. Trina's expression proves it. "Where are they?"

"One's on my chest. They other is on my knee."

"Come with me." She pushes up from her chair, shoves her book in her bag, and grabs my hand.

She tows me along through a maze of hallways. When we finally stop, she stands close to me like she did before our kiss. "Let me see."

"See what?" I ask.

She eyes my chest. "Your scars."

"Are you trying to get me naked?"

She laughs and tells me to shut up. I make sure the hall is vacant before stripping off my T-shirt.

"You like what you see?" I say to mess with her.

She rolls her eyes, but her face flushes. She trails her finger across the lesion. "It's warm."

Her touch has me thinking things I shouldn't, especially after what happened during our last kiss.

She looks down at my legs, or in that general vicinity. "The one on your knee?"

"It's the same. Identical, actually." I pause, and then immediately want to break the uncomfortable silence. "You want to see?" I joke, but after the words are out, I'm a nervous that she may actually say yes.

She acts like she's considering, but thankfully says, "I'll take your word for it."

"Any theories about what would cause this?"

She shakes her head. "No. None."

Figures.

"I can check around," she offers.

"No!"

She steps back and I force myself to chill the heck out. "Sorry. I don't think it's a good idea for this to get out."

She leans in like she's sharing a secret. "You're probably right. If upper management found out, they'd send you off to the Probing Department."

I double-check that we're still alone. "You're kidding?"

"Yes, I'm kidding! You need to unwind." She steps closer and spreads her hand over the middle of my bare chest. "Seriously. You need to calm down."

Embarrassingly, my heart drums faster.

"Do you want to try again?" she whispers and leans

closer to my face.

I'm unable to speak. Of course I want to kiss her again, but I'm terrified of the results. We remain motionless for a long time until I wrap my hand around her warm neck and lean down.

She tastes like vanilla today. When I pull her closer, she moves her hand from my chest so our bodies are touching. She pushes my hair behind my ear and then everything feels wrong.

I try to push her away gently, but she stays glued to me while the heat in my scars ramps up. When I finally break free from her grasp, she stumbles back from the force. I manage to apologize before the pain takes over.

Trina's voice is far away. "Grant! Grant, look at me."

I can't get past the burning to open my eyes.

"Grant!" her shout echoes and my face is yanked upward. "Look at me!"

I open my eyes and concentrate on her face, which appears to be vibrating. I'm not sure how I even got to the floor. When the burning lessens enough to breathe and there's just one of her in my vision, I begin to relax.

Trina's sucks in air. "What's going on with you?"

That seems to be the question of the week.

⁓⁓⁓

After I get my shirt back on, Trina and I spend the rest of break sitting in the hallway staring at the opposite marble wall. She invents a few theories about my scars, none of which

I like. By the time she mentions that maybe my scars are possessed, I have to tell her to cool it.

"I'm just trying to help."

Helping is the last thing she's doing. I'm feeling more like a kook by the minute.

A few silent minutes go by. Trina breaks the awkward tension with, "The kiss was nice."

"It was." Before my scars tore in half.

"We could keep trying. Maybe we could find a work-around," she jokes.

My eyes can't stay off her lips, but the thought of more pain is too scary. "Not today." I think I do a decent job at keeping my voice light, and then go for a subject change. "How long have you been here?"

"Forty-three years." She pauses. "Some of my assignments seem like centuries ago, especially my pre-Elite ones. I really miss my Tragedies sometimes."

"What about Maintenance?"

Trina picks at the frayed canvas of her slip-on shoe. "Twelve of my pre-Elite Tragedies are dead. The five who are living are well enough that they don't require Maintenance."

I think of Ryder. "Shouldn't you check in anyway?"

"Being an Elite doesn't allow for much time off."

"How'd you die?"

"I don't remember." She shakes her head like this frustrates her. "I heard you had cancer."

"Melanoma." The image of the little boy that passed me when Meggie and Brody were leaving the hospital enters my mind and my stomach tightens. "Do you remember anything from your life?"

"I have a twin brother. I was twenty seven when I died and he and I were really close. I can't imagine what my death did to him."

Heat crawls into my scars, nothing like before, but unsettling nonetheless.

Trina watches me rub my knee. "You all right?"

"Yeah. Did you have a husband, or boyfriend, or anything?"

"No. Not that I remember, at least."

I exhale, not realizing I was holding my breath.

"You sure you're all right?" She grabs my hand, and her touch makes my heart race. With each beat, my scars get hotter.

I ignore the pain, furious that it's interfering with a perfectly good moment, and I don't pull my hand away until my calimeter buzzes. Trina pushes the face of hers as I'm quieting mine.

"I'll see you in training?"

I dig the tarnished heart out of my jean pocket and nod. "See you then."

I fight not to flinch from her hug, but the burn intensifies.

She lets me go and begins walking down the hall.

"Aren't you displacing?" I call after her.

She turns to face me, walking backwards. "Not today. I have to meet Jonathan."

"Trading assignments?"

She nods.

My scars hurt even more when she flashes her beautiful smile. "Displace," I mutter through clenched teeth and fall through the floor. The whooshing air covers my groan as I drop to Earth.

"I missed you at break," Elliott says before my feet even hit the dated carpet.

I didn't miss him, but instead of saying so, I grunt.

"Liam had an idea. This one's really good."

"I have to get my reading done. You should probably do the same."

Elliott pokes his head into the kitchen, sighs, and pulls out his book. Three minutes later, his book thuds closed and he's off. "Liam thought I should share stories of when you and Tate were together since I'm not getting anywhere with the general stuff. I wasn't there for most of these experiences, but, lucky for you, Tate shared a lot of them with me after you died."

Right, lucky for me.

"Oh, boy," Lawson mumbles with a hint of sympathy is his voice.

Elliott disregards this. "She kept me up every night telling me stories the whole week after you died. Talking about you was therapy for her, even though she and I were the only ones who saw it that way. My parents kept pushing her to see a real shrink."

My scars prickle with residual heat from being with Trina. To ignore Elliott and his increasingly grating voice, I focus on Meggie who's working hard to fill out thank you cards at the table.

"Tate told me about a time you guys got locked in Busch Wildlife."

"What's that?" I ask, strictly out of curiosity.

"A public conservation area with a bunch of lakes. She told me you two had been fishing." He makes mock quotations in the air and then flinches. "I don't care to know what you were really doing, so if you do remember, you can keep that to yourself."

I can't help but laugh along with Lawson. The guy is talking about his sister, after all. If I actually believed any of this garbage, I'd throw in a comment about how hot she is just to see him squirm.

"So you guys were done fishing…or whatever," he's squirming now without my help, "and you were heading back to our house. Tate still had a twelve thirty curfew even though my parents liked you. *Nothing good happens after midnight* is what my dad would say. She despised the curfew, but it never bothered you. You actually agreed with our dad, which infuriated Tate, and put you one notch higher on my parents' list. Neither you nor Tate realized that the gates of Busch Wildlife locked at ten."

Elliott pauses to block when Ryan focuses too long on the refrigerator photo of the twins. It takes a minute for Elliott to collect himself before he picks back up with story-time. "The bordering trees were too thick so there was no way around the gates. Tate said you kept your cool, but she could tell you were wigging out about getting her home in time."

"What happened?" Asking the question proves I'm paying attention and I immediately regret opening my big mouth.

"You drove every gravel road in the place until you finally found a narrow service road out. Tate was only fifteen minutes late. My parents didn't even notice. By that point, they liked you so much, you probably could have had a slumber party out there and they wouldn't have cared."

Elliott allows a welcomed silence for an entire minute. "Anything?"

The guy just isn't getting it. When I don't answer, he moves on.

"When my Grandma died, my sister was a mess."

I rub at the heat in my knee.

"Tate broke as soon as she walked in the viewing room at the visitation. You held her together."

The temperature is rising.

"She said she wouldn't have survived that without you."

"I'll be right back."

I jump through the front door to the three-by-three concrete slab that's barely a porch. Hunched over and trying to catch my breath, I lift my head and blink back stinging tears. I blink again when I see a girl sitting on the hood of Ryan's SUV.

The girl shades her eyes, focused on the dilapidated house across the street. "Look at them."

Chills run down my body, cooling my scars, when my head makes the connection. It's the voice.

The house that has her attention is just like every other on the vacant block. I walk towards her. "Who are you?"

She acts like she doesn't hear me.

"Hey!" I yell and grab for her. "Who are you?"

Before my hand reaches her elbow, she melts into the hood of the car like wax, until she disappears completely. Trying to make sense of what has happened, I force air into my lungs to keep calm. What's really worrying me about her disappearance is that I've never felt so empty and dead.

⸺⸺

"What did she look like?"

"Huh?"

"Tate," I say out of breath to Elliott. "What did she look like?"

His eyes widen, probably because I'm coming unhinged. "She was beautiful."

"Features!" I bark. "Give me features!"

"Oh."

Come on already!

"She has reddish-brown, curly hair. She's a little shorter than you, not stick-thin, well, until after…"

I stop listening.

My fingers twist into my hair when I slide down the wall and try to catch my breath. Elliott's voice morphs into a strange, slow-motion echo.

She's real.

13. *I was looking forward to a good fight*

It about kills Elliott to leave before getting an explanation for my outburst, but he has no choice. Ryan is already halfway down the block and I have yet to find my voice and explain my temporary insanity. These days, the insanity is feeling more permanent. My scars throb like the after effects of a bad burn and Meggie's slow day couldn't have come at a better time. She's asleep by seven, largely due to the sleeping pill and anti-depressant cocktail. However she finds peace is fine with me.

The sound of the T.V. spills in from the living room, but I zone in on the even rise and fall of Meggie's covers and try to find an explanation for today's events. Ticking through what I know—or, at least, think I know—I come up with a list of facts: Tate's real, even though I don't remember a thing about her; I've seen her, or some screwed up hologram version of her; she's the voice from coding who is ripping me apart, and she's somehow linked to my scars.

In a game of holes verses pieces, the holes are schooling their competition.

Needing a distraction now more than ever, I dig through my bag until my hand finds what it's searching for. When Meggie lets out a muffled snore, I'm more at ease with my decision.

"Displace," I whisper into the darkened room. Instead of falling or being yanked upward, I'm pulled horizontally at a speed that morphs the trees, mountains, and homes that I travel through into blurred streaks.

My muscles relax in the familiar home. The only change to the living room is an addition to the wall of memories. Ryder and Hannah are over-the-top happy in a black and white photograph, blending well with photos of Willow, Troy, Mya, Mya's husband, Lucas, and her son, Lennon.

In the flesh, this couple is even more radiant, parked on a plaid blanket in the middle of the room amidst mismatched furniture. Their makeshift picnic includes a six pack of beer, a bag of cheese curls and a Monopoly board. Hannah's stack of money is three times thicker than her fiancé's.

Ryder straightens his right leg and massages his thigh like anyone might do after sitting for too long. In his case, though, the cause for the muscle stiffness is my fault. Why can't I remember the events leading up to his—

"I passed go again. That's another two hundred dollars for me! Sorry, honey," Hannah jabs.

"Good, you can use that towards the ridiculous ice sculpture you want for the wedding."

"It's a champagne fountain, and it's going to be beautiful." Hannah leans over the board game and plants a kiss on Ryder. "You don't think it's a good idea?" she says against his smiling lips.

"Whatever you want."

Their spring wedding plans are documented in Ryder's book, and from what I read, the day is going to be perfect. There's no question that Ryder will give her all she could ever want and more.

I play the part of Monopoly spectator for the next fifteen minutes while Hannah shares more of her decorating ideas for the big day. I would have thought a conversation like this would bore me out of my mind, but with everything going on between my scars and Meggie, I need an escape.

Ryder and Hannah engage in what's quickly escalating to a make-out session that's inappropriate for me to watch. When Hannah pushes aside the Monopoly board and the game pieces, property cards, and money go with it, I take that as my cue to leave. Being subjected to these marathons when Ryder was my Tragedy was one thing. Now I'm free to go more than a wall's thickness away for refuge, and frankly, I like now better.

I turn my back on the happy couple and displace, but I can't deny that I'm smiling. It's nice to see Ryder and Hannah genuinely happy.

Meggie's still sleeping when my body stops jetting across the Earth and lands in her dark bedroom. I park in the corner chair and close my eyes to let my mind go blank. Turns out, this is easier said than done because the image of the phantom girl takes over. Tate. Why is her name so hard for me to think? *Tate. Tate. Tate.*

I'm bombarded with questions and don't have a single answer. What had her attention across the street? Why do I feel like I should know? Was she real or am I seriously losing it? How did she manage to look so happy and sad all at once?

With a frustrated groan, I'm up and pacing for the remainder of the night.

Just after the sun comes up, the front doorknob jingles.

"Awful early for a visit," I say to Elliott when I get into the living room, even though I knew he would be here.

"Ryan wanted to check in on them and drop off breakfast before he went to work," Elliott says. "What the heck happened yesterday?"

Lawson moves back into the bedroom and my eyes fall to the tan carpet. "It was no big deal." No way am I going to tell him what happened. If he thinks, even for a minute, that his story telling is working, I'm done for.

Ryan roots quietly through the kitchen and the coffee maker clicks on. My stomach kicks at the scent. I'm not thirsty, but I want some. Badly.

"I've got another one for you."

I force my mind off the coffee I can't have. "Another what?"

"Story." Before I can even form an expression, Elliott begins. "At one of Tate's music recitals, there was a guy from her music class who was into her. He didn't try to hide it, either. Apparently you weren't very intimidating." He pauses, finding more humor in his joke than I do.

I force my fisted hands open. I have no idea why this bothers me.

"During his own solo, his eyes stayed on Tate the entire time he was playing."

"Let me guess, he played guitar?" I can picture it now,

rock star steals girlfriend from ordinary, boring guy.

"Drums," Elliott corrects.

Mental kick. Why do I even care?

"At the end of the recital, he came over to our group and went on and on about how great she did, directing most of his words and all of his sight to her chest. Tate didn't notice, though. She was too busy trying to reclaim her fingers from your death grip. She finally had to mouth the word *stop* before you broke her hand."

I almost smile, not that I remember any of Elliott's story, but the reaction sounds like me.

"Tate cut the guy off and he finally left after she had to whisper to you to behave. My mom kept her eyes on you like she was afraid you were going to jump the dude. My dad thought the whole thing was hysterical. It was a shame, actually. I was looking forward to a good fight."

I fail at smiling and I focus on the scent of coffee again.

Elliott's voice gets quieter. "Tate told me about when you were diagnosed. The doctor said the words, said that you had cancer, but she didn't really hear him. She couldn't hear anything. She said it was like the world had stopped. While the doctor was explaining everything, she was in pain. She couldn't look at you. She said she would have broken in half if she'd seen your face at that moment."

I don't notice I'm gritting my teeth until Elliott finally shuts up and then I find myself in the tiny master bathroom, not even sure how or why I moved.

Elliott must have followed. "You all right?"

"I need a minute." Using the pedestal sink for support, I

focus on the black and white tiles. He doesn't take the hint. "Get out!"

When he retreats, I try to breathe through the flames of pain in my scars. Blinking back tears, something in the tub catches my eye.

What the—

"Do you believe in fate?" the girl whispers from the pink water. Her hazel eyes, clear and intense, are focused on me.

Red trails float through the water from the deep lines in her wrists. I reach into the water to pull her free, but the liquid becomes thick red jelly, swallowing her. I jump into the goo, frantically digging for her. I know I'm screaming. I have to be.

When I blink, the tub is empty and my jeans and arms are clean. I suck in a breath, and another, and another, before hurling into the sink. My watery vomit vanishes as soon as it touches the green porcelain.

I force my body to move slowly into the living room. "Liam said Tate slit her wrist."

Elliott and Lawson are both there, seemingly waiting for me. Elliott's expression is downright scary. I suspect I'm looking pretty scary myself.

Elliott nods.

"Did it happen in the bathtub?"

He swallows and nods again.

"It's working."

"What is?" he manages, though I think he knows.

"Your stories, or whatever. I don't know. Something is

making me see her."

"Are your memories coming back?" There's hope in his voice.

I shake my head to answer and decide to add, "But I'm seeing her. She was on the hood of Ryan's SUV yesterday and I just saw her in the bathroom." I slide down the wall, having to sit while the images of Tate play over in my head.

"You all right?" Lawson whispers.

I can't answer. I'm a lot of things, but all right is not one of them.

———

Elliott, using his better judgement, stays quiet until he and Ryan leave. Lawson does the same and the house is silent until Meggie and Brody wake. I wait in the bedroom while Meggie showers. After that, she brushes her teeth and her hair. In another step in the right direction, she surprises me by wearing something other than sweatpants. This is huge progress.

After assuring Brody that she'll be fine, Meggie and I are off to the hospital in her mom's compact car, keeping good on a promise Meggie made to Janine.

"Stop in for twenty minutes, that's all I'm asking," Janine had said. "The other nurses need to know you're OK. They don't believe me and want to see you for themselves. They miss you."

Prepared from my earlier reading, I perform my first block as soon as we get through the hospital's sliding doors, the second when she sees Janine, the third when she sees a few other nurses, and the fourth, fifth and sixth when she sees the elderly doctor who delivered her kids.

There are a million places I'd rather be this afternoon. Actually, any place would be better. The image of Tate in the jelly goo fills my head. Strike that, any place but one.

When I've lost count of blocks, Meggie and the compact car freeze a quarter mile before the neighborhood entrance. I shut my calimeter off and displace to my room.

Must. Code. Now. There's no way around it.

I drop my bag at the door. On my walk down the hall, my feet move as if enclosed in mafia-style, swim-with-the-fishes concrete boots. I park myself on the mat and try to recognize the exhausted guy staring back at me from the mirrored wall. I use both hands to comb through my hair and then close my eyes.

Everything goes exactly as I expect. The binds release when I'm in my tree stand and I feel briefly, falsely great before the usual nightmare steals it away. Funny thing: even when prepared for the ice followed by the scorching branding iron, the torture still hurts worse than I had imagined.

"I can't go on without you," the flame whispers in the girl's—Tate's—voice.

I'm screaming before my eyes even open.

After a change of clothes and with a desperately needed coffee in hand, I jog across the expansive field to Trina. She's in the middle of blocking Jackson. The other Elites are already working as well.

I'm out of breath when I reach her. "I need to talk to you."

Trina turns to me in mid-block and the bubble that was formed around her and Jackson fades away. "I need to talk to you, too."

She doesn't realize Flannel King is about to maul her so I put my body between them. Jackson slams into my chest with the force of a fly. My coffee doesn't even spill. Only when his head hits my scar do I flinch.

When the stunned look clears from his face, Jackson becomes flustered. "Where'd you come from? I mean, I'm sorry! Are you OK, man? That was some hit I gave—"

I hold up my hand to stop him. "I'm fine."

"Are you sure? I mean I really hit you—"

"One hundred percent sure. Can you give us a minute." This does not come out as a question.

"Oh yeah, totally. I'll just be right over here waiting. Just right over by—"

"Goodbye, Jackson."

He shuts up, but before I can spew everything I want to tell Trina about Tate, Jonathan steps between us.

"Grant, I'm glad you could join us. Are you feeling ill?"

Mental sigh. "I'm fine. I just need a minute with Trina."

"So she told you the good news? Excellent."

Her face contorts like she's been punched in the stomach. "I'm a Legacy now."

If Trina looks like she got punched in the stomach, my

expression would be more of a steel-toed boot to the groin. I'm surprised I don't actually stumble backward.

Jonathan, completely oblivious, couldn't be happier. He may as well be yelling: *Best news ever!*

Trina and I don't share his enthusiasm. I want to wrap my arms around her, maybe even kiss her again, but then Jonathan reminds me he's still here.

"Grant, are you feeling up to being blocked today?"

When I finally pull my eyes off Trina, I sigh, which he takes as a yes. Could this day get any worse? With just the blow of a whistle, Jonathan has everyone lined up.

"Why are you still training?" There's a misdirected venom in my voice and Trina seems fragile when she shrugs.

"I don't know what else to do. Jonathan said it was OK for me to be here. What am I going to do?" Her eyes are desperate, searching me for an answer.

Now I do hug her. Screw what anyone else thinks. "It'll be all right." Her curly hair is extra wild today, like she just woke up, and the stray pieces tickle my chin.

"Ready?" Jonathan asks.

I let go of Trina and mope through the ten steps it takes to face the line. Reed is waiting like he's bored.

"Go left?" he asks.

I nod.

He yells the first order and I hardly notice the dark, cold wall. Reed's thoughts are easy to distinguish and I fight against them with almost no effort. When my blue filter clouds my vision, I walk left with as little enthusiasm as possible.

"Great job," Jonathan says.

Evelynn is next. She smiles—*glint*—and doesn't give an order at all. She doesn't need to. We both know which direction she's going.

She says, "Haze," still wearing her smile and little else. The ensuing blackness is more dominant than with Reed.

With the process even more familiar, I pluck out her foreign thoughts and fantasize about reflecting the block back to her so she'll kiss Jackson instead of wanting me to kiss her. Jackson would love that. Of course, then he'd have to tell me how much he loved it and, chances are, he wouldn't do that in three words or less.

When she severs the command, I come back from Fantasy Island and stand like a department store mannequin. Her bright white teeth show again, she shrugs, and moves to the back of the line.

I almost smile with relief for the chance to rid myself of some pent-up aggression. "I'm coming after you," I growl at Billy before he can even get into position.

His response is equally hard. "Good luck."

"I don't need luck." I can't wait to pummel him.

Which I do.

Hard.

I match him swing for swing and get a few good blows in before Lawson and Reed peel us apart.

I spit a glob of red to my left, but the cut is almost healed when my tongue slides across my gum line. Jonathan isn't happy about our display and is equally unhappy when I ask for another try with Billy.

Lawson is next. I refuse to go after him and we opt for the trusty *go left* bit. Before Jackson can step up, Jonathan releases us.

I stay close to Trina when she walks, zombie-like, along the stone path. Once we're through the doors, out of sight of Jonathan, I grab her arm. "Come with me."

I release her arm to shut my calimeter off while we run. She perks up, grabbing my hand, and we sprint through the hallways. We don't stop until we're so deep into the maze, no one could possibly find us.

I push her against the wall and kiss her. And keep kissing her. Her fingers grip my back and she pulls at me as if it were possible to get closer. As much as I kiss her and want to want her, and this—I can't fool myself.

I feel nothing today. Strangely, my scars don't even burn.

We're both breathless when I pull away, but only one thought swims in my head: Tate.

14. I'll punch you in the face if you take your pants off

I wipe Trina's cherry lip gloss from my mouth with the back of my hand. "I'm sorry."

"For what?" she asks, still out of breath.

I shake my head. "This. Us. You being a Legacy. Everything."

Trina's eyes are sad when she puts her hand on my chest. "How are your scars today?"

"Better," I mumble.

"That's good." When she drops her head, her curls cover her face. "What am I going to do?"

I pull her chin up and try to sound convincing. "You'll be fine. You're going to start another life."

She shakes her head. "I don't want another life."

After a short silence, I ask, "Who are you joining?"

"My brother. He'll be dead in a few days."

"That's great!" Did I really just say that?

She cracks a smile. "Dork."

I lean away and put my back against the wall beside her.

"You said on the field you had something to tell me,

too?"

"I don't even know where to start. Remember I told you about Elliott trying to jump-start my memories?"

"Yeah."

"It might be working." I try to explain the unexplainable. Trina listens without interrupting until I've wrapped up the bathtub scene. I neglect to add my vomiting episode; some things are better left unsaid. I tell her how strong the incessant fire in my scars is, not only when I code, but also now just before I see a vision of Tate.

"Has the pain increased?"

"If you mean, do the lesions feel like they're ripping me in half, then yes."

"Have you looked at them lately?"

I shake my head. "I've tried not to since the other day when…well, you know."

Her face brightens a little and I wonder if she's thinking about our kiss. "Yeah, I know. Let's see them."

I raise my eyebrow. "Trying to get me out of my shirt again?"

"Trust me, if I wanted to do that, I wouldn't use an excuse," she jokes.

Grinning, I pull my sweatshirt off. My chest tenses when Trina's finger trails along the raised welt.

"Yowch!" She jerks her hand back and puts her index finger in her mouth.

"What?"

"It's two hundred degrees, that's what!"

I touch the bright red scar, which is slightly warm.

"You're being a little dramatic."

"Really?" She turns her finger so I can see the white, raised blister on the pad.

I grab her hand. "Holy—"

"Tell me about it!"

"It doesn't burn me." I touch the scar, leaving my finger there to prove my point while she watches in disbelief.

"You really are a freak," she whispers.

Amen to that.

"I can't stop thinking about her now. Tate, I mean."

"Are you saying that whatever this is…or we are, is over?"

Somehow I know our almost-romantic-relationship has to be severed. Willow's right, I don't need any distractions. And now I have this Tate thing to contend with. "I'm sorry."

Her expression makes me wish Elliot had kept his sister out of my head.

Trina tilts her chin upward and kisses me. Even though my lips move with hers, Tate's image wraps itself around every fold in my brain and I pull back. "I really am sorry."

"Me too."

We put more space between us. I push my hands through my hair and catch a glimpse of my calimeter. "Crap!"

Trina jumps. "What?"

"I gotta go! My calimeter," I say in explanation.

"Oh. Oh! Go!"

"I'm really sorry," flies from my mouth for the umpteenth time while I fight with my uncooperative sweatshirt sleeves.

"Shut up and go!"

My fingers fumble in my pocket and the command is out as soon as my hand closes around Meggie's locket.

I'm grateful that Meggie is just pulling into the driveway when I land in the compact car. The last thing I feel like doing is explaining my tardiness to Lawson.

Brody welcomes Meggie home by warming up dinner and Lawson and I have a minimal word conversation. Sharing assignments with him certainly has its advantages.

The couple endures an uneventful night with a few tears shed from each of them.

The next morning, when Meggie and Brody are at the kitchen table with coffee, Lawson says, "Your head is somewhere else."

It takes me a minute to register what he's said. I shrug, though I really should be agreeing. I know my head is in another place. Like on this girl I don't remember.

Lawson doesn't press for more, but warns, "You'd better keep your focus on the game."

I internally battle with myself on whether or not I should talk to him about what's been happening. After about an hour, I make my decision. "You know Elliott's little experiment?"

When Lawson says nothing, I stand up and start pacing, wondering where to begin. Deciding to go with a direct approach, I pull my sweatshirt off. I kneel down a foot from him and point to my bright red scar. "Feel this."

"You'd better step back, bro," he warns in his baritone voice, wearing his best WTH look.

"No, I'm serious."

"So am I. Get your bare chest away from me."

"Come on," I urge.

Curious enough to bite, his finger reaches to the raised welt. He pulls back immediately after coming in contact with my scar and shakes his hand in the air. "What the—?"

"Exactly." I pull my shirt back on and sit beside him so we both have our backs against the island in the kitchen. I'm sure Lawson would agree our proximity is closer than the two of us prefer, but the size of the kitchen doesn't allow for much else. "I have an identical scar on my knee."

He turns to me with a dead-serious look. "I'll punch you in the face if you take your pants off."

Even through the absurdity of what's happening, a grin escapes. "One run-in with a giant per day is enough for me."

Lawson studies the new blister on his index finger while I wonder why my scars don't cause such a reaction when I touch them.

"You're a messed up dude, you know that?"

Huh, you think?

Lawson's welt has already decreased by half and should be completely gone within the next fifteen seconds. "What's this have to do with Elliot's stories?"

"I've been having these—I guess you could call them visions—of his sister. Before this, though, I started hearing a girl's voice while I code. I think it's Tate I'm hearing and my scars don't like this very much. There's a connection between her and my wounds, there has to be."

Lawson sits for a minute like he's mulling this over. "I thought for sure Elliott was wasting his time."

"Me too." Or wished, at least.

"You really are a messed up dude. At least you have the bonus of keeping people out of your head."

There's that, I guess.

"I've tried using your advice to fend off blocks in training, but I can't do it."

Hello? The real problem isn't blocking; it's that my skin has the side effect of burning people.

Meggie grabs her keys off the counter, kisses Brody and opens to door in the kitchen that leads to the carport.

I slap Lawson's knee. "That's my cue. Keep trying with the blocking, man. I'm sure you'll get it."

Instead of sticking around for Lawson's reply, I plunge through the front wall. Meggie is already buckling herself into the car, so I fly behind. My heart leaps when we pull into the grocery store. She's doing something normal!

When we walk through the sliding doors, I realize that I haven't done my reading. Sheesh! Lawson's right, my head's got to get back where it belongs. I catch up on the day's events in the produce department, after noting that the fruits and vegetables are sad compared to what we've got in Progression.

I thank the big man that I didn't procrastinate any longer because two minutes later, I'm preparing for an upcoming block.

Five, four, three, two…

"Hey Meggie! How are you, honey?"

The woman puts her hand on Meggie's arm, but this isn't what sets Meggie off.

"Haze," I yell.

Be strong, be strong, be strong…

The pain hits me, but I'll happily take the torment if it helps Meggie. Gritting my teeth, I sever the connection.

Meggie turns away from the little girl in the cart who's chewing on her own shoe, and gives what I assume is suppose to be a smile. Her expression is frightening, but better than crumbling into a sobbing fit in the middle of the supermarket.

"Hi Jody," Meggie's voice cracks, but she's mostly keeping herself together.

"I just can't imagine what you must be going through…"

Really? The woman couldn't just talk about the weather or something? Politics, religion, anything else? To make things worse, the crazy lady goes on and on about how sorry she is, blah, blah, blah. She says nothing that actually helps, like *this is complete crap,* or *someone should suck it hard for putting you through this kind of hell.*

Meggie's glassy eyes are so distant I almost reach out to be sure she's standing in front of me. The little girl says gibberish words that make no sense to anyone but a two-year-old and stretches her arms out to Meggie.

And there goes Meggie.

I say the command.

Time to go, time to go, time…

When I sever the connection, Meggie manages to say, "Sorry Jody, I really have to go," and all but sprints her cart past the deli. She stops when she reaches the chip aisle, probably because it's vacant, and zones in on a bag of pretzels for an excessive amount of time.

After a few deep breaths, Meggie adds a bag of chips to the cart and wanders through the store. There's no rhyme or reason to her mad shopping spree. She goes up one aisle, passes five and goes down another. Then she backtracks to the aisles she skips. After we've made at least two trips up and down each lane, she abandons her cart of seven items at the register.

I follow her outside, wanting to tell her she forgot to check out, or she's leaving her groceries, or she's lost her mind. Obviously, she wouldn't hear any of these things so I consider blocking her to go back, but what's the point? A jar of olives, a bag of chips, and five pounds of bacon won't fit in her already-full fridge or freezer.

She makes an emergency stop at Doc Arnoldson's office and he spends thirty-five minutes with her. From there, we drive to Pine Grove Cemetery and devote the rest of the sunny afternoon to lying on the ground that shelters her kids and her mother. Without grave markers or grass covering the fresh dirt, the four rectangles sit like healing wounds.

When my calimeter buzzes, it's hard to tell that the scene freezes because Meggie is so still to begin with. I displace and see Lawson a few miles away, burning red through the atmosphere. Green and orange blurs, Elliott and Whitfield, are further to my left.

After landing, I opt for coffee instead of coding and I'm crossing through Benson in under five minutes. Even making good time, the place is crowded. Trina is missing from her reading corner so I head to Willow's table. She and Liam are at it again, but now my arrival doesn't stop them. When Willow raises her head, I almost fall backwards. The woman looks like she's fifty-years-old! Owen, Anna, and Clara are watching them chinwag back and forth while I slide into a chair to do the same.

"…the second time she's tried to slice herself. One of these times, we're not going to be so lucky," Liam is saying.

"I know." Willow sighs. "We just need to keep watching her."

"Christ, woman, we've been watching her!"

There's a heavy exhaustion in Willow's voice. "She's in a rut, that's all."

"This is more than a bloody rut. She's not functioning anymore. She's consumed with him, with the idea of joining him." Liam's eyes dart to me, but move away just as fast.

"Well, she can't," Willow says matter-of-factly. "Our job is to be sure she doesn't."

Lima's pathetic sigh isn't as dramatic as he probably hoped.

"Is there anything I can do to help?"

All eyes turn on me like I've just announced my coming out or something. No one responds, until Willow opens her mouth, but before she can vocalize anything, she's interrupted.

"Mind if I join you guys?"

I turn at Trina's voice. "Sure," I say quietly. "You guys know Trina?"

They all nod like I'm stupid. Clara is the only person who doesn't say hello. I move my chair over a couple inches to make room for Trina and she scoots a chair in from the neighboring table. Our close proximity, mixed with Clara's obvious disapproval, makes me uncomfortable. Plus, I think everyone is still shocked by my offer to help Tate. To be honest, I'm surprised myself. The idea is stupid, really. What could I even do that would aid in her healing?

Willow tries to appear happy, but her voice lacks enthusiasm. "Hey girl, how's the team?"

"The same." Trina shrinks further into her chair. "I just found out I'm a Legacy."

"Sweet! Another Elite opening!" flies from Owen's mouth.

Willow is apologetic when she turns back to Trina in full Momma mode. "I understand how you're feeling and I'm sorry."

"Sorry? Are you kidding? That's great news." Liam uses more enthusiasm than he's had all month.

Willow and Trina look at Liam likes he's wearing nothing but pink underwear.

"He's kidding, right?" Trina asks Willow.

Willow shakes her head. "I know it feels wicked rotten now, but it's not that bad. Really," she adds to Trina's skepticism. "I felt just like you when I found out. Trust me, you'll be fine."

Trina sighs.

"Who's joining you?" Liam asks.

"My brother."

Willow consoles her. "Your memories will come back."

"I hope so."

"They will." Willow nods to drive her point home.

"'Sup?" Rigby asks, happy as Willow usually sounds, probably because he and Whitfield are linked together at their hands. He gauges the small space between my body and Trina's. "Sorry about the other day, man. I overreacted. Whitfield explained everything."

Whitfield smiles at me and then makes a *shh* gesture. Seriously, why the secrets around here? Things would be a lot easier if we had the freedom to talk about our assignments. If I had said, "Hey Rig, Whitfield winked at me because she's on an assignment connected to mine. So yes, we know each other," I probably wouldn't have gotten pummeled by the guy.

Owen whispers the good news to Rigby about the Elite position, but Rigby is indifferent.

Elliott joins our already crowded table and manages to squeeze a chair in beside Willow.

"Tate was a book nut. She read all the time, anything she could get her hands on. She read to my brother, Fischer, every night. She read to you, too."

Willow cuts in when Elliott decides he needs oxygen. "This guy doesn't give up, does he?"

"It's working," Elliott counters.

"I didn't say it was working." Did I? "Something's

happening, yes, but there's no proof that my memories are coming back, or that your stories have anything to do with it."

"Tate used to spend hours reading to you," Elliott continues.

"Probably because the guy is illiterate," Owen says just after he's shoved a handful of Cheetos in his mouth.

Elliott goes on. "You'd stay silent while she read until she'd finally say something like, *Are you even paying attention?* You'd nod, but could never tell her what the story was about. She read to you anyway because she liked the way you looked at her." This last part seems hard for him to say.

"How'd I look at her?"

"I don't know."

Rigby, knowing I'm screwing with Elliott, smiles.

"Like I wanted to get some?"

The elbow to my ribs reminds me that Trina is here. I lean down, grabbing my side, and whisper my apology to her, but she still disapproves. Glancing at Clara, I can see that she also disapproves, but her problem seems to stem more from my exchange with Trina, and less from my previous comment.

Elliott ignores me and goes on. "I don't know how you looked at her, I'm just passing along the story. So, moving on, you had really bad reactions to your cancer treatments. You were seriously disgusting."

Talk about knowing how to kill the mood. Elliott flattens it.

"A few times when you were bowing down to the porcelain god, Tate read to you. Every time you'd come up for air while you were hugging the toilet, she'd stop and wipe your forehead. You'd always tell her to keep going so she'd read and read while you hurled and hurled. How she put up with the stench of you is beyond me."

One of my typical snide comments is lost because I'm trying too hard to ignore the burn.

Elliott gets quieter. "She didn't know where her strength came from. She also didn't know if she could handle things getting worse for you. Turns out, she got the opportunity to find out."

Standing, I'm unable to say anything because my jaw is clenched tightly enough that my teeth might break. I sprint out of Benson figuring there's no point trying to act normal anymore. I catch the elevator and am through my door minutes—though it feels like years—later.

This, whatever this is, will not control me.

IT WILL NOT CONTROL ME!

I sit on the mat and the unrecognizable face in the mirror stares back at me. I close my eyes, not even sure if I'll be able code in this state.

I do. Easily.

The pain that pulses through my body numbs to nothing, but I know the reprieve is only temporary so I'm braced when the forest passes the baton to my old bedroom ceiling. For the first time, I am able find my voice instead of just screaming while the lead weight pummels me.

"What do you want from me?" My yell echoes as if my old bedroom was a steel box.

"Come back to me," the fire whispers, making my skin

melt from my bones.

"How?" I echo back.

"Pleeeeease," the fire begs.

"Tell me how!"

The agonizing temperature steals away my voice. When my scream finally comes, the noise bounces off the walls of the coding room.

"Grant! Look at me!"

I try to orient myself by uncurling from the fetal position, but the pain is overwhelming. Screams at eardrum-damaging volume flood through the mirrored room. Only when I see Willow's lips moving do I realize they're mine.

"Grant!" her distant voice yells. "Calm down!"

My voice silences, but my body convulses from the fire. "The scars," I manage through my teeth.

Somehow Willow gets me into a sitting position. I think my calimeter buzzes, but the buzzing stops before I can be sure. A minute later, Willow has my shirt off and is staring at my sweaty chest.

"Oh my God. How long has it been like this?"

"I…told…you…about…them," I manage through my trembling.

"Is the one on your knee the same?"

I suck in a shaky breath and nod.

She pushes up from her knee. "This is absurd."

When she disappears out of the room, I watch the empty doorway. Does she expect me to follow her? There's no way I have the strength to get up right now.

Letting my head fall, I gasp at the sight of the glowing

ember that was once my scar.

Willow returns and throws a T-shirt over my head, shoving my arms through the sleeves. Her hand dives into her bag and reappears holding a child-sized necklace. She pushes the thin piece of gold that says *#1 Daughter* between our hands and entwines her fingers with mine. Her lips move and we're plummeting to Earth.

.

15. She's forcing me to hang with the carnies tonight

"Where are we?" My voice is as unsteady as my legs and my scars feel like they're burning through my T-shirt and jeans.

Looking around, the far corner by the dresser houses the only visible piece of carpet in the small bedroom. The rest of the floor is covered by piles of black clothing.

Willow doesn't answer me and stays focused on the bed.

"Willow—"

"Shh!" she hisses and then turns her attention back to the lump under the covers. "Step back a little. I'm not sure what's going to happen."

"What's—"

"*Shhhhh!*"

When the lump shifts, Willow takes a defensive stance. Her bare arms are tense, defining her muscles.

A mess of hair similar to Trina's, but on a really bad day, emerges from the covers first. If I wasn't expecting a person, I'd call an exterminator.

When the girl's face appears, I stumble backwards.

Willow's gaze darts back and forth between the girl and me.

"Willow! What are we doing here?" I demand.

"Shhh!"

I've about had it with the shushing.

I try to find a memory, a real memory, but all I know of the girl is from my demented ghost visions and Elliott's stories.

"Why are we here?" I ask again while Tate stands and stretches. When she's not melting into a vehicle or submerged in a tub of goo, she's a beautiful sight, crazy hair and all. She'd be even hotter if she wasn't wearing so much black.

Willow sucks in air and whispers, "Unbelievable."

"What?"

She finally answers with something other than a shush. "She's smiling."

"And?"

"She hasn't smiled in a long time. I think it's working." Willow's traveled all the way to Loonyville this time.

"What's working?"

"You being here."

"That's it folks, check her into the ward!" I sing. "Willow, that's the craziest thing I've ever heard."

"Really? How would you explain the sudden mood change?"

"I don't know, she had a good dream? She got a break from you for a few minutes? There could be a million reasons."

"It's because you're here."

I leap back before Tate walks through me, but she stops

six inches from my face.

"Grant," Tate breathes. "You came back."

"Did she just say…" I break off, staying focused on her intense hazel eyes while mentally fighting the increasing pain of my scars. If my clothes haven't burst into flames yet, they're about to.

"Yeah," Willow answers, not noticing my agony because she's beaming at Tate, who's also beaming. It's a collective beaming party for everyone but me. I'm burning into ash.

A funny thing happens while my lesions are scorching. My world shifts. I don't know anything about this girl who's ripping me apart by my scars, but I suddenly don't want to leave. No, it's not that I don't want to, more that I can't. I'm damn near igniting into a fireball, but the pain doesn't matter. As long as she's smiling, I'll willingly burn to nothing.

"I knew you'd come back to me," Tate whispers.

"You brought him," Liam's voice morphs after he drops from the ceiling. His body stays blurry in my peripheral vision even after he's stilled.

Gritting my teeth doesn't contain my scream any longer and Willow notices me now. She'd have to be blind and deaf not to.

Somewhere in the echo of my yell, I notice Tate's fear. I want her to smile again; I'd give anything. To shut myself up, I bite through my tongue and swallow the heavy flow of blood.

"Give me your hand!" Willow demands, now right at my side.

"Can't. Leave. Her," I say through my teeth.

Willow death-grips my wrist and says the command before I can yank free and we shoot into the sky, away from Tate.

"Take me back!" I scream at Willow, wishing my scars would magically heal like my tongue.

"Are you crazy?"

Maybe. Probably. "Take me back!" My mind is wired like a crack addict. I have to get back to that girl.

"No way! That could have destroyed you. I can't believe I was so careless." She shakes her head. "I'm so sorry."

"I have to go back!"

"I'm not taking you back! Ever! It was a mistake. I should have never listened to Liam."

The adrenaline pulsing through me makes me more agitated and aggressive. "No, it wasn't! You said yourself she smiled because I was there. I need to go back to her." I must get back to her.

"No. Drop it!"

"I can help you. Maybe another visit would make her even better," I say, hoping Willow bites.

She doesn't. "Take your shirt off."

"What is it with everyone trying to get me naked lately?" I try to joke, but can't keep the pain out of my voice.

When my shirt is over my head, Willow claps her hand over her mouth.

Turns out, I was right about my flesh igniting. Ash flakes to the floor when I push my finger into the quarter-inch-deep, blackened hole. The shape is the same, resembling a teardrop, except three times bigger. My jeans have a two inch charred hole at the knee and there's no need to examine the area. I know it's the same; they're always the same.

Willow slowly lowers her hand from her mouth and tears pool in her eyes. "I'm so sorry. What have I done?" Her hand resumes its position over her mouth, but the attempt to conceal her shock doesn't matter. Her wide eyes say everything she doesn't.

"I'm fine," I insist in the kitchen where Willow is banging through the cabinets for God knows what.

"You're not fine." Her eyes drop to my chest, but my new shirt hides the evidence. "Those wounds are not fine."

My voice is hard. "I have to go back."

"There's no way in flaming Hades I'm taking you back! It was a mistake. A horrible mistake."

"Dammit, Willow, I said I'm fine!" Furious now, I can only think about getting back to that girl. I don't know why, but I have to be with her. Every cell in my body is screaming so.

"You're not fine! Now go!" She points her finger down to the floor. "You need to get back to your Tragedy."

It kills me that she's right. Meggie's been unattended for who knows how long. I don't even remember when my calimeter went off, but surely well over an hour has passed. "This isn't over." I grab the heart-shaped locket and say the command that drops me through the floor.

Thankfully, I haven't missed anything that would make Lawson lay into me again, but the sky is already darkening. In Meggie's car, still parked in the cemetery lot, her sniffles are the only noise. I try to read, but my mind has trouble staying focused on the words because Tate's face is swirling around in my head. Amazing what a day can change; I'm actually excited about Elliott's visit later. The reason for him dropping by is something I'm not so thrilled about, though.

Meggie turns the ignition over and the engine seems to be roaring in the still night. The ride home takes less than ten minutes and that's only because we get stuck at three red lights.

I follow Meggie through the carport door and into the kitchen. "Honey, I'm home," I say harshly, unhappy about the situation we're walking into.

Brody picks up the third of five shot glasses lined up on the counter, sucks the amber liquid down, and moves on to the fourth.

Behind him, Lawson can barely stand. He manages to say, "Haze," but the filter barely ripples around him and Brody. When the connection is broken, Brody, who's concentrating much too hard, starts refilling the mismatched shot glasses. At least half of what he pours isn't caught by the glasses. No worries, though, because he proceeds to slurp up the spillage from the countertop like a dog.

Meggie is about as joyful as I am when Brody resumes pouring, making the liquid level flush with the top of the fifth shot glass.

"Brody!"

Brody's eyes raise and amber liquid pours onto the counter. "Hey, baby."

Meggie's crying now. "Stop it!"

"Oh, I'm sorry, baby. You want one, too?"

Meggie crosses around the tiny island and snatches the bottle from him.

"Careful, you're spilling it," Brody says in a whisper, forcefully taking the bottle back and cradling it like a baby.

Amber liquid sloshes onto Brody's sleeve when Meggie yanks the bottle away again. "Brody, you have to stop this!"

"Shhhh." Spit flies around his finger. "You're going to wake up the kids."

Meggie is full-blown bawling now. "The kids are dead!" She needs to be blocked, but knowing what's coming, I'm afraid to look away from Brody, even for two seconds.

Brody's glazed eyes squint and he points at Meggie. "Don't talk about my kids like that! They're not dead! Do you hear me?"

Meggie trades the bottle for the cordless phone on the counter. Her eyes dart between the numbers and Brody while she dials. Meanwhile, Brody appears to have forgotten where he is.

"I need you!" Meggie hisses into the phone. "Brody's bad. Hurry!"

Brody steals the phone away. "Hello? Hello? No one's there baby," he says calmly to Meggie before—BAM!—pieces of the phone rain down from the force of hitting the far wall in the kitchen.

Lawson's blocking again while Brody chooses personality number seventeen. He plucks the bottle from the counter and leaves a trail of alcohol when he stumbles toward Meggie.

"Haze," I say.

Run, run, run...

The current his me. "Block!"

Meggie turns and runs toward the bedroom. Brody chases after her with Lawson and me following behind them both.

"Do something!" I yell to Lawson.

"I'm trying!"

Brody doesn't even flinch when Lawson completes another block. Meggie moves faster because Brody is stumbling and she manages to lock herself in the bedroom. Brody slams on the door, screaming to be let in. I stay on the other side with Meggie, blocking her so she will calm down. When Brody finally stops the banging, the house is silent. After five uneasy minutes of monitoring Meggie, I walk into the kitchen and am immediately disgusted at the sight of Brody opening another bottle.

"You need to stop him," I demand to Lawson.

Lawson, trembling in the corner, appears to be lacking the energy to muster another block.

As Brody fills a shot glass, I hear the door click open. Lawson raises his head and I run out of the kitchen.

I'm in the middle of blocking Meggie so she'll go back into the bedroom when she runs right through me and makes me lose my concentration.

"You have to stop!" she screams at Brody. "*Our* kids are dead and no amount of alcohol will bring them back!"

Brody raises his eyes from the counter. "What did you say about my kids?"

"Our kids, Brody! Ours! They're dead! They're all dead!" She sobs and wipes snot away with the back of her free hand.

His silence makes me edgy. Meggie sniffs twice and turns away from him, but Brody already has his pitching arm drawn back, loaded with the heavy, brown bottle.

"No!" I lunge and push Lawson out of the way, forming my energy around Brody.

I shove Brody hard to the side with my shoulder and he crashes into a kitchen chair. At the same time, the bottle smashes against the wall just inches from Meggie's head. Part of the liquid that managed to miss her leaves a urine-colored stain on the celery green wall.

My shoulder feels like it's boiling, but I'm so used to burning lately, I hardly notice.

Meggie's expression is a mix of disbelief and disgust. The chair is in three pieces and Brody isn't in much better shape. Lawson, standing back up, is clearly not happy with me, but Ryan and Elliott charge through the front door before he can say so.

Ryan, wearing a formal suit similar to his funeral attire, stops abruptly at Brody's body. "What did you do to him?"

Surprisingly, Meggie doesn't look shocked or confused because her disgust has taken over. Certainly she'll be questioning how Brody smashed into the chair, but at this moment, she apparently doesn't care.

Ryan looks from Meggie to Brody and then to the stained wall while I wonder how much trouble I'm in. Meggie's head is still in one piece, so any consequence will be worth it.

"Are you OK?" Ryan asks.

Meggie nods.

"Did he hurt you?"

Meggie shakes her head.

Ryan loosens his tie on his way over to Brody. "Should we call an ambulance?"

"Probably." Meggie glares at Brody from her place by the living room entry while Brody rolls into a fetal position and moans. The revulsion melts from her face and is replaced by so much sadness my heart breaks for her.

Ryan watches Meggie for a few seconds before going for the phone. He finds the mutilated phone on the floor, curses and disappears into the living room.

"What happened?" Elliott asks.

"What the heck is wrong with you?" Lawson roars at me before Elliott gets an answer.

"How about a thank you?" My word choice probably could have been better.

Yes, word choice definitely could have been better.

Lawson lunges but I'm in the living room and over the sofa before he can catch me. He could come through the furniture if he wanted to, but he doesn't. With narrowed eyes, probably debating if I'm worth it or not, he opts for not worth it and his puffed up body relaxes. Elliott's does the same.

"If you think I'll stand back while he crushes her skull, you don't know me at all."

Lawson ignores me and proceeds to park himself on the far side of the room.

Ryan appears from the hallway, announces that an ambulance is on the way, and stalks into the kitchen. The wall separating us muffles his low voice, but not completely. "If you try to touch my sister again, I'll kill you. Do you understand me?"

Brody's so inebriated, I doubt he can understand anything, but he groans what I guess could mean yes.

While I'm ignoring Elliott's relentless questioning about the event, three paramedics come through the door. They each nod to Meggie like they know her and then survey the kitchen. It doesn't take a rocket scientist to put together what happened; just the stench alone is enough, but every one of their assumptions is wrong. No one in their right mind would guess it was a ghost who crushed Brody and the chair.

One of the blue-uniformed guys asks Ryan what happened.

"Brody got drunk and went after Meg."

When Meggie opens her mouth, Ryan jumps over Brody and puts his arm around his sister, squeezing her shoulder. "I'm just glad I got here when I did to keep him off her. I may have pushed him a little too hard in the process."

The guys take in the sight of Brody and the busted chair six feet away and the replay flashes through my head. Who knew the human body could bounce so high?

"Meg, are you all right?" another one of the uniformed

guys asks.

Meggie hugs her arms around her frail body. "I've been better."

"Did he hurt you?" the same guy asks.

"Not physically." She turns to Ryan. "I'm going to go lay down. Can you handle this?"

Ryan nods and she disappears into the hallway. From the bathroom comes the sound of a pill bottle shaking and the water turning on and off. The bed squeaks a minute later.

Brody groans, reminding everyone why they're here, and the medics start the process of transferring Brody's body to a stretcher. Ryan follows the guys out to load Brody into the ambulance.

Elliott finally speaks. "What the heck happened here?"

"Yes, Grant, why don't you enlighten Elliott on how Brody fell into the chair," Lawson suggests on his way to the front door.

"I pushed him."

Elliott's confused. "How'd you push him?"

I take two strides toward Elliott and nudge my shoulder into his. His left foot goes back to catch his balance.

"Like that, only harder," I pause. "A lot harder."

"This isn't a joke," Lawson scolds from the doorway.

"I know it's not a joke!" I erupt and take two steps toward Lawson. "You saw that bottle, how hard he threw it. It would have broken her skull and you know it!"

Lawson focuses on his fisted hands while I try to calm my temper.

"I wish I didn't have to push him, but your blocks

weren't working. I get that you're angry with me, but you need to understand I can't let him hurt Meggie. She's been hurt enough."

Lawson is unreadable when he steps outside to be with Brody. With Elliott and me now silent, the conversation on the porch is audible through the open door.

"I should be asking Meggie this, but considering the situation, I'll defer to you. Does she want to press charges?" one of the medics asks.

Another guy's voice answers. "Come on guys, this is unlike him. Every one of us knows that. What they're going through…"

"We have to ask. You know that," the first medic replies.

"I could kill him." Ryan's voice is full of hate.

After a pause, a lowered voice says, "Ryan, he's not your father,"

Ryan clears his throat. "She won't press charges."

"Are you sure?"

"I know my sister. I need to check on her. Are we finished here?"

After a short pause, Ryan comes through the open door.

"Call any of us on cell if you need anything," a voice says from outside.

Ryan slams the door hard enough to make the walls shake, and heads toward the bedroom.

Elliott watches Ryan stomp by and I follow. From the bed, Meggie looks up at her brother. Her eyes and nose are red and she hugs her arms around her knees like the scared child she was so many years ago.

Ryan tries to offer comfort. "I'm staying the night. I'll call Nancy and let her know."

Meggie wears a dead expression and says nothing. I was expecting an argument; in fact, I would prefer an argument to make her seem alive again. I leave the room feeling hopeless, knowing there's nothing anyone can say or do that will make her situation better.

"Looks like we're having a slumber party," I say to Elliott, who's seated cross-legged on the floor in front of the chair.

"Really?" He reaches into his bag and skims a page in his book. "That's strange. I knew about the argument and that Ryan was coming over here, but he and Nancy are supposed to attend a company dinner tonight. They were going to show up late because of Meggie's unexpected phone call."

"Brody wasn't supposed to be making a trip to the hospital either. I guess my actions changed things up a bit." I try to be nonchalant, though a part of me is worried about what I've done. The argument should have ended with Brody passing out and Meggie crying to Ryan for about an hour before forcing him to return to his company function.

"How'd you push him?" Elliott asks a few minutes later.

The subject change Elliott is offering is better than making myself crazy thinking about the undocumented events that have unfolded. "I focused my energy around Brody's body and then used my shoulder to hit him. I still can't believe that works," I say more to myself.

"I had no idea we could touch living people. You're nuts. You know that, right? Not that I'm surprised. You've never been one to follow the rules."

Maybe Elliott really did know me in real life. I cross to the sofa and sink into the cushion. "I need to know more about Tate." I need to figure out what this sudden connection to her is all about. I need a memory to stick.

Elliott appears shocked, not that I blame him. I never thought I'd be voluntarily asking him about his sister.

"OK." Elliott fidgets with the shoelaces of his black Chucks. "Tate loved carnivals and would insist on going every time one came to town. You hated them. Actually, loathed would be the better word. *Save me, man. She's forcing me to hang with the carnies tonight,* you said to me more than once before you left our house."

"Let me guess, you didn't help me out?"

"Wasn't my problem. She'd make you ride the Tilt-A-Whirl about a hundred times by calling you a chicken. And she'd always come home with some obnoxious stuffed animal that you'd end up spending two hundred bucks to win." Elliott's face brightens. "Sometimes I really wanted to tell you to grow a pair, man. You were like a puppy around her."

"She was probably putting out," I say to even the blow.

The color of Elliott's face seems to be directly affected by my grin because the wider I smile, the deeper red his cheeks get.

Obviously pissed, his next story starts with, "When you had cancer and were a bald-headed mutant," if that doesn't scream mad, nothing does, "Tate was going to shave her head. She would have done it, too, if you hadn't held her down and pulled the clippers out of her hand. She thought if she looked like you—you know: a freak—people would stop staring at you all the time. You told her it would make them stare more because you'd be the misfit couple. I told her you really were a sissy if you couldn't handle a few looks."

"Thanks."

"No problem. You really were decrepit."

"Bet I still looked ten times better than you," I jab back.

"Ha, hardly!"

Something makes his eyes sad. "She really thought you were going to beat it. When you died," he pauses, "when you died, a part of her died, too. She became a different person, not just in appearance, but inside. She was never right after that. It started at your funeral, which was a cry-fest, by the way. Jeez, there were so many people there."

"Really?" I don't remember knowing more than a handful of people. "Who?"

"Lots of patients from the hospital. You made a lot of friends during your treatments. People were drawn to you, although I still don't get why. It's not for your charm, I can tell you that."

I half smile.

Elliott continues. "Everyone from your dad's company was there and most of our high school teachers came. My extended family took up a lot of space, too. Tate did all right during the visitation, but not on the day of your funeral. In the middle of your burial, she took off running through the cemetery. I was able to convince my parents to let me go after her instead of them, which was good because your mom really leaned on my mom for support that day. Your dad was worthless in that department. He couldn't stop crying long enough to do anything. I found Tate hiding behind a headstone on the other side of the cemetery. She was gasping for air. She begged me to…"

He stops talking for a few seconds.

"She begged me to make the pain go away. She said she was burning from the inside out."

As if on cue, the pain of my scars steals my breath away. I bite into my fist to keep myself from screaming. "I need a minute," I croak into my hand and spring up from the sofa.

In the backyard seconds later, the yellow light collects gnats while I try to catch my breath.

"You ready?"

When I spin around, my mouth won't work. When my lips finally move, my voice is just a whisper. "Tate?"

Wearing an electric smile that brightens the yard more than the whitish-blue tint of the moon, she laughs and throws a kernel at me before shifting the bowl of popcorn in the crook of her elbow. "I've got the movie in already."

My voice won't work.

"Are you feeling all right?" She cocks her head to the side. "That was a pretty strong treatment you had today. We can just sleep if you want."

I swallow.

She rests the back of her hand on my forehead and her touch is cool against my skin. "You're really warm. I'll go get your pills."

Her face turns dark first, and then the rest of her body follows. The ash crumbles to the ground and blows away with a breeze that didn't exist a minute ago.

I search for a trace of something, anything, to prove she was here. Of course, there's nothing. She's more of a ghost than I am.

I take over twenty minutes trying to sort out the anomaly before going back inside.

I sit on the sofa and try to remain calm. "Tell me more."

Elliott spends the rest of the night telling me stories about birthday parties, weekend trips, and family things. He tells me how much time Tate and I spent together, about my treatments, about all the movies we watched, but nothing he says triggers any burning or weird visions.

He and Ryan leave in the morning without giving me what I need: another vision of Tate. Ryan promises to be back as soon as he gets off work so at least I'll get to push Elliott for more later.

Meggie sips the coffee Ryan has made for her and picks at a burnt piece of toast without taking a bite. After a shower, as documented, she spends the rest of the day at the hospital, but not for Brody. I'm more than a little relived that she's back on the path her book has shown.

I only have to block her twice in the baby nursery. Instead of devastating her, the tiny people have the reverse effect. At one point, her smile actually touches her eyes.

When I leave, Meggie freezes with her arms wrapped around a baby boy.

16. That reaction is appropriate, given the circumstance

Even though I actually want to, burning pain and all, I decide against coding, but only out of fear that Jonathan may get suspicious if I'm late for training again. I change clothes, grab coffee, and am on the field in less than ten minutes. My stomach knots together at Trina's absence and I avoid eye contact with Lawson.

Jonathan is all business today. His eyes are tired when he says, "Pair off and begin blocking drills. Billy, please be our Watcher today. Grant, I need you to come with me."

Jonathan walks off the field. When I realize I should probably be walking with him, I jog to catch up.

"Everything OK?" I ask, trying to keep my voice steady.

Jonathan doesn't answer.

This has to be about Willow. She probably ratted me out because she's worried about my scars. *When I see her, she's done for,* is what I'm thinking as I follow Jonathan silently down the Orders hall.

With each of his three knocks on a vacant, gold desk, a chime echoes around us and a marble wall panel slides away.

Jonathan, a man of few words today, walks through the new doorway. I almost prefer to stay in the Orders hall, but curiosity makes my feet move. The marble booms closed behind us and Jonathan walks past a small seating area.

I follow Jonathan through a maze of bright but narrow passageways. Even given the circumstances, I can't help but admire the turn-of-the-century, decorative woodwork along the walls.

After what seems like a half mile later, Jonathan stops in front of a pair of seeded glass paneled doors tall enough to make the courtyard entry seem toddler-sized.

"Is everything all right?" I ask Jonathan, feeling nervous and edgy from his silence.

He steps back to allow door number one to swing open. "Excuse me for a moment." When he steps into the room, the door closes too quickly for me to see what is on the other side.

Willow is so going down for this.

Jonathan returns a minute later, says, "This way," and directs me through the door.

The architecture is magnificent enough that the elaborate hallways may as well have been an afterthought. The arched columns that serve as walls around the ceiling-less room expose a landscape of tall grasses beyond them. In the distance past the fields, forest and mountains pierce the blue skyline. An evergreen-scented breeze passes through. Our muted rubber soles on the tile are the only sound in the room. Even the scarlet tanagers are quiet, perched in long lines atop the arches. Their heads turn to follow us as we walk through the pathway between a large outer and inner circular desk structure.

When we stop on the sunburst design in the center of the tile floor, one of the archways in the far corner swings inward and a long line of people file in and fill the gold chairs surrounding the desks.

I clear my throat and shift uncomfortably, wondering why I feel like I should know this place. I consider asking Jonathan—who hasn't made eye contact since the field—where we are, but I am interrupted by the audience settling into seats.

"Hello, Grant. I'm Landon."

My eyes move to the guy sitting at the elevated portion of the inner desk. He broadens his shoulders and, though he may be trying, his smile is not friendly.

"A situation has been brought to our attention."

Willow, you are so dead.

He goes on. "You used unnecessary force on your assignment. This is an offense we cannot take lightly." Goodbye fake smile.

When his words fully register, ten seconds later, I try to hide my relief and swallow. "Yeah, uh, I'm sorry about that." I run my hand through my tangled hair. "It was necessary to keep Meggie safe. Who are you again?"

"I'm Landon."

Jeez, I'm not the biggest idiot in the universe. "Who are your friends?" I ask as hundreds of eyes stare at me. I hope the guy gives me a little more than the people's individual names.

"We are the Schedulers," he says bluntly.

Oh crap!

"That reaction is appropriate, given the circumstance."

Did I just say that out loud? "Huh," is my Einstein reply and my tense shoulders fall in relief that Willow didn't rat me out. I'm sure I would be in a lot more trouble if they knew about my scars.

"What you did is unacceptable and threatens the core of this program. Mistakes of this nature make it difficult to keep our existence concealed. Certainly you can understand how that would be problematic."

"Oh, well, there's the confusion. It wasn't a mistake," I reply easily.

All of Landon's cronies shift in their seats and Landon's mouth presses into a hard line. He sucks a deliberate breath through his nose like he's trying to stay calm.

"Meggie was about to get her head bashed in with a whiskey bottle," I say as an explanation. And a darn good one at that.

"Your actions threatened our entire establishment."

"My actions saved her life!" *Relax, relax, relax,* I think to myself.

Landon gains control of his tight fist under his chin, letting his fingers relax. "We will not allow such risky behavior."

"I get it. It won't happen again." *So long as Brody keeps his hands—and his bottles—to himself.* I think better of adding this part.

"I'm afraid it's not quite that easy." Landon leans forward on his elbows. "We are placing you on probation."

"Fine, whatever. Can I go now?"

"You are suspended from this assignment until further notice."

It takes a second for my head to register his statement. "What?"

"You are terminated from Meggie's assignment until we feel confident you have more control over your actions."

"You can't do that!" *Get a grip on your volume, man.*

"As it is your second offense, the panel has decided this is the necessary action needed for you to understand the severity of your conduct."

"My second offense?"

"Yes. You have received a written warning once already, have you not?"

Dang. The note in my assignment book. "I won't do it again. I swear," I lie.

"I'm sorry. The decision has been made."

My head snaps up. "Come on, cut me some slack here! Meggie needs me."

When he doesn't reply, my anger builds. "I can't leave her! What if Brody gets drunk again?"

The committee surrounding Jonathan and me remains seated and calm like I'm using a normal voice. *Breathe, Grant, breathe.*

After the minute they've obviously given me to collect myself, I turn back to Landon. "What's going to happen to her?"

"Another Satellite will be put on her assignment until you have more control over your actions."

I shake my head and laugh. It's not the right response, but it's either that or jump over the desk and wrap my hands around Landon's thick neck.

"We will send word when we feel you are ready to accept the full responsibility of being a Satellite."

"With what? An owl?" I mock.

The large group remains unsmiling.

"Thank you for your time," Landon says. "You are free to go."

"To do what?" I spit out harshly and start toward the doors.

"To reflect on your choices," he counters back.

I growl my response.

"Please give your tocket to Jonathan on your way out."

I stomp back to Jonathan and dig in my pocket, slamming the tarnished heart into his open hand. Then I resume my raving-mad pace to the doors. When I finally exit the room built for a giant and return to the human-sized hallway, I slam my palms against the wall.

Behind me, Jonathan uses a consoling voice. "Please realize this is for the best."

He can't be for real.

He says nothing else and leads me back through the labyrinth.

"What am I supposed to do now?" I ask him when we're finally in the Orders hall.

"I'm sure you'll think of something." He walks away, leaving me staring, open-mouthed, behind him.

I'm flicking my fingernail on the glass of my frozen calimeter, willing the silver hand to move to at least tell me when break is. I've been staring at the useless watch since my last trip down to Benson. I sigh and push myself up from the sofa for another visit because I don't know what else to do with myself.

The eating hall is empty when I get there, which I already knew because the hallway, elevator and lobby were also deserted. I slowly drag myself back to my room.

In the kitchen, my scars prickle and I'm suddenly overwhelmed with wanting—no needing—to make some kind of connection to Tate. Since I won't be able to hound Elliott for stories anytime soon, I decide to try my only other option. Who cares if I ignite into flames doing so? I'm obviously not needed around here.

In the coding room, I strip my off shirt so it won't end up sweat-soaked, and I close my eyes. Everything plays out as expected. After feeling relaxed in my tree stand, the painful paralysis arrives. The flames grow hotter as they climb higher and higher up my chest, to my ear.

"Come back to me," the fire whispers. "You know how."

As badly as it hurts, I don't want to leave. I keep my eyes squeezed closed until the pain is too much and I'm forced to open them. This returns me to the coding room.

Panting and fighting against the flames, I catch a glimpse of my bare, wet skin. It's like someone used my chest to snuff out the largest cigar ever. I curl on the hard floor and convulse until my temperature cools to tolerable. When I'm able to stand, I yank my jeans off and push my finger into the charred burn on my knee. I have to be the biggest oddity around here. Considering the competition, that's saying something.

I throw on new clothes and think about chugging a pot of coffee, but I don't want to risk missing anyone. Now that my calimeter is useless, and because so much time seems to be lost while I'm under, there's a good chance I coded straight through break.

I almost yell with joy (yes, joy!) when I enter the busy hallway. I ride the elevator down with two other Satellites and cross the lobby while my mind works out the details of a plan. There's no way this is going to be easy.

Half-hidden behind the third arched entrance of Benson, I fidget with the bottom of my T-shirt, bounce my foot up and down, and wait.

And wait.

And wait.

By the time the first Satellite disappears, the hem of my shirt is torn.

"Hey, you know Willow?" I ask a dark-haired girl walking into Benson.

"Yeah, sure." Her arm muscle tightens under my grasp.

"Sorry." I release my hold. "Can you tell her Grant needs to see her in the lobby?"

She nods and blushes.

"Tell her it's urgent," I yell after her.

When the girl turns back to me, her face reddens even more.

I rub my palms together and then along my jeans to dry the sweat. The heat from my knee is still radiating.

When Willow gets up and walks through the emptying room in my direction, I push myself to the side of the archway. When she walks into the glass-tiled corridor, I twist around the column into Benson to keep myself hidden. I peek around and she doesn't disappoint, staring into the lobby from the corridor and shaking her head. She's so predictable.

When she steps further into the lobby, my mind battles with itself.

There's no way this is going to work.

Try, dammit!

After a deep breath, I creep up behind her and she gives the cue.

Wait…

Wait…

Wait…

GO!

I reach under her elbow when her hand pulls free from her pocket, barely getting my finger around the dangling chain before she says the command.

———

Willow reaches for my arm like I knew she would and her volume makes my ears ring. "What in Christ's name are you doing?"

"Thanks for the ride, babe. I owe you one." I smack a kiss on Willow's cheek to make her even more furious and lunge through the wall. Willow wouldn't be Willow if she didn't chase after me. I'm hoping the kiss was enough distraction to give me a lead.

I sprint across Tate's front yard. Jumping into the air as soon as my feet hit the pavement, I play the fastest memorization game in the world to burn the aerial view of Tate's house in my mind.

"Stop!" Willow is shouting behind me as we fly over the cookie-cutter houses in the gridded neighborhood.

I push myself faster and the neighborhood below is replaced by the green and tan curves of a golf course. When I'm over a cluster of more houses, I bank left on instinct and drop my elevation into the area that's part forest, part field and dotted with black lakes.

When my feet pound the grass of the dam, Willow is still in the sky, streaking like an airplane contrail, except purple instead of white. I sprint across the thin piece of land that separates the twin lakes to hide in the thick, wooded area.

What's the plan, what's the plan? runs through my head with each steady breath. I weave further away from a hiking trail through the dense forest and lean against one of the fatter trees for a minute.

I cautiously jump up to the tops of the trees for a better view, just in time to see the purple streak bank a one-eighty, sending Willow back in the direction we came from. That's a winner, folks.

Back under the canopy of the trees, I'm feeling successful. The forest continues on with the party like I'm not here. Tree limbs creak under the weight of the hyper squirrels, and birds flutter and chirp around me. A small doe walks through the trees, just barely turning her head my way when she passes. I slide down the rough bark and settle onto the dirt ground. Now what?

⸻

A couple hours later, when the sun is gone and the crickets are awake, I weave through the trees back to my landing spot on the dam. My night vision becomes unnecessary in the clearing because the moon is as effective as stadium lights. At the edge of the closest lake, a jumping frog ripples my reflection in the water. The water settles and the moonlight gives my skin a sickly blue tint. Even though my muscles are large and defined, my pale skin is an unwelcome reminder of the diseased body from my past and I turn away quickly.

The uneasy feeling that I've been here at this lake has me pacing the bank. This could be the place Elliott talked about, Make-out City, but the memory doesn't root like it should. The story itself resonates so little that I still can't help but harbor doubts that Tate and I were really an item. The pull I now feel towards her, however, makes me think otherwise. I spend the entire night searching my head for a solid memory, hoping something will stick. Unfortunately, my head remains empty. Oh, the fun Willow could have with that one. Man, she's going to kill me, which is all the more reason being caught is not an option.

Just before the sun rises after a forever-long evening, I switch my mind to Meggie instead of Tate.

After about ten minutes, it occurs to me that this train of thought doesn't help at all. I've failed Meggie. No way do I regret what I did, though. In fact, I'd do the same thing a hundred times over to keep Meggie from getting hurt. My stomach twists with the realization that I might never see her again.

Crunching gravel interrupts my horrifying, worst-case-scenario game of what could happen to Meggie. When a rusty, brown Ford stops, my overactive imagination accepts the reprieve. I massage the bridge of my nose while the vehicle's driver, a white-haired man, pulls a tackle box, a fishing pole, and a chair out of the bed of his truck.

Because I have nothing else to do, I plant myself on the ground in a mix of clover and grass a few feet away. While the man reels in half a dozen nice-sized crappie, I cover the blades of grass around my legs with my blue filter and pull the roots, one by one, from the earth.

When the sun is finally overhead, I get up. A circle of dirt that was green two hours ago compasses my picnic spot. Oops.

"See you later," I say to the old man like he can hear me.

An easy hop puts me thirty feet over his white head. A few seconds after leaning sharply forward, the lake-spotted area is behind me and the golf course and neighborhoods are blurring below. Not willing to take any chances, my feet hit the pavement a few streets away from my destination and I search for a hiding place. A pink Barbie clubhouse wouldn't be my first choice, but it suits my purpose.

Having made it this far, getting hauled back would be devastating, so I try to make the best of my shelter. My shoulders curve inward to stay hidden within the tiny space. At least the playhouse is bigger than the backseat of Meggie's first car. A little, anyway.

A smile creeps onto my face while I'm squatted down and waiting for my signal. Oh, if Billy could see me now; the princess tea set beside me would send him into overdrive.

By the time the signal finally comes, hours later, my nerves are shot and I'm craving coffee.

Less than a mile away, Willow and Liam streak into the sky. I'm in the air and moving over the houses before they're out of sight, figuring I have a minute, maybe two, max. The adrenaline my pounding heart pushes through my veins does nothing to help my nerves.

Finding Tate's house from memory of the grid system isn't difficult because of the dry-rotting deck. I lower myself to the ground at the appropriate time, landing in her backyard. I'm through the kitchen wall and up the stairs in a matter of seconds. I pick the first door on the left. No good, bathroom. Door number two, however, is a winner.

I stop short and mimic Tate's frozen stance by the dresser. The silence makes the entire situation feel surreal, almost unnatural, but my scars don't heat up so I shouldn't complain.

My boots feel like they're nailed to the floor and it's not until I stop looking at Tate's face in the mirror that I'm able to move closer.

Over her shoulder, I recoil from the image on the taped-together photograph and my hand clamps over my mouth to smother my gasp. Could that ashy monster really be me beside the bright and beautiful Tate?

I check the mirror to be sure there's no traces of that past disease. My reflection beside Tate's appears more balanced now, though she still has the lead…even with the black eyeliner. What would this girl have seen in a guy like me?

My increasing heart rate forces me to snap out of memory-lane mode (which consists of no memories at all) and jump. I'm through Tate's ceiling, but have used too much force and am on the roof instead of in the attic. The purple and green colored dots in the sky are doubling in size, tripling…

I suck in a breath and bounce lightly to drop through the shingles, hoping the glowing lights haven't seen me. The fiberglass insulation in the attic remains motionless under my boots, and the dust, thick enough to roll into a snowman, stays settled. I move to a rafter and perch on one of the two-by-fours with my legs swinging under me. Listening for voices below, so far I hear nothing but silence.

I focus my energy on the wood beam beside me and trace my finger through the dust. After making a *G*, I complete the rest of my name. I add *& Tate*. My name and hers fit surprising well together.

When Willow's voice carries through Tate's ceiling, her

tone is not cheerful. "I can't believe he would just leave his Tragedy hanging." Long pause. "Actually, never mind."

I think of Meggie and have to force myself to stay in the attic. How could Willow think I would leave my Tragedy alone by choice?

She goes on. "We've got to find him. Any ideas?"

"The bloke's lost his mind," Liam's voice muffles.

"You have no idea."

"Oh, I reckon I have a bit of an idea."

While they go on about how crazy I am, I'm overcome with the urge to sneeze. Really? Come on, I'm dead! The dead should not sneeze! I cover my mouth and pinch my nose closed.

No dice, I'm gonna blow. Desperate, I leap through the roof and push off of the shingles, flying as far as I can before the first sneeze belts out. Followed by another. And another. So much for my hiding spot.

As I'm dropping back down to Tate's, Liam appears out of the siding and falls effortlessly to the ground.

Brake, brake, brake!

I freeze twenty feet above him and hover without breathing.

Ah Choo!

Seriously?!

Liam's head snaps up. "Grant!" he hisses.

With the advantage of already being in the air, I push forward and don't dare look back. I lower when three large oak trees get closer and I whiz through them, hoping they'll offer camouflage. I hit the ground so fast my legs have to work in double-time to keep my upper body from crashing forward.

Jumping into the closest house puts me in someone's kitchen. Using the yellow curtain over the sink to stay hidden, I see Liam's green streak continue on.

Whew, saved. For now, anyway.

The closeness of the houses work to my benefit and I move through the walls quickly, making my way in what I think is the general direction toward Tate's. Most of the kitchens are full of dinner time activity and the evening news fills a few of the small living rooms. I move faster when I reach a bedroom hosting a make-out session.

Only knowing what Tate's home looks like from above means I have to go up. Here goes nothing. The very moment I realize I'm floating over the house right next door to Tate's, her laughter carries through her open window. That's not what gets my attention, though. It's Willow's voice that catches my off guard.

"I don't believe it," she says.

Thinking of only my heating scars, I lose my concentration and fall to the ground while I rub at my T-shirt and jeans in effort to conceal the rancid, burning smell of flesh. Willpower I didn't know existed keeps me from leaping into Tate's bedroom. A dangerous move like that would be the end of Tate and me...whatever we are.

I cautiously step through the wall into the garage, and then into the kitchen. A woman, Tate's mom I'd guess from the resemblance plus twenty years, is coming down the steps.

"She asked Fischer if he wanted to play a game," the

woman says to the man who must be Tate's dad.

The man's fingers pause on his laptop keyboard. "You're kidding."

When the woman smiles, I move up the steps in slow motion and stop at Tate's door. Without breathing, I push my face through the white wood until I can see her room. Someone has thrown me a bone because Liam is still M.I.A. and Willow, sitting in the far corner of the room, is focused on Tate and Fischer, both of whom are laying on the floor with a stack of playing cards between them.

Willow seems relaxed for the first time in weeks.

I smile, despite the fact that my scars are on fire. The smell alters my mood and panicked adrenaline slides through my veins.

Put out your smoking clothes, you idiot!

I jump out of the house and sprint down the street. With no sign of Liam, flying is the fastest choice, and I beat my own record speed back to the lake.

Five seconds later, I'm diving down to the bottom of the lake where the coolest water should reside, though I can't feel a change in temperature. My skin and hair remain dry, but the fire eases while I'm under. Not completely, but enough.

I could fly out of the lake, but I swim to the bank instead, wanting to feel more human and wishing I could feel the coolness of the water. Lifting my burned shirt, I check out the scar on my chest. Ash flakes to the ground and my finger disappears up to the first knuckle. My knee is the same.

I can't go back to Tate, not yet anyway. Being close to

her made the world feel strangely whole again, just like last time, but there's a good possibility my scars are going to burn clear through me. The longer I can prevent that from happening, the better.

Ignoring the charred holes in my T-shirt and jeans, I spend the evening determining the right thing to do and wondering why this pull is so strong. Elliott's stories made me see visions of her, but they haven't made this girl any less of a stranger to me. Even so, there's no denying I'm drawn to her. Obviously, or I wouldn't be here burning to death.

Sitting in the dark with my broken calimeter, a sigh escapes. I wish my watch were working. I wish I could go back to my regular life as a Satellite. I wish I were still watching over Meggie. I wish, I wish, I wish…

But do I really?

No. I don't wish for any of those things. I wish I were with Tate right now. I'd spend the last minutes, hours—however long I had—clinging to her while my body incinerates to ash.

This seals my decision and a second later I'm soaring over the trees, the darkened golf course, the glowing houses and street lights.

Now or never, I decide when I drop to Tate's street, hoping I'm fast enough to stay out of Willow's grasp.

My stance is defensive when my feet hit Tate's floor.

"See there, Liam, I told you the kid would come to us eventually."

I ignore Willow to watch Tate for a second. She hovers over a game board with a brown-haired boy, setting rectangular pieces of red plastic on one of the squares. Her laughter eases my nerves, but the branding iron has already started to warm.

When Liam bounces up, I jump back against the wall, prepared to bolt if needed.

Willow's voice is emotionless. "Chill, Liam. Let the kid talk."

"I need to be with her," I explain, surprising myself with my directness.

Liam falls on the bed and sighs. "Bloody hell! Not this again."

"Not what again?" I ask.

Willow laughs. "I'm telling you, you're nothing if not predictable."

I believe I said the same about her not too long ago.

"Willow, let me spare you the rest. He can't be without her, he's not strong enough, et cetera, et cetera," Liam mocks and shakes his head.

I open my mouth and then snap it closed because what I was going to say is pretty much along those same lines, although I wouldn't have sounded like such a sissy saying them.

Tate's laughter stops and she clears her throat. We all freeze, the brown-haired boy included, and our attention transfers to Tate. She breathes deeply and then closes her eyes and smiles. After a long pause, she collects the dice and resumes her game.

"Oh good, Psychic Sylvia Brown knows you're here," Willow says.

"I can help her."

"You can't save the world, kid."

"I just want to save her," I whisper.

"Yeah, well, to do that will destroy you. And once you're destroyed, she's going to have to deal with your loss all over again. So it's up to you really. It all comes down to if you want to get out alive or not."

"I'm helping her. And I'm not alive, anyway."

"You're going to have to leave her eventually," Willow says.

"I won't. I won't ever leave her." Seeing her here, so close, the pull is stronger than I've ever felt.

"How are your scars?" Willow asks sourly.

She's figured it all out. Willow knows everything that I've already put together. What's so hard to swallow is the fact that she's right. Willow…right. As usual. The truth makes my blood boil.

"They'll destroy you. Do you know that?"

I swallow.

"Not like death, kid. They will literally turn you to dust. Forever. You willing to give up eternity for her?"

I swallow again. How can I be willing to give up my existence for her, for someone I don't even know? Still, I nod, because somehow I've never been more sure about anything.

Willow stands and paces the room. "Don't you get it? Don't you see? It doesn't matter. Once you're gone, she'll still have to face your loss. You gain NOTHING!"

It doesn't matter. Knowing I tried is everything, all I need, all I'll ever need to be truly fulfilled in my life, in my existence.

Willow continues pacing and biting into her thumb. "I was going to give you the choice. I thought that would be easier; that you would accept this truth and let her be. But you," now she's pointing her finger into my chest. "Dammit Grant, you're choosing wrong!"

She wraps her hands around my neck to choke me and, instinctively, my hands grip around her wrists to stop her.

"Displace," she says too fast and we're rocketing into the sky.

———

"No!" I roar into my empty room and kick the horrid sofa over. "No!"

I pace the living room, wishing I knew where Willow has displaced. There's nothing I can do now to get back to Tate.

I don't even know this girl, this stranger, but deep inside a mocking voice is screaming at me, resonating from the place where my heart once was, the place that is now nothing but a black hole. "Tate was mine!" the voice says. My life, my reason for existence, is alive on Earth and I can't be with her. Doing so will obliterate me.

I jog down the hall and sit on the mat in the coding room to welcome the burn. I hope that the fire is enough to destroy me.

17. That boy is gonna be the death of me

Willow

"That boy is gonna be the death of me," I scoff when I land back in Tate's room.

"Says the girl of bad puns."

"Liam, he's impossible!"

"You're preaching to the choir, sister."

"How is she?"

Liam nods toward the game in progress.

I put the necklace back in my pocket before dropping my bag and parking in my usual spot in the corner. I pull my dreadlocks into a ponytail and rest my head against the wall.

"She's laughing again, Willow. That's big."

I don't answer, but I know he's right.

"He can help her, you know?"

I sigh. "I don't understand how she's getting through to him. I was on board with Elliott when he was trying to bring back the kid's memories, but I should have never brought him here. It was a mistake. A selfish mistake."

"It wasn't selfish," Liam says naively.

Of course it was selfish. Tate and Grant were more intertwined than any couple I've ever witnessed. When he lost that connection, *I* was the one who couldn't accept it.

"His presence changed her."

"His presence about destroyed him!"

Liam's shoulders fall. "I know. If we could just find a way for him to be here with her."

"Jonathan was right. It is necessary and safest for Grant to forget." I pick at the remaining orange nail polish on my index finger. "Wait a minute. You were the one that wanted him gone last time and now you're his biggest cheerleader? What gives?"

"She's different this time." Liam's attention turns to Tate and Fischer. "She's happy. Maybe she was grieving too much before. Maybe she thought pushing him away would help her. Who knows? But we have proof now that she can sense Grant's presence and I think she's reconnecting to him somehow." Liam pauses while I continue mutilating my nail polish. "I know that sounds absurd, but there's no other explanation."

"That doesn't sound absurd. I believe she's reaching him, too. I don't know how it's working, but Grant's experiences with coding proves it. I think every time Tate puts something back together from their past, she connects with him." My voice lowers. "Maybe we should stop her from putting their memories back together."

"No!"

Liam's dramatic response makes me jump.

"That's not fair, and you bloody know it!"

I use a calm voice, hoping my demeanor will transfer to Liam. "It's hurting him, Liam."

Liam throws off his ball cap and scrapes his fingers

through his hair. "It's helping her, though."

Liam sits on a pile of black clothes and talks into his knees. "Their connection is making her better."

"And the stronger it gets, the more it's destroying Grant."

We both stay quiet for a long time.

"So, who do we sacrifice?" I ask more to the air around me than to Liam.

Liam remains silent.

———

Tate gets more rest than she's had in a long time. The only time I can recall her sleeping more soundly was when she was aided by sleeping pills. Her mom and dad stop in her room separately before they leave for work. Neither stays more than a minute, but both seem relieved to see her sleeping so peacefully.

When Tate finally wakes, well after ten, she's not only lacking her usual scowl, but she begins gathering her clothes from the floor.

"Wow," Liam says in a tone that sounds as surprised as I feel.

Liam shoves his red bouncy ball into his front backpack pocket and we both stand up quickly to follow Tate out of her room. When she dumps the armful of clothes in the hall closet laundry basket, Liam and I nod to each other in approval.

Tate makes a stop in the bathroom to brush her teeth.

She pulls her hair into a ponytail and even takes time to pull a few curls out behind her ears. She still uses way too much black make-up for her beautiful face, but at least she's made a few steps in the right direction.

Downstairs, Tate stops at the kitchen table and tells Cutest-Kid-Ever that maybe they can play another game later. This worries me because if she goes back on her word, Fischer will be crushed. His current exuberant expression says so.

Tate leans down and kisses Cutest-Kid-Ever on the cheek and tells him she'll be back later.

"Field trip," I announce with enthusiasm.

Liam rolls his eyes, but half-laughs.

Liam and I follow behind Tate's car because we both enjoy the freedom of flying on sunny days. Tate pulls into the familiar single car driveway, knocks on the front door twice to announce her arrival, and then lets herself in with her key.

"Hey hun. How are you doing today?" Mrs. Bradley asks from the kitchen.

Tate shrugs and settles into one of the swivel chairs at the bar-like counter. "How are you?"

Mrs. Bradley smiles. It's the smile she uses a lot, the one that takes a whole bunch of effort. "I'm doing good today." Her eyes always sell her out. God love her for trying to stay positive. "Honey, how many times do I have to tell you? Black is not your color."

"I think that's like the five hundredth. How many times do I have to tell you I dress like I feel inside?"

"I think that's like the five hundredth," Mrs. Bradley jokes.

"It's your lucky day," I yell to Liam who's already parked himself in the small living while the theme song of his favorite game show sings from the T.V.

He shushes me.

Tate never needs to be blocked when she's here at the Bradley house. It's a good break for everyone involved.

I bounce down the single step off the kitchen and plop onto the sofa next to Liam. I'm not a fan of the game show, but love driving Liam crazy by belting out wrong answers to all the questions.

In the kitchen, Tate and Mrs. Bradley talk about an upcoming job Mr. Bradley's company just received and the pending bids that have gone out to other companies. When Mrs. Bradley asks about Cutest-Kid-Ever, my mind leaves the game show and focuses on the conversation about the kid I love so darn much.

"He's OK," Tate answers. "We played games yesterday."

After a pause, Mrs. Bradley's voice says, "Oh, Tate, that news makes my day."

I get up quickly to peek around the living room wall. I smile when I see Mrs. Bradley because her happy expression reaches all the way to her eyes.

"That's really great. Really, really great."

"Momma B, it was just a couple games," Tate counters in a teasing voice.

Mrs. Bradley rubs Tate's arm. "You know I worry about you and Fischer; the two of you used to be so close. He misses you so much."

"How could he miss me? My room's next door to his."

Mrs. Bradley turns serious. "Physically being there doesn't matter much if you're emotionally and mentally absent."

"I'm scared," Tate finally says in a broken voice. "I'm so scared of losing him, too," she whispers.

All the air seeps out of my chest. When I refill my lungs, a tear rolls down my cheek as Tate silently cries into Mrs. Bradley's sweatshirt.

"You have to let him in," Mrs. Bradley is saying. "It's been long enough. You have to live again, Honey."

After a few minutes, Tate pulls her head back from Mrs. Bradley shoulder. "Do you think he's with us?"

Mrs. Bradley pulls Tate close again. "I want to believe he is. I get out of bed everyday because I know that's what Grant would want." She pauses. "He'd want you to be happy. If there's anything I'm certain of, it's that."

"I can feel him sometimes."

Mrs. Bradley loosens her hug. "Don't ever let that go. Hold on to that feeling, and he can always be with you."

I wish that were true.

An hour passes quickly and soon we're flying behind Tate's car again.

She makes the expected detour to the cemetery and my muscles recoil.

"I'll go," Liam says.

"You're a dream. I owe you," I reply with sincere gratitude.

"Yeah you do. I'm keeping score." Dread erases his smile when he walks around the car to follow Tate.

They close the distance to Grant's and Elliott's tombstones, fittingly side-by-side.

I sigh and lean against the car, wondering how Tate and Grant will ever live without each other.

———~~~———

When the day's assignment ends, I swallow down a quick cup of green tea in my room while I tick through my to-do list: coding, checking on Grant, and seeing Troy. Troy tops my list because he's, by far, the sexiest choice of the three. Plus, he always knows the right words to say to mellow me out.

"Don't you boys ever hang with your families?" I ask when I step out of my door.

My Legacy buddies, Jordan and Shane, are hidden behind goggles in the common area, ignoring me because they're entranced by a video game.

"Watcha playin'?" I ask.

"Elite Force," Jordan says from behind his goggles.

"Who's winning?"

"I am," Shane replies without breaking his movements.

"Shut up," Jordan sneers.

I grin. "You picked Reed again, didn't you, Jord?"

"I don't need your two cents."

"No wonder you always lose. For the love of all that is holy, if you want any kind of fighting chance, choose Jackson next time."

"Negative, Hippy."

Jordan's response makes me smile wider. I reposition my bag and maze through the hallways to the back part of the building where my hall awaits.

"Good day, friends," I say like I always do to the photographic collage of all my Tragedies printed on the wall. When I exit through my private door, I stop and let the sun warm my skin. As much as I love being a Satellite, I equally love escaping for a while. Going back to my human senses, especially on warm days like this, reminds me that when my assignments end, spending an eternity with Troy isn't going to be so bad.

I wrestle my sweatshirt off and tie it around my waist. It's a tank-top kind of day, which always adds a higher bounce to my step. I follow the granite path to my own slice of heaven. Troy has added another window planter, complete with purple wildflowers, to our comfy stone cottage. The other three windows are complete, leaving just one planter left in his so-called summer project.

Inside, I unsling my bag from my shoulder. "Hey Babe, I'm home!"

Troy's arm appears around my stomach and he spins me around. My trusted corduroy satchel drops to the floor and I shriek happily. Yes, he is exactly what I needed.

I twist under his arms and plant a huge kiss on his cheek. "How ya doing, baby?" I ask when I'm done showing him how much I missed him by giving him a kiss with more bang.

"Better now. How about you?" His forehead creases when he steps back to make sure his wife is still in one piece.

God, I love this man.

My whole body relaxes. "I'm better now, too."

"How long do you have?"

At this moment, I wish I had eternity. "Not long enough."

"I was hoping I'd see you today. I made coffee."

"I already grabbed some tea. Thank you, though."

"No problem. I already drank half of it anyhow."

"So you didn't really make it for me?"

He smiles. "Sure I did."

I mimic his expression. "Uh huh."

The corners of his eyes crinkle even more when he laughs. "You sound just like Mya."

My gaze falls to the gray stone hearth and I try not to be sad. I'm so entirely happy and fulfilled with my life, now more than ever, but a small hole inside me sometimes feels very empty. "You did something right, then," I whisper and kiss him again.

He shakes his head. "When are you ever going to understand? Every decision I made in their upbringing was wholly entwined with you. I couldn't even buy toothpaste without questioning which kind you would choose."

"You always got Tom's of Maine brand, right?"

He laughs and buries his face in my hair. "Yes, Babe. Always."

It's a funny thing, how something so minuscule can make me feel so good. Leave it to Troy to always say the right thing.

It gets harder and harder for me to leave Troy behind, even though I know he stays plenty busy. Between fixing up his car in the back shop and his trips to the ocean, how he finds time to entertain is beyond me, but he's doing just that today. A group of Satellite widows (temporarily, anyway) are stopping by later for a barbecue and the baseball game.

"Baseball?" I question.

He laughs while he mixes up his top-secret marinade. "Yeah. We're streaming the Sox game…you know, via satellite."

I shake my head at his bad joke. "Really?"

"My wife, the hater. When you finally get some free-time, I'll make a Sox fan out of you, too."

"Doubtful," I say on my way out the door.

"Love you," he calls through the kitchen window screen.

I throw up my hand in a wave. "Love you, too." More than you'll ever know.

Back in the building, I check my calimeter and opt for the shortcut to the lobby. No sense prolonging the inevitable visit to the kid. The glowing rectangular sensor beside the golden door accepts my hand print, making the mural of my Tragedies' faces split. I grip my satchel tightly to my side and step into the narrow shaft. The invisible force grabs hold and pulls me through the constricting space. While my eyes instinctually search for light, I imagine Grant's reaction to my preferred mode of travel and my laugh trills through the tunnel. The exhilarating sensation would certainly make that lightweight hurl.

The force halts and leaves me standing behind the ancient, gilded door. I straighten my bag on my side and tighten my sweatshirt sleeves around my waist.

"Have a fabulous day," Lavender's voice chimes and, right on cue, the door slides up.

I step out and walk down the marble hallway and into to the lobby, skipping across the expanse to the B corridor with the memory of Troy's kiss still fresh in my mind.

Before stepping into the elevator, I turn at the sound of my name.

"Hey Jonathan, what's up?" I ask, still smiling.

"Glad I caught you."

I try not to laugh. It's not like he'd ever fail to catch someone he was searching for.

"Could you accompany me on the field?"

"Are the Elites there?" I ask.

Jonathan answers with a nod. I need to talk to Grant anyway so this saves me a trip to his room.

"After you," he says and motions me to go first.

I walk past him, wanting to ask if everything is all right, but judging by his lack of small talk, the odds of getting an answer are slim to none. I pull my hair tie free to release my dreads while we walk across the lobby.

He pulls the wooden, sculptured door open for me. The old gang, minus Trina, are working in pairs. Gosh, I miss this. Not the pain part, but the comic relief.

Jackson just made Billy skip across the field. Yes, I definitely miss this.

"What's up guys? Go ahead, tell me how much you've

been pining for me," I say after Jonathan collects the crew.

"Hardly. We've been enjoying the silence." Billy's a terrible liar because his python arm wraps around my shoulders as we walk toward the bleachers.

"With your mouth, I doubt it." I counter.

After my quick hellos to the others, they welcome me back like only they can, with rude jabs and snarky remarks. Evelynn stiffly asks how I've been and I gather all of my play-nice feelings to shrug my reply.

I lean over and ask Reed, "Where's Grant?"

"You haven't heard?" he whispers back.

"Heard what?"

"Rumor has it, he's on probation, which I'm guessing is true seeing as he's not here."

"Probation?" My whispers hisses out, loud enough for the others to hear. "For what?"

Billy leans my way. "Probably for being such a pansy."

I know he's kidding, but my momma-instincts take over for the kid that I'm actually extremely fond of. "Watch it Billy, he kicked your tush in sprinting drills."

"He got lucky," Billy rebuffs.

When Jonathan clears his throat, I decide to ask him about Grant's absence, but then he looks at me…wearily? Nah, I'm sure that's just my imagination running amok. If Troy were here, he'd remind me that my hyperactive mind always gets the best of me.

I open my mouth at the same time Jonathan does, and he wins. "A special circumstance has surfaced and the Schedulers and I have agreed that an intervention is necessary.

We are requesting your aid in facilitating an experimental mission. We cannot be sure of the outcome; however, we have all agreed that the measure is worth the risk involved."

Everyone gets excited. Even me. OK, I'm not gonna lie, especially me, despite the fact that I have zero spare time at the moment. I'm nothing if not a workaholic.

Troy is not going to be happy. The beauty of my husband, though, aside from his obvious physical traits, is that he'll understand. No one gets me like he does. And, boy, does he—

Reed jabs his elbow into my side.

"Huh?" I mouth when he pulls me from my better-than-great daydream.

Reed jerks his head towards Jonathan.

"As I was saying," Jonathan goes on, which really means *Pay Attention!* "Willow will be an asset to us in this mission."

I sit up straighter. Jonathan, knowing that flattery and I go together like chocolate and peanut butter, must be cooking up something really good.

"Effective immediately, replacement Satellites will take over your current assignments. All of the selected Satellites have been briefed on the specifics of your Tragedies. I have no doubt each will do a fine job."

Oh, rubbish! Liam's going to be on his own. Even if he's not, he's going to have to start at square one to build the seamless routine we have. I can hear him now. He's going to be "bloody thrilled" about that.

"If you will follow me, please." Jonathan makes his way

to the doors.

Obedient pupils that we are, we keep pace behind him. There's a charge of excitement in the air. Even from Billy, who's practically bouncing across the lawn beside Jackson. Side-by-side they're like David and Goliath. I smirk. Yes, it's definitely good to be working with the old crew. Well, most of them.

Evelynn sweeps past me when we get through the door and, liking her even less since her kissing episode with Grant, I remind myself not to say anything if I don't have anything nice to say. Thinking of my time with Troy earlier does the trick in bringing my happy thoughts back.

"I missed the joke. You know I love a good joke. Are you going to spill? Come on, spill." Jackson delivers his words in a speed that only he can.

"Sorry, no joke. I was just daydreaming."

"That reminds me, I heard a new one the other day. A joke, I mean. Want to hear it? It's a really good one. One of my better one's actually. You'll think it's hysterical. Trust me, it's really, really—"

"Do you know why Grant's on probation?"

"Oh, um, no. I mean there's been talk that he didn't follow the rules on his assignment, but you know how Satellites talk. You can never be sure what's true and what's not. I, for one, have a hard time believing Grant would break any rules. He seems like a straight shooter. You know what I mean? I'd never—"

"Let's hear your joke," I interrupt because Jonathan's eyes have moved to us. The man that hates gossip is wearing his disapproval all over his face.

Jackson is excited to tell his joke, God love him. As we walk and he rambles, I think about Grant. Of course the kid would break the rules. I know that better than anyone.

"…who walks into a bar. Or maybe it was a girl. Shoot, which one was it? It's probably not important. We'll say it's a guy. So the bartender asks what he wants to drink. Oh shoot, no it was a girl. Sorry, It was definitely a girl. Forget what I just said, I'll start over. So this girl—"

"What I am requesting will not be an easy task." Jonathan's words rescue sweet Jackson from his botched joke as we walk. "The Schedulers and I cannot foresee if this undertaking will be successful. Because the outcome remains uncertain, I ask that you all be particularly alert through this process. Instinct is your greatest guide in what you do each day. If, at any point, you experience anything that feels out of the ordinary, I ask that you report the situation immediately." He continues leading the way down the vacant Orders hall.

Get to the goods, I want to say, but keep my lips buttoned.

"You must first become acquainted with your Tragedy." Jonathan climbs the bookcase ladder and returns a minute later, waving in the air what he's retrieved. "This will be phase one in our experimental mission."

Jonathan flips past the first page before setting the book on the golden desk. Then he flattens the binding with his palm and unfolds the paper like a magazine centerfold, minus the naked gal. When Jonathan stops unfolding, the connected six pages each include the outline of a hand.

Our expressions are comical as we size up the extended paper.

Jonathan's voice sounds apologetic. "As you can see, some modifications were necessary."

I can't say that I'm surprised. Nothing around here surprises me anymore. What I find hard to wrap my head around is how this is actually going to work. I mean, I think I can guess, but in my vision, it's going to be extremely… crowded.

I strategically position myself between Reed and Jackson because they're the smallest of the guys. That, and they're not Evelynn. She's been known to have clothing malfunctions, and with my luck, one of her girls would pop out in mid-fall and smack me in the face.

In order, Lawson, Evelynn, Reed, Me, Jackson, and Billy stand along the desk. Apprehensively, we place our hands on the appropriate outlines.

"I'll see you soon," Jonathan says.

My palm sticks to the dry paper like Velcro. Two seconds later, the book sucks us in, mashing us together like we're trying to swirl down a sink drain.

The feeling is worse than I could have imagined. What I hope is someone's cheek presses against my own. When I pull back, the sequined material of Evelynn's dress scrapes across my face. Then, in a turn from bad to worse, the sole of a large boot catches me in my mouth and smashes against my lips. Gross!

When we finally land, we're a mess. Hair is mussed, clothes are strewn and, yes, a boob makes an appearance.

Thank the Lord the referenced body part is Reed's, not Evelynn's.

We straighten ourselves and our clothing. Looks like Jackson had a wardrobe malfunction as well, albeit not of the *Janet* Jackson nature. The sleeve of his flannel shirt is torn clean off, exposing his thin arm.

There's very little space in the circular room and even when we get close enough to touch our right shoulders together in a flower-like formation, the stone is less than two inches from our left arms.

Lavender comes on the intercom. "Welcome."

After her long pause, we all laugh, though the sound we make is more uncomfortable than happy. Apparently, she doesn't know how to address a group this size.

She sighs. "Please hold while I configure your assignment."

Our laughter is sharply cut off when the room starts spinning. We press closer together. We may heal quickly, but that doesn't mean getting our skin scraped wouldn't hurt like— *Hello!* I gasp. Yep, the stone wall definitely hurts. I wish I had put my sweatshirt back on. I try to press in closer, but the allotted space makes that impossible.

When the wall abruptly halts, we all relax a little.

"Your assignment begins in the year 1985 with the introduction of your Tragedy, Tatum Lewellen Jacoby. Please proceed through the door ahead."

Air rushes audibly into my lungs, but this is not why the five pairs of eyes are on me.

18. No offense, but this isn't going to work

Willow

It's safe to say everyone knows who Tate is and how she's connected to Grant. Their story is like an unhappily-ever-after fairytale around this place. It's also obvious the Elites know I've been on her assignment.

A crowded room can be a wicked lonely place. "Are you all just gonna stand there?" I push past them toward the door I've already been through once in my afterlife.

The doorknob zaps me, our obnoxiously sized group enters the hospital like the contents of a clown car filing into a jewelry box, and scene one plays out: Tate, meet world. World, meet Tate.

We're pulled back into the stone room with very little order. Our bodies knit together when the merry-go-round starts again. I'm sure to keep my hands, feet, *and* arms inside the vehicle at all times.

The wall halts and we enter scene two: toddler Tate welcomes baby Elliott into her world. Back into the room we're sucked and around and around we go.

Scene three: pretty much identical to scene two, only

welcome Cutest-Kid-Ever instead of Elliott.

And…repeat.

Scene four: Tate learning to drive. This is a very funny thing to watch. Her dad is not laughing, as he buckles his seatbelt because he drew the short straw. Literally. Both her parents were dreading getting in the passenger seat. The straw idea was genius, in my opinion. Especially since sly Mrs. Jacoby cheated. God love her.

Scene five: first date with Grant. Wow, what a charmer the kid was. One word could sum up the entire night: shower! Mud-covered and persistent, he may have charmed the pants off Cutest-Kid-Ever, but I can't believe he managed to score another date after that disaster.

Scene six: the iconic exchange of *I love yous* and another disaster for the kid. The last time I saw this play out, Grant's painful expression before Tate said anything back, made me laugh so hard I thought Tate and Grant might actually hear me. The kid is terrible with women. He's lucky he's got his good looks going for him. The others share my initial humored reaction.

When we're canned like sardines back into the round room, I prepare for our release from Lavender, but instead she keeps going, which I take to mean we're going to be here a while.

I try to fool myself into believing this is a good thing. Might as well get this part knocked out. In truth, the first time is about as fun as cramming for a final exam. The second time downright sucks eggs.

Scene seven: sappy engagement. All right, this was

actually kind of a good one. Plus, seeing the kid sweat is worth watching again.

Scene eight: D-Day. I mash myself in the far back corner of the tiny doctor's office and am the first one out as soon as the Doc's diagnosis speech is wrapped. Tate's expression, bent over and pained like someone just slammed a knife into her gut, has already been burned into my brain. Luckily, Grant was too busy staring blankly at the doctor to notice his unhappy fiancée.

Scene nine: drum roll please…and gasp. The Elites don't disappoint. Not that I blame them. Seeing Grant now, no one could imagine he was capable of such frailty. We're all holding our breath to fight against the rancid vomit smell until we're back in the stone room.

Scene ten: another ugly Grant day with Tate trying like the devil to be supportive and helpful.

Scene eleven: the kid's death.

I try to be better this time, I really do, but the scene knots my stomach just like the first time when I stood by Grant's side on Earth during his real death, and the second time when I had to watch this same movie reel after Rebellion Tate was assigned as one of my Tragedies. Seeing the scene in person wins the title "worst day ever," but the saying "third time's a charm" holds no water in making this any easier.

Sure, there are a million similar scenarios like this in my long list of Tragedies, but Grant's gets to me more than the others. Maybe because actually being there, witnessing it in person, makes the emotions more real. Or maybe because when the kid says goodbye to Tate, there's still a spark in his eyes. I saw it when I was there with him during his death, when

I relived it again during Introduction to Tate, and now here, the sentiment is still unmistakable. He's not at peace with leaving her.

I close my eyes when the monitor flatlines and Grant's mom whispers, "Be good."

The first time around, I got to leave as soon as Grant was released from his diseased body. Unfortunately, the second and third time require that I stay to see Tate go ape-crazy. When she's finally sedated by injection, our large crowd is released.

Evelynn is sobbing loudly when the wall spins around us. I cried, too, the first time. And the second. And a little bit the third.

Scene twelve: Grant's funeral. Again, sad. This seems to be the theme. All six of us watch Elliott chase and then try to console Tate as Grant's casket, back in the distance, is lowered into the ground.

Lucky number thirteen…and thankfully the last: the kitchen massacre. The phone rings and news comes through the line about Elliott's death. Tate's mom goes ballistic, Tate's dad goes ballistic, Tate goes ballistic, and finally Cutest-Kid-Ever goes ballistic. The end.

Dramatic, exhausted sigh.

Back in the round room, I get ready to sing Lavender's closing words like I always do, T*hank you for your time and best of luck in your assignment,* but instead the room spins again and then stops with another door.

What in the world?

Lavender's voice breaks the silence. "The doors that follow represent Tate's post-Satellite journey. To protect the privacy of the Satellite and uphold the integrity of this organization, the Satellite will remain invisible."

Sweet Lavender must be unaware that no one's keeping secrets these days.

I shift in the tight space, wanting to disappear, or at the very least stretch my arms more than an inch, while Lavender directs us to the next door.

There won't be any stretching happening in this hallway, that's for sure. The real scene is playing out through the doorway, but our crowd is too big to squeeze into the bathroom.

We do our best to move around so everyone can get a peek. Poor Jackson's jumping up and down to try to see over Billy. I'd offer to put him on my shoulders if I didn't think it would hurt his ego.

On the bathroom floor, Tate's dad is rocking her like a child. My glimpse of the bathtub turns out to be a mistake. I hate blood.

I jerk my face away from the pink water and the blood-streaked tile floor and swallow bile. Lawson, the Godsend who he is, pushes his shoulder against mine to shove my body away from the door. He keeps his body pressed against me, purposely making a wall to shield Jackson from the gruesome scene as well.

"Tate, come on baby, look at me!" Tate's dad says and then yells for Tate's mom to call 911.

Mrs. Jacoby runs through all of us before disappearing into the master bedroom.

Liam explained this scene to me before, minus all the

gory details. How strange knowing both he and Grant were here for this.

When we're thrown back into the stone well, the Elite volume is set to mute.

Next scene: same year, same house, different room. Mental Tate is back with a vengeance. She cracks a vase into the wall, screams at Mom, then at Dad, and then at—Oh no she doesn't! Bejesus Tate!—Cutest-Kid-Ever.

We enter the circular room like dirt into a vacuum. We exit like zombies.

The next three scenes are all the same: Tate destroys things. A burned photo album follows smashed CDs and a few broken picture frames. I play a game of Find Liam, but he wins. There's no trace of him anywhere in the room.

We go in, we come out.

The next door is different because before the movie reel plays out, I know what's coming. I stole Liam's tocket and ended up in this same place with Tate. It feels odd to be watching now. In a second, Tate's going to bash her engagement ring on the bridge railing with a hammer. The diamond that must have cost a modest carpenter a whole bunch of money will drop into the river. The gold band will follow, along with Tate's breakdown of the century. Watching now, I can pick out the moment my block gets Tate off the railing before she darn near follows the ring. There's not a doubt in my mind that the poor girl would do anything to have that ring back now.

Lavender announces our last door. Hallelujah!

From where the six of us stand in Tate's parent's bedroom, Tate is a dream in her white, fairy tale dress. Lawson and Billy step closer to the bed before Cutest-Kid-Ever walks through them.

Cutest-Kid-Ever stops, frightened beyond words. When the bride turns away from the floor length oval dressing mirror, the picture-perfect image is gone. The thick globs of black make-up around her red eyes have run down her chest and bled into the satin bodice.

"Are-are you OK?" Cutest-Kid-Ever stammers.

"Get out!" Bride of Frankenstein yells.

Cutest-Kid-Ever leaves, but he sobs louder than he can run.

I'm not heartless, I'm really not, but when Tate hurts her brother like this, I'd like to put my boot straight up her—

The stone chamber sucks me in before I can finish my thought. This is probably for the best.

Mentally exhausted, I sing the words with Lavender in my head instead of out loud. "Thank you for your time and best of luck in your assignment."

The six of us become Play-doh again, mashing together like the Spaghetti Factory in reverse as we're jerked upward. My arm intertwines with someone's knee and pops. I'd scream if a miscellaneous elbow weren't shoved in my mouth. I hope that's just an elbow, anyway.

"You all have some kinks to work out," Lawson says to Jonathan when we finally land.

Jonathan takes inventory of our pipe-cleaner-like bodies and nods. "My hope is we won't be repeating this process in the near future."

I second that.

Using my left hand, I untie my sweatshirt and roll the sleeve into the best ball I can manage. I shove the thick material into my mouth after saying, "Fix me."

"With pleasure M'lady," Billy says.

My scream is muffled when he snaps my shoulder back into its rightful place. Twenty seconds later, I'm pain-free. I spit my sweatshirt out, tie the sleeves around my waist, and mumble my thanks to Billy.

"Let us make our way back to the field," Jonathan says when we are all healed and standing upright.

We follow him along the trek I've made so many times I could walk it blindfolded. Like always when I'm around Progression during working hours, the silence in the usually busy lobby makes me lonely.

The fresh air relaxes me when we step through the courtyard doors because the breeze smells amazing, like laundry and sunshine. Troy, of course, would say sunshine doesn't smell, but it absolutely does.

Jackson skips beside me. "What's so funny?"

"Nothing." I push away my thoughts of Troy and hope Jackson's not going to fall into another joke telling fit.

Jonathan points us to the bleachers, throws a black T-shirt at Reed and flannel button-up at Jackson, neither of which he was carrying a minute ago.

"New ink?" I ask when Reed strips off his torn shirt. Woven fluidly through his other tattoos, an emerald trail of smoke runs diagonally down his back. It ends at a vibrant teal star on the side of his ribs.

He nods. "You like?"

I approve. "Very fitting."

"Hey guys, I was thinking about some ink myself. What do you think?" Jackson shows us his boney torso in all its glory.

I mockingly shade my eyes with my hand. "Forget the tats, Jack. Go for a little Vitamin D, instead."

Jackson sizes up his own pale chest. "I'm serious."

"So am I!"

Jackson laughs at my joke while Reed hops up and sits on the bleacher behind me.

"I was thinking about a skull. You know, something really manly." Jackson raises his arm over his head, making his ribs jut out. "A samurai sword would be pretty tight. Or maybe a snake. Or I could work them all in. Maybe something like—"

Jonathan clears his throat and Jackson obliges, buttons up his new shirt and sits next to me. Lawson sits on my other side, sandwiching me like meat between an elephant and a mouse.

"As I mentioned, this is experimental. We cannot be sure about the effectiveness of this method, nor the outcome. This is new territory for all involved." Jonathan pauses. "We believe Tatum will attempt to take her own life within the next twenty four hours. We have four Satellites on her assignment to delay this action so we can properly train. For the first time in our Satellite history, we are going to perform a group block."

A group what?

Jonathan, unlike the rest of us, remains cool and collected. "Let me correct myself, we are going to *attempt* to perform a group block."

No way! Getting six people to block at the exact same time will be impossible.

"As you can imagine, a block of this magnitude will be difficult."

No, Jonathan, impossible. It will be impossible!

"The thought transfer has to be precisely timed. We have two purposes for this block. The first and foremost is to keep Tatum alive. Secondly, we must break the connection between her and Grant."

My expression betrays me, which doesn't go unnoticed by Jonathan.

"This is the only way that Tatum Jacoby will be able to move on and live out the path intended for her."

I barely hear him. "It's not possible," I whisper before I can stop myself. My voice is laced with hope. There's no way this could really work, could it? I shake my head. No, no way.

"Willow's right," Evelynn adds.

Billy clears his throat. "Yeah, it's not like we're trying to make the girl dance. You're talking about some serious mind bending."

"Indeed. Which is why it will take so many of you, and also why we chose our best team for this task. The Schedulers and I share your concerns. Tatum is an interesting study. We expect Tragedies to stray from their course and we plan accordingly. Tatum has diverted from her course before,   but we managed to steer her back. Now, despite our interventions, she is again breaking away from her path,   and this time she is more reckless than ever. We cannot allow her to be a danger to herself. Her life is too significant."

But Tate's actually been better the past few days. I have to tell Jonathan this.

Jonathan rubs the bridge of his nose. "There is an inexplicable connection between Tatum and Grant that is keeping us from making progress. We do not know how a block of this magnitude will affect someone's mind, but we must take that risk. The Schedulers and I agree this is our only option."

No one says anything. I gulp loudly when I try to swallow down my conflicting thoughts.

One of my first conversations with Grant was about his memories. He was terrified when I told him he was going to forget Tate. How can I be a part of breaking a connection that shouldn't have been broken to begin with? Or should it have?

What will happen to Tate if I do? She's showing real signs of recovery when Grant is there. What will happen to Grant if I don't? Just being in her presence is destroying him. The guy may burn to death, and he doesn't even seem to care.

"I would like to open this session by blocking in groups of twos and expanding from there," Jonathan says. "Billy and Jackson, please block Evelynn; Lawson and Willow, block Reed. Let's begin."

The group dismantles as instructed. I stall by putting my sweatshirt on.

"Can I talk to you for a minute?" I ask Jonathan when the others are out of earshot.

"Sure."

"Tate's getting better."

Jonathan pauses a moment. "How so?"

"Her attitude has improved. She's even playing with Fischer again."

"Have you noticed what may be contributing to this change?"

I study the spiky blades of grass around my left boot. What can I say? *Actually, yes, Jonathan. I brought Grant with me and his presence brightened her mood.* Yeah, no.

"I think if she just had a little more time…" Why can't I just tell him? Sure, I'll be in trouble, but he'll at least know that Grant can help Tate. Maybe he could even fix Grant's scars so Grant could visit Tate on a regular basis.

What am I thinking? That's the most absurd—

"Do not be deceived by a few good days. Tatum's lack of progress is worrisome and her future is beginning to shift. It is paramount that we intervene now before the opportunity to do so is lost."

Maybe Jonathan is right. Maybe this is what needs to happen.

"Do you have something you'd like to say?"

I remain mute for an uncomfortable amount of time. Eventually, I shake my head and walk away.

"How do you want to play this?" Lawson, asks in his get-down-to-business way when I reach him and Reed. His eyes, though, are extra glassy.

"You want me to come at you guys?"

Lawson agrees and they both mistake my silence as a yes. My intuition rebels because breaking the connection between Grant and Tate feels so fallacious.

Looking at Evelynn, Billy, and Jackson, already working

far away, I change my thought pattern to something more helpful. *I think I can, I think I can…* my thoughts repeat like *The Little Engine That Could,* Mya's favorite bedtime story.

Lawson and I stand side by side about fifteen yards from Reed.

"One, two, three," Lawson counts.

"Haze," we say in unison.

The rippling bubble forms around me and shoots across the lawn to my target. Lawson's filter does the same. When my filter overlaps with his two feet in front of Reed, the ripples move strangely faster.

I jump when Lawson's voice echoes in my head. "Stop, stop, stop," he repeats.

Stop, stop, stop, I think along with Lawson, but his deep voice is distracting and my thoughts are unable to get in the same rhythm.

Reed runs through Lawson's filter before I can yell "Block."

My filter disappears and I lunge in front of Lawson, making my shoulder connect with Reed's.

Reed trips and stumbles into Lawson's chest. "Dude, you're a horse."

Lawson gives his best smile, which is about half of a normal person's. "Seriously, sister, you didn't think I had that?"

Of course I knew he had it. "Just trying to get in on the fun."

Reed straightens his shirt. "I could hear your voices in my head. It was weird."

"Interesting." Jonathan says from behind us. "Did you

feel persuaded?"

Reed shrugs. "Not really."

"Try again," Jonathan says sternly and begins walking toward the other group.

We do as we're told, with the same results.

"I think the problem is our timing," I explain to Lawson. "I can't get in tune with you. How about this? After we give the order, count to three in your head before starting your thought."

Lawson agrees and we go again. This time Lawson's voice plays along with mine, but before I feel any pain or break the connection, Reed smacks into Lawson's chest. No good.

Rinse, lather, repeat.

I shake my head. "We're not convincing him."

"Maybe we need to be louder," Lawson offers.

"Worth a shot, I guess."

When we go this time, I refrain from jumping a foot in the air when Lawson's roar intertwines with my higher pitched yell. The jolt that hits me sends my body flying backwards.

Beside me on the grass, twenty feet from Reed, Lawson groans and rolls to his side.

We both manage to sit up in time to see Jonathan jogging to us. "What happened?"

"Dude," Lawson mumbles.

Still feeling stunned, I take Jonathan's outstretched hand. "That block gave us a zap from Hades."

Jonathan hoists me up and then helps Lawson.

"Did you sever the connection?" Jonathan asks us.

"The pain was too much," I explain.

Jonathan rubs the dent in his chin for a full minute.

"No offense, but this isn't going to work."

Jonathan is not happy with my statement. "Failure is imminent if we are not united with a concordant goal." The whole gang has gathered around and Jonathan's intent eyes stop on mine. "Are we in agreement regarding the purpose of this mission?"

The others silently agree with their heads, but I remain motionless.

"Willow, a word, please?"

I trudge behind Jonathan, away from the others. He stops and puts his hand on my shoulder.

I swallow. "I still don't believe Grant and Tate's connection is meant to be broken."

"Their connection is inhibiting Tatum from following the path she needs to lead now."

"Grant is a part of her. He's wrapped around every darn cell in her body. She needs him."

And he needs her. The image of the disgusting lesion on the kid's chest creeps in my head. I don't dare mention this to Jonathan now. The man doesn't need any more fuel to feed his plan.

Jonathan pauses for a long time. "Would you agree that Troy is a part of you?"

"Yes, of course, but what—"

"What happened with your connection to Troy when you joined us?"

Oh, for the love—fight fair!

"I forgot him," I whisper to my boots until I find my full

voice. "This is different. Their connection should have been broken the natural way, not the way Tate ripped it apart. Now she's trying to reconnect with him. Jonathan, she needs him. They need each other. Why can't you see that?"

Jonathan remains unnervingly calm.

"Come on, Jonathan! Why can't you see this for what it is?"

Maybe he's uncertain, but he stands his ground. "This is necessary for Tatum. She's not in a healthy place. You know that as well as I do. She will still remember Grant. We are only removing the emotional connection she feels towards him."

"These measures are extreme."

"Without an intervention, we risk her life ending prematurely."

"It hasn't been that long."

"Willow," he pauses sympathetically. "Tatum's made very little progress and her condition is deteriorating more each day. Keeping her alive must be our top priority now. Given the circumstances, I understand the emotional strain this places on you and I will respect your decision if you choose to decline. The choice belongs to you, and you alone."

How can I say no? What kind of impression would I be giving the others? What if I'm wrong about Grant and Tate?

"I'm in," I finally whisper.

When I look back up at Jonathan, his nod is solemn. "Please understand as we move forward, there's no room for indecision."

"You have my word," I mumble and try to ignore the regret that's snuffing out my intuition.

19. I think you broke me

Willow

Three times now, Lawson and I are knocked on our backsides, unable to sever the blocking connection with Reed. In the distance, it appears that Evelynn, Billy and Jackson are having about as much luck as we are.

This time, I try to be ready. Actually, I've tried to be ready every time. My back foot is wedged in the thick grass for more traction, but my legs feel like silly string in combat boots. The voltage delivers a deadly shock, so painful I hardly noticing my flight through the air. When I land, the current doesn't stop like it has before, but, Holy Mother, I wish it would! *Labor, labor, labor…* I think, in effort to deflect the pain.

"Block!" I yell from my curled position on the ground.

The voltage releases me and my raw throat tells me that I've probably yelled really loudly, even by my standards.

Everyone on the field is staring at me, including Reed, who has stopped in mid-stride.

Jonathan's the first one to move and he crosses to me. There's a sick excitement in his voice. "Excellent! Can you share what was done differently?"

Lawson shakes his head and I say, "I don't know," with

a croaky voice.

"Keep trying until you figure it out," Jonathan urges.

Oh sure, that sounds like a bang-up time. "Don't you think we should give Reed a chance to block?" I plead as Jonathan is walking away.

"It's all about stamina," Jonathan says over his shoulder and then, "I saw that," when I roll my eyes.

After two more tries, I lift my head in time to see Reed stop and then I allow myself a well deserved minute to get my bearings.

I announce to Jonathan that I think we've done it and he has the Legacies gathered around me a minute later.

"Willow, Lawson, please perform another block while we observe," Jonathan says.

For the love of St. Therese!

"Wanna mix it up?" Lawson asks in a tired voice when we're crossing the lawn.

After agreeing with Lawson's whispered plan of attack, my voice belts out in unison with his. "Haze!"

One, two, three.

In my head, our voices scream simultaneously, *Bunny hop, bunny hop, bunny hop.*

The force throws us both into the air and my hands ball into fists. I stay focused as my body bounces off the ground. "Block," I manage.

Reed, sideways in my vision, makes me want to laugh, but my back hurts too badly. He hops between Lawson and me like he's in a potato sack race.

Jonathan watches him cross the lawn. "I'd venture to

say that block was a success."

As usual, my mouth works faster than my head. "Success, my—"

"Eh hem."

"Sorry," I reply to Jonathan with very little sincerity as my muscles continue to quiver sporadically.

Jonathan shades his eyes and turns in Reed's direction. I'm able to get up on one elbow just as Reed stops at the edge of the field, freezes, and scratches his head. In the time it takes him to cross the expanse of the field back to us, Lawson gets himself upright and offers me his giant hand.

"You all right?"

Certainly he can see the worry in my eyes. Everything about this is a bad idea.

"Billy, Reed, and Jackson, why don't you block Evelynn?" Jonathan circles back to Lawson and me. "Any helpful advice you can offer?"

"Your thoughts have to be in unison. Agree on the outcome and make a plan, by counting or whatever, so you can transfer the thought together."

"Yelling the thought seems to be helpful, too," Lawson adds.

"When you say yell do you mean out loud? Because I can totally do that, but I don't want to be the only one shouting. You know what I mean?"

I jump in when Jackson takes a breath. "Just think it loudly in your head."

Billy, Jackson, and Reed huddle together about twenty feet from Evelynn. When they break apart, they command the haze and the rippling effect is even weirder from the outside. The usual water bubbles stretch out from each Elite and across the lawn, but when they merge around Evelynn the enclosure moves faster than Niagara Falls. Inside, Evelynn is barely a magenta blur.

As if a bomb explodes, Billy, Jackson, and Reed are blasted backwards. When they hit the ground, Billy's filter dissolves. Jackson's and Reed's filters are still stretched to Evelynn and don't separate until both guys yell, "Block."

Evelynn begins cartwheeling across the lawn with her back to us. Beside me, Lawson chuckles as Evelynn continues across the field like a magenta bicycle reflector. Yikes!

"What happened to your filter, hot shot?" I yell to Billy.

He rolls to face me and answers with a mean glare.

Jonathan passes Billy on his way to Jackson and Reed and asks Reed to block Evelynn, probably so she'll stop mooning us each time she's upside down.

When we've all regrouped, Jonathan orders Billy, Evelynn, and me to block Lawson. We choose a friendly outcome and begin. The next thing I know, everything's dark.

I try to turn over, but can't move. Dear God, I'm paralyzed!

"No you're not," someone muffles, answering the statement that I must have said out loud.

When a weight lifts and frees me, I raise my head and spit grass and dirt out of my mouth. "You oaf! What the heck is wrong with you?" If I wasn't dead already, the giant would have killed me.

Beside me, Billy groans, apparently hurting, too.

"I think you broke me," I whine to him, but get no reply.

Jonathan reaches us with Jackson and Reed trailing behind. "Good work."

Sure, now that I'm as flat as Stanley, Jonathan approves.

Billy moans.

"Oh, suck it up." My voice is too weak for the dig to have the full effect.

"Shut up."

I laugh, instantly regretting it because he laughs, too. Feeding off each other and unable to stop the convulsing movement of our guts, we're both holding our ribs in pain. Finally, the pain wins. I can't take anymore.

We watch Lawson from a distance while he twists the day away. What I wouldn't give to have a recording of him. I'd have blackmail forever. Then again, he's seen me do things I'd be happy to forget. One thing's for sure, the guy's got some killer dance moves.

Evelynn stumbles over to us and sits beside me to watch the show.

Reed turns to Jonathan a few minutes later. "How long are we going to watch him?"

Jonathan, entranced by Lawson's swinging hips, pops back to reality. "Go ahead and block him."

When Reed completes the block, Lawson continues dancing.

Reed tries again. Nothing.

Jonathan puts his hand up. "Hold on, Reed. Jackson, would you please try?"

Jackson's already working before the words are out of Jonathan's mouth. After Jackson fails twice, Reed isn't quite as disappointed in himself.

"Reed and Jackson, together please."

They do as Jonathan instructs. My dreads blow back when Jackson and Reed are thrown fifteen feet behind me.

"You boys all right?" I ask when Lawson finally stops dancing.

Reed's voice is muffled by the crook of his elbow. "I'm not sure."

Jackson's speechless, which is alarming.

"Promising," Jonathan says to himself. "The results seem to be as lasting as we hoped. The more Satellites that are involved in the block, the more, it seems, are required to undo it. Promising, indeed."

Regret is performing a hip-hop dance in my belly. What we're doing is wrong.

I gave Jonathan my word. I cannot go back on that.

While my head houses the boxing match of my thoughts, Jonathan calls Lawson, Reed, Evelynn, and Billy to the field. I should have guessed who'd be on the receiving end.

At Billy's request, since he almost crushed me on the last round, the group forms a circle around me. A minute later, they are all floundering on the grass. I march past Jonathan to my prize: Jackson.

I bend down and kiss him full-on. I've never wanted anything more. Jackson's eyes pop from their sockets. I would laugh at his ridiculous expression if my mouth weren't otherwise occupied. When he gives in and closes his eyes, he's on his toes so I don't have to bend down. At barely five feet tall, I've never had to bend down for anyone in my life.

His tongue moves around my mouth as fast as he talks. I can't stop kissing him, so I try to keep up. Around and around we go like a game of tag. Or hide-and-go-seek.

What the—

"What are you doing!" I push the leech off me and spit onto the grass before using the back of my hand to wipe the slobber off my face.

"Sorry. Really I am. I didn't know—it was them!" He points across the field. From where she's resting on the ground, Evelynn smiles at me. Reed, Lawson, and Billy are much further from us, probably from undoing the block, but also on the ground and barely moving.

Jackson is still rambling. "...honest, I didn't know. I really didn't. But I was all right, right? I mean, the kiss, was it good for..."

"Not now Jackson!" I stomp over to Evelynn.

"Willow, I would advise keeping your cool," Jonathan warns as I pass him.

When I reach her, I fist my hand around her long, gold necklace. "That's how you did it with him, isn't it?"

"What?" The little siren is actually confused.

"With Grant. You blocked him so he'd kiss you."

Wounded for half a second, she recovers. "He begged for it."

"Willow!" Jonathan's voice is close now.

I release her necklace. "You wish."

The boys find enough strength to gather around us in record speed. True to form, they would never miss some girl-on-girl action.

No doubt Jonathan wants to shift the focus to something constructive by saying, "We won't know the true effect until we perform a block with all six of you."

What's with all this "we"?

"Please form a circle around me."

The others register what's happening about the same time I do.

"Jonathan, we—" Reed starts to say.

"I promise this will be your last block."

Of course it will, because this one will probably kill us for real.

After we decided on the trusty go-left bit, Billy starts the count. When he hits three, we all belt out a pathetic, "Haze," in unison.

I count along in my head and then the noise is so loud I cover my ears. I think I'm chiming along, but I can't hear myself over the others.

A force rockets me backwards and I happily succumb to the darkness.

20. They want to destroy us

Grant

My muscles don't have a chance to relax while I code. In less than five seconds, the forest scenery shifts, but not to my old bedroom as I was expecting. I'm not paralyzed like before and nothing hurts. This is a good day!

Sitting on the tailgate of a parked pickup truck, my eyes follow the line of mature trees bordering the narrow gravel road. Aside from the two bikes laying on the rocks, the road is deserted.

"Dance with me."

My head jerks to the voice behind me. "Tate?"

Standing in the scratched, white bed of the truck, she smiles down at me and ruffles my hair. "Dance with me."

Before I can answer she takes my hands and pulls me to her.

"There's no music." Really? I have a million questions to ask this girl and that's what I come up with?

Her hands release mine and half of her body disappears into the sliding back window of the truck. The radio kicks on. Tate returns, lifts my hands from my side, and wraps them around her waist. She steps closer and I automatically tighten my grip. This makes her smile, so I tighten my embrace even more. Her hand cups my neck and she rests her head on my shoulder.

"I love you." Again, where the heck is my obscene word choice coming from? I realize I don't regret saying these words, but they catch me off guard.

"I know," she whispers and kisses my shoulder. "I love you, too."

We move together for a few minutes and my world feels whole. I'm never letting her go. I breathe deeper, wanting more of her scent.

She stops moving and laces her fingers firmly around my neck.

Her head lifts off my shoulder and she studies my face for a few seconds. "Something bad is about to happen." Her hazel eyes are dark when she focuses on the sky.

I want to erase the worry from her face. I'd give anything to do so. "I don't understand."

"They're coming. They want to destroy us."

My anxiety increases with my heartbeat. "Who's coming?"

Her eyes fill with tears.

"Don't cry. Please." My arm muscles tense to keep a strong grip on her. "Please, Tate, tell me who's coming."

"They're going to destroy us. They don't want us to be together. It's too late."

"It's not too late. You need to tell me who!"

Her fear morphs to anger. "You already know!"

"No, I don't." *Please calm down!*

"Your friends." The expression on her heart shaped face

is pleading. "Grant, I love you. Hold me. Please don't ever let go."

I push a curl off her wet cheek and cup her face with both hands. "I won't, Tate. I won't ever leave you. I'm here, I'm right here! I love you." And I do. Even without any solid memories of her, the words are so easy to say, so true.

She buries her face in my neck and I hug her hard, locking her body to mine. "Please don't cry."

"Come back to me," she pleads. "Please, come back to me."

My arms squeeze tightly around her, but hit my chest.

She's vanished! I spin around the empty truck bed in panic.

"Tate!" My yell echoes like I'm in a cold cave. "Tate! Come back!"

The gravel road is gone an instant later, leaving me panting and gawking at my wild reflection in the coding room.

As if Tate put it there, an idea materializes in my reeling head. I can almost hear her voice. I know what I need to do.

21. What if we destroy their connection forever?

Willow

Wake Up! Wake up! Wake up!

I open my eyes to stop the sound of my own voice screaming in my head. From my back, I push up onto my elbows and squint into the blinding sun. The shadow above me moves and the form comes into focus. "Rig?"

Rigby grabs my hand and yanks me up. I groan and massage my upper arms before moving to work on my shoulders. Rigby moves behind me and takes over.

I carefully move my head side to side to stretch out my neck. "Your hands are genius." I roll my head down. "What happened?"

"You took a good hit while you were blocking. Jonathan pulled us from break and brought us here," Rigby explains.

"Us?" I raise my head and scan the field. Well would you look at that; the whole darn gang is here. Anna has her attention on Lawson while he rubs his neck. Elliott is standing over Reed, who must have just come to. Owen is talking to Billy. Clara is helping Evelynn fix her wardrobe malfunction, and Liam appears to be trying to tune Jackson out.

"A group block? Girl, that's insane!"

I rub my temples and the pulse beats into my fingers. It's insane, all right.

"Everyone please join me over here," Jonathan hollers from the bleachers.

In true gentleman form, Rig helps me across the field even though I could manage on my own. Probably. The teeth clenching seems to help with the pain. I won't lie; my legs are thankful when Rigby and I sit on the bleachers beside Owen and Billy. Owen won't take his nervous gaze off Anna when she comes our way, not that I blame the guy. Lawson is staggering beside her like an intoxicated Incredible Hulk. If Lawson falls, Anna will be buried alive.

When the others have piled onto the bleachers, I try to rub my headache away while Jonathan talks.

"Our group block was as successful as I had hoped. We have some unexpected side effects to contend with, but I think this just may work."

"Did we block you?" Billy asks. I can only assume the others remember as much as I do, which is basically nothing. I don't even remember saying "Block."

"Yes. Quite well actually."

Jonathan's about to go on, but I cut in. "How did you stop?"

He leans forward like he didn't hear me. "What's that?" A classic case of stalling.

My famous Willow-volume is in order. "How did you stop? It would have taken five Satellites to reverse the block. If you were walking, how did—"

"Tsk-tsk, Willow," he says, "you know I never reveal my tricks."

If that's not the truth. I'd give my left arm for just a tiny glimpse into his head. OK, not the whole arm, but a few fingers maybe.

"Phase two is complete. We have finished the necessary training," Jonathan states.

We relax like we were all holding our breath. Another day of that kind of torture and I'd need to be committed.

"Some modifications are necessary to the original plan. Each of you will be accompanied by a partner. Since there seems to be no secrets among this group," he swoops his eyes over each of us and his expression is unreadable, "we may as well include you all."

Jonathan brings the new arrivals up to speed in regard to our upcoming assignment. Beside me, Rigby sits up straighter. "Your assignments will be filled temporarily by other Satellites. Your job will be to block our Elites awake like you have just done. Simple enough?"

They nod.

Jonathan steeples his fingers. "Great. I would like each of you to get in a coding session before your departure. I ask that you meet back here after break, which is currently in progress. Any questions?"

He gets no response.

"Great. See you all soon." With that, he heads off the field.

"Hey, Willow, wait up!" Jackson yells from behind me.

"What's up, Jack?"

"Listen, I'm really sorry about earlier."

Earlier, earlier, earlier…what the heck happened earlier?

He's still rambling when it hits me: *the kiss.*

"…to get weird between us. I mean, I can understand if it stirred some feelings for you, but you're a married woman. Troy will—Oh no! Troy! He's not going to hurt me is he? Oh jeez, I didn't mean to—"

"Chill, Jack, it's all right, and Troy will be fine. I'll try my best to put my feelings to sleep." I do a decent job of keeping a straight face, if I do say so myself.

Jackson brightens. "I owe you one! I really do. Thanks so much. I mean it."

I purse my lips. "Mmm hmm."

"And for the record, you're a pretty good kisser yourself."

Oh gosh, I'm gonna blow. "Thanks, gotta run!" I pick up my pace faster than his short legs can carry him. When I'm out of earshot, I crack up. At the same time, I want to scrub my tongue with bleach.

Once I'm through the courtyard doors, I jog to the target that catches my interest. "Yo, Elliott!"

He stops and waits for me in the middle of the lobby while I snake my way through the crowd.

"Hey, how you doin'?"

He shrugs.

"You know this is about…" it's too hard for me to say her name, "your sister, right?"

I immediately regret asking the question. When he

finally nods, I nod with him.

"Are you cool with doing this?"

He takes a breath and shoves his hands into his pockets. "Do I have much of a choice?"

"You always have a choice, El. Are you going to be able to do this?"

Instead of answering, he asks, "Are you?"

I squeeze the jewel on one of my dreads until it stabs into my thumb. "It's going to keep her alive."

"Jonathan says this is the right thing, that this is the only way. We have to trust him." The guys sounds an awful lot like he's trying to talk himself into something.

"He could find someone else if you think—"

"How could I say no? She's my sister. I want to see her again," he pauses. "Their bond was strong, Willow. Really strong."

I reach out and rub his forearm. "I know."

He chews on his lip for a few seconds. "I guess I'll see you later, then?"

"Looks that way."

Taking the scenic route back to my room, I use the time to convince myself that I shouldn't go see Grant. This turns out to be easy because I don't know how I'd face him.

Will I ever be able to face him again?

"Hey, Willow."

I almost run head-on into Trina. "Sorry, I'm out of sorts today. You're looking better."

Trina smiles. "Programming is going well, though it's exhausting."

"I hear you. How's your brother?"

"I haven't met him yet. I'm still in the process of getting my memories back."

"That's running smoothly, then?"

"It is. Programming is wild, huh?"

"It's definitely that. Life on the other side is good." I think about Troy. "It's a funny thing, how much we fight against the change to defend our Satellite life, but then we get our memories back and everything changes. At least it did for me. I didn't realize how much good stuff my head was missing until I went through Programming. When I met Troy here, my world became whole. I felt good. Really, really good. I know it will be the same for you."

"Do you still feel good?" Trina's forehead creases. "I don't mean to pry, but you seem sad today." She smiles, but it's an empathetic grin. "You were never like this when we trained."

"Today is…" I'm not sure how to finish. Boy, I'm off all right; I'm never at a loss for words.

Trina squeezes my arm. "It's none of my business. Just know I'm here if you need anything."

"Thanks. I'd better get going. Good luck with the rest of Programming. You'll have a lot of catching up to do with your brother. Enjoy it, sister. There's nothing better."

As I walk away, my thoughts shift back to the daunting task ahead. Once in my room, I sit on the rug by my sofa, ready to clear my guilty mind. My muscles relax as soon as I close my eyes and the ocean fills my view. The waves crash against angular chunks of granite, occasionally spraying me with cold water. My muscles relax further. I inhale the salty air and bring myself back a smidgeon early, knowing a quick conversation with Troy will get my mind in the right place better than coding.

I say hello to the gamers on my way out and weave quickly through the mazing corridors of Programming. "Good day friends," I mumble to the walls when I reach my own hallway.

My stomach summersaults when I enter my paradise. The sky is hazy, making the colors duller than normal. The air here is similar to my coding destination and I breathe in the smell of the northeastern coast.

"Babe?" I yell into the quiet house, dropping my bag on the stone foyer floor. I walk into our bedroom where the sheets are still tangled from earlier.

The noise of a coughing motor cuts through the silence. Bingo. I use the French doors in our bedroom and follow the curved granite path through the backyard.

The weathered barn door is slid open to expose most of Troy's shop. An overhead light shines on him and my breath hitches. I don't care for the car, really, but seeing him like this, covered up to his elbows in grease and twisting a wrench in the innards of the old Chevy, gets my heart racing.

He catches me staring and his voice carries over the sputtering engine. "Hey babe!" He wipes his hands on the bandana he's taken from his back pocket before reaching through the driver's side window. A second later, the car is silent.

"Sorry, I'm a mess." His gray eyes take inventory of my

body as he walks toward me. "It's a shame I can't touch you when you look that good."

I lean over and kiss him, lingering. When I pull back, his smile is seductive.

"I could go wash up real quick," he offers.

"Nah, I can't stay long."

"It'd only take a second."

I kiss him again. "It's tempting, but it would take more than a second."

"You're right," his lips mumble against mine.

My teeth scrape against his when I smile before pulling back. "I need your advice."

"I'm all yours. What's up?" He uses the bandana to wipe more grease off his hands while he follows me to the oak tree beside the barn.

I sit on the wooden plank and grip the ropes of the swing. My boots kick around until dust clouds form while I attempt to skirt the real issue. "I kissed Jackson today."

Troy rests his back against the wide tree and laughs.

"You're handling this better than I thought."

"If you're going to cheat, you could at least chose someone," he pauses, "taller."

God love this man.

"So what's really going on?" he asks.

"The guys blocked me into doing it," I explain.

Troy's smile doesn't crinkle his eyes like it usually does and he stops wiping his hands. "What's really going on with *you?*"

"Jonathan's put me and the Elites on a super-secret

mission."

"So you can't tell me about it?"

I roll my eyes. "Of course I can tell you about it."

"But you just said—"

"Babe, around here, confidentiality died with the Egyptians. Anyway, you're my husband so technically it doesn't count."

He thinks about this and nods. "All right, shoot."

"Just between us?"

He huffs out a chuckle. "You're really something, you know that?"

"Stop hitting on me and listen!" He's impossible sometimes.

"Sorry. I'm all ears."

"Tate's been trying to reconnect with Grant, and it's been working. Jonathan just finished training us for an assignment that involves breaking that connection. I don't even know if it will work." I kick at the dirt and squint up at him. "I don't want it to work."

Troy nods, but says nothing.

"I gave Jonathan my word that I would try. I can't go back on that, but I feel like we're messing with fate, or nature, or something. I don't know. Their connection is so strong. Grant didn't forget her like he was supposed to, and now, even though she's erased his memories, he's still weirdly drawn to her. She won't let him go unless we intervene, I know that, but what if we're doing the wrong thing? What if I'm doing the wrong thing?"

"You rarely doubt Jonathan."

I shake my head.

"Why now?"

I shrug. "Instinct, I guess."

"You've always had great instinct," Troy agrees. "What's your biggest fear about this whole thing?"

I take a slow, deep breath. "That it will work."

"And if it does?"

I kick the dirt harder this time and say nothing.

"You forgot me." Even though his delivery was sugar sweet, Troy's words cut through me like a searing knife.

"It wasn't my fault!"

"Whoa, that's not my point. What I mean is, you forgot me because it was necessary. Here we are, though, back and better than ever."

I want to smile with him, but can't. "The way I forgot was natural, like all Satellites. The way we're planning on severing Grant and Tate's connection doesn't feel right."

A gray haze blurs the horizon line between the sky and the mountains. Troy remains patient and, ultimately, I expose my real fear. "What if we destroy their connection forever?"

Seeing Troy didn't make me feel any more certain about my decision like I had hoped it would. Even my balance feels off, like I'm walking a tightrope in a hurricane.

Get in game mode, Willow, I scold and sit on the bleachers with the others.

"Everything all right?" Lawson whispers.

I nod. It doesn't feel as much like a lie if I don't use words.

"Welcome back," Jonathan says. "You all look well. I trust you have coded and are ready for the challenge ahead."

His audience is eerily silent, but, unlike me, the others probably stay button-lipped because they're remembering the pain from the block.

"We need to discuss the logistics before your departure. I have instructed Liam and he will be there waiting for you. We are going to need an open space so you can surround Tatum accordingly. As luck would have it," he grins at his joke; there's no such thing as luck and we all know it, "Tatum is going to be in the wildlife area close to her home this afternoon. Elites, Tatum stepping into the open field will be your cue to surround her. Billy, you're the loudest so I would like you to count. Just like you trained, on Billy's count of three, your energy should be collected and you will summon the Haze. Then, Billy will count to three in his head before you all transfer the thought. As practiced, the thought needs to be sent loudly and in unison."

Jonathan pauses long enough to intensify the suspense.

"'Let go of Grant before you destroy him.' These are the words that must be repeated."

My breath is forced out like I've just been flogged.

Before *she* destroys *him?* This isn't about Tate at all.

Jonathan's mouth is moving, but I can't hear him. I can't hear anything. This isn't right, it can't be. I squeeze my eyes closed to fight back the stinging tears. When I open them, Jonathan's lips start to produce sound again.

"…will block your partner awake. We will convene back here when the assignment is complete. I trust each of you will perform to the best of you ability." Jonathan focuses on me when he says this. Apparently we're over the subtleties. "I am optimistic about the outcome. Willow, the necklace please."

I get up with the others and force my fingers to work, digging slowly through my bag. We form a tight circle and the eleven of us loop a finger around the chain.

"Good luck," Jonathan says.

I refuse to say "thanks" like the others. I gave him my word and intend to follow through, but I don't have to be all cool about it.

"Displace," I whisper.

22. *Bloody hell*

Grant

"Hey man, got a minute?" I stay calm by keeping my hands in my back pockets, but continue to pace the deserted hallway. "I really need to talk to someone."

My banging heart must be working to my advantage because, after a double take, Liam approaches me when he steps out of the elevator. "Bloody hell. You all right?"

"No, I don't think I am."

My hands are shaking when they come out of my pockets. Liam's eyes dart left and then right like he's measuring the five-foot distance on either side of us. He steps back until he hits the gold elevator door. "What's up, mate?"

I jump towards him, knowing his white-knuckled fist could be wrapped around his tocket, giving him a way to flee. I pounce before he can displace and slam him against the gold door.

"What's going on?" I bark two inches from his nose.

He's either in shock or playing dumb; I'm too ramped up to tell which.

I get a better grip on both of his shoulders. "She told me something was about to happen."

"Who?"

"Tate." When I say this, Liam's eyeballs are about to spring out of their sockets.

I loosen my grip long enough for his muscles to relax under me and then I slam him into the elevator door again. "Get your tocket."

My volume makes him flinch and he swallows loudly before shaking his head.

"Now!" After taking a few seconds to realize his options are slim, he digs into his jeans.

"Open it!" I say, glaring at his fisted hand.

Gauging the size of the silver ring, I try to work out the logistics. I grab his hand so the ring is pressed against both our palms. "Displace before I break you!" I growl through clenched teeth, digging my fingers deeper into his knuckles.

He struggles under me, but my hold is too strong. The angry expression I'm wearing must tell him how determined I am. I *will* break him if necessary.

"Displace," he finally says.

23. This whole time, you were fooling us all

Willow

We fall through the grass and plummet into the atmosphere like a circle of skydivers, eleven of us connected to Tate's thin chain. When we land in a clearing, our feet don't disturb the loose ground like they would if we had any real weight. We're invisible, nothing but ghosts about to cause some serious damage.

"What the— What's going on?" a panicked voice shouts loud enough for us all to hear. A panicked voice I know too well.

I spin around and my eyes dart to Liam. "What's he doing here?" I demand in a pitch even I don't recognize.

"He ambushed me! There was nothing I could do!" Liam yells back, out of breath.

I'm equally frantic and staring at Grant. "We've got to get him out of here!" Oh God, this can't be happening.

Grant walks from the side of the lake into the clearing, more pallid than I've ever seen him. "You'll never catch me," he says dryly. "Trust me, Liam's been trying. You gonna tell me what's going on, or what?" His eyes race around our large group; his peers, most of them his friends.

"You need to get out of here." I hope he can hear the warning in my voice. "Please, Grant."

Tate crosses the clearing from the opposite direction carrying a tackle box. She's going fishing? Suicidal my—

"Willow! Tell me what's going on!" Grant's eyes are on Tate and his voice is shaky.

The Elites have already circled her, conveniently positioning themselves so I don't have to move.

"What should I do?" Liam asks.

He can't be here! "Grant, please go!"

"What are they doing?" Grant zeros in on me and his brown eyes are filled with terror.

"One…" Billy has started the count. "Two…"

My tears pool, making the purple translucent ball in my vision blurry. "I'm so sorry."

"Three!"

"Haze!" our six voices yell together.

The filters pour out of each of us and merge around Tate. I try to blink my tears away so I can see, ignoring Grant's frantic shouts while Billy's voice counts in my head. Grant sprints to Tate, disappearing into the rapid waterfall of our filters.

Confused by the sapphire blue cloud that emanates from the waterfall, I try to concentrate. There's so much noise, I almost lose the thought.

But I don't.

The words, my words, everyone's words, bounce around my skull like thunder. *Let go of Grant*—I'm lifted into the air with the force of a tornado before I can complete the sentence.

—⁓⁓—

Wake up! Wake up! Wake up!

I open my eyes in hopes that the screaming in my head will stop.

Rigby is standing over me and the dark expression he's wearing doesn't fit him. "She's coming around," he yells over his shoulder.

I squeeze my head with both hands, afraid that my pulsing brain is puncturing my skull. My whole body aches when I sit up.

"Did it work?" I'm afraid to hear the answer that I already know. Elites don't fail.

Rigby nods just once.

"Where is everyone?" I ask, wondering the same thing about myself.

Jonathan appears at my side and hands me a cup of coffee. He sets it on the end table when I don't take it. "They are resting in their quarters."

Realizing I'm in my room, I grab my head again. "How'd we get here?"

"You wouldn't wake up," Rigby says as if that explains everything. "No one would," he whispers.

"How are you feeling?"

"Where's Grant?" I demand, ignoring Jonathan's question.

"He went back to his assignment."

"So that's it? Things just go back to normal?"

He nods. "Yes. That's it."

"And Tate?"

"Everything appears to have gone as planned."

Well pin a rose on me. How perfect. "I feel terrible."

Poor Rigby is desperate for something to do. "Can I get you anything?"

"I feel terrible for what I've done," I whisper for clarification.

Jonathan is the picture of calmness. "You did well."

I shake my head in anger. "I've ruined them. This was never about Tate. This whole time, you were fooling us all. The kid is good and you couldn't risk losing him as one of your own."

Jonathan stays quiet.

"Do you realize what we've done? We've destroyed them! All because you want him in your collection of Satellites."

"Willow, he was destined—"

"No!" I scream, on my feet now, and Rigby takes a step back. "No! He was destined for her! Don't you see that? He's not right without her."

"This sacrifice was necessary. Think of the lives that are to be changed. Someday I hope you will understand the necessity…"

I ignore the rest of his words while pain digs into my brain. I will never understand this.

24. The guy never looks fine

Grant

Back at Meggie's, she and Brody are curled together on the sofa. Meggie's puffy eyes reveal that she's had one heck of a crying spell.

"Lawson?" I yell.

No answer.

I make a fast sweep through the place and conclude that Lawson is missing. Strange. Parking myself on the chair, I turn my attention to the uneventful evening news after catching up on my reading. It feels good to be back.

An hour later, Lawson drops from the ceiling.

"I'm back!" By his shocked reaction, my joke doesn't fly. Maybe a different approach is in order.

"Look, I'm sorry I left you hanging. I know I shouldn't have pushed Brody like I did. I'll try to contain myself in the future." My insides rebel against my statement, knowing that I'll have a tough time standing aside if Brody tries to hurt her again.

Lawson's mouth hangs open.

"I said I'm sorry." Sheesh. "Being pulled from this assignment made me adjust my thinking. I have to be here with her." Being close to Meggie drives home my decision.

"So, like I said, I will try to contain myself in the future."

Lawson finally mumbles, "Uh, so…what, I mean, where…"

I raise my eyebrow, wondering what's wrong with him.

"What did you do while you were gone?" Lawson manages to get out.

Now that I think of it, what did I do? I can't remember anything solid except the headache that has finally dulled. I push away the unsettling feeling, happy to be back here, and shrug my answer.

Lawson cracks his knuckles like he's nervous.

"Where have you been?" I ask.

"Oh, ah, Jonathan needed to see me." He shifts his focus to Meggie and Brody. "How are they today?"

I watch the couple for a few seconds, happy to see that Meggie is comfortable enough on Brody's arm, and that Brody seems mellow enough not to punch her. "They seem better, actually."

Lawson's shoulders relax. "Brody's recovery in the hospital had the added benefit of a good detox. He needed it. He's been clean for a week."

"*A week?*" I wasn't gone that long.

Instead of answering, Lawson parks himself on the living room floor.

A week? I look back at Meggie, glad that her eyes are still dry. "Has she been OK?"

"As OK as anyone can be in her situation."

Fair enough. "Well, like I said, I'm back. Lucky you." I

study him, wondering why I can't get the guy to crack a smile. "What's your problem, man?"

"You remember anyone named Tate?"

My finger runs over my T-shirt, tracing the raised scar on my chest. "Who?"

The silent tension becomes uncomfortable. "No one. Sorry, must have you mixed up with someone else."

He's acting even weirder, but seems stressed out enough that I decide not to press him any further.

Meggie gets up from the sofa, which is my cue. When I follow her into the bathroom, she actually fills the tub with water. This is promising! Waiting while she bathes, I think back to my follow-up meeting with the Schedulers and Jonathan. They acted like they had forgiven me for my interference, though I was definitely not asking for forgiveness. Talk about a one-eighty. Landon seemed like he'd even call me his friend at one point while he was giving me a "quick refresher" of our rules. I kept quiet about the fact that the "handbook for dummies" was still in my backpack and let Landon carry on like I had broken the rules out of ignorance, not disregard. I still don't believe I did anything wrong, but I wasn't about to argue. I'm just glad to be back on my assignment.

I flex my arm muscles, which feel rested and strong. Trying to find something conclusive about where the week went, my brain keeps returning its focus to the strange headache I had.

I get up from the bed and walk to the bathroom door to peek in on Meggie when I hear her crying. Tears stream down her pretty checks and roll into the bubbles at her neck. I want to fix this poor woman so badly.

"Haze," I say quietly when my sight is veiled in blue.

The filter never extends out from me to Meggie.

"Haze!" I yell since my quieter tone didn't work.

As soon as the waterfall surrounds me and starts toward Meggie, my head is assaulted by a sledgehammer. I cover my ears to be sure my brain stays inside.

Meggie's tears ramp up, but I only know by the expression on her face, which is blurry since my eyes won't focus. I can't hear her over the jet engine that is rumbling in my head.

I turn away from Meggie, causing my blue sight to disappear before I can say "block." The screaming in my head relents a little, but not to a level I'd call comfortable.

Meggie doesn't stop crying, and I try again, which ends with another failure and even more pain centered in my skull. When I walk back to the bed and squeeze my temples, I notice Lawson, standing very still in the doorway.

"Problems blocking?" he asks.

"No. Why?" My voice is defensive even though I'm certain that my failed blocks are a fluke. Probably I'm just out of sorts from my time off.

Lawson goes back into the living room and Meggie, thankfully, calms herself down without my help. She finishes her bath, brushes her teeth, and talks Brody into going to bed early.

I change my focus, hoping for a reprieve from my throbbing head. "They're sleeping together?" I ask Lawson when he follows Brody into the bedroom.

Lawson nods.

In the bed? This is serious progress!

I try to make small talk with Lawson after we take our respective corners for the evening, receiving snippy, one-word answers in return. I take the hint, shut up, and spend the rest of the night convincing myself that my ability is fine. Around three, I almost ask Lawson if failed blocks are normal after having some time off, but ultimately decide against it, fearful of the answer he might give. Certainly I would have been warned about this in training.

Only the occasional roll from Meggie and Brody disturbs the quiet evening. While they sleep, I focus my energy until the blue filter clouds my vision a dozen times just to be sure it's still there. I don't dare say "haze" because the pain in my head has finally subdued to a dull ache.

———

The next morning, Meggie and Brody don't get up until well past nine. By noon, the house is full when Max, Ryan, and Nancy show up as documented. Before I have a chance to greet Whitfield and Elliott, Lawson pulls Elliott into the bedroom for some top-secret conversation.

"What's with them?" I ask Whitfield.

She glances toward the hall that leads to the bedroom. "Who knows. You talk to Rig lately?"

I shake my head.

"He's been acting weird. He says he's fine, but I can tell

he's keeping something from me. You don't think he's into someone else, do you?"

Before I can answer, Meggie starts to cry.

"Haze," I say out of instinct when my blue vision comes.

Ahhhhhhhhh!

Whitfield breaks the connection by jumping in front of me and grabbing my shoulders. Her lips move, but I can't hear her.

"You all right, hon'?" her voice finally muffles in a slow, underwater kind of sound.

My eyes dart around her to Meggie, but Whitfield moves, putting her nose an inch from mine. "Grant, what's the matter?"

I swallow. Why can't I block?

Whitfield's even more worried. When I find my voice, I mumble that I'm fine, but she doesn't release my shoulders for another whole minute.

I try to rub the pain from my temples as Nancy consoles Meggie. The hug does more for Meggie than I'm able to. Nancy helps get Meggie settled into a chair at the table.

While Nancy rummages through the pantry, Meggie spins the placemat with her finger in the same way that my fingers work on my head. She closes her eyes, her finger stops moving, and she appears to be practicing some deep breathing exercise. I consider trying the same thing in hopes of lessoning my pain.

"My parents are coming down from Michigan this week. They'd love to see you," Nancy says, turning on one of the burners while I pull my energy in again.

Meggie keeps her eyes shut, but nods when I say, "Haze."

After another excruciating attempt, I feel Whitfield's eyes on me.

"I'm fine," I insist.

"You don't look fine. Does he look fine to you?" she asks Lawson and Elliott, who have entered the kitchen.

Lawson forces a smile. "The guy never looks fine."

"Funny," I manage in an even tone despite the fact that I'm internally falling apart.

———

The rest of the day plays out around the television. Elliott has very little to say to me or anyone else and spends most of his time watching a survival show with Brody and Ryan. In the kitchen during a commercial, he has better luck blocking Ryan than I had with Meggie, meaning he actually succeeds. All I have to show for another failed attempt at blocking is a headache, and Elliott and Whitfield are *both* worried about me. At least Lawson wasn't in the kitchen to see my blunder. He turns out to be the luckiest, not having to block Brody at all this day.

My calimeter frees me in the middle of the third episode, taking place in a desert instead of a forest like last time. Feeling worthless, I hitch on my backpack and adjust the straps. "See you later, man."

Elliott nods.

I say, "Displace," under my breath and it's up I go.

My quick coding session doesn't make my nerves feel as calm as I'd like, but I hope the time in the woods is enough to help me block again. On my way to training, I'm determined to talk to Jonathan about this problem, but when I step on the field, all thoughts of blocking are gone. Instead my cheeks burn from the attention everyone has decided to give me. It takes a great deal of self control not to reach down and make sure my fly is up.

As I get closer to the group, the unrelenting stares are enough to make my hand twitch toward my zipper.

"What?" I say to Evelynn because she's the first person I reach.

Her tongue slides over her teeth, but there's no smile or glint from her bright teeth. Instead of her usual revealing getup, her body is respectfully covered by black sweatpants and a plain white T-shirt.

Jonathan's voice diverts their attention from me, but I can still feel tension zinging through the air. "Now that we are all here, let's begin, shall we? First, I'd like formally introduce our newest arrival. This is Morgan. She will be replacing Trina." Jonathan goes on with the introductions. We all shake Morgan's hand as he ticks off how long each of us has been an Elite. My stint as an Elite is the least impressive, with less than a year under my belt.

Morgan combs her hand through her straight, brown hair and her fingers knot into the ends just below her shoulder like she's nervous. I can sympathize when I think about my first day, but selfishly, I'm glad the others' attention is off of me.

"Lawson, please pair with Morgan today," Jonathan directs after he's given Morgan the rundown about how training works. "Evelynn, why don't you pair with Grant? Jackson, please work with Reed. Billy, I'd like you to be our Watcher."

Everyone divides into pairs to take their places on the lawn. Evelynn sneers, "I don't really see the point," to Jonathan as we walk away. Very much out of character, she doesn't make a single flirtatious advance towards me on our way to the right side of the field.

"You look nice today," I say to start conversation.

She huffs like she's insulted.

"Go left?" she asks when we've stopped.

Go left? That's as out of character as her clothing, not that I'm complaining. "Perfect."

She nods and takes a few steps back, putting about fifteen feet between us. "Haze," she says when she's in position.

I concentrate on going left. My muscles tighten in anticipation and my vision dims with my blue filter.

Instead of stepping to my left, I run to her when she falls. On her knees she holds her head with both hands, making a half-angry, half-pained moan.

Before I can ask if she's OK, she yells, "Again, Jonathan! I told you something was wrong!" She's all kinds of ticked off.

Jonathan jogs over to us, followed by all the other Elites.

"I can't block!" Oh yeah, all kinds. "What the heck is an

Elite suppose to do when she can't block? This is madness! Fix me, damn it!"

Jonathan skirts around her like he's comforting an aggressive horse. "Calm down. Nobody can block Grant, remember?"

"It's not just Grant!" she yells.

"She's right. Something went wrong." Billy's anger is muted compared to the bar Evelynn has set.

"We cannot be certain of that," Jonathan answers.

"Come on!" Billy throws up his hands and his temper is more in line with what I would expect from him. "How else would you explain our sudden inability to block?"

"He's got a point," Reed agrees as he rubs his own temples just as I was earlier.

Jonathan stands there like nothing is wrong while the others come apart around him, making similar accusations.

"What are you talking about?" I demand, unable to contain my voice any longer.

And...silence. Like, eerie, awkward, all-eyes-on-me silence. Morgan is the only person who seems as oblivious as I am.

Evelynn's the first to speak. "Tell him."

"Yeah, I think we should. I mean, he should know what's going on, too. Don't you think? Something is—"

Jonathan raises his hand and Jackson stops.

"May I have a word in private?" Jonathan asks me.

I follow him, but can hear Evelynn behind us. "Unbelievable! He's not going to tell him!"

"Let him handle it," is Lawson's reply, though we're too

far for me to hear the others.

I stop and put my hands on my hips. "What aren't you going to tell me?"

Jonathan takes a long, slow breath through his nose. "How is your head?"

"What does this have to do with my head?"

"I suspect you have been suffering from headaches?"

"What's going on?" I say instead of answering his question.

"The team of Elites seem to be having difficulty blocking. Have you noticed this with Meggie as well?"

"I don't understand. Jonathan, tell me what's going on."

He's focused on the mountains. "I will. In due time, I will."

"No, now! I need to know what's wrong with me."

He has the nerve to start walking away!

"Jonathan!"

No answer.

"What the hell am I suppose to do to protect Meggie?"

Shoulders slumped, he no longer carries himself with confidence. I want to chase after him, but I'm too stunned to move. He walks past the others and says, "You're dismissed from training for the day."

Everyone but Morgan explodes with questions and rebuffs, following Jonathan up the hill. Jonathan continues as if he can't hear them.

My feet finally move after them.

"Grant?" Morgan's voice is panicked when I stalk past her. "Are you able to block?"

I stop and turn. "Are you?"

Her thin eyebrows knit together. "I haven't been released to my new assignment, but I think so. I was able to block fine on my last assignment." She pauses. "Lawson chose to block me first today. Jeez, I don't know. The last time I blocked was almost week ago. Oh no. What if I can't?"

I anxiously watch the courtyard doors as Reed and Jackson are pushing through after the others.

"Can I try blocking you?"

I have to catch up to the others. "Now's not really a good time."

I make the mistake of turning back to Morgan just as her eyes fill with water.

"Please," she begs. "What if I can't block? How am I suppose to be an Elite if I can't block?"

My mind scrambles. I have to find out what's happening, but Morgan is about to lose it. "Calm down."

She pushes up her thin shirt sleeves. "I can't calm down. I'm not cut out for this! An Elite! Why would they choose me? I don't have what it takes to be an Elite!"

"You'll be fine," I say quickly, as the courtyard doors close.

"Please, can I try and block you? I need to be sure I still can."

"OK, but we have to make this fast."

"Thank you!" She moves a few paces away from me. "Stay standing, all right?"

I glance again at the doors and nod.

"Haze," she orders.

Because I'm too preoccupied to pull my energy in, everything darkens to black and the temperature drops for an instant. My knees willingly buckle in order to stop my own screaming voice in my head commanding me to sit.

"Oh, thank the Lord!" Morgan is shouting with her hands over her head. "Thank you, Grant! Thank you so much!" She bends down and her lips peck my forehead before she runs across the field. I dumbly watch her as she skips up the stone path.

"Thanks again, Grant!" she says.

My foggy head registers that I've been blocked. Not because I remember, but because of Morgan's response. I push myself up from the ground and sprint to the door, maneuvering between Morgan and a leafy plant on the landscaped walkway.

The courtyard hallway is vacant, but down the corridor the lobby is buzzing with loud voices. Among the crowd of people, I have no luck spotting any of the Elites.

I cut a path through the groups of Satellites and head towards Benson. I need to find an Elite who will give me answers, seeing as Jonathan was zero help in that department. Once I'm in the crowded dining hall, another blow. I can't find a single Elite when I pan the faces. Even worse, my usual table of friends is vacant.

I keep searching, focused on the doorway in the back of the room in hopes that someone, anyone I can talk to may exit. Nothing.

"Have you seen Billy or Evelynn?" I ask a guy who is on his way out, figuring I'll go after the two Elites that seemed the angriest at Jonathan, and therefore, the two who may be most willing to talk.

"They just took off with some Elites. Willow, and a few others were with them."

"Did you see where they went?"

He raises his Indians ball cap, pulls it back down, and shakes his head. "Sorry. All I saw was them heading toward the lobby."

The informant must think I'm the rudest guy ever when my boots pivot and I sprint away. Not caring, I don't stop until I reach a group of about a dozen Satellites in the lobby. "Have you seen Billy or Evelynn?" I blurt out.

By their reaction, they must think I've escaped the asylum.

"How about Willow? Or maybe Rigby or Owen?"

Nothing.

I move on to the next group and get the same empty results. It's not until I reach my eleventh inquiry when someone is finally able to point towards the Y Hallway branching off the marble lobby.

I run there, murmuring my apologies when I bump a few people along the way.

Bingo.

There at the end of the hall, close to the gold cherub elevator, is everyone I've been searching for. All the Elites, minus Morgan, along with my usual Benson friends are collected in a tight huddle. I can't make out what's being said, but I easily recognize Willow's voice doing the talking.

"Hey!" I yell.

I'm about tired of this look from everyone today.

I stalk towards them. "Will someone please tell me what the hell is going on?"

"Oh, for the love," Willow mumbles and shows her usual annoyance by my dramatic approach.

Evelynn steps back from the circle, making room for me to join them. "He needs to know."

"I don't think that is a good idea. Jonathan would have told him if he needed to know. I don't want to go against Jonathan here. I mean, he always has his reasons for—"

"Shut it, Jackson," Billy says. "I agree with Evelynn."

"I don't know, man, Jackson might be right." Lawson says.

"Why shouldn't he know?" Clara asks. "This is about him."

"Yeah, he's the reason we can't block," Billy adds.

My anger ramps up. "How am I the reason?"

Anna repeatedly taps her toe on the floor and glances down the hall. "What do you think, Willow?"

Willow doesn't answer.

"We should tell him," Elliott says.

Liam is as nervous as Anna. "I don't know…"

Rigby pulls the toothpick from his mouth. "He's going to find out eventually. I mean, how long can Jonathan keep this from him? Look at you all. None of you can block and Whitfield confirmed that Grant can't either. She suspects something is going on and it's only a matter of time before others are going to catch on as well. I'm tired of lying to my girl. If you don't tell him what's going on, I will. I'm not keeping this secret."

"Let's vote on it."

Everyone, myself included, freezes on Jackson because he's never made such a direct statement. As long as I've known the guy, at least.

"Fine. We'll vote. Those in favor of telling him?" Willow purses her lips and waits for a show of hands.

Rigby's and Evelynn's go up, followed by Billy, Clara, Elliott, and mine—assuming my hand counts.

I wait for Willow to make a move. Finally, her hand rises into the air as well, breaking the tie.

Then, with the worst timing ever, my calimeter buzzes.

The others reach for their watches.

A slow breath goes through Willow's nose. "Saved by the bell. Let's meet here at next break."

There's no way I can wait until break. "Tell me now!"

"Sorry, kid, but duty calls. Next break it is. See you all then."

Before I can argue, Lawson and Liam have dropped through the floor and the others follow one by one. Owen and Anna kiss goodbye and are the last ones to disappear, aside from Willow.

"See you later, kid. Chin up, 'K?"

"Willow, come on! I'm going to be worthless back on my assignment."

"Seeing as you can't block, I agree. It won't hurt to keep trying, though."

"Won't hurt? My head might explode off my neck!"

"Don't be so dramatic," she tries to joke.

"Seriously, Willow, what about my Tragedy?"

Willow is speechless. This is worse than I thought.

"What about you? Can you block?"

Willow shakes her head. "I'm sorry, Grant. I really am."

"What are you sorry for? Give me something here!"

She takes three strides and wraps her arms around me. "Better get back to your Tragedy. Do your best today, kid. I'll see you at break." With that, she releases me and starts toward the lobby.

Tempted to go after her, I choose Meggie instead. Even if there's nothing I can do for her, the pull is still there to try and protect her the best that I can. Problem is, without my blocking ability, I have no idea how.

I land at Meggie's and make a quick plan B. Maybe Lawson or Elliott will be willing to give me something.

Maybe not.

"Please," I beg the guys after they both tell me no.

"We'll discuss it as a group," Lawson says in a firm voice.

Whitfield paces the small living area in front of the T.V. If she were human, she'd surely have Brody, Ryan, and Max yelling at her to get out of the way. "I knew something was going on! Rigby's so distant lately. Is this why, whatever *this* is?" She freezes with her hands on her hips.

Without a word, Lawson pushes himself up from the floor and walks into the kitchen behind Brody.

"You are so infuriating! Just tell the guy what's going on. I want to know, too!" Whitfield yells after him.

"He won't talk." I've known the guy long enough to

know that much.

"Elliott?" Whitfield directs.

"Sorry. I would, but I have to stick with the group on this. We'll tell him at break. I'm sure Rigby will fill you in soon."

"Tell him what?"

"I really am sorry." Elliott says to me, and then disappears into the kitchen with Ryan.

What's with all the apologies? And how could I have anything to do with everyone's inability to block?

Instead of making myself crazy mulling this over, I read Meggie's assignment book and learn that Brody is returning to the highway department tomorrow. I worry about how Meggie will handle being alone all day. The next paragraph answers my question. Just as I feared, she's going to struggle. A lot. My nervous stomach begins to cramp. How am I going to protect her? Before I can dwell too long on that, Meggie falls into her first crying spell.

"Haze," I say, silently praying that my Satellite ability will miraculously reappear.

It doesn't. All that I'm left with is the headache of the century and an irate Whitfield.

Nancy comes to the rescue for the second time, consoling Meggie the best she can. I follow the girls into the kitchen, ignoring Whitfield's fifty questions along the way. Lawson watches me with pity in his eyes, which makes me even angrier. My only saving grace is seeing Brody pour a Coke, straight up. If the guy was still drinking, I'd be in a world of hurt.

After successfully ignoring Whitfield's questions—not a difficult task seeing as I don't have a single answer to what's going on with me—the party ends an hour later. My head still hurts and I'm all for some quiet time.

"I'll see you at break. I really am sorry, Grant. I need you to know that. What we did…" Elliott trails off. "I'm sorry." He's broken enough that I can't push him for information even though every part of me is screaming to do just that. Whitfield's on it, though, following Elliott with a slew of questions pouring from her mouth, most of which are "tell me what's going on" phrased a bunch of different ways.

Brody gathers the last of the empty pizza boxes before taking the trashcan out to the curb.

Meggie and I head into the bathroom where she starts filling the clawfoot tub. I silently excuse myself before she gets undressed and sit on the bed while she bathes. Brody comes in ten minutes later and joins her in the bathroom.

Lawson sits beside me.

"So you can't block either?" I ask after a few silent minutes.

He shakes his head. "I've been fortunate that Brody has had a couple decent days. I've only had to try a few times."

"When did you first notice you couldn't?"

He takes his time answering and the secret they're all keeping grates on my nerves.

"The day before you came back on assignment," he finally says.

"The others, what they said…how could this possibly have anything to do with me? I was on probation. I wasn't even around!"

Lawson takes a deep breath. "I have a few theories. They seem to be in line with what the others think."

Whitfield was right, Lawson is seriously infuriating! Break can't come soon enough. Knowing I'll never get Lawson to talk, I decide to drop it. "So Brody's going back to work?"

Lawson nods. "Tomorrow. He's going to be part-time for a while. You think Meggie will go back soon?"

"I have no idea. I hope so. I thought being around babies would be awful for her, but when she spent an afternoon visiting them at the hospital she actually seemed peaceful."

"Maybe that's the way it was supposed to work, you know? Maybe that's why she does what she does."

"Are you really giving me the whole 'everything happens for a reason' bit?"

Lawson shrugs his massive shoulders. "Who knows. Maybe."

Yeah, maybe. Or maybe her kids could have *not* burned to death. I decide not to open my big mouth and instead, our conversation ends.

About an hour later, when Brody's deep breathing has fallen into a solid pattern, Lawson leaves the room, probably to avoid another line of questioning. I stay parked in the corner of the bedroom, worrying about tomorrow. Watching Meggie sleep, the question lingers in my head: how will I help her?

The next morning Brody makes Meggie breakfast before kissing her goodbye and heading off to his first day back in the field. He looks nervous, either because he has to leave her or because he's trying to meld back into normal life. Probably both.

Meggie busies herself with laundry and cleaning the house. She talks to Janine for a while on the phone and then takes a nap. After waking from a nightmare, she makes a late lunch, and does a better job of mutilating her sandwich than actually eating it. After an hour, she gives up on the crumbled bread and washes her plate. Her composure breaks when she's at the sink.

"Haze!"

More Pain!

Damn it!

"Haze!"

Ooooouch!

Meggie's knees buckle and she slides her back down the cabinets, hitting the vinyl floor. She cries and cries. And cries. And cries.

After three more attempts at blocking, I cannot physically continue. I hold my ears, certain that something—blood or maybe my whole brain—is oozing from them.

Meggie gets up and I convince myself that she's going to pull herself out of this.

She slides open the utensil drawer and her hand disappears inside, emerging with a sharp knife.

"Meggie, no!" I roar, forgetting all about my head, and cross to her. My body ghosts through hers in my effort to take the knife away.

Focus, Grant, focus.

"Haze!"

Oh, it hurts!

Through my watery eyes, Meggie is blurred as she turns the knife over in her hand, examining the sharp blade.

"Meggie, please! No!" I plead, now crying with her. "No, no, no," I sob.

A different approach comes to mind. I focus my energy and try to hug the color around the knife. The filter is too weak and only tints the silver in the lightest blue. I take a shot anyway, grabbing for the knife. Like my body, my hands ghost through the blade.

I yell out a final plea when Meggie rests the shiny blade on her wrist. "Somebody help me!"

Sinking to the floor in pain, exhaustion, and despair, I cry into my knees. "Please, Meggie! Please don't do this. Oh God, don't do this. Brody needs you. Those babies need you. This world needs you." This is all true. I know deep in my core that there is a reason she must live through this hell. She MUST! "Meggie, please," I sob.

"Shh, it's OK," a whispering voice says. "Mom, it's OK. I'm here. I'm here for you now."

My head lifts slowly because I know that I'm delusional. It couldn't possibly…

The guy standing beside Meggie pushes his blond hair

off his forehead. My eyes grow wider and I use my palm to push away the pooling water, sure that I am hallucinating.

"It's OK, you're going to be all right. Can you feel me here with you? I love you, Mom. Please don't do this to yourself." His deep voice throws me off, but the resemblance is there.

The sound of metal hitting the countertop makes me jump. Air gurgles through Meggie's runny nose and she wipes her eyes.

"Josh?" she whispers.

I have brain damage. It's the only explanation.

"I'm here! I'm right here, Mom."

Meggie begins sobbing again, but this time her cries are different, hopeful, maybe even happy. She comes down to my level on the floor and wraps her arms around her legs.

Josh kneels in front of her and tries to hug himself around her. Instead, he ghosts through her legs and makes a sour face. When he recovers from his obvious frustration, he puts his face close to hers.

"I love you, Mom. I miss you so much, but I'll see you again. You have to stay strong for me. You have to stay strong for Sophie and Harper. They love you, too."

My mouth moves, but no sound comes. When I'm finally able to talk, my voice cracks.

"Josh?"

The guy looks over at me.

"How did you get here?" I ask, surprised that my voice even works.

He puts up his index finger and raises it to his lips in a *shh* gesture. Then he returns his attention to Meggie, trying to wrap his arms around her again. He awkwardly holds his head on her knee as if resting it there, close to Meggie's face.

25. Oh, honey, his trouble started way before becoming an Elite

After landing in my room, I head straight to the Y hall. I'm out of breath when I reach the others. Everyone but Rigby is already congregated in a tight group.

"Josh came back!" are the first words out of my mouth.

Lawson is the only one who understands what I'm saying.

"Meggie's son, Meggie's *dead* son! He's older now. Shoot, maybe thirty even, but he was there in the kitchen with her!"

"That's impossible," Lawson says.

"It was him, I know it was. He helped Meggie. I couldn't block her, she was about to…he saved her life!"

"Her son? On Earth?" Willow questions.

"Are you sure it was Josh?"

I nod to Lawson, ignoring the doubt on his face, and then turn to Willow. "Tell me what's going on."

The others become very still after turning to Willow.

"Lawson told me you don't remember your fiancée." Willow lifts her eyes to the ceiling. For a second, I'm not sure if she's talking to me or someone else. "I figured as much, but that hasn't always been the case. You didn't forget Tate when you got here." Willow continues, despite my glazed over expression. "You broke the rules and went back to see her during your last assignment. Something I wasn't all that thrilled to hear."

The disappointment on her face pains me. "Willow, I wouldn't have left Ryder—"

"You did," she says sharply.

I wouldn't have done that to her, or her son. No way. She has to know this. "Willow, I would have never—"

She cuts me off again. "Tate broke your connection to her by destroying all of the material things you gave her. You forgot her. I wasn't thrilled about that either, but that's how things are supposed to happen here, right? Each of us forgets our previous life." She takes a breath. "I didn't accept this so I took you back to her, which was a huge, careless mistake on my part. And just when I thought things couldn't get any worse, you connected to her again."

Rigby joins us, but is as silent as everyone else as Willow talks.

"Jonathan convinced us all that Tate was getting worse, that your connection to her was the reason. He convinced us all that we had the power necessary to break the connection again. It was a lie. He just wanted you to be like the rest of us. It had nothing to do with Tate."

Liam takes a step forward. "Willow, you're out of line. She *was* getting worse."

"That wasn't Jonathan's motivation."

"You don't know that," Liam argues.

"She got better when Grant was there. You said so yourself." Willow pauses. "Anyway, Jonathan conjured this mission for us. He trained us to preform a group block. It would have worked, too, if you hadn't intervened. You showed up and none of us were prepared for that."

This girl has officially gone *muy loco*. "What are you talking about?"

The others nod, backing up Willow's crazy story. I would remember. Wouldn't I?

A small voice in my head reminds me that I don't remember being blocked by Morgan. Could Willow actually be telling the truth?

"You used your special power, kid."

"What special power?"

"You blocked our block," Evelynn says in explanation.

"And stole our ability!" Billy's expression says he and I are not, by any means, BFFs right now, and probably never will be.

"That's our theory," Lawson adds.

Liam clears his throat. "It's not a theory, it's the truth. Tate still remembers Grant."

Willow is all kinds of angry. "In essence, Jonathan's plan worked. He got you back." She taps the back of her boot heel on the marble floor. "What he didn't consider was that when he got you back, you'd be worthless."

"Or that Tate would still be messed up," Liam whispers.

"He didn't consider we'd all be worthless!" Billy adds.

"Seriously? *None* of you can block?" No way.

Elliott scratches the top of his head. "Only the ones who blocked you."

"Who blocked me?"

"All of the Elites and I," Willow explains in a lowered voice when a couple Satellites come off the elevator and walk past us.

Willow turns away from me. "I'm sorry. Jonathan convinced us it was for the best."

I try to take the information in. It doesn't make sense because I remember nothing, but at the same time, the proof is in my inability to block. And no one is wearing a face that's about to say "gotcha." Instead, they maintain their seriousness; Willow, Clara, and Anna even look sad.

"What about the rest of you?"

"They were there to wake us up," Reed explains. "Through our training, we learned that a group block is not only painful, but it knocks us out. Literally."

"You all took part in this," I whisper, more to myself.

No one says anything or makes eye contact with me. Everyone except Billy, that is, who I think wants to cut me up and grill me for dinner.

"Why would you do that?"

Jackson plays with the cuff of his plaid shirt. "We trusted Jonathan. I mean, why wouldn't we? He's never steered us wrong before. Right guys? We didn't know what was going to happen. We didn't know you were going to be there. We didn't—"

"It's your fault!" Billy says with venom. "If you hadn't showed up everything would have gone as planned. You stole our ability!"

Lawson vice grips Billy's arm when Billy lunges forward. "Cool it, man. It's not his fault. He didn't know this would happen either."

Billy struggles against Lawson. "Princess, here, has been nothing but trouble since he became an Elite!"

"Oh, honey, his trouble started way before becoming an Elite," Willow says dryly.

"Hey! I didn't even want to be an Elite!"

Billy fights against Lawson when I say this. "You've got a lot of nerve!"

"Seriously, Grant, insult to injury," Evelynn feels the need to throw in.

"Shouldn't *I* be the one angry? I'm assuming you were all willing to play out Jonathan's little mission?"

"We weren't all willing. We just did what was asked of us," Elliott argues.

"It's true," Anna agrees. "None of us could have known what was going to happen. Not even Jonathan."

We all settle down after getting eyed up by two Satellites passing by. Billy straightens his collar when Lawson lets him go.

Not sure where to go with this new information, I ask, "So now what?"

No one answers.

Willow breaks the long silence. "Who do you think sent Josh?"

"If he was really there."

Lawson's dirty look gets under my skin. Why would he

doubt me?

Willow paces the small space between the others. "I can't see Jonathan doing this. It messes too much with people's destinies."

"That's obviously already happened. Surely Jonathan would be concerned about damage control now," Reed adds.

"Who cares who sent the guy?" Evelynn chews on her bright pink thumb nail. "There has to be a way for us to get our ability back."

"Jackson, you said you felt stronger when you coded, right?" Willow asks.

"A little stronger, maybe. I felt relaxed for sure, but I wasn't able to block any better. Willow, how are we supposed to help our Tragedies?"

"Well, seeing as we don't have many options here, I think you should all go code before heading back to your assignments. Let's meet on the training field at break."

Anna goes to work twisting her hair into a ponytail. "What about us?"

"You guys, too."

Anna finishes the last wrap of the rubber band and slides her hand along the top of her head. "Are we allowed to be there while the Elites are training?"

"At this point, training is a waste of time, so what's it matter?" Billy says.

Owen nods. "Good point."

"I'll give Jonathan the heads up that you're all coming." With that, Willow turns and begins walking toward the lobby. Reed follows, and the others take his cue.

I grab Lawson's arm and pull him closer to me. "It was Josh. I swear it."

Lawson shakes his head. "I don't get it. How is that possible?"

"I don't know, but having him there saved her life. I was worthless."

He nods, though I'm still not sure he believes me.

"How was Brody's first day back on the job?" I shout down the hall after him.

"Apparently better than Meggie's day," he hollers over his shoulder.

I make the trek back to my room and think about the information Willow shared. The story sounds far-fetched, but I have no more theories and the others seemed on board with her. Nerves make my stomach knot up because I have zero recollection of any of it, not even the part about me being engaged.

I drop my backpack inside the door and head down the hall, figuring I'll change clothes after I code. I've noticed the girls around here start to look at me funny when I wear the same outfit for days at a time. Silly, really, considering nothing I wear ever gets dirty and always smells decent.

When I'm cross-legged on the mat, I close my eyes to my reflection in the mirror. Yes, the clothes are fine. My hair, on the other hand, could benefit from a combing.

My body relaxes as I count down from ten. By the time I reach number four, I'm in my tree stand on the edge of the overgrown field. When the monster buck crosses the clearing, my muscles are like wet spaghetti.

Something at the wood line catches my attention, but I can't get my eyes to focus on the bright pink blur of color.

"Hello?"

The buck doesn't startle at my loud voice.

I blink to get my eyes to work, but when I open them, the shape is gone. Or maybe it was never there in the first place. The latter is probably more likely. Regardless, I feel too relaxed to overthink anything. This may be the first time in days that the dull ache in my head is completely gone.

Feeling good, I watch the buck eat from the field for a few more minutes.

When I pull myself out of my head and back into the coding room, I stand and stretch my arms, which feel as limber as when I was in my tree stand. I pray that the coding session has helped. Maybe today will be different; maybe my blocking ability has returned. I swallow the lump in my throat that's telling me otherwise.

As planned, I make a quick wardrobe change in the closet, which consists of a lighter pair of jeans and a red T-shirt instead of blue. I opt to keep the same pair of boots. My calimeter buzzes when I'm finishing my coffee.

I drop from my kitchen into Meggie's. She's in the same place I left her, hugging her knees on the floor. Unlike before, though, Josh isn't here. Despite this, Meggie seems better. When she comes back to life with the lights, she wipes her eyes with her palm and sniffs a few times before using the counter to pull herself up.

I read through the day's events quickly, learning that Brody will be back within the hour. I wish Josh were here to prove to Lawson that I'm not crazy. Meggie digs in the fridge and pulls out a package of ground beef, compliments of one of Janine's food deliveries. Then she actually opens the package and fires up the stove burner. To see her do anything normal is promising. Could Josh's visit have helped that much?

By the time Meggie is finished making tacos, Brody's home.

"Dinner?" Lawson sounds as surprised as I was when he walks in behind Brody.

"I know, right?"

"Did you block her?"

I shake my head and hope the look on Lawson's face goes away.

"How about you? Did you have to block Brody yet?"

"No, not yet, but I will soon."

"Great," I mumble.

Brody seems excited about dinner. He thanks Meggie, kisses her forehead, and tells her he's going to go change clothes.

Lawson takes a deep breath. "That's my cue. Wish me luck."

"Changing clothes is going to set him off?"

"The routine of it. He would always play with the kids for a few minutes before dinner."

Oh, jeez. "Good luck," I say with one hundred percent sincerity.

Meggie is filling two taco shells when Lawson runs into the kitchen. I almost jump out of my boots from his baritone voice.

"They're here!"

"Who?"

"Harper and Sophie! They're in the bedroom!"

I bump Lawson's shoulder in my hurry to get past him. The girls at Brody's feet are not the girls I saw in Meggie's past. The two blondes, roughly in their mid-twenties, are thin like Meggie with sharper cheekbones and fuller lips. One has hair bluntly cut just above her shoulders; the other has the same straight hair, but down to her waist. Both are in the middle of a quiet rendition of *Twinkle Twinkle Little Star*. Normally, I would find it strange to see two grown women singing at someone's feet, but under the circumstances, witnessing this is actually kind of beautiful. Brody takes deep breaths during the serenade while tears stream down his face.

"We love you, Daddy," the girls say in unison when the song is over. This seems to spark more tears from Brody.

"Don't cry, Dad, we're right here," the short-haired girl says

The other girl laughs, "I don't think he can actually hear us, Soph."

"Sure he can." She watches Brody for a few seconds. "See, he's smiling."

"I don't believe it!"

I turn at Lawson's voice. "I don't either. It's working, though. They're making him better." Before I can say anything to the girls, they zoom upward and disappear into the ceiling.

Lawson and I are quiet—presumably he's as dumbfounded by all of this as I am—while Brody changes clothes. We follow him into the kitchen and he gives Meggie a kiss with more oomph this time.

"You believe me now about Josh?" I ask, although I already know the answer.

"I can't believe how much they look like Meggie," Lawson whispers, but says nothing else for a long time.

"We've got to talk to Jonathan about this," I tell Lawson while Meggie and Brody eat.

"You think?"

"He sent them."

Lawson is skeptical. "We don't know that."

"Who else could it have been?"

"I'm not sure. If it is Jonathan behind this, he should probably be told their presence, whatever it means, seems to be working for these two."

"So, at break we'll tell him."

Lawson nods and then the two of us silently watch Meggie and Brody finish their dinner.

———

Lawson and I get to the courtyard doors at the same time during break. Walking onto the field together, we go straight for Jonathan, who appears to be doing crowd control for the larger than normal group. Morgan, new to this mess, stays at a safe distance outside of the group.

"What are we supposed to do?" Evelynn is shouting. "My Tragedy is a mess!"

"This is madness!" Billy hollers over Evelynn.

Owen's voice is as loud as the others. "You have to

listen to them. Something has to be done."

"Jonathan, a word?" Lawson's deep voice is enough to silence the others, and Jonathan seems relieved to get a break from the chatter.

"I know you are all anxious for answers, but please excuse me for a moment."

I put my hands on my hips. "No, here."

"I would like to speak in private," Jonathan asserts.

"Come on." Lawson motions me with a head nod to the right.

"No. This is affecting all of us. No more secrets."

Willow takes a step forward and there's poison in her frown. "I second that. No more secrets."

Jonathan's eyes are tired, and he takes a long time before answering. "Fine. Here, then."

"Sophie and Harper were there today."

Silence follows, but Jonathan does not appear shocked by this news.

Reed steps further into the haphazard circle. "Who are Sophie and Harper?"

"My Tragedy's daughters," after a few seconds, Lawson adds, "His dead daughters. Did you send them?" he asks Jonathan.

Willow twists a dreadlock between her thumb and index finger. "Grant, didn't you say, some other kid was with your Tragedy earlier?"

I nod. "Josh. Sophie and Harper are her kids, too."

"Wait, I don't..." Anna's mouth drops open. "She lost three children?"

"Their children couldn't have been there. That's impossible, right Jonathan? Or are they Satellites? Even then, though, how could they—"

Jonathan raises his hand to stop Jackson.

"Our Tragedies got better without any interference from us," I blurt out.

Jonathan's expression is hard to read as we all wait for him to say something.

"I'm going to assume what you are describing is mere illusion. In the meantime, keep doing your best. Liam would you please come with me?"

That's it?

"Our best?" Evelynn shouts to Jonathan's back as him and Liam walk toward the doors. "We can't block!"

"It wasn't an illusion! Meggie's kids were there!" I yell.

Jonathan ignores us both. Liam turns to Jonathan while they walk, probably waiting for an answer like we are.

Frustrated, my attention returns to the group. Morgan would obviously rather be anywhere but here, and I can't blame her. Billy is uncharacteristically speechless. His face says enough, though, and I half expect him to charge Jonathan.

"Now what?" Lawson asks.

Evelynn's blue dress catches the sun when she spins around, making the material look like rippling water. "Now we continue to suck! This is ridiculous."

Clara uses a consoling voice. "Jonathan will fix this."

"Easy for you to say! You can still block!"

When Clara recovers from Evelynn's bad attitude, she

asks, "When has he ever let anyone down?"

"There's a first time for everything." Evelynn stalks off toward the trees.

Willow parks herself on the ground. Jackson and Billy follow, joined by Elliott who goes to work at mindlessly picking blades of grass.

"So your Tragedies' kids really showed up, huh?" Willow asks.

Lawson and I sit, and the remaining members of our group—Liam, Rigby, Clara, Anna, Owen, and Morgan—do the same.

Lawson squeezes his forehead. "I didn't believe it until I saw them myself. The girls are grown up now, so I wasn't sure at first, but they share so many of their mom's features, I knew. They really helped Brody, I'd venture to say even more than my blocking." He focuses on the mountain range in the distance. "When my ability actually worked, that is."

No one speaks for a long time until Lawson says, "I'm sorry, Grant. What Jonathan made us do was wrong. We should never have gone along with it; it never felt right to me."

"Me neither," Elliott adds in a quiet voice.

"What will we do if we can never block again?" Jackson's eyes are pleading as he searches Willow for an answer.

"I don't know, Jack." Willow turns over her flip flop with her bare foot. "I just don't know." After a few minutes, she stands up and slides her shoes back on. "Let's try some blocking drills."

"What for?" Billy grumbles.

"You got something better to do? Come on, get up. Evelynn, we're going to practice!" Willow yells across the field.

Evelynn ignores her. Billy shares Evelynn's sour attitude, but the rest of us stand.

"Should I go?" Morgan questions.

Willow turns to her. "Have you begun your assignment yet?"

Morgan shakes her head.

"You should stay. You're going to want to build up your tolerance for what's ahead. Reed, would you work with Morgan?"

Reed nods and Morgan follows him to a vacant place on the field.

In true Willow form, she takes the lead and breaks the rest of the Satellites—minus Evelynn and Billy—into groups. She sends me across the field with Anna.

After some small talk, I try to block Anna three times with no success. The only thing that comes from my attempts is the feeling that my skull splitting in half. During a much needed break, we watch the others work. Willow, Lawson, and Jackson are having the same bad luck. Lawson is rubbing his temples and, by his angry expression, I'd say he's feeling about as good as I am. Evelynn and Billy must have decided to join in the fun, because Billy's stomping his feet in a toddler-like rage when Evelynn stands up and gets back into a position to be blocked.

Morgan is the only Elite making any progress with

Reed. Jealously roots and makes my throat tight.

Before I succumb to another failure, my calimeter buzzes, sending my migraine into overdrive.

Anna mimics my movement, reaching for her watch. "We'll keep trying."

Her words make me want to punch something, while the empathy in her voice makes me want to hug her. Anna is so selfless, and ultimately, my emotions get the better of me and I do hug her.

"Thanks," I say into her hair.

She wraps her arms tightly around me, which eases my nerves. "We'll figure this out," she muffles into my chest. "I'm sorry this happened, Grant. I wish you remembered Tate. Elliott and Willow both say you loved her so much. I don't think it's right to have such strong feelings about someone and then just forget them. I can't believe we all agreed..." She pulls away.

"You did what you had to. You're a good person, Anna, and a really good friend."

A tear rolls down her cheek. "You're a good friend, too." She pauses and half laughs. "We'd better get over to Willow before her arms fall off."

Over my shoulder, I can't help but grin. Willow is flailing her arms, presumably to everyone on the field, in a motion that says "come here."

Willow's already begun her speech by the time Anna and I reach her. "...must get back to your assignments. Let's get together in the Y hall at next break. I'll let Liam know where we're meeting. Morgan, even though this doesn't directly affect you, you're welcome to join us if you'd like."

"This doesn't have anything to do with her."

Billy's icy tone toward Morgan is uncalled for and Lawson gives him a disagreeable look. "I think what Billy means is, you may want to avoid getting involved in this mess. You'll have plenty of other things to worry about soon."

"I, for one, say there's nothing wrong with including another mind, hers especially. She has the advantage of not being directly involved and may be able to give us some fresh insight," Willow says.

Elliott seconds. "I agree."

"Of course you do, you always agree with her!" Billy jabs.

"Do not!" Elliott argues.

"No, dude, you actually do." Lawson smiles and his delivery lightens the foul mood enough that even I'm laughing.

Willow clears her throat. "Morgan, you're capable of making your own decisions. Know that you are welcome, if you choose to join us." Willow's eyes circle around the group. "Good luck, everyone."

26. Dear God, you're rambling like Jackson

When we've landed back on Earth, Lawson confirms that his head feels about as good as mine. Through the dull throbbing, we try to come up with ideas for how to resurrect our blocking ability while Meggie and Brody clean up the kitchen from dinner. Our conversation doesn't go very far because the only things we can think of are more coding and practice, neither of which have helped so far. This is bad news because tomorrow Meggie and Brody are both going to have a tough day. At least Brody has the day off work.

I turn my attention to Meggie when she tells Brody she's been thinking about going back to work herself. She's planning on calling the hospital in the morning to see about picking up a few part-time shifts.

Remembering Meggie at the hospital nursery holding the newborns raises my spirits. I'm up for anything that may help her get through this horrible time in her life. "That'll be good. She's a sucker for babies."

Sitting on the counter, Lawson crosses his legs and messes with an unraveled string from his shoelace. "You'd think a job like that would be tough for her, considering what she's lost."

"I would have thought the same thing, but you should have seen her the day she visited the nursery. She seemed almost happy." I pause. "What are we going to do tomorrow?"

"I guess we can only hope that their kids show up. We're surely going to be worthless."

I nod and watch Meggie scrub a pan. She and Brody are now as silent as Lawson and me. At least none of us are crying. That's a big win.

After the kitchen is clean, Brody turns on the sports channel and Meggie gets on the computer to pay a few bills. They both give in to sleep around nine-thirty and the night, thankfully, is relatively nightmare free.

The next morning, Meggie calls the hospital while Brody makes omelets. She shares the phone conversation with Brody while she picks at her eggs. Meggie's manager has been understanding about Meggie's schedule and will welcome Meggie back whenever she is ready. Brody and she discuss this for a while and Meggie decides she'll work on the same days Brody is working.

"We may as well share the same shifts," Meggie is saying, "seeing as we no longer have to worry about daycare." After the words are out, her face contorts in horror.

"Oh, no," Lawson whispers.

Tears spill down Meggie's cheeks and Brody grabs for her hand. Meggie pulls away hard enough to bump her drink, which results in the trill of breaking glass.

Brody scoots his chair out. "It's OK, Meg, I got it."

"It's not OK! Nothing will ever be OK!"

"Haze," I say out of habit and instantly regret the order.

Through the pounding in my head, my expression is pleading. Lawson, however, has no help to offer.

Meggie continues to escalate and I continue to panic.

"Lawson, what do I do?"

Lawson covers his face with his hands, making small circles with his fingertips on his forehead. My eyes burn into him, wishing he had an answer that would fix this mess.

"Mom?" The higher pitched voice carries over the chaos.

Meggie freezes at the same time Brody pauses over the glass fragments. Lawson lowers his hands to see the two girls and guy that I'm seeing.

"Mom," the short-haired girl says again. "It's OK."

Meggie's breathing slows and more tears fall from her eyes as she stands frozen by the table.

"We all love you, Mom. We miss you so much, but you have to stay strong." Almost a head taller than his mom now, Josh bends down to put his face close to Meggie's after his arms ghost through her shoulders once.

A loud, single sob escapes from Meggie.

"Do you feel that?" she whispers, prompting Brody to stand. "I can feel them."

"Mom, we're right here." With similar difficulty to what Josh had, the long-haired girl's hand slips through Meggie's upper arm.

Her twin lifts her hand so that it rests inside Brody's hand, and Brody looks down at his daughter, though there's no way he could really be seeing her. "The kids?"

"I can feel them," Meggie repeats and takes a long breath.

Brody walks around the glass to get to Meggie with the short-haired girl close by his side. The girl steps back when Brody wraps his arms around his wife. Josh and the long-haired girl stand close to their mom and dad, seeming pleased by their parents' embrace.

"The family is together again." I don't mean to say this out loud.

"And it's working," Lawson whispers.

"Josh, can you hear me?" Lawson asks.

Josh doesn't turn away from his parents, but nods.

"Did Jonathan send you?" is Lawson's next question.

Josh finally speaks. "Who are you?"

I don't know what to say, so it's Lawson that speaks first. "We're Satellites. We were sent here to watch over your parents after your deaths."

Josh steps towards me. "Then why aren't you doing that?"

"Josh!" the short-haired girl hisses.

"Something happened. We're usually much better than this," Lawson assures.

"Why can't *they* watch over their parents?" my voice says before I can stop myself. "Don't give me that look!" I say to Lawson. "Seriously, consider what they've done in just a few short minutes compared to what we've done, and we've been here for months!"

Lawson uses a low voice like the others won't hear him.

"Because that's not the way it works."

"But it could." I pause. "I mean, why couldn't it?"

"That's not their purpose."

I turn back to Meggie's kids, though they are now grown adults. "What's your purpose?"

The girl with the long hair answers first. "I'm a Tocket Hunter."

Josh doesn't take his eyes off Meggie. "I'm a Guardian."

"What's that?" I ask.

With some effort, he finally turns away from his mom. "I intervene before bad things happen. Kids getting pummeled by baseballs or semi-trucks, that sort of thing."

"Huh," is my only response. Willow said everyone has a purpose, but I had never put much thought into other departments. "Where do you live?"

"In Progression."

Confused, I defer to Lawson.

"Progression houses the departments in different wings," he explains.

"No way," I mumble. "That would mean Progression holds hundreds of thousands of people."

Lawson agrees like this is no big deal.

Forcing my mind off the mere size of Progression, I ask the short-haired girl, "What do you do?"

"I'm a Scheduler."

My eyes about bounce off the linoleum. Even Lawson can't hide his shock.

"Er, a Scheduler-in-training I guess is more appropriate."

Lawson shock turns to awe. "You've landed a heck of a

job. What's it like?"

"There's a lot of research involved: studying family histories, relational interconnections, that sort of thing. Recently, I've been learning the stages of grief." Her expression turns to sadness, but then lifts. "I'm having a problem with the guess work involved in planning someone's life. The other Schedulers tell me this will become easier through the years. I'm Sophie, by the way." She crosses to me and shakes my hand, then moves to Lawson for another formal introduction.

Josh and Harper follow her lead. I drill into my head which twin is which, Harper with the long hair, Sophie with the short hair. *Harper Long Hair, Sophie Short Hair…* I repeat in my head to remember for the future.

"Did you all lose your memories as well?" Lawson asks.

"We're supposed to."

"Supposed to?" I ask Josh.

"Someone had to pull a few strings for us to be here." He pauses and his voice gets quiet, "We wouldn't do much good if we didn't remember our parents."

"So you have your memories still?"

Sophie Short Hair taps on her forehead. "All there. They were gone for awhile, until we went through Programming."

"Sophie!" Harper Long Hair gives her sister the shut up look.

"Has having your memories affected your jobs?" I ask to no one in particular.

Lawson shifts his position on the countertop, straightening his broad shoulders. "We shouldn't be talking about this."

Irritated by all this hush-hush crap, I can't keep my mouth closed. "Why not?"

Lawson hops off the counter and hits my shoulder when he walks by me. "A word?"

"Have you not learned anything?" he hisses in my face when we're in the living room.

"Hey, there's nothing wrong with a little curiosity. What's with this place, anyway? No one questions anything. We just go about our business because that's the way things are? I'm sorry, but I don't like the way things are. Why does it have to be this way for Meggie and Brody?"

Lawson appears to be trying hard not to roll his eyes.

"Those kids shouldn't be dead!"

"This isn't just about their purpose, it's about Meggie and Brody's purpose, too. Don't forget that. You can't change the way things are written. Nothing ever changes, so you just need to go with it."

I chew on my lip and my anger is apparent to Lawson.

"Come on, man, this is our job."

"We're worthless here! Those kids have done more good for Meggie and Brody than we've been able to do in months. What does that tell you about our job?"

"It is what it is."

"It doesn't have to be!" I say this to Lawson's back as he's walking through the kitchen doorway. He doesn't even pause, which infuriates me more.

The adult kids stay close to Meggie and Brody for the rest of the afternoon and I keep my questions to myself because none of the answers are satisfying. Lawson and I continue to play the silent treatment game since we seem to be so good at it.

When it's time to go, I blurt out the question that's been stuck in my mind for an hour. "If you had a choice, would you choose to be dead?"

Josh, Sophie, and Harper exchange a look that says they're considering whether or not they should answer. Lawson rolls his eyes.

Josh bites. "My work as a Guardian has been cool and I'm excited to learn more," he pauses, "but, no. I would never choose this for my parents. I want to help them." He turns to Meggie and Brody, frozen on the couch with Meggie's head resting on Brody's shoulder. "I hope we can continue to help them."

After the three of them say goodbye to their parents-turned-mannequins, Josh disappears into the kitchen. When he comes back a few seconds later, the palm of his right hand is just under his nose and he's concentrating comically hard. When he reaches the coffee table, he lowers his hand, turns his wrist, and something small drops from his palm with a tiny clink, too quiet for Meggie or Brody to notice. Then he grabs Sophie and Harper's hands and the three of them whisper the magic traveling word that makes them disappear into the ceiling.

I raise my eyebrows at Lawson on my way to the table. There, in front of Meggie on the dark wood, Josh has left a penny, heads up. I displace before Lawson can notice the tears stinging my eyes.

Above me in the clear sky, three bright yellow streaks are close together and moving upward like rockets. All around me, as far as I can see, are the colorful trails of other Satellites, including the two closest to me, Whitfield and Elliott.

After landing in my room, I bypass the coffee maker and head straight to the Y hall. Willow, Elliott, Anna, and Owen are already waiting. Liam and Evelynn come in behind me, followed by Lawson, Jackson, Clara, and Reed.

"Morgan's a no show, huh?" Reed says.

"I'm here!" Morgan hollers from down the hall, walking with Rigby.

"Should have stayed away," Billy says from behind her. Everyone ignores him, Morgan included.

"Looks like we all made it," Willow starts. "How did your assignments go?"

Mumbles and groans confirm that the other Elites had the same bad luck with blocking.

"The kids were back today," I tell Willow.

Lawson clears his throat. "Jonathan sent them again."

Willow ties her yarn-like hair into a ponytail. "Did they tell you that?"

"Not exactly."

Willow's skepticism prompts Lawson to go on. "I know you're not the biggest Jonathan fan right now, but who else would have done it?"

Willow ignores the first part of Lawson's statement.

"Did they help?"

I step back to let Morgan into the haphazard circle we've created. "In two visits they've helped Meggie more than I have since I started her assignment. That house fire was a mistake, Willow." My voice rises. "They shouldn't have died."

Clara's voice has an edge like mine. "My Tragedy should have never lost her brother. Nor the one before who lost his son...but car accidents happen, right? And then there's Sarah who lost her six year old and Janet who lost her husband a month after she miscarried. You want me to go on? I'm sure whatever purpose they had could have waited."

Anna steps forward. "Umm, should we be sharing all these details about our assignments?"

Billy takes a step closer into the circle. "Jonathan didn't care when he shared Grant's sob story with us. Besides, what's it matter now? I can't block for anything, so I figure my days are numbered."

Willow rolls her eyes. "Your days aren't numbered, Billy. Quit being such a drama queen. I'll agree, though, what difference does it make if we know details about each other's assignments? I, for one, would have loved to know that Grant was my son's Satellite."

Boy, does Willow know how to silence a room.

She grins and shakes her head. "That's right, Grant watched over Ryder when Troy died. He didn't do too bad, either, though I'll admit, I'm relieved that was before he lost his ability." Her carefree expression goes away. "When I think about Ryder, it worries me that none of the Elites can block."

"Willow, I'm ready to fight."

"Pardon?" I think she's about to laugh at me.

"We should fight for Josh, Sophie, and Harper. They should be with Meggie and Brody. They can help her better than we can. Lawson can back me on this."

Lawson steps in. "I told him it doesn't matter, things aren't done that way around here."

"Lawson's right," Owen agrees.

"Why? We could change things," I argue.

Willow crosses her arms. "It's just the way it is, kid. There are reasons beyond what we know. I realize you don't think the children's deaths were justified, but it was necessary, if not for the kids, then for Meggie and Brody. There's a reason Meggie and Brody are going through this, whether it's because they will make a difference in the world or a difference in the life of someone who will need them. This experience may be necessary for them to relate to another family struggling with loss. Regardless, I refuse to believe people die for nothing." Willow focuses on the dark marble floor. "We have to have faith in the system."

"I say the system is jacked. Let's fight it. Come on, strength in numbers, right?" I start pacing. "If we all join in, maybe something can change. Maybe the deceased can watch over their own loved ones. Why not?"

Reed steps forward, forcing me to stop. "And then what? What about us? What's our purpose then? If that happens, then we've all died in vain. No thanks."

"Yeah? How's your purpose working out for you right

now?"

Reed lunges, but Elliott catches him before his fist kisses my cheek. "You have a lot of nerve, you know that? You're the reason we can't block!"

"Me?" I spit back. "I didn't make you do what you did! You all decided to be Jonathan's puppets and I'm not taking the blame for that! In fact, I should be blaming you! I've lost my ability, too, and I never even agreed to your little mission."

"Settle down. Come on, we're all in this together."

"Says the hippy. 'Can't we all just get along'?"

Willow is unenthused about Billy's comment. "So not funny."

Rigby pops his mouth closed to keep his toothpick from falling out. When he recovers, he half-grins and says, "It was kinda funny."

When the tension cools, Elliott lets Reed go. Morgan and Anna step closer into the circle after having jumped back to steer clear of any swinging arms.

"Things can change around here, and we can make it happen." I scan the faces staring at me.

Liam, Reed, Elliott, and Morgan remain silent. Billy and Lawson laugh, though Billy's laugh is more along the lines of him thinking I'm a fool, whereas Lawson's is more like I'm a lunatic. Rigby, Clara, Anna, and Evelynn seem somewhat interested in entertaining the idea. Owen looks like he's... hungry? Jackson appears to have a million things he'd like to say, but doesn't know where to begin. Willow is unreadable.

"Willow, what do you think? Can something like this be done? I mean, if we had the numbers, could we make a difference around here? Would the Schedulers listen to us?" Dear God, I'm rambling like Jackson.

"Dear God, you're rambling like Jackson," Willow says.

"Hey!" Jackson rebuffs, making me disregard the way that my thought and Willow's were eerily synchronized.

Something stirs in my core and adrenaline pumps through my veins at the thought of taking on the Schedulers. I'm not sure why, but I feel like I have something to settle with them. The only thing they've done to me was pull me briefly from my assignment, and that was because I'd broken the rules. Still, they were wrong. I saved Meggie's life, or at the very least, prevented her face from being bludgeoned by a whiskey bottle. "The Schedulers have to know the difference Meggie's kids are making. We have to tell them so they'll see."

"It won't change anything," Lawson counters.

"And what about us? What will we do for a living?" Reed questions.

I shrug because I haven't given much thought to us. Who cares, really, if our Tragedies have a better life because of it?

"Maybe we could visit our own families," I blurt out before thinking the idea through. I barely remember my life. Would I go visit a fiancée that I know nothing about; someone I'm not even sure really exists? And then there's my dad. Would my presence make a difference in his life? My mom, however—God, I miss my mom and would love to see her. More than that, I'd love to have more memories of her; memories that would actually stick and feel real.

Liam steps forward. "Count me in."

Willow shakes her head. "Hold up, everyone. Grant, what you're proposing is ridiculous. Impossible, actually." Willow turns on her mom voice. "Listen, kid, I don't mean to sound harsh, but you're only one person. Even if you got all the Elites in, there are thousands of Satellites who still have their ability. You're going to have a wicked tough time convincing other Satellites of your plan."

"We don't need to convince all of them. If we catch the new ones just coming in, they'll be on board. I wasn't thrilled when I first got here. Were you? And what about the rest of you? How did you feel when you found out you were going to lose your memories?" I surprise not only Willow, but also myself with my argument because it's a darn good one. "Willow, we could actually make this happen."

"I've thought many times you were losing it, but this time I seriously think your mind has—Poof!" her hands flutter open beside her ears for effect, "vanished altogether. Do you even grasp what you're proposing here? It will never happen. Think about it, kid. Taking on the Schedulers… it's career suicide."

I make eye contact specifically with Evelynn, Billy, Reed, Jackson, and Lawson. "Yeah? Exactly what kind of career do we have ahead of us?"

Willow narrows her eyes. "Dear Christ, you're serious." She takes over my habit of pacing the hallway, pointing her thumb over her shoulder. "The kid's actually serious!" she blurts to Lawson.

Reed takes a half step forward. "Just so I understand,

what *exactly* are you proposing?"

I take a minute to form my words correctly. "I'm proposing that we join together and demand more answers than we're getting. I'm proposing that we stop being puppets in this circus and take control over our own destinies." I take a deep breath. "I'm proposing that we start a little rebellion of our own."

27. It's protocol

My intestines are in knots on my way to meet Jonathan in the courtyard. I just want to get to the Y hall and attempt, once again, to rally the others to join in my plan. For the past week, Elliott has been trying as hard as I have to get the group to at least consider the idea of going up against the Schedulers. Liam has been the only one to bite so far, but I think we may have won Evelynn over after training yesterday. She's probably only entertaining the idea because of her frustration after an hour and a half of failed blocks. Regardless, I'll take anyone I can get on my side right now. I'm thankful—and shocked— that both Liam and Elliott are willing to help, especially since they still have their blocking abilities.

Opening the massive carved door, brightness hits me and my eyes narrow. I walk down the stone path, meeting Jonathan beside one of the giant landscaping pots halfway to the vacant field, and wondering why he wanted to meet me here. "What's up?"

He takes a slow breath. "Hello Grant. Thank you for coming."

Looking closer at his face, it's not just tiredness there; it's something more. I swallow, recognizing the look. Meggie had it during the burials, as if she was finally realizing her children and mother were gone. I'm so grateful that her kids have been coming back every day. I hope to never see that dead expression on her again.

"Jonathan?" I ask, becoming worried.

His hand appears from behind his back with a book and he smiles. Not one of those friendly type smiles, more of a smile of... *pity?*

"Your service as a Satellite is complete." He grips the book with both hands. "Welcome to the Legacy program."

When the statement roots in my head, all the air rushes from my lungs. I can't imagine the look on my face: shock, pain, anger? Ironically, Jonathan's expression is saying all these things.

He avoids eye contact when he says, "This is your Legacy book. Everything you need to know about the Satellite you will be mentoring is in here. Also included is information about Programming, which you will begin in a few days. This will be the last book you'll receive, signifying the close of the Satellite program for you."

"Programming?" With a million thoughts swarming in my brain, mostly of Meggie, I spit out the one thing that seems to be the least relevant. "I just got here. I've only had two assignments. Who will I even be reuniting with?"

He swallows. "No one."

"No one?" I start pacing. "What about Meggie? What will happen to her?"

"Another Satellite will be placed on her assignment. You should feel proud of how you have helped Meggie. She has reached a point in her healing where an Elite is no longer necessary."

I'm not sure why my blood is pumping so quickly, or why I'm losing control of my emotions. Without my ability, I should have known this was coming. Isn't this what I want: for Meggie to be protected? No, I'm panicking because I want change. I want Meggie's kids watching over her.

"I didn't help her to heal. It was her kids. You have to see that!"

He takes a deep breath. "I don't know what you're talking about."

"Why are you—?"

"Grant, please—"

"You sent her kids, I saw—"

"Enough!"

Hurt, I stumble back at his tone.

His voice and expression soften. "As I mentioned, in the coming days you will be meeting the Satellite you are to mentor and will also begin Programming."

"Why am I going through Programming if I'm not reuniting with anyone?"

"It's protocol." Jonathan scratches at his short beard. "I'm really sorry, Grant."

I can't come up with anything more to say.

"The others have been told as well."

"The others? Why would you tell the others I'm being pulled from the program before telling me?"

Jonathan doesn't answer, but acts as though I should know something he's not saying.

"You don't mean—the other Elites are becoming

Legacies, too?"

Jonathan gives me the sympathy look and I feel like an idiot for being surprised. Of course the others would be pulled from the program as well. None of us can block.

"How Jonathan? Tell me how this happened." My anger spikes. "I want to hear you say it!"

"It seems that protecting Tatum with your block…" he trails off. "Your ability is stronger than we have ever seen."

"Was," I correct. I feel lightheaded. It isn't that I hadn't believed the others, but more that I was holding out hope that they were lying, that this really couldn't have been my fault.

Jonathan's eyes move across the field to the mountains far in the distance. "This program is losing a significant amount of talent."

I begin pacing. "I've ruined six lives for a girl I don't even know! The fact that this place steals our memories is bogus! Would it have really mattered if I remembered my life? Would it have really affected my purpose that much? The Elites wouldn't have been forced to break our connection by that asinine group block. I wouldn't have destroyed the others' abilities with my block. They would all still be OK!"

My boots stop and I dig my heel into the stone path as the new reality sets in. "The Elites are going to hate me."

"Don't blame yourself. We all had a part in this. The others were willing participants."

I can't think of anything else to say, so Jonathan stands silently beside me for a long time. At one point he puts his arm around me and squeezes my shoulder, but this does nothing to console me. In fact, it makes me angrier.

Since my Satellite career is ending anyway, I figure what the hell. "Ending so many human lives is unfair enough, even if there is a purpose for it. At least let us protect our own families. I know you sent Josh and the girls. If you could see how much they've been helping Meggie…why can't it be like this for everyone?"

Jonathan pushes the book against my chest, forcing me to take it. "I suggest you begin your reading. Good luck." With that, he's gone, leaving nothing but the door swinging closed behind him.

Epilogue

Landon, seated along the elevated portion of the double-tiered circular desk, addresses Jonathan. "Just as we suspected, the Elites have gathered."

Holding the attention of Landon and one hundred and sixty-four other Schedulers, Jonathan crosses his arms in the center of the sunburst on the patterned tile floor. "Not surprising, now that they have become Legacies. Excuse me for sounding crass, but I don't see how this is a threat to our program."

"Two other Satellites are on board as well."

Despite Landon's increasing panic, Jonathan remains calm. "I am unconcerned with Liam's and Elliott's involvement."

"Do you realize what this could do to our establishment?"

"You're giving Grant much credit. As I recall, you doubted him and his abilities not long ago."

"His blatant neglect for the rules is dangerous. He has jeopardized this program on two occasions. I do not doubt his abilities, only his motives, which is why myself and the others are in agreement that we should not disregard what he is proposing."

"The Elites are upset, but the action you're proposing is unjust. Grant is a Legacy now and has earned his right to complete Programming," Jonathan says.

Landon stands, putting his hands on the desk, and leans forward. "Returning his memories will only give him more motivation. Certainly even you can see that."

"I dislike your tone, friend." Jonathan's expression hardens. "Legacies deserve to have their memories back after all they have done for this establishment. To say otherwise is treacherous."

"He's right. We cannot keep something of Grant's that is rightfully his."

Landon straightens and looks down to his left. "Wynn, to stand by and do nothing would be irresponsible of us. What Grant is proposing—"

"Exactly. *Proposing.* Nothing will come of it," Wynn says.

"You cannot be certain of that," Landon argues.

"I agree with Landon," a voice says from the right side of the circular desk.

"Me, too!" another voice shouts, causing the disruption to elevate.

In a matter of seconds, the room is flooded with the chaos of arguments until Wynn is the only person still seated at the desk. The volume of the Schedulers increases.

"It's unsafe…"

"You can't keep those from him…"

"Something must be done…"

"He's dangerous…"

"He cannot be allowed to have his memories—"

"You're not keeping his memories!"

Jonathan's booming voice silences everyone. The Schedulers, one by one, sit back down in their seats, until Landon and Jonathan are the only two in the columned room who remain standing.

"You seem to be in the minority, my friend."

Jonathan's voice is as sharp as Landon's. "We are finished here. The Elites will continue with their Legacy program, Grant included. If any of you disagree enough to stop that, then I say good luck to you."

Jonathan pivots in the starburst and walks toward the seeded-glass doors.

"We will not allow this!" Landon yells after him. "Grant Bradley will not have his memories back," he says under his breath.

A small grin plays on Jonathan's face as he shakes his head and pushes the doors open.

To be continued…

1. Still have that great sense of humor

My door flings open and in comes Willow. After enduring these typical entrances from her, I don't even spill my coffee.

Her ratty, brown bag thuds against the floor. "What's up, kid?"

As she makes her way toward me in the kitchen, the metal charms in her dreadlocks clink together. Willow, along with everything she owns, is loud.

I move over as she helps herself to a mug from the cabinet over the sink.

Her eyes scan me up and down, certainly in effort to gauge my well-being. She's such a mom sometimes. "You look decent, considering the Legacy news."

"Wow, no sarcasm. What's got you in such a great mood?"

She shrugs. "Troy and I just finished watching the baseball game."

I almost choke on my coffee. "Baseball?"

"It was a great game," she says like this shouldn't be such a stretch to believe she's into sports. "I'm becoming rather fond of the Red Sox."

"You've always had poor taste, so I guess that makes

sense."

The knock on my door interrupts before she can shoot back a reply. By her feisty expression, I'm sure it would have been a good one.

"Come in," I say over my cup.

A second later, Jonathan is stepping over Willow's bag. "Willow, Grant, very nice to see you both."

Willow's mood sinks, along with her shoulders. "Jonathan."

He reacts to Willow's sour tone with a tired smile. "Grant, I need you to begin your reading as soon as possible. It's imperative that we get you into Programming right away."

"What's the point?" Willow mumbles.

Oh, this should be interesting.

Jonathan raises his eyebrow. "Pardon?"

Willow balances the empty seashell coffee cup handle on her finger, making the mug sway back and forth like a clock pendulum. "What's. The. Point?"

Jonathan's voice remains calm. "The very same reason you went through Programming, of course. To recover memories."

"No Jonathan, the reason is different, or have you forgotten? Grant isn't reuniting with family. He, along with the other Elites, is only doing this because of what you made us do."

"Let's be clear: I did not force your hand, Willow." Jonathan uses a kinder tone than I would choose if I were being so blatantly challenged. I want to interject and remind them both that this mess is all my fault, but Willow's already running her mouth.

"Are you telling me if I would have said no, your little experiment would have never happened? Cut the crap, we both know if I had refused, you would have found someone to take my place."

As if Willow hasn't even spoken, Jonathan says, "Grant, please begin your reading as soon as possible." He turns to Willow and nods once. "Goodbye, Willow. Please send my best to Troy."

"Mmm Hmm." Willow's tone is flat, but her volume increases. "You must be pretty special, kid. Usually you'd just get a note to begin your reading," she says before the door clicks closed.

"Way to go. You ran him off before I could talk to him about Meggie again. Every time I tell him how much Meggie's kids were helping her, he ignores me. Why won't he listen—"

"What's he expect you to get out of Programming? More importantly, what the heck are you supposed to do with your time once you've completed the process?" She reaches over me and fills her cup with coffee.

Sometimes I wonder if Willow and I are even in the same room. "You should get over your beef with Jonathan. We could use his help right now."

The bottom of Willow's mug clinks against the counter and fresh coffee spills over the top. "I'd think you, of all people, would have the bigger problem with the guy. He's the reason the Elites are all in this mess."

"Him or me?" I mumble.

Willow squeezes my forearm. "You can't really believe this is your fault?"

I hop myself up on the counter. "Billy would disagree."

"The Elites are understandably upset. But if you're going to say this is your fault, you could just as easily say it is my fault. We all went along with Jonathan's plan." Willow grabs her cup and slurps her first sip. "He should have never asked that of us. He put us all in a rotten position."

"Look, I'm about as happy as everyone else with what's happening, but to continue your wrath against Jonathan—I mean, come on, do you think he knew it would turn out like this? It's Jonathan we're talking about."

"Exactly my point." Willow stares back at me for a second before rolling her eyes.

"Stop pouting. You're just looking for someone to blame. Use that energy to help me. Blame the Schedulers! We can fight them. Wouldn't you love to see Ryder again?"

"Of course I want to see my son!" Willow barks back. She sucks in a deep breath and lowers her cup to the counter.

"So help me. We've got Elliot, Liam, and Clara."

"Clara still wants you, so she doesn't count," Willow interrupts.

"That's not true. We're just friends."

Willow's narrow, doubting eyes force me to change the subject. "I think Anna's got Owen talked into it. Plus all the Elites are in, even Billy."

"Yeah, and what about your buddy Rigby? Why isn't he as enthusiastic as the others to join your futile scheme?"

I hide how much the blow about Rigby affects me. Despite our misunderstandings about my feelings for Clara (or lack thereof) and how I knew his now-girlfriend, Whitfield, from sharing an assignment, Rigby was my first friend in Progression. I thought he'd have my back. "He says he has his reasons."

"Reasons like, *this isn't going to work.* I can see how you swayed the Elites. Without their blocking abilities, their futures as Satellites are over."

She may as well punch me in the face like she did when we first met. The sting would be the same.

"Sorry, I didn't mean…" Willow's words trail off.

I pull away from her when she tries to rub my arm. "No. You're right. I'm not a Satellite anymore. I get it. That's not why I'm fighting for this, though."

Willow's expression remains sympathetic. "You're a Legacy now. You're still an integral part of this program. Being a Satellite is forever, kid." Willow's grin is forced. "Certainly I've shared this with you before."

I shake my head. "Not when your ability is gone. I can't even perform maintenance. At least you still have that."

Willow turns away from me, using a coffee refill as an excuse despite her cup being three quarters full. "Maintenance doesn't require blocking. Listen, what you're proposing is career suicide for an active Satellite. Rigby's not an idiot. He knows that."

"So, you think our other friends are idiots for joining

me?"

"No." She turns back to me with her full cup. "But I think they'll regret their decision."

I glare at Willow and she mimics my expression. After a minute, she softens, but I hop off the counter and step away when she tries to hug me.

"I get why you're doing this, I really do, kid. It won't work, though. This program, the whole establishment, it's bigger than you and me." Her voice raises as my proximity to the sofa grows closer. "You can't change something that has been working for centuries. It's impossible."

"Nothing's impossible." I can't believe I just said that. When have I ever been the glass-half-full guy? It's this horrid sofa. I know it. Not only is the thing too darn comfortable to part with, but now it's turning me into Willow.

"I respect your passion and even applaud you for it, but listen, kid, you're setting yourself up for failure and it pains me to watch. I love you, I really do, and if you were asking anything else of me, I'd stand by you with guns blazing."

If she's waiting for me to turn around, she's wasting her time. I have zero plans of unlocking my eyes from the bookcase.

"But this—kid, you've got to give up on this." Willow pauses. "You're putting the others in a bad position. You're messing up their careers. Please think of them. I know the Elites are done, but the others don't have to be. They still have their ability to block. They have futures ahead of them,

Tragedies whose lives are dependent on them, destinies they have yet to fulfill."

"I have no intentions of ruining anyone's future, but I disagree with you. There are other options for Tragedies, other options for us. We would all love to see our loved ones, to visit them after our deaths, to help them heal." OK, fine, she wins. I'm only turning around to plead my case, though. "Willow, please, having you on board would mean everything. You know so many Satellites. People would listen to you."

Willow belts out a long, dramatic sigh. "We'll have to agree to disagree on this one."

I stare at the seashells on her mug, wishing she would change her mind, but knowing she won't.

"You'd better start your reading. You wouldn't want to make Jonathan mad."

"You don't have to go," I say, wanting more time to plead my case.

Cut the crap, Grant, you just like having her around, my brain argues.

"I should get back to Troy." She lifts her mug. "I'm stealing this, by the way. Actually, never mind, it was mine to begin with, so I'm just taking possession of what I already owned."

Her shoes make the funny flip-flop noise when she comes towards me. "Please think this through, kid. If for no other reason than to consider how this will negatively affect the others."

"Send my condolences to Troy," is my reply when she

leans down and hugs me.

Willow pulls back and smacks my head.

I can only force half a grin because I want her to join us so badly.

She returns my expression with a full-on smirk. "Still have that great sense of humor."

"Oh, that wasn't a joke."

She flip-flops herself to the door and scoops up her dilapidated bag. "Please think about what I said. Thanks for the coffee." She lifts her cup in a *cheers* motion before pulling the strap of the ratty bag over her head.

"Anytime," I mumble as she's closing the door.

I chew on the inside of my lip, missing her already. I settle deeper into the green cushion, wishing I had a diversion other than the black book staring back at me.

Is this really it, the end of my short-lived career? I spent most of my first assignment fighting against being a Satellite, and now I don't want the work to end.

This isn't the way things should be, the louder voice of truth says in my head, drowning out the other until every molecule inside me joins in. Just because we're dead, even if there is a bigger purpose for ourselves or our loved ones, we shouldn't be kept away from the people in our lives, the people we love who have made us who we are. We shouldn't have our memories stolen from us. No one deserves that.

I put my focus on the book. Sitting there on the trunk, the thing looks innocent enough, yet reaching for it, my fingers retract like the black binding will bite me. I realize I don't want to know what's in those pages. I don't want to know what the future holds for another Satellite—or what my future holds, for that matter.

The most disturbing reality yet hits me: someone is about to die, and someone's family is about to suffer. A lot.

Breathe, Grant, breathe.

I scoot to the edge of the sofa cushion and lean my elbows on my knees. Still staring at the book, I bite my thumb knuckle. Why is this so difficult?

A minute later, I'm up and pacing. Instead of allowing visions of what the unfortunate future holds for an unnamed family, I tune in to the movie reels of my short Satellite career: meeting Willow, training, learning to block, protecting Ryder, becoming an Elite, fighting against other people's blocks, helping Meggie, losing my blocking ability as a result of a supposed fiancée I don't even remember—

I snap the book up from the trunk.

Why can't I remember my life?

The word *Legacy* shines, holding my eyes there the same way I'm holding my breath. I want to remember my life.

Shouldn't I be happy? I'm about to go through Programming. I *will* remember my life soon.

Nerves make my stomach muscles clench. A minute later, my anxiety mixes with anger and the book is skating across the hardwood floor. After a light thud, the book stills at the base of the bookshelf.

What is wrong with me? This is good news. I'll complete this Legacy thing and be free to lead a rebellion against the Schedulers.

Yes. I'll complete this Legacy thing.

A coffee run to the kitchen and a few deep breaths later, I return to the living room where the book has magically returned to the trunk. Figures. Like my regular assignment books, the gold text is bracketed by wings. Line one: *Grant Bradley*, line two: *Legacy*.

Legacy.

Legacy.

Legacy.

I reach for the book—still half-expecting the thing to bite me—and will my fingers to work. I manage to flip to the first page, which, like the cover, states my name above the word that is sounding more terrible by the second. Not because of what it means to me, but what it means to whoever is in this book. They will lose their memories and be separated from their family the way I was.

I swallow and turn the page, which displays a handwritten letter from Jonathan.

Dear Grant,

With enormous gratitude for your service as a Satellite and an Elite, I welcome you to the Legacy program. You have proven to be exceptional in your abilities. I trust you will continue performing increasingly amazing feats.

I am hopeful you have found the Satellite program to be a rewarding experience. The coming weeks will be challenging. Like many others before you, I realize the task of letting go of this life may be met with a touch of resistance. Let me assure you that your future will hold abundant happiness, and that this closing chapter marks the beginning of a life filled with exceptional possibilities. If you should need assistance at any time, please do not hesitate to contact me.

All My Best,
Jonathan Clement

I look up at the ceiling. This is really happening, not just for me but for all the Elites. My teammates are facing this emotionally grueling task right alongside me, and I'm the reason why. Billy's initial reasons for wanting to kill me when I became an Elite were unwarranted, but now the guy actually has a decent motive. If I were him, I'd want to rip myself in half also.

Thinking about Billy, along with Lawson, Reed, Jackson, and Evelynn—yes, even Evelynn—having to give up the only life they know, I slam the book closed and send the thing back on the familiar course across the room.

Want to know how the series ends?
Grab your paperback or ebook of Legacy, the final installment in the Satellite trilogy, at www.Amazon.com!

Acknowledgments

I am very thankful to those who continue to cheer me on in this venture. I am honored, humbled, and astonished by the encouraging feedback Satellite has received.

To: Linda, Mary, Wendy, Sherry, Shelly, Pat, and Joao who have been patiently waiting for the release of Elite, and who have continued to ask when they can get their hands on a copy, I'm elated to finally be able to answer that question!

A giant thanks to my editor, Debi. You were highly recommended by two of my most trusted friends and did not disappoint. This book could not have been what it is without you. Your time and efforts are enormously appreciated.

Kelli and Lacy, you both have a true talent for catching typos and I'm grateful to have your extra set of eyes in this project. And to the fastest beta reader ever: Robert, your advice and professionalism are top notch. Thank you.

Alec, Ben, and Will, you are the loves of my life and my motivation for completing projects like this one. I am so lucky God has entrusted the three of you with me. May your dreams always be within reach. Dan, we survived yet another novel. Two down, one to go.

And to Heather: all I can say is, you've done it again. Thanks for making life awesome!

About the Author

Lee lives in Missouri with her husband and three sons. She received a BFA with a Graphic Design emphasis from Lindenwood University in 2000. She spends her days as a graphic designer for a billboard company that makes having a day job not so terrible. You can usually find Lee hanging out with her boys—preferably by a body of water, hidden behind her laptop, or conversing with her dog, Dixie. Satellite, Lee's first novel, was selected as a quarterfinalist in the 2012 Amazon Breakthrough Novel Award contest. Visit www.leedavidson.net for social media links, book updates, and more.

Made in the USA
Coppell, TX
28 May 2020